Juli Flintoff is an English artist from West Yorkshire. Initially studying drama, she obtained a Bachelor of Arts from Sunderland University. For several years, Juli was a successful Community Arts Development Worker facilitating workshops throughout the Bradford, Calderdale, Leeds, Wakefield, and Kirklees areas. After exhibiting five large banners at Bradford's International Youth Event attended by delegates from all over the world, she became involved with projects for young offenders. This led her to train as a Prison Officer and later a Drugs Dog Handler. In 2010, she began caring for her elderly father and since his passing in 2011 she has dedicated her life to supporting, caring, and advocating on behalf of her mother who lives with dementia. *The Daisy Chain* is Juli's third publication preceded by *Blame, Shame & Guilt,* a heartbreaking tale of child abuse, and *The Secret Back Door,* an inspiring book depicting the struggles of living with dementia.

In loving memory of Audrey Swaine 14.03.1967 to 20.06.2023, a beloved mother to Myer, and cherished grandmother to Louisa, Phoebe and Ethan.

May you continue to sparkle in Heaven as you always did on earth you beautiful, vivacious lady.

Juli Flintoff

The Daisy Chain

To Steve with much love & appreciation

Austin Macauley Publishers
LONDON * CAMBRIDGE * NEW YORK * SHARJAH

Copyright © Juli Flintoff 2024

The right of Juli Flintoff to be identified as author of this work has been asserted by the author in accordance with sections 77 and 78 of the Copyright, Designs and Patents Act 1988.

All rights reserved. No part of this publication may be reproduced, stored in a retrieval system, or transmitted in any form or by any means, electronic, mechanical, photocopying, recording, or otherwise, without the prior permission of the publishers.

Any person who commits any unauthorised act in relation to this publication may be liable to criminal prosecution and civil claims for damages.

This is a work of fiction. Names, characters, businesses, places, events, locales, and incidents are either the products of the author's imagination or used in a fictitious manner. Any resemblance to actual persons, living or dead, or actual events is purely coincidental.

A CIP catalogue record for this title is available from the British Library.

ISBN 9781035857593 (Paperback)
ISBN 9781035857609 (ePub e-book)

www.austinmacauley.com

First Published 2024
Austin Macauley Publishers Ltd®
1 Canada Square
Canary Wharf
London
E14 5AA

Thank you to the team at Austin Macauley Publishers for their outstanding appraisal of *The Daisy Chain*; it is one thing to have your work validated but to have it recognised so descriptively literally blew me away. Thank you for affirming its potential and for your continued support, guidance and expertise along the road to publication.

Thank you to my beautiful boys, Coban and Corai, who provided much support, positive encouragement, the time and space to write, along with numerous cups of tea and hot water bottles. A massive appreciation to my lifelong friend, Mary Dolan and Emma Wilson, who eagerly proofread my manuscript, provided outstanding feedback and avidly encouraged me to pursue its publication.

Lastly, thank you to my sister in Christ, Dr Jacqueline Matthews for your support in the final proofreading and your dedication to ensure I met my deadline. Greatly appreciated!

Table of Contents

Prologue: Cassandra Matthews: 31 December 2000   13

Part One: New Year's Eve 2000   19

   Chapter 1: Gerald Matthews: 'What Are You Doing?'   21

   Chapter 2: Cortina Matthews: The Keepsakes   26

   Chapter 3: Cortina: Please God   29

   Chapter 4: Barry Jarman: Pitstop Alley   31

   Chapter 5: Jacobi, Parker and Williams: 57 Park Grove   34

   Chapter 6: Happiness, Leonard and Barry: The Aftermath   40

   Chapter 7: The Little Boy: The Stranger   43

   Chapter 8: Shona Williams: Doubts   45

   Chapter 9: Shona Williams: Rest Day   51

   Chapter 10: Shona Williams: Making Enquiries   55

   Chapter 11: Dr Richard Carmichael: Woodpecker Mode   59

   Chapter 12: Sally Carta: The Past is the Past   66

   Chapter 13: Jonathon Carta: A Little Mixed Up   69

Part Two: Fourteen Years Later   75

   Chapter 14: Cortina Matthews (March 2014): Life Goes On   77

   Chapter 15: Mick Denby: A Day Off   80

   Chapter 16: Mick Denby: The Stranger   85

   Chapter 17: The Stranger: In the Shadows   87

Chapter 18: Cortina Mattews: Don't Let Go	92
Chapter 19: Gerald: Bath Time	97
Chapter 20: Cortina: Happy Birthday Cort	99
Chapter 21: Cortina and Gerald: A Blast from the Past	102
Chapter 22: Tony Lloyd: Not Funny	105
Chapter 23: Emma Boulden: How Truthful are You?	111
Chapter 24: Gerald and Cortina: Playing Games	118
Chapter 25: Sally Carta: Living It Large	120
Chapter 26: Sally Carta: Just Breathe	124
Chapter 27: Sally Carta: Confusion	128
Chapter 28: Sally Carta: Pain	130
Chapter 29: Sally Carta: Torment	133
Chapter 30: Mick Denby: The Luckiest Man Alive	136
Chapter 31: Shona Williams and Dion Jacobi: Let the Investigation Begin	144
Chapter 32: Shona Williams and Dion Jacobi: Two for the Price of One	151
Chapter 33: Shona Williams and Dion Jacobi: Establishing the Facts	161
Chapter 34: Mick Denby: An Unfortunate Encounter	171
Chapter 35: Mick Denby: In the Execution of One's Duties	178
Chapter 36: Nina "Bloody" Spalding: Playtime	183
Chapter 37: The Investigations Continue	187
Chapter 38: Meeting the Governor	193
Chapter 39: Damien Clarke: The Investigation Hots Up	203
Chapter 40: The Prison Revisited	207
Chapter 41: Out in the Field	213
Chapter 42: Searching	217

Chapter 43: Breaking the Bad News	*223*
Chapter 44: Revelations	*234*
Chapter 45: Full Disclosure	*237*
Part Three	**239**
Chapter 46: Cortina Matthews: Something is Missing	*241*
Chapter 47: Gerald: Mirror, Mirror on the Wall	*248*
Chapter 48: Tony Lloyd: Pointless Protests	*250*
Chapter 49: Cassandra Lloyd: In Control	*253*
Chapter 50: Gerald: Present Day	*255*
Chapter 51: Emma Boulden: The Millennium NYE	*257*
Chapter 52: Malcolm Carta: The Sad Truth	*259*
Chapter 53: Sally Carta: Let the Party Commence	*262*
Chapter 54: Malcolm: Putting on a Brave Face	*266*
Chapter 55: Emma Boulden: Being Useful	*268*
Chapter 56: The Party	*272*
Chapter 57: Gerald: Present Day	*276*
Chapter 58: The Guests	*278*
Chapter 59: Gerald: Present Day	*283*
Epilogue: Twelve Months Later	**291**

Prologue
Cassandra Matthews: 31 December 2000

Cassandra Matthews paced back and forth, her anxiety levels spiking to an all-new level, where the hell was the doctor? She took another deep drag on the roll up between her yellow stained fingers and blew it out just as rapidly, spitting the loose bits of tobacco from her mouth. Her head was swamped with a multitude of "what if's" that she furiously tried to shake away but their onslaught was overwhelming. She glanced for the 50 millionth time towards the clock but it had barely seemed to have moved where the heck was, he? She grabbed her glass off the cluttered coffee table and downed the full contents before reaching for the vodka bottle, refilling it then downing it again. She strode over to the lounge window, threw back the net curtain and peered up and down the night lit street. There was not a soul in sight but somewhere in the distance she could hear the faint hum of music from some party no doubt looking to enjoy the New Year celebrations.

Cassandra turned back to face her pitiful, bleak home with its worn-out carpet, sagging settee and oddments of second-hand furniture, oh how she hated it, but what could she do? She had no money and the bit she'd had coming in from the surgery looked like it was going to dry up pretty soon. Why the hell should she have to live like this when only 12 months ago her life had been perfect, she had been married to Tony Lloyd and had everything she could ever have wished for.

She suddenly remembered the kids upstairs so shot up the steps two at a time knowing full well the fireworks would soon disturb them. She thought back to the birthday parties she had hosted and how they had brought each New Year in, together as a family, with Tony always initiating the countdown. She used to love the concept of letting go of the old year with its regrets, hurts, fallouts and drama's yet at the same time welcoming in a new one with renewed hope and dreams for a better future. She quietly slid open the bedroom door and carefully peered her head around it to see the gentle rise and fall of the children's covers.

Good they were sound asleep; she did not want them to stir when the doctor arrived. She dipped into her own bedroom and was just taking a strip of her medication out of its box when she heard the familiar rattle of the back door. She shoved the whole strip of tablets into her right cardigan pocket there was no time to mess about now then she lightly sprinted down the stairs. Cassandra turned the key in the lock, quietly shifted the bolt at the top of the door and slid back the chain revealing Dr Carmichael standing on her top step.

'It's about time,' she said turning and making her way back towards the lounge expecting him to just follow her. She picked up a small tin containing pre-made, hand rolled cigarettes, popped the cap, selected one, lit it, then poured another glass of vodka downing it before turning back round to face him.

'What the hell is she doing here?' Cassandra screamed, directing her anger at Carmichael.

'Cassandra, I can see that your annoyed but Dr Carta and I felt it was imperative that she accompanied me on this house call,' Carmichael informed her.

'House call, is that what we are calling this?' Cassandra said angrily.

'There is no need to become hostile, Cassandra, I think things have already become way too out of control don't you?' Dr Carta asked.

'Out of control, actually I think it is time for them to spiral beyond your wildest dreams,' Cassandra stated.

'Oh, here we go again with the threats,' Dr Carta said loftily. 'I had thought by now Cassandra you would have realised they do not get you anywhere.'

'Threats? I am talking about action not threats and he knows I mean what I say otherwise he wouldn't have brought you here as back up,' Cassandra said referring to the suddenly mute Dr Carmichael.

'What is it you actually want from us Cassandra because I have got to tell you I for one are fed up of living on the knife edge of your control, wondering which way your precarious little mind is going to flip next!' Dr Carta said directly.

'What I want is for you two to tell the truth so that I can have some peace of mind,' Cassandra blurted out.

'But Cassandra I remember what we all agreed and quite frankly it is way too late to go back on your word now,' Dr Carmichael tried to coax her.

'You can save your breath neither one of you are wheedling your way out of it, this time I have nothing left to lose,' she ventured.

'And yet we have everything to lose, our jobs, families, reputations basically everything we have worked our entire lives for, why on earth can't you just let sleeping dogs lie?' Carta asked.

'I think you know the answer to that question, I have lost everything yet you who have caused so much distress to protect your own, have lost nothing,' Cassandra spitted at them.

'What is it going to cost us Cassandra?' Carta asked as Carmichael shot her a displeasing glance, 'everyone has a price.'

'The price I have been forced to pay has been endless, each minute of every day for the past 12 months has been agonising torture knowing I should have spoken up. Knowing I should have stopped Tony from taking Malcom's money, knowing I should not have allowed you to emotionally blackmail me or allowed you to manipulate us,' Cassandra said broken and crying at her own weakness.

'You made the right choices based on the circumstances at the time, we all did,' Carta began. 'It is easy to look back with hindsight searching for ways to escape your own wrongdoing however this situation is bore out of your emotional state.'

'Damn right I am in an emotional state, I am going out of my mind yet you two don't seem to give a crap,' Cassandra screeched.

'That's not true, Cassandra we are here, aren't we?' Dr Carmichael tried to sound soothing.

'You're here but not for me, you are here because you know damn well you are about to be exposed and you want to shut me up, again!' Cassandra stated.

'Yes, Cassandra your right, we do want to shut you up because no good will come from you talking to the police all it will do is bring devastation to too many people, including yourself,' Carta stated dispassionately.

'I fail to see how it could possibly affect me any worse than the lies you manipulated everyone to tell,' Cassandra told her.

'Is this really how you see the situation that 'I manipulated everyone to tell lies,' wow, you were a willing participant when it suited you. Just because you cannot live with the decisions that you made it doesn't give you a right to keep holding it over our heads. You're not the victim here Cassandra if truth be known isn't it you who is manipulating us with your threats dictating we come here in the middle of the night to dance to your tune?' Dr Carta told her accusingly.

'You have absolutely no compassion nor care for another human being, have you?' Cassandra began, 'It is beyond me how you ever thought a medical career was the correct vocation for you. You talk of my emotional state as being irrational that is rich for someone who is completely devoid of any love or empathy,' Cassandra told her boldly.

'There is no need to become personal Cassandra maybe the tablets Dr Carmichael prescribed for you are not working and we need to look at an alternative,' Carta responded patronisingly.

'What is not working for me is you two coming round here and failing to listen yet again. So, let me make it abundantly clear, you are no longer in the driving seat, I will be making an official complaint about your conduct, I will get them to open an investigation into what happened and by the way,' she said over her shoulder as she grabbed for the vodka bottle again to refill her glass. 'I do not give a shit how it affects either of you two,' Cassandra stated.

'I do not see any purpose in talking to her whilst she is in this state,' Carta told Carmichael, 'There is no reasoning with her.'

'No reasoning with me? I take it you do know what tonight is?' she screeched as a little face came to the door.

'Mummy,' the little girl whispered as she rubbed her tired little eyes.

'Shush it's alright sweetheart come on let's get you back to bed,' Cassandra told her daughter who readily allowed herself to be lifted and carried back up to her bedroom. Cassandra took a little time to settle her daughter down in order to also give herself a breather, she needed to regain her composure whilst the doctors whispered downstairs.

When Cassandra rejoined her now unwanted guests, she could feel that there had been a shift in the atmosphere. Dr Carta was stood near the mantlepiece whilst Dr Carmichael had taken a seat on one of the hard chairs next to the settee. She approached the coffee table, picked up her glass and took the whole contents in one gulp.

'Can we start again Cassandra, please?' Dr Carmichael implored. 'Whatever you choose to do tomorrow is entirely up to you but tonight it's New Year's Eve so let's at least be civil and raise a glass together.'

Cassandra walked into the kitchen to retrieve two glasses but as she was pouring the vodka Carta said, 'Not for me thank you. I am driving.'

It didn't matter one bit to Cassandra the last thing she wanted to do was waste her vodka on the aloof Dr Carta. She couldn't believe how she had once looked up to her, admired her and was so desperate to be seen by her, hoping to fit in and be accepted. Seeing Dr Carta stood at the mantlepiece now though with that haughty look upon her face smirking at her like she was a piece of dog dirt made Cassandra Matthews want to fly up and smack that smug bitch square in the face.

She felt a little light headed, maybe she needed to ease off the vodka but the doctor had poured her another and it would be rude of her not to toast the New Year in with him. Afterall in the grand scheme of things, he was only the puppet on Carta's very short strings so yes, she would have a drink with him. She leant forward to take hold of the glass but her hand eye coordination was way off and she couldn't tell which of the glasses was the real one. She opened and closed her hand like a crab snapping its pinchers with her spatial awareness also seeming shot. Cassandra glanced up to see the Dr regarding her with deep intent she could see his mouth was moving but she could not process anything he was evidently saying.

She opened her mouth, her head lolling from side to side, her vision blurred, she tried to shut her mouth but her tongue felt thick as though it was expanding. Cassandra instinctively knew that this was not the affect from the vodka so she desperately searched Carmichael's face her eyes imploring him to help her but he was not forthcoming. She tried to concentrate her energy on Carta but her eyes could not bring her into focus, her mind was whirring, her mouth dry and sleep was begging her to join it. With little resolve, her eyes closed, her body slouched back onto the settee and then a new sense of peace flooded her system as she submitted to its enticing pull.

Cassandra Matthews had made several mistakes that evening, the first was to make a call to Carmichael, the second was to allow Carta to gain access into her home before making angry threats to ruin the doctors' lives. However, her biggest mistakes were not realising she had dropped her strip of tablets when she had picked her daughter up, of downing the contents of the glass that she had not poured and of underestimating how far the doctors would go to save their own skin.

It is true that people who have nothing to lose can be a dangerous commodity but those who have everything to lose can be even more treacherous. Now there would be no more threats, no more looking over their shoulders and no more fear of what might happen when a loose tongue talked because that tongue would never utter another word.

Outside the window, a face was watching the events in front of him unfold a scene that would scar him for the rest of his life. He stumbled backwards glancing towards the bedroom above wondering what would become of the two children asleep upstairs?

Part One
New Year's Eve 2000

'The sins of our fathers
Are as great as our mothers
We may sleep in blissful ignorance
But the day of reckoning shall soon prevail.'

(Juli Flintoff)

Chapter 1
Gerald Matthews: 'What Are You Doing?'

From a young age, Gerald liked nothing more than sitting on the floor of the bedroom he now shared with his sister Cortina playing with his Brio train set. This had been the only present that he had received for his 6th birthday so it had become his pride and joy. Each morning he would jump out of bed race to the bathroom to relieve himself, shoot downstairs for the cold toast that would have been left on his "Thomas the Tank Engine" plastic plate since his mum had dumped it there hours earlier. It was always dry and tasteless apart from the slightly burnt edges and at the side would sit a plastic beaker of half full room temperature milk. It was not the most appetising start to his day but it was all that he had come to know since his mum and dad had separated.

Gerald was a quiet boy, though inwardly content, who enjoyed to watch the people around him. His sister Cortina was very different she was more active, chatty and made friends very easily. Gerald did not. He had few friends because he wasn't as outgoing as the children around him so his teachers described him as a loner. He was not. Gerald didn't prefer solitude over the company of those around him he longed to be a part of his peers' games he just had not developed the social skills that the other children had.

The unfortunate outcome for Gerald was that he was persistently overlooked because he was quiet by nature. So, he began to take a 3rd party interest in the world around him by becoming an observer. Through this method he was able to sense his environment and experience it indirectly through a type of a second-hand, measured system. In other words, he felt the thrill of the little boy racing his bike down the hill as he watched him but when he fell off and hurt himself, he was able to eradicate this experience. The way that Gerald was processing events in this detached way resulted in him having little emotional connection with anyone, that was apart from with Cortina. With Cortina, he was totally unable to block anything out. There was no filter process, no barrier, in fact no protection at all as Gerald was unable to stop himself from feeling everything that Cortina felt.

On the morning of 31 December 2000, Gerald finished the meagre ration that was his breakfast and raced back up the stairs. He knelt down beside his bed, carefully slid the box out from under it and shuffled himself slightly backwards in order to give himself enough room. He checked over his shoulder to make sure he hadn't woken his sister; she did not stir, so he carefully lifted the box to allow its contents to slowly slide out. Gerald glanced over his shoulder again to see her roll over on to her side so she was facing the wall but she did not make a murmur. Delighted he began to separate the curved pieces of the beechwood track from the pile in front of him and placed these to his right.

He selected the long plastic red suspension bridge the focal point of his set and together with the two solid raised pieces that formed the bridge he placed them at arms-length in front of him. He located the little black engine of the railway train with its red protruding funnel along with the three different coloured carriages of a blue tipping truck, a green and a red animal car. He then sourced their removable loads, one a yellow cylindrical shape which had a hole width way through it allowing it to easily slide onto the black carriage. He found the giraffe and the elephant (unbeknown to him parts from the Brio circus set) and he carefully slotted their feet into the spaces that held the animal on their respective cars.

Once he had constructed each part, he allowed the magnetic force to pull them together to connect them as one full train. He loved to hear the slight click of the small, round metal parts as the magnet attracted its counterpart so he would pull them apart just to hear the connection snap back into place, over and over again. His desire satisfied he moved on to begin to construct the track itself.

Gerald always started with the suspension bridge that he'd balance upon the two wooden supports before carefully taking the curved raised pieces which he would also place upon the supports before slotting them into place. He loved the smooth up and down slide that it created at either side of the majestical red bridge and the rush it gave as the train swept downwards.

Gerald lost himself creating two outwardly sweeping tracks away from the bridge that circled back around towards each other before shooting back towards the bridge, delving underneath it then connecting together in one last arch. So deep was he in his own little word of creativity that Gerald had completely forgotten he was not alone.

'What you doing, Gerald?' Cortina asked sleepily.

Startled, Gerald turned around before composing himself and said, 'Just playing Cort, do you want to help me?'

Cortina got out of bed and crept down onto the floor next to him waiting for him to offer her the parts he was happy for her to use. Cortina knew that Gerald loved his train set and although he had welcomed her to play with him, he was very protective of it so she would never upset him by bulldozing her way in. Cortina was always mindful not to upset her brother in any way and was always respectful of him and due to this Gerald felt safe around her and was able to fully let his guard down. There was another reason Cortina was careful and that was because she had seen many underestimate the quiet boy sat in the corner who peered over the top of the book in his hand.

Teachers assumed he had no social skills, that he required assistance on how to play and join in or worse still that he was shy. Children who did not know him would tentatively try to encourage him to play with them or worse he would attract the attention of bullies and become their new target. Cortina had witnessed on many occasions how their misinterpretations had landed them in deep water when the demon that could be Gerald retaliated. Although she had to admit that when it came to the bullies, she would secretly watch and wait for that moment when the switch would flip.

Sometimes it was a particular look he got in his eye other times it was a twitch at the right side of his mouth and then he would spring into action. He was like the little frog, jump up toy she had gotten for Christmas, you pressed the frog down and without warning it sprung back up. Her and Gerald got different ones which they would take in turns to try and catch when they sprang up. She would pay close attention to it to see if the bottom was moving to indicate it was about to pop up, but it didn't, you just had to be on your guard, ready. Gerald was like that pop-up toy, the only problem was the assailant failed to keep their eye on him so they were never ready for the bullet when the trigger was inadvertently pulled.

Gerald passed Cortina one of the last two curves to put in place to complete the track. Cortina looked at her brother waiting for him to urge her to take her turn then permission given she secured the piece like a jigsaw puzzle to the next. She knew that Gerald would want to put the very last piece in place so he could revel in the finished article and salivate on his creation. She had seen him do this every morning since their birthdays on the 5 March, so she knew exactly how to support him to the fullest and therefore how not to cause him distress but more importantly not to be on the receiving end of that distress.

Gerald sat back to purvey his work like an artist standing back from the canvas to get a better view. He carefully walked around the masterpiece to where his little train engine and its carriages sat and with both hands, he picked it up as one whole piece to place it on to the track but the little elephant slipped through his fingers.

Cortina still knelt on the floor could never have anticipated her brother's action and therefore was totally bewildered by his response. Gerald's anger at the sudden imperfection of his action immediately ignited the sleeping demons deep within that even he was unable to control. He threw the tiny train, with its little carriages with such force at the track that the red funnel of the engine broke off, some of the wheels bent and the giraffe splintered as it ricocheted up.

It was Cortina who wasn't quick enough because this time the rage had occurred instantly and without warning before the elephant had even touched the ground. The giraffe caught Cortina on her cheekbone just below her eye before finding its resting place along the centre of the red suspension bridge. At the sight of the giraffe laid where it was not supposed to be tainting his beautiful centre piece, Gerald's rage continued to spiral to catastrophic levels. Cortina scrambled for the safety of her bed and the protection her sheets would afford, unable to stop Gerald as he systematically decimated what had earlier been his pride and joy. Only when she could hear his sobs begin to subside did she know it was safe to lower her covers to take a peek.

Gerald was sat by the door on the only bit of carpet that did not have bits of what was once a train set. His mind was blank, his arms tightly wrapped around his knees in a protective foetal position as he gently rocked back and forth his eyes staring wildly ahead. Cortina knew she could not approach him so it was also impossible for her to get out of the room safely, so all she could do was hold tight and wait.

Gerald sat for several minutes, his body still in reactive shock at his own rage, his pulse and heart racing, tension convulsing through his veins. Gerald was only able to mentally return to the room as the tingling in his fingers generated a connection with his brain that there was a physical sensation. His rocking body slowly ceased allowing him the ability to unlock his arms and stretch his legs forward.

As his feet began to touch the broken pieces of track the result of his spiralled display of anger the reality of its brokenness smashed him in the face like a baseball bat. Cortina waited. She knew that she had to wait for the pinnacle moment before she dared to approach him and then from under the covers where she had laid as still as an inanimate object came the guttural wail. She leapt out of bed, momentarily taking in the scattered parts of Gerald's once pride and joy side stepping them to get to him. She was as much taking comfort from him as he was from her glad that the episode was over knowing that the sobs would subside and then there would be the depressive aftermath.

Gerald allowed her to envelop him, allowed her to rub his back and to shush him just as she had seen their mother do many times before. They may only have been 6 years of age but both Gerald and Cortina knew that there was no longer any care, comfort or love being bestowed upon them other than from each other. Their father had left 9 months earlier just after their birthday and now it seemed their mother no longer had any time, patience nor affection towards them. Gerald and Cortina had been existing in a living hell of having to fend for themselves whilst their mother took to the bottle night after night.

She no longer had that spark she'd once had, no longer had a zest for life nor a perceived reason to get up for. In fact, to Gerald and Cortina it seemed to them that all her fight and everything that she had once stood for had left in the bags that their dad had packed. So, they had been forced to cling to one another exactly as they were right now, sat on the carpet littered with broken tracks leaning against the door of their bedroom. The sad truth was that unbeknown to either Gerald and Cortina this would be for the last time as soon their entire lives would be sent like a bowling ball careering down a whole new trajectory.

Chapter 2
Cortina Matthews: The Keepsakes

Cortina cared deeply for Gerald but when he became enraged as he often did, she was out of her depth, adults hadn't created effective methods to help Gerald so how was she supposed to navigate her way through. She sat with him until his little sobs subsided and then she slightly pulled away, it made her heart ache to see his tearstained face. She gently put her little fingers under his chin to raise his face up but it was fruitless as he was not ready to face her so he heartily resisted her pull.

'Come on Gerald,' she urged him, 'I am not cross with you.'

He tilted his head keeping his eyes closed unable to meet her questioning gaze his little lip protruding ever so slightly.

'Gerald,' she said again, 'if you are the big boy who can smash up his toys then I don't want the little boy to pretend he isn't brave enough to face his actions.' This was the phrase that Cortina had heard her mother say on so many occasions so in the absence of a parental figure she was now assuming the role. 'Gerald, I want you to look at me.'

'I am looking at you Cort only I have my eyes shut,' he told her.

'Ok Gerald,' she played along, 'even if you have your eyes shut, I know you can still hear me,' she began. 'You know Mummy will be angry because you broke your toys again. We will have to clear all those pieces up and put them in their box then take it out to the bin and throw it in to the trash.'

'But I don't want to Cort,' Gerald said, I don't want my lovely train track to go in the bin, I love my train track it was my birthday present.' He started to wail again but this time Cort was not going to allow him to feel sorry for himself, he had scared her with his anger and he needed to know.

'If you loved your train track, you should have looked after it, Gerald, you really scared me and look you hurt my face,' she said pointing to her cheek.

Gerald pulled himself up from the comfort of his sister to look at her not feeling deserving of her love if he had hurt her. He began to wail again as he saw the welt on her soft porcelain skin, he knew it would leave a scar and then it was his turn to hug her. Cortina stood up now and offered Gerald her hand which he obediently took pulling himself up. From this view point, he could see the entirety of his expelled rage.

'Sorry, Cort,' he said simply.

Without another word both Cortina and Gerald worked together to force all the bits of the strewn track back into its box. Once they had finished, they struggled with the box sliding it across the carpet down the stairs to the front door. Gerald climbed from the bottom steps up on to the little window sill besides the front door to release the latch so they could get out, as he had done many times before. Once outside, they grappled with the box to get it to the wheelie bin where they propped it up behind it ready for the dustbin men to remove. On the way back up the path, Gerald turned to have one last look at the box no longer full of his pride and joy knowing that a bit of himself was leaving with it.

Cortina, aware that Gerald would be devastated by his actions had kept two special pieces as a keepsake whilst she had helped to pick the bits up from the carpet. 'Gerald,' she said to him directly, 'I have something for you,' and putting her hands into the two tiny little pockets at the front of her nightie she pulled out the objects. 'I want you to keep the giraffe Gerald so that it reminds you that your anger hurts and I am going to keep the elephant as a reminder that mistakes happen. You have one and I have the other so whenever we are apart, we will remember that we are always part of a set,' she told him.

For the rest of the day, Cortina kept touching the little elephant in her pocket prompting her to think about Gerald and of the times when she felt close to him, the times she had been afraid of him and then times when she just wanted to run away from him. It was confusing, if Cortina didn't like someone at school, she would go to great lengths to avoid them but with Gerald she had no choice he was her brother. Cortina wished that her dad was here because then her mum would be well again and maybe together, they could help Gerald instead of her feeling like it was her job.

Maybe if they hadn't gone to that stupid party last year then her dad wouldn't have met Emma and would have loved them enough not to leave them. Maybe if Cortina hadn't told her dad that she hated him when he had explained he didn't love Mummy any more he would have stayed. Maybe it was all Cortina's fault and that was why Gerald behaved the way he did because he blamed her too. She did try to behave, she tried so hard and prayed to God every night to bring her daddy home but he hadn't done it yet. Cortina decided she would pray extra hard for her daddy to come home, for her mummy to stop drinking and to start to love them again and for Gerald that he wouldn't be so angry.

Yes, tonight she decided she would go to bed early because she had a lot to talk to God about, He would listen, He always did and she would leave it for Him to sort out. Little did poor Cortina know but that night there would be a catastrophic turn of events, maybe God was listening but it would not turn out the way she was expecting.

Chapter 3
Cortina: Please God

When Cortina lay in bed that night, she pulled the covers over her head and poured her heart out like never before. She told God how helpless she felt how she wished she still had her old life where her mum and dad lived together. She asked God why her mum didn't love her anymore and dared to ask what her heart feared, whether it was her fault that her parents had split up. She prayed and prayed until her tiny eyelids began to feel ever so heavy and her thoughts began to fade before sleep finally took over. It was a few hours later that she was abruptly awoken by the loud bangs and screeches of rockets as the night sky was filled with an array of blasts and colours. Cortina lay rigid, unable to overcome the fear that succumbed her. One after the other, she could hear the bangs before the bedroom was awash with vibrant colours of red, green and amber. She tried to block the infernal noise by placing her hands over her ears and delving further down beneath her bed sheets counting to 10 then starting at 1 and counting all over again.

However, the fear was like a coiled spring and before she could resist it any further, she flew up out of bed and ran through the door to find her mother. She ran to her mum's bedroom hoping to snuggle in to gain comfort if only from the body heat of being next to her but the bed was intact, still made and her mother was nowhere to be seen. Perplexed and disorientated in her sleepiness, she ran to the top of the stairs unsure whether to seek out her mother, unsure of what state she might find her in or whether to slip into bed next to Gerald. Tentatively, she took a step down, then came an almighty bang from outside that seemed to shatter the glass and she was off down the stairs without further hesitation.

Cortina Matthews stopped in her tracks no longer due to the succession of loud bangs or the cast of the lights throughout the hallway. No, it was due to the long black shadow that had caught her eye across the floor which thanks to the lights of the cascading fireworks had extended across to the opposite wall of the hallway. Cortina did not want to turn around, terrified that the body shaped shadow was an intruder yet comparably also feeling compelled to do so. She was momentarily rooted to the spot fear coursing through her veins, eyes wide, aware that her chest was rising rapidly and then falling heavily. Cortina turned but was so shocked by the sight that fell upon her eyes she ran to the window sill by the door, climbed upon it, slid the latch and ran out, screaming.

All around her the sky was being lit by a splendid palette of colour but the only noise she could hear now was an internal scream penetrating her brain. Cortina ran as fast as her little legs would permit her bare feet immune to the little stones and debris along the pathway. She ran through her gate in no particular direction, just a desperate yearning to get away from the new horror of her wakefulness blinded by the terror her eyes had bestowed upon her. How she wished she had stayed in bed, how she wished she had slid in next to Gerald and not gone downstairs, this is your fault Cortina Matthews, this is all your fault, you made this happen and now not even God will forgive you.

Chapter 4
Barry Jarman: Pitstop Alley

Barry Jarman had been out with work friends celebrating the New Year and was thoroughly inebriated. He smiled at the thought of the young blonde in the office who had finally succumbed to his advances and given him a New Year's kiss. He said kiss, but boy it was a full-on snog about as passionate as it could possibly be. He staggered from side to side propelling himself along the ginnels between the houses on the back route home with the biggest grin plastered across his smug face. He hoped that she wouldn't regret it or worse still she could be snogging everything that moved because then she would forget about him. However, after tonight, he knew he wouldn't be able to forget her, he was as smitten as a schoolboy with a crush and no mistaking it. Barry Jarman slipped into the "pitstop" alley as it was called locally namely because it was a place where most folk on their drunken walk home would make a nightly "pitstop" to have a pee.

He repositioned his tackle, pulled up his zip and wiped the excess pee on the leg of his trousers before continuing on through to the end of the ginnel. He was in a jovial mood when he stepped out of the other end on to Park Grove in order to make the last 50 yards towards his home when he was nearly knocked off his drunken feet. As he looked down to his right, he was stunned to find little Cortina Matthews in nothing but her nightwear screaming hysterically. Not wanting to add to her distress, he bent down next to her.

'Cortina,' he said as softly as he could but she was simply screaming. Resisting the urge to slap her face to stop her as he had seen in the movies he said her name again, but a little more sharply, 'Cortina!'

She still kept on screaming so he did the only thing he could and he scrabbled her up in to his arms and carried her to the nearest door that had a light on.

The door was answered by a burly man in his early 30s in the background there was idle chatter emanating from another room the man had a huge grin on his face as the door swung open, and he automatically began with, 'Happy New Year!' believing it was other revellers coming to join the party. He stopped half way through his greeting when he found Barry Jarman stood at his door with a child in his arms sobbing. He stepped aside to let Barry in and called to his wife, 'Happiness, you had better come here.'

Happiness entered the small dining kitchen where Barry could see held half eaten plates of food, half empty bottles of spirits and a bin overflowing with empties. 'Oh no, now what do we have here?' Happiness declared in her south Nigerian enunciation.

Happiness lent forward into Barry so she could see the little one's face and then told her husband to take the girl so she could tend to her, 'In here' she stated as she walked through into the lounge expecting her husband and Barry to follow.

'Turn the music down,' she instructed no one in particular and knelt on the floor near to the top end of the now vacated settee. He carefully laid the child down, 'Hello, my darling now can you tell me your name?' the child stared without seeing so Happiness turned to look at Barry to fill in the gaps.

'Her name is Cortina she lives just up the street at number 57 on Park Grove,' Barry said having quickly sobered up. 'I was on my way home when she came flying down the street and nearly knocked me off my feet. I have no idea what on earth has happened but she was hysterical,' Barry told the anxious crowd.

'Leonard, you and Barry need to go up to number 57 to see if her parents are anywhere to be seen?' Happiness then turned back to Cortina, 'Come my lovey can you tell me what has happened, a little one like you shouldn't be out on the streets gone midnight!' Happiness tried to coax but there wasn't even a flicker of acknowledgement.

Happiness sat rubbing the back of the girl's hand to let her know she was safe though being very careful to lean back so not to overwhelm her. The guests began to make themselves scarce the New Year celebrations apparently over. After what seemed to be an age and a half to Happiness, Barry and Leonard returned with ashen looks on their faces.

'The police are on their way,' Leonard delivered. 'The poor mite,' he finished shaking his head as he went back into the kitchen to pour both himself and Barry a brandy.

Happiness did not want to leave the little girl as perplexed as she was by her husband's lack of explanation so she stayed where she was to give her the comfort that she obviously required. A few moments later, she could hear sirens in the distance, the little girls hand tightened in hers, 'It's ok, my lovely there is no need to worry.' But the girl began to cry again and Happiness was sure that she had heard her faintly whisper, 'But it is all my fault.'

Chapter 5
Jacobi, Parker and Williams:
57 Park Grove

It was a good half hour or more before patrol officer Dion Jacobi and his colleague Jenson Parker entered the house on Park Grove where the little girl was said to be. They tapped lightly on the partial open door, entering stating their presence and introduced themselves to Barry and Leonard who were still in the kitchen.

'Where is the little girl now?' Jacobi, an officer for many years began. 'Do we know her name.'

'Yes, it is Cortina Matthews,' Barry offered. 'I was the one who found her and brought her here.'

'Yes, then both Barry and I went up to the house to find out why she was on the streets so late at night,' Leonard stated.

'And what are your names?' asked Jenson opening a little black pad noting their names, movements and the address he was now at.

'Has she said anything at all?' Jacobi enquired.

'No, not to my knowledge she was just hysterical literally racing down the road and nearly knocked me off my feet,' Barry explained.

'We were in full swing of our celebrations when Barry here knocked on our door, that was the first we were alerted that there was a problem,' Leonard told them.

'What made you come to this door Barry; do you know each other?' asked Jacobi.

'It was the nearest house where I could see that the lights were on and I didn't want to be caught with a screaming kid in my arms, in case people thought I had done something to her,' he said earnestly.

'We do know of each other living on the same street but just to say hello to,' Leonard told the officers, 'Like putting a hand up if we are driving past each other that kind of thing.'

'Yeah, we are law abiding citizens that happen to live in the same street, wave, nod to or say hello to,' Barry stated, feeling the pressure of suddenly being involved in a police investigation.

'So where is the girl now?' Jacobi asked.

'She is in there,' Leonard nodded towards the lounge then added, 'with Happiness, my wife.'

Jenson tilted his head with a questioning look upon his face one that Leonard had seen and had to explained many times before, 'Happiness is Nigerian.' The police officer was thankful, gave a thin smile in response and proceeded to make a note in his pad.

Jacobi peeped around the door frame to see a much smaller child than he had expected laying on the settee with whom he presumed was Happiness sat beside her on the floor. Happiness looked over her shoulder at the intruder a pensive look upon her face as her shoulders shrugged up and down as if to say I have no idea what is going on. Jacobi turned back into the kitchen and told the others that he felt they had better wait for his colleague, Shona Williams to arrive as she was better equipped to deal with these matters. The aura of a white flashing light panned across the kitchen closely followed by red ones.

'Looks like the paramedics and fire brigade are here,' Jenson stated to Jacobi as Barry and Leonard glanced at each other with a puzzled look across their faces.

'In instances of this nature, it is protocol for the paramedics to attend to confirm life is extinct and the fire brigade are in attendance to safely cut the body down thus alleviating any further damage or bruising. We also have to preserve the knot that was used to create the noose as it forms part of our investigation. Our scenes of crime guys are busy detailing the area, photographing any evidential information that would help to establish exactly what has occurred,' Jacobi casually informed them.

'What's occurred,' Leonard blurted out. 'She's fucking killed herself, that's what's happened.' He finished the remnants of his glass and took the bottle to pour himself another.

'I know this is very difficult sir but might I ask you to go easy with the bottle we may need to take a statement tonight and I need you to be in a fit state, if you don't mind,' Jenson said easing the bottle away from Leonard's hand and placing it back down onto the counter. There was a tap at the door.

'Come in,' Leonard said. 'You might as well join the party as well.'

Shona Williams poked her head around the door, recognised her colleagues then stepped fully into the kitchen, 'what do we have guys?' she enquired.

'This is Barry, he was on his way home from the pub when he came across a young girl Cortina Matthews running down the street in a hysterical state. He knocked on the first door that he could see still had lights on which was this one, occupants are Leonard here and his wife Happiness, she is in the lounge with Cortina,' Jacobi said giving a nod towards the lounge.

'Both Barry and Leonard ventured towards the girls home,' Jenson began then checked his pad, '57 Park Grove to find a woman suspended by the neck from the banister. At this point, it is suspected that the victim is none other than the child's mother Cassandra Matthews, given the child's age; I wanted to wait for a more senior officer with specialised training to attend before approaching the child.'

'Thank you,' Shona nodded. 'Is there anything else I need to know before I talk to her?'

'No, I think that is everything,' Jacobi said looking at the other 3 gentleman to see if they had anything else to offer, they didn't.

Shona Williams gave a cursory look around the kitchen noting that a party had obviously been occurring so made a mental note that the names of the guests would need to be identified for questioning to verify the events she had been told. She lightly tapped the glass of the partitioning door and noted the black lady sat holding the little girl's hand, she remained where she was. Shona approached slowly, careful not to scare the little girl who was wearing a thin cotton nightie. Her right hand was gripping the black lady's hand whilst the other was tucked in a small pocket to the left of her nightie, it also appeared to be clutching an object. She made a mental note to seek what was so important to the child that she had grabbed it before she had left the house.

'Cortina,' Shona said softly. 'My name is Shona and I work with the police.'

The girl seemed to become agitated at the knowledge she was a police officer so Shona tried a different approach. 'Cortina I am here to help you and to find out what has happened tonight.' A tear dribbled from the corner of the little girl's eye but no sound passed her lips; she just stared incessantly at the ceiling. 'Cortina, do you think we could sit you up, would that be alright?'

'Would you mind bringing her a drink of juice and maybe a biscuit if you have one or anything sweet for that matter?' Shona asked Happiness. She nodded and tried to pull away from Cortina but she just gripped tighter onto her hand. 'It is Ok Cortina,' Shona said prising her fingers from Happiness's hand. 'She will be coming straight back in a moment.'

Shona kept hold of the little girl's hand continuing to quench her need for human contact until Happiness had returned then she motioned for her to sit on the settee. Shona carefully assisted the little girl to a seating position, then once upright near to Happiness she nestled in next to her not wanting her face exposed. Shona waited a moment then motioned to Happiness to entice the little girl to take a drink so that she could gain her trust.

'Come on little one it's time to have a drink,' Happiness told the girl guiding Cortina to the glass of orange liquid. 'Come,' she urged, gently lifting her right shoulder to ease the girl closer towards the glass.

Cortina tentatively took the offering in her shaking little hands; she had a sip before greedily drinking the rest of it down.

'There you see that is better, now here,' Happiness said giving her the biscuit.

Cortina held the biscuit for a moment staring at it as though she had never seen one before then like a mouse, she carefully nibbled around the edge of it her rigid body, slowly beginning to relax. Shona waited patiently for her to finish the entire biscuit not wanting to interrupt the focus of her complete concentration before she attempted to speak again. Shona knew full well that despite her urgency to investigate what had happened it was more important not to rush the little girl who was as much a victim as her mother.

'Cortina I am Shona I have come to talk with you so we can find out what has happened to your mummy, a friend of mine from social services will be here any minute to help me, to help you. Is that, ok?' Shona asked.

The little girl gasped slightly but then gave a weak nod. Shona could see her beginning to fidget with whatever it was that she had in her pocket so she decided to distract her by reverting her attention to this. 'Do you have a treasured possession you're holding on to that you would like to show me, Cortina?' Shona asked kindly.

She nodded before pulling out her hand to reveal a small wooden elephant and then she said, 'Gerald.'

'Is that the name of your elephant? Gerald,' Shona asked.

'It is the name of my brother,' Cortina spoke in a hushed voice.

'Where is Gerald?' Shona asked.

'In bed, asleep,' Cortina said and then she began to silently cry, the tears coming thick and fast.

Shona retraced her steps to the kitchen to address Jenson, 'Would you mind checking for other occupants at number 57, it appears, the little girl has a brother, Gerald who may be asleep in bed. Also ask one of the paramedics to come down will you I think she could do with a once over and a blanket for when we leave.'

'On it,' Jenson stated and promptly darted out through the door as Samantha James the duty social worker arrived. Shona greeted Samantha, introduced her to Barry, Leonard and Jacobi before taking her into the lounge to Cortina.

'Cortina, this is my friend Samantha that I was talking to you about, she has come to ensure that all your needs are met and that we take good care of you. We will have to go with her now so that Happiness and Leonard can get some sleep, you must be shattered too,' Shona said.

Cortina simply repeated, 'Gerald.'

'I have sent my colleague to fetch Gerald so he should be waiting for us by now, don't worry, Cortina you will not have to go back into the house,' Shona informed the little girl as she took her hand and gently eased her off the settee. A paramedic arrived at the back door with a blanket for the little girl which he wrapped around her before scooping her up and carrying her up the road to an awaiting ambulance. On her way through the kitchen, Shona quietly motioned Jacobi to the lounge to ask Happiness her view of the events and to enquire whether Cortina had said anything. Shona then accompanied Samantha out into the back yard to the bite of the cold night air, 'It is going to be a long night,' she said.

'It is going to be an even longer one for those poor little kids,' Samantha said shaking her head. 'Whatever has driven the mother to do such a terrible thing will affect those poor little mites for the rest of their lives.'

'Let's hope we can piece it together and quickly for their sakes,' Shona suggested.

'Is the children's father still on the scene?' Samantha wondered.

'We are making enquiries to ascertain it along with a last known address as we speak, I just hope he can give the children the support and security they need because if not I dread to think what will happen to them,' Shona said.

'They will end up as wards of the court and be placed in care if we cannot locate him, so let's just hope it's a positive outcome for their sake,' Samantha said out of experience.

Shona Williams and Samantha James walked the rest of the way in silence both deep in thought at the prospect of what might happen to the children whose lives had been blown apart due to the tragic decision their mother had taken. Neither one relished the prospect of the night's occurrence nor the path the children had subsequently been cast upon. However, both were mystified at what could have driven a mother to not only have taken her own life but to have not protected her children from witnessing it. Shona Williams hoped to be able to get some answers quickly and Samantha James just wanted to get the children settled so she could get back home to bed.

Chapter 6
Happiness, Leonard and Barry: The Aftermath

As their uninvited guests finally left, Happiness remained at the back door for a while staring out in to the night sky, the fireworks had all but stopped bar for the odd one. When she did turn back into the kitchen it was as though she had seen a ghost.

'What do you make of all that?' she asked.

'Horrendous!' was the only word that Leonard could find. Barry to her right was suddenly feeling awkward, here he was on the most celebrated night of the year stood in a stranger's kitchen.

'One for the road?' Leonard asked noting his discomfort.

'Sorry, yes if you don't mind,' he said, 'I was so keen to get home before…well you know…before all this but now it's the last place I want to be.'

'Yes, tonight hasn't quite turned out the way any of us expected, has it?' Happiness agreed walking through into the lounge, 'That poor child.' Leonard poured them all a drink.

'I cannot get the image of that poor woman hanging out of my head, I do not know what I expected to find but it wasn't that,' Barry said truthfully.

Noting that Barry needed to unburden himself, once Leonard had poured the drink, he motioned Barry to collect it and follow him through to the lounge. Happiness may not have seen what they had seen but Leonard knew how sensitive his wife was and that she too would be in need of his support. They found Happiness sat at the opposite edge of the settee from where the child had been lying, simply staring at the now vacant spot. Leonard sat on the hard arm part next to her. As if sensing Leonard's reluctance to take up the child's empty spot Barry was also loathed to, so he chose instead to hover at the doorway.

'What do you think will happen now?' asked Leonard.

'From what the little girl said she has a brother who was still in bed when she fled from the house. She must have been absolutely terrified; it doesn't bear thinking about I make no wonder you found her in such a hysterical state, Barry,' Happiness said shaking her head.

'That policewoman sent one of the fella's up to find the lad, apparently the little lass had just bolted,' Leonard stated. Barry pictured the little girl's face when she had bumped in to him coming out of the alley. The room was silent for a few minutes as each of them pondered their own involvement in the night's occurrences, then it was Leonard who broke the ice.

'When Barry and I walked up to number 57, I have got to say I was a bit annoyed at having to seek the kids' parents and them not taking care of the lass. I was well and truly going to give them a piece of my mind, a lass of that age out on her own,' Leonard admitted.

'You and me both Leonard, here I was on my way home in a good mood having had a great night when boom,' he clapped his hands together for effect, 'She literally came from nowhere. When we were walking up to the house, I thought we would find a party in full swing, the adults that pissed they hadn't noticed the kid was missing,' Barry said.

'To be honest, even as we went up the path it never dawned on me that there was no music or people milling around, I just saw the door open, fuelling my anger and I was about to charge in when I was stopped in my tracks,' Leonard's voice faltered.

'Where was she?' Happiness asked in a quiet voice.

'She was hanging in the hallway from one of the balustrades,' Barry offered. 'Still, just hanging, no movement at all. That will be one image I will never be able to erase!'

'The house was so quiet, there were fireworks going off all around me but I didn't hear a thing, my eyes were just locked on to the bairn's mother,' Leonard said downing his drink in one gulp.

'Oh my,' said Happiness, 'and now they are going to fetch the little lad down past his mother I hope they cover his face.' Then she buried her head into her hands, small sobs escaping intermittently, with Leonard rubbing her back for comfort.

'I am sorry to have brought this to your door,' Barry suddenly found his voice.

'Bloody hell Barry, don't you go feeling bad about it, you weren't to know what the little lass was running from. No, you did the right thing mate, you found yourself in a predicament and needed to get the lass some help. I am glad we were all able to do our part for her but there is no mistake none of us could have predicted the outcome.' Leonard told Barry as Happiness began to sit back up.

'Yes, Leonard's right, we have all been able to work together to do our bit but it's what happens now for the children that worries me,' Happiness sniffed.

Again, the three of them contemplated the thought before Barry thanked them again, said goodnight and made his way the short distance home.

Chapter 7
The Little Boy: The Stranger

The little boy was in a deep, restful sleep when the stranger walked into his bedroom, he did not stir. The stranger crossed the room and gently shaking him by the shoulder he softly spoke the name Gerald, but he did not stir. The stranger pulled back the covers wafting cold air across the young boy's body, consequently initiating a response as his hand reached blindly for the covers that were out of his grasp. The little boy shifted his position bringing his knees up to his chest in an attempt to protect himself from the draft. Again, the stranger tried to awaken him, 'Gerald,' he said again a little louder. An eye sprung open, then the other and without warning his legs kicked out hitting the stranger full pelt in the chest as he screamed out. Taken aback, the stranger took a moment to compose himself but it was enough time for the child to spring up from the bed and to run out on to the landing. His first instinct was to find his mother but there was an abundance of activity downstairs with lights of varying colours skimming continually across the hall and casting a glow up to the top of the stairs.

At the bedroom door, the stranger loomed so the child ran down the stairs wanting to be in the thick of the commotion rather than on his own cornered by the stranger. Instantly he wished he had stayed where he was tucked up in the warm comfort of his bed. In front of him was a lifeless body suspended by the neck, her facial expression contorted in agony was pale, her eyes bulging, her mouth gaping and her head held rigid to its right. He screamed into her face, a mask of horror just like the ones he had seen during Halloween. He screamed and he screamed at the horror directly in front of him but he couldn't overt his eyes, he couldn't close them only stare unblinkingly at her.

The little boy did not know how long he had stood on the stairs he did not know how long he had stared death in the face only that he would never be able to erase the nightmare of what he had just witnessed. And then he was thankful to the stranger who scooped him up into his arms finally severing the invisible umbilical cord that had kept him bound like concrete to the spot. The devastation, shock and fear that coursed through him perpetuated his fragile mind rendering him unable to stop himself from struggling in the wake of the terror that engulfed him. The stranger gripped him tighter, fleeing out through the front door like a fire fighter rushing his hose to a fire wanting to get him to the safety of an awaiting ambulance.

The little boy caught sight of Cortina, 'Cort,' he screamed as he kicked and struggled, 'Cort, Cort,' but she did not come to his aide, she did not stop the stranger from taking him, she did not help him perpetuating his anguish even further.

As the stranger reached the awaiting ambulance a blanket was quickly thrown around the little boy swaddling him in its soft fleecy embrace, yet he still had the power to struggle. The paramedic was powerless to treat him in his current state so unfortunately, he was forced to administer an injection to sedate him. It was not long before he succumbed to the warm comforting peace that began to radiate throughout his entire body until finally, he was able to let go and embrace the soothing, relaxed state of sleep. He lay in the back of the ambulance his face no longer a picture of anguish, the stark lights dimmed to offer a semi-shadowing glow. He would sleep for a number of hours only to wake to the same torment of a mind permanently affected by the witness to a suicide.

On the night of 31 December 2000 when the clock struck 12 the cogs shifted for two young children that would send them into a spiral of court hearings, care and foster home placements lasting many years. Their mental health's would be compromised causing both children to plummet into depths of despair few will ever come to realise. The trauma of not only seeing a mother's lifeless body but coupled with a continual revolving door of homes and ultimately their forced separation would affect them for the rest of their whole lives. As Gerald slept peacefully in the back of one ambulance and Cortina in the back of another, what neither realised was that the nightmare had only just begun.

Chapter 8
Shona Williams: Doubts

Shona Williams, Dion Jacobi and Jenson Parker were on the scene at 57 Park Grove until 06.35 hrs collating evidence and trying to make sense of why a mother of 6-year-olds would commit suicide. Unfortunately, a suicide note had not been found but on her bedside table there was a packet of amitriptyline tablets. On the box, Shona Williams noted that they had been prescribed by a Dr Richard Carmichael on the 28 December 2000, only 3 days before. Shona understood enough about the drug to know that it took time to work and if Cassandra Matthews had only been on it for a few days, it was not long enough for her to have felt its full benefit. She made a note to speak to Dr Carmichael because it was possible Matthews had been on the drug longer and this was just a repeat prescription. The other fact that Shona was aware of was that alcohol increased the sedative effects of the drug hence why the label states not to operate machinery, drive or drink whilst taking the drug due to its drowsy affects. The box stated that there should be 5 blister packs each containing 10 tablets yet only 3 full packs were evident with a fourth only having 7 tablets in. Therefore, if Cassandra Matthews had taken a tablet each night since she had been prescribed them, then there were 10 tablets unaccounted for.

Shona checked the contents of the bin in Cassandra's bedroom there was no blister pack discarded in there, so she checked the waste paper bin in the bathroom along with the one in the kitchen. Not only did she find the empty packet but she also found an empty bottle of vodka. Shona imagined Cassandra Matthews being at home, alone, on New Year's Eve depressed and sick of the life she was living, no husband and of being left to raise her children as a single parent. She tried to visualise her swallowing the tablets down with gulps of vodka, was she intentionally contemplating suicide from the outset or hadn't she realised what she was doing. Then as the effects began to take control had the pain been numbed to such a degree that she was unable to consider the affect it would have upon her children when they found her.

Afterall, there was no one else in the house at the time so it was bound to be one or both of them that would make the grim discovery. Or did she just not care because she was so consumed by her own pain or self-pity. Shona concluded that she may never get the answers to the tragedy that had occurred at 57 Park Grove but she knew it would be that one case that she would never forget. Once the body had been cut down, the doctor had certified what everybody already knew, that she was in fact deceased the coroner was then permitted to take the body to the hospital mortuary. He would then decide whether it was necessary to open an inquest, do a post mortem or register it as a suicide.

It was clear from Shona's preliminary investigations that a break-in had not been detected, there were no signs of a struggle and there were no marks to the body that suggested Cassandra had put up a fight. Although Cassandra had failed to leave a suicide note stating her intensions by walking around the place, Shona could see her lifestyle spoke volumes. From what Shona had seen the children themselves were unkempt, their clothing and bedding were filthy, pots and pans filled the sink and the place hadn't had a good clean for months.

Cassandra was obviously living on the bread line her ex-husband had a new life shacked up with someone else, she was on antidepressants and everything had become too much for her. It was a very sad state of affairs where Shona could not help but have empathy with the woman even if she had ruined her children's lives by her actions.

Shona and her team found Cassandra Matthews passport, bagged it, sealed it then labelled it for identification purposes, a formality but it would save anyone from having to view her body. The knot and noose part of the rope was processed in the same way. She took one last look around the property before closing the door, locking it and then automatically retrying the handle as she always did with her own home just to be on the safe side it was definitely locked. Shona slid down into her red 2-seater MR2 the only guilty pleasure in life that she allowed herself. She loved its sleek dashboard with the 2 pop-up concealed compartments, it's small neat, smooth steering wheel, the soft leather seats and its swift change gearbox.

Shona loved nothing more than blasting out some tunes whilst reconnecting with her first love, especially after a difficult, shift. She would take the long way home or go for a burn out along the motorway clearing her mind of the day's events by simply enjoying the feel of the car on the open road. Better still was a moment like today where she could drive to her favourite spot overlooking the sea and watch the sun rise. In the summer, she liked nothing more than flicking the switch to release the roof letting the wind blow through her shoulder length hair.

Shona Williams arrived at her one-bedroom apartment, swung into number 34 her designated parking spot, jumped out secured her car then made her way to the car park lift. She took the lift to the 3rd floor briefly checking her make-up out in the lift mirror enroute and once the door had pinged open, she stepped out and made her way along the corridor towards her apartment. She was within 10 yards of her door when a thought struck her, there were no glasses.

Surely Cassandra Matthews wouldn't have drunk straight from the bottle and besides, the house was so messy so it would make sense that a glass would have been left out somewhere. In her depressed, intoxicated state there was no way Cassandra would have washed up the glasses when the pots and pans were still in the sink. That was unless someone had been drinking with her and they had washed them to hide the evidence.

It was no good, there was no way she would relax unless she went back to check her theory so she took the lift back down to her car. She smiled at the MR2 again it was weird the feeling of greeting it never got old and besides where was the hardship when she got to drive her beloved car again. When Shona arrived back at Cassandra Matthew's front door, she was initially puzzled at not being able to get her key into the lock, that was until she depressed the handle, found it to be open and a key lodged in the lock from the other side. No one had any rights to enter the property so she took her time to carefully and quietly make her way in. Initially she visually scanned the hallway instinctively focusing on the area where Cassandra Matthews body had been suspended.

'Police, show yourself!' she asserted then paused, listening, there was silence. In to her radio, Shona said, 'This is Officer Shona Williams I am at 57 Park Grove that is figures 5,7 on Park Grove, the Cassandra Matthews residence, send back up immediately,' she instructed. With her heartbeat thudding in her chest, she carefully took a step inside being sure to keep the door wide open and her body close to the wall. She glanced into the lounge, then making her way along the hall, she kept scanning up the stairs then back down to the closed door of the kitchen in front of her, maintaining an "high alert" status the entire time.

The kitchen door was ajar although she was sure it had been fully open when she had left it earlier. The downstairs appeared clear.

'Police,' she stated again. 'Come out with your hands up, officers have been dispatched.'

She was sure she had heard some movement coming from the upstairs floor, her eyes scanned across the ceiling as though she could see through the floorboards like a thermal imaging camera locating the person through their body temperature. She couldn't detect whether it was the mother's bedroom or the children's room. Shona eased her way to the bottom of the stairs and began to slowly climb her back hugging the wall as her left foot took a step then her right crossed to the next step. Slowly, deliberately and with care she maintained her full attention continually glancing between the upstairs doors.

A "click" sounded she couldn't be sure if it was a gun cocking or a door handle, she hesitated with bated breath as the children's door began to open. Shona could hear the approaching police cars but knew her position was compromised; she could take a bullet before they had even got out of their cars. The door opened followed by a young woman's scream and then instinctively she closed the door again.

Shona was confused, who was this person? 'Hello, you in the bedroom, this is the police, come out with your hands up!' Shona tried again.

The bedroom door tentatively began to move until the young woman was fully visible. 'Come out and put your hands on to the banister in front of you,' Shona told her. The woman did as she was instructed so Shona quickly took charge and cuffed her to be on the safe side.

Whilst they were making their way down the stairs two officers appeared at the front door, 'Everything Ok?' One asked.

'Yes,' Shona replied. 'I had to return to the house and found this young woman here rummaging around upstairs, do you want to explain who you are and what you are doing here?' Shona addressed her.

'I am Emma, Tony's partner, a social worker rang to ask if we could pack some things for the children. Tony is on nights so I came over to get them some,' she explained.

'So, you have a key to the property?' Shona asked.

'I don't, it's Tony's, he and Cassandra are still married, *were* still married,' she corrected herself, 'this was still his house and he needed the key because Cassandra was sometimes too drunk to answer the door.'

'Did the Social Worker explain what has happened here today?' Shona asked.

'Not to me, Tony just rang and said could I come over to pack some stuff for the kids, but to be honest there isn't much worth packing. It is either dirty or stuff you wouldn't even donate to a charity shop,' Emma said truthfully.

'Why didn't you answer when I called out?' Shona enquired.

'I had my earbuds in,' Emma said. 'They are in my jeans, back right pocket.'

Shona checked the area and found two kidney bean shaped ear buds.

'Can you remove the cuffs now?' Emma asked.

'Sorry it was just a precaution,' Shona said removing the cuffs and replacing them back upon her belt. 'Thanks lads,' she then said to the officers, 'false alarm.'

As the officers made their exit down the path Shona decided to take the opportunity to learn as much information about Cassandra Matthews life as she could. According to Emma, Cassandra and Tony had not had a very happy marriage, they had only been together for a couple of months before Cassandra had revealed she was pregnant. Tony had done the dutiful thing and had married her though predictively declared to his new mistress 'he had never loved her'. Emma and Tony had been together for only a year and having found the separation very difficult, Cassandra had subsequently made their lives hell.

Apparently, she would get into a drunken stupor most nights and then ring Tony's number which at first, he started answering primarily out of guilt but then the abuse had started so he refused to entertain her. He tried to ignore her but her calls became incessant every single night until at breaking point, he would finally answer it. If he switched his mobile off, she would ring Emma's house phone so they would unplug it but then she had started coming to the flat where Tony now lived with Emma. Tony had tried to get her some help he had called her doctor but he wouldn't talk to Tony even if it was in Cassandra's best interests.

He had looked into counselling; he had tried reasoning with her, threatened to take the kids when she had left them home alone anything to get her to stop but nothing worked. It seemed that in Emma's own words Tony and her were at the end of their tethers which in Shona's view could push them over the edge enough to stop her, permanently. Shona made a note to look into the relationship to see if there were instances in their marriage that Tony had been abusive, to enquire about any reports filed regarding Cassandra's harassment and also to investigate their whereabouts last night.

Once Shona had got as much information as she possibly could she supervised Emma to get a few things for the children although as she had stated there wasn't really anything decent enough to take. Before locking up, Shona did another cursory look around the house and checked the reason, she had initially returned, whether there had been any drinking glasses. There was nothing on the cluttered coffee table, or at the side of the sink, the living room floor, the bedroom side tables nor discarded in the bin. Perplexed, Shona opened the kitchen cupboards there were two sat side by side like someone had placed them there together having picked them up with one hand a finger in each.

At the bottom of one was a tiny clear residue, obviously this could be water but there again it could also have been vodka. Shona returned to her car for an evidence bag, she dispensed two disposable latex gloves from the cardboard box of her briefcase, donned them and returned to the kitchen. She cautiously manoeuvred the two glasses into the bag, sealing the top and labelled it appropriately. It might be nothing but Shona was as fastidious in her work as she was in her personal life and she knew it would niggle at her if she didn't check every detail.

Whoever Cassandra had become at the breakdown of her marriage and whatever she had done to leave her children without a mother was of no consequence to Shona, she had a job to do. Whether Cassandra Matthews had committed suicide or had her life taken was the one question that Shona had to find out and come what may she would do it to the very best of her abilities.

Chapter 9
Shona Williams: Rest Day

Once Shona had locked Cassandra Matthews house, she swung by the station to drop the two glasses into the evidence suite and then took herself home, she needed sleep. She caught the lift back up to the 3rd floor and unlocked the door of number 34 swinging it wide to reveal her pristine, highly desirable apartment with its perfectly placed designer furniture and classy open-plan grey kitchen. She hung her jacket on the vintage coat stand and placed her shoes upon the designated shoe rack before moving across to her Wurlitzer jukebox at the far end of the lounge. The vibe she had gone for was a contradiction between old, vintage, maybe even quirky mixed with a contemporary feel in the quality of her designer settee and kitchen units. One style she really hated was traditional, the old look of yesteryear or the cheap pine shit she'd had in her bedroom as a teenager. Her parents small house had been full of huge mahogany picces stood on a multicoloured flowered carpet with a deep maroon background. To say it was dark and dingy was an understatement, it was like a dungeon, dreary and claustrophobic being hemmed in with too much furniture in such a small space.

    Shona enjoyed living on the third floor where she could see out over the neighbouring park with its miniature railway, swings, football field and tree lined horizon. Shona hated being cooped up if she couldn't get out in her car with the top down her second choice would be to surround herself with nature. She enjoyed exploring the maze of paths, the little duck pond with its centre island of numerous species, the botanical delights of the public greenhouse and observing the multitude of visitors. Shona didn't know if it was a natural instinct of hers to enjoy people-watching or if it had been born out of her police training to observe, analyse and deduce but she found sitting on a bench in this park relaxing. If she ever needed to distress, this was where she could be found.

There again if she was puzzled by a case or needed to let her thoughts run wild for a while this was where she would come. There had been many occasions Shona had taken to a particular spot and then ping, the answer had sprung at her like a ball from the tennis courts.

Today she needed to hear a fistful of her favourite tunes in the form of some Indies rock music of the 80s so she put a compilation of Talking Heads, The Smiths, Jam, Joy Division and The Cure to play one after the other. She loved programming the Wurlitzer then hearing it kicking into life with its flashing lights and mechanical arm responding to her commands by pinpointing and selecting the right track before setting it in its place to play. She took a cold bottle of Bud from the drink's fridge under the kitchen work surface, popped the top and glugged deeply straight from the bottle. Amazing she thought, here she was drinking straight from the bottle so why did she find it doubtful that Cassandra Matthews might have done the same. Afterall, the empty vodka bottle had only been a smaller half-litre measure so she had to concede it was possible but her suspicions would still have to be explored even if they were extinguished either way.

Shona finished her drink as the second disc hit the turntable Suffer Little Children by the Smiths maybe in light of the night's events it wasn't very respectful so she ejected it. The next wasn't much better with "Love Will Tear Us Apart" by Joy division so she changed it up a gear to The Jam's "A Town Called Malice", it would have to do she decided. She took her bottle to the dual-purpose bin and placed it in the recycle side before making her way to the bathroom. She turned the dial of the shower to let it run whilst she slipped out of her clothes, used the toilet and stepped under the soothing hot droplets of water.

The magnitude of power that the sports shower pelted her with was exactly what she needed to wash the grime from her hair and body that she had felt from being at Cassandra Matthews home. It was the type of place that ordinarily you might wipe your feet from on the way out so it had definitely left her with the feeling that she needed to scrub herself. She allowed the water to minister to her with its therapeutic, rhythmic flow before thoroughly shampooing her hair, rubbing and caressing her scalp to get a deep clean. She rinsed it off and applied the conditioner, taking her shower comb to ensure the mixture was applied the entire length from roots to tip before lathering her body with an exfoliating sponge.

She rinsed herself but then decided to repeat the process methodically soaping beneath her armpit and down her left arm, across her chest, beneath and around her boobs, her belly, down each leg and foot before changing hands to do her right arm and back. She squeezed the excess soapy liquid from the sponge and wiped across her face then re-soaped and finished her routine by attending to her private areas.

Shona rinsed the conditioner from her hair, raised her face to the water then allowed it to wash over her before turning the dial to shut it off. She felt fresh, clean and relaxed so taking up her towel she wiped herself dry, cleaned her teeth and made her way into the bedroom to slip into her pyjama shorts and t-shirt set. She sat on the edge of the bed flopped her hair forward and gathered it up in the towel she had just been wearing and threw it over her head in a kind of turban to allow it to dry. Shona was far too tired to mess about with a hairdryer even if she would look like something from the Hair Bear Bunch. She pulled back the edge of the quilt and slid in loving the feel of the soft, clean Egyptian cotton sheet. She kicked off the bottom edge of the quilt so that her feet could stick out, winter or not, she couldn't abide anything on her feet and then like a switch her eyes closed and she was gone.

When she awoke 4 hours later, it was to a cold breathy atmosphere. She checked the thermostat in the lounge to find it was set correctly but for some reason the boiler had not automatically kicked in. These apartments may have been newish but the boilers were not the most reliable, at least hers wasn't. She looked outside to find there had been a scattering of snow along the hardened ground of the park. She yawned, loudly, a habit that had really irritated her mother when she had lived at home. So, she did it again just to prove to herself she could do whatever she wanted in her own place, she visualised her mother raising her eyes at her and that made her chuckle to herself.

Shona decided to spend a couple of hours pottering around the house trying to find something to tidy but as she lived alone and kept it pristine it was difficult to find anything remotely out of place. She filled herself a bowl of Bran Flakes then added a gush of skimmed milk before standing to eat them looking out of the window. There were only a handful of people in the park today mostly exercising their dogs or the odd adult with a child on a bike or some battery-operated ride-on that they had undoubtedly got for Christmas.

She finished her cereal, had a quick wash, cleaned her teeth, got changed and slung her work gear from yesterday into the washing machine. Restless, she decided to take a walk in the park before settling herself in front of the TV with a quilt around her and another endless Christmas film. She could not have told you what the film was about because her mind had been focused on the "suicide" of Cassandra Matthews, her conversation with Emma Boulden, and the "to do" list she was conducting in her head for the following day.

Chapter 10
Shona Williams: Making Enquiries

During the days that followed Cassandra Matthews untimely death Shona made a few enquiries just to satisfy her curiosity in between her caseloads. She contacted Dr Carmichael's secretary requesting he give her a ring about an ongoing investigation but didn't feel it important to share any further details. She checked the police database to see if there were any complaints lodged by Tony against his wife, there had been an informal chat with Jenson Parker so she made a note to talk to him. It didn't turn out to be of any use has Emma had stated Tony was fed up of her harassing him but was reluctant to go to the extent of getting an injunction against her. So, she ran a check on Tony but all that came back was a speeding offence for travelling 37mph in a 30 zone and then it had been from several years earlier.

She rang Tony's place of work, a huge distribution centre at the other side of town where his boss had said not only was he doing the night shift on New Year's Eve, 10pm to 6am but he had gone in early to cover a guy who had gone off sick. His boss, who had a thick Yorkshire accent praised his employee describing him as being exceptionally reliable, punctual, hardworking and very conscientious. The only snippet of information she didn't know was that Tony had huge debts due to his ex-wife's ability to spend, she had also gained the impression that it had not been a happy marriage.

When Dr Carmichael finally rang Shona back, he was able to collaborate that Emma's story was true, he had taken a call from Tony regarding his wife and that he was at his wits end with her. Dr Carmichael recalled Tony stating that he thought the children in her care were at risk due to her erratic behaviour and excessive drinking. Dr Carmichael couldn't discuss the matter due to patient confidentiality but he had offered an appointment for Cassandra Matthews with the view to direct her to targeted support. Cassandra had failed to keep the appointment. With regards to the amitriptyline, he was able to confirm that she had been prescribed the drug for four months with a review appointment having been scheduled for 28 January 2001. She had been given the drug due to her low mood and subsequent depression pertaining to the breakup of her marriage. She had also complained of an acute inability to sleep. So, no leads there. Shona had thanked him for his time and wished him a good weekend.

With so much to cover and not enough hours in which to investigate, Shona coerced Jacobi and Parker to call into Leonard and Happiness's house along with Barry's to see if there were any other details they could share about the family or the mother. There wasn't anything that shed any light on why Cassandra may have taken her life or of there being any issues with other people within the community only that she was often seen inebriated. A very sad revelation was that little Cortina had assumed blame for her mothers' death by stipulating it "was her fault". Leonard had provided a full list of names and contact numbers of the guests at his New Year's Eve party whom Jacobi and Parker quickly rang through but there was nothing new to report.

Shona then contacted social services wanting to obtain an update upon the children and immediately wished she hadn't bothered. Samantha James wasn't available so she was put through to a snotty nosed, unemotional arse who was the duty social worker he informed her in a matter-of-fact manner that it had been impossible to place the children together and that the father lived in a one-bedroom flat with his new partner. The children had been temporarily placed in emergency care with different families but that was the only information he had available.

When Shona got off the phone, her heart began to ache for the two little kids whose lives had been devastated only a few nights earlier. She sat momentarily perplexed by the body of power that could rule in matters to destroy these two little lives as if they hadn't gone through enough with the trauma of coming face to face with her hanging motionless in death.

Poor Cortina running wild into the night believing it was her fault and Gerald taken from his bed the fear of being ripped from his home and his sister. These two little kids each experiencing more than their little eyes should ever have seen, then not even allowed to comfort one another in the aftermath. She had to admit the system could do with a complete overall one that was less emotionless where the true needs of the child were at the forefront to support them and see it through their eyes. One where the children were given a voice and were able to express it openly. She was sure that if she were in their position she wouldn't care if there wasn't a spare bedroom at her dads she would sleep on the settee or even the floor if it meant she could be cared for by the person that loved them.

Shona felt despondent and let down by the system for them and made a mental note to check in on them as the case progressed. The one thing that the snotty nosed duty social worker did inform her about was the plan for grief counselling along with additional ongoing emotional support, once they had a more permanent placement. When Shona ended the call, she said out loud, 'No shit Sherlock!' As far as she was concerned it was the very least Cortina and Gerald would need, she just hoped for their sake it would be sooner rather than later along with them being reunited with each other.

Shona decided to check Cassandra's mobile records to verify what Emma had also told her about the excessive phone calls, this also panned out to be the truth. As a formality Shona also rang the contact number that Emma had provided to substantiate her whereabouts on New Year's Eve, a Sally Carta. She was able to confirm that Emma had arrived around 6pm, that together with Sally's partner, Richard they had eaten a Chinese, had drinks then they had brought the New Year in.

Five days after Cassandra Matthews had been cut down the coronial post mortem had been concluded. The report noted that toxicological tests taken from tissue samples and bodily fluids showed that she had alcoholic poisoning. The high presence of amitriptyline was consistent with her having being on the drug for a number of months although a spike of the drug was noted. It was also interesting that he had specifically noted that there were no solid tablets found in her stomach. Shona felt this could still prove her theory that it was consistent with them being crushed and ingested with the alcohol. Although has her boss stipulated, no one could know for sure if it was Cassandra who had made that decision or a third party.

The coroner had studied photos of the scene, he had examined the ligature from around Cassandra Matthews neck and completed a thorough examination of her body. He concluded that although there was no evidence of a gravitational drag from the weight of the body nor breaks to the neck whilst suspended it would suggest she didn't jump over the banister. However, her neck did have abrasions consistent with ligature asphyxiation including markings of splintering in the direction towards the back of her neck from being suspended. Therefore, given all the information that had been presented to him he determined that Cassandra Matthews death had been the result of suicide.

With regards to the residue in the glass, forensics had been unable to detect the presence of any drugs which did turn out to be water. More surprisingly was the fact that there were no traceable fingerprints upon either of the two glasses. This did generate a big fat question mark over the case for Shona and whether someone was trying to cover their tracks. It was possible that Cassandra had been drinking alone, that she had intentionally taken too many amitriptyline tablets resulting in her making an impaired choice to take her own life.

However, it was also possible she had been making someone's life a misery whether it was or wasn't Emma and Tony's and they had subsequently encouraged her to keep drinking. It was also possible that the tablets could have been crushed, her drink spiked and that she had been unconscious, placed on the floor in the hall and hoisted up to the position she had been found in. However, her boss, her colleagues and the coroner all disagreed with her analytical mind so it was one case she would have to chalk up as experience and forever puzzle its mystery.

For Shona Williams, there would always be an invisible question mark hovering over Cassandra Matthews *"suicide"*, one that would remain in place for many years and from time to time she would find herself thinking about it. For now, though she had absolutely no leads, no backing and nothing to substantiate her line of enquiry, so the case was closed. But what if there were elements of truth in Shona's suspicions?

Chapter 11
Dr Richard Carmichael: Woodpecker Mode

Richard Carmichael was an impressionable and easily manipulated young man who had only recently qualified, fulfilling his late mum's dream to have a son who was a doctor. It didn't matter whether the role suited his character, that the hours would be long, medical school gruelling or if it was his true vocation, he simply walked the path that she had put him on. His mother a very strong overbearing woman had used and abused her son for her own amends on a daily basis throughout his childhood and beyond. If friends or colleagues ever questioned her behaviour, Richard was quick to jump to her defence; that she meant well, she just loved him, was protective and that she only wanted the best for him. In reality, she coerced him into anything and everything she could knowing full well he was too kind to refuse her demands never realising she was taking advantage of him in order to benefit herself. So, if his grades were not quite good enough, she would drill it into him that he could do better but only if he aspired to be better.

Richard worked hard; he studied hard applying himself to strive to be the best that he could be because he wanted to make his mother proud. Richard went to Sheffield University to study the primary undergraduate degree MBChB (Bachelor of Medicine, Bachelor of Surgery degree). However, after 5 years of intensive studying just a month before he was due to receive his degree certificate his dear mother ended up having a massive heart attack and died. Poor Richard was beside himself not only at the death of his mum but that she wouldn't witness his success and at suddenly finding himself alone in the world. Perhaps these were the reasons he became so infatuated by an older woman who worked at his first GP Surgery.

Sal Carta was so self-assured, she literally oozed with confidence. She was funny, smart, had a great laugh and was a joy to be around everything that the newly qualified Dr Richard Carmichael's mother wasn't. One thing they did have in common though was the ability to make men do exactly what they wanted them to do. In Sal Carta's case, she used her feminine magnetism to seduce with insinuation rather than direct emotional blackmail and she didn't falter, she had the opposite sex literally eating out of her hand. Dr Richard Carmichael had no experience with the opposite sex nor an ability to regulate his emotional boundaries so he became as compliant as a puppet on a string.

Sal Carta was used to her subjects having at least some resolve and resistibility but Carmichael had neither where she was concerned. He was in awe of the way she could command a room full of people to respond almost instantly to her demands and as far as he was concerned, she was stunningly beautiful despite the 20-year age gap. Carmichael was smitten and unable to hide his feelings, whenever she walked into the room he was like a dog on heat, falling over himself to pull a chair out for her, to open the door or get her a coffee. At first, Sal Carta loved the attention as it gave her kudos a new level of self-satisfaction until he became a bit of a lap dog and then it became embarrassing. Sal started to make an effort to avoid the young doctor that was until there was a conference in London and then she only ended up waking up next to him.

Over the next couple of days Carmichael focused on the variety of meetings, lectures and on networking with his peers, as for him, the conference was a very important opportunity to further his career. However, his reaction gave Sal Carta the misconception that she had lost her touch with him not appearing to be so cow eyed since he had slept with her. Sal Carta couldn't have been more wrong.

Apart from the fact Carmichael was trying to make a good impression in his new career he was also exceptionally embarrassed and found himself unable to face the woman he had fallen head over heels for. So, he did his best to keep out of her way, worried that she would burst his bubble with a few harsh words or a dismissive wave of the hand. Through his lack of experience and courage, he chose to hide away from his feelings rather than to confront the situation and be direct. This apparent disinterest created a totally new concept for Sal Carta who suddenly found herself being the huntress rather than the pursued, not a position she felt comfortable with. The confidence she generally exuded transcended into a determination to snare the young doctor at all costs before the end of the conference.

On the very last night as doctors, surgeons and other high-ranking professionals finished dinner and made their way to the hotel bars Sal Carta grabbed the young doctor's hand, led him to the lift, snogged him all the way to the fifth floor then guided him to her room. That night she redefined who was in charge, the problem with her actions was it ignited a spark in her heart that would soon provoke a fire and in turn would detonate a sequence of events. Like a domino effect, their lives would start to fall when their status was threatened so Dr Carmichael and Sal Carta would stop at nothing to keep the plates spinning. The little white lies dripping from their tongues would literally devastate the lives of those around them. They will do whatever it takes to protect their careers, their reputations and each other until they have become intertwined so tightly together it would bind them together forever.

So, when Dr Richard Carmichael received a message from his secretary informing him that a policewoman by the name of Shona Williams had contacted him with regards to one of his patients, fear gripped him. He held his breath in anticipation waiting for the name of the patient then when he heard 'Cassandra Matthews', he almost fainted.

He did his best to sound nonchalant, to sound professional, matter-of-fact, as he gave the officer the basic details that she had requested. Inside he was exploding with panic, so as soon as he had replaced the receiver, he did what he swore he wouldn't do and immediately contacted Sal Carta.

'They are on to us!' Carmichael blurted out.

'Good morning to you too, Dr Carmichael,' Sal responded.

From the tone in her voice and reluctance to discuss anything he surmised, she must have had a patient in with her. 'Call me when you are free,' he said, then as an afterthought stressed the word, 'Please!'

The doctor leant back in his office chair pushing the boundary of its backrest to an unnatural angle, his mind awash with numerous possibilities, the panic rising. He knew his body would be sending adrenaline and cortisol into his bloodstream and that soon his blood pressure would spike. And there it was causing his heartbeat to race faster and the muscles in his entire body to tighten.

He knew he had to calm down as having been born with a heart murmur during times like this, he could go into what he called 'woodpecker mode.' This was when sharp, knifelike stabs followed in a continual succession in his chest like a woodpecker was actually trying to dig a hole through to his heart. He checked the clock above the door it was only 10 minutes since he had made the phone call but it felt like a lifetime.

He tried to bring his thoughts into focus having to skim across the lino floor in his chair to the windows to let a little air into the room that now seemed to be suffocating him. He slid back the window, stuck his head out and took a few deep breaths before reseating himself facing back into the room. He glanced again at the white-faced clock to the far-right corner of the room. It hung just above the door, where he had purposefully placed it so that when he was looking at the patient, he could discreetly check over their shoulder to ensure he didn't overrun. His desk with its light-coloured Formica top stood to his right the monitor and keyboard still positioned where the evening cleaner had left them. Everything had a place, untouched, unmoved until the first patient entered each morning and then his workstation came to life.

Life, that is what he was responsible for, the delivering of life, the saver of life, the managing of life's illnesses, the preservation of life. Yet he was also guilty of the taking of life. He glanced around trying to ground his thoughts in an attempt to capture the ones he knew would want to take him through the bowels of hell. Anything was preferable than the one-way ticket to purgatory, he knew his mental health would not afford him a return trip a second time. He counted 1 to 5 as he slowly breathed in and then again as he exhaled intentionally, blowing out more strongly, he opened his eyes not having realised he had shut them. He needed to be very careful, he knew from personal experience it was so easy to pass the fine line of sanity. In his mind's eye, he could see himself teetering on the edge of a cliff like some wing suiter about to plummet off, only he was not a willing participator. He also knew that should he fall there was little support, no parachute and should he get into difficulty there would not be a safe landing.

Dr Carmichael's thoughts were going into overdrive, he had his foot on the accelerator and like an automatic it was changing the gears rapidly without any ability to slow down. He could see where he was heading and wanted to shove his foot on the brake but it was stuck rendering him incapable of being able to take control of himself. And then the telephone came to life piercing his destructive train of thought, physically scaring him like any good jump movie.

His arm automatically shot out barely enabling him to co-ordinate any purposeful direction to grasp the receiver towards his ear. 'It's about time,' he said as the door swung open revealing Sally Carta. He looked at her in disbelief, confused at why she was standing in his doorway when he was on the phone to her. That was until he heard the faint mumblings of the caller coming from the mouthpiece that he now found in his hand resting on his lap. Befuddled, he redirected the phone to his ear and said, 'hello?'

'Dr Carmichael, I was asking if you were ready for your first patient, clinic started 15 mins ago?' Janet the receptionist enquired.

Dr Carta entered the room and quietly hovered around appearing agitated.

'I am sorry Janet but Dr Carta needs my attention regarding a patient I will ring through when I am available. Please make an apology on my behalf and cite a medical emergency. Let them know we will be with them as soon as we can,' he told her then ended the call without taking his eyes away from Sal Carta.

As soon as it was safe to speak Sal Carta began albeit in a hushed voice, 'What the fuck is wrong with you? Just look at the state you have got yourself into, thank goodness the police didn't come to the surgery to see you,' She delivered without mercy.

'What is that supposed to mean?' he enquired.

'You have got guilt written all over your face, pull yourself together people expect us to be calm, in control able to deal with all of lives emergencies.' She urged him.

'That is easy for you to say it wasn't you that the police contacted,' he spoke.

'Well, what exactly did they want?' she asked.

'They wanted to know about Cassandra Matthews,' he said.

'From the panic in your voice, I didn't think it was about anything else but the Matthews woman,' Carta said dismissively. 'So, what specifically did the police say?'

'It was a woman, Shona something, I didn't catch her name, anyway she wanted to know if I had any recollection about Tony Lloyd her husband, contacting the surgery. I said I did remember him it was about some erratic behaviours that she was displaying and of her excessive drinking. I explained that he had wanted me to intervene because he thought the children in her care were unsafe. I offered to make an appointment with her to refer her to supportive services but that she hadn't turned up,' he told her.

'Sounds like you handled it well,' she said.

'I also confirmed that she was on amitriptyline, how long she had been prescribed it, that it was for mild depression associated with the breakup of her marriage and the planned review date,' he stated.

'Perfect, so if the police think there are any suspicious circumstances around either death their first suspect will be the husband, so why have you got your knickers in such a twist?' she demanded.

'When you put it like that, I can see that maybe I was a bit too reactive, it just rattled my cage that's all especially the knock-on effect it could have on all our lives if the truth got out,' he told her.

'I think you are being a bit over zealous if not dramatic, this Shona woman was obviously just making preliminary enquiries to satisfy her curiosity about who Cassandra Matthews was. Nothing more, nothing less so let's move on and get on with our day,' she said turning and leaving his office.

Carmichael sat for a moment bewildered by Sal's ability to detach so quickly then put it to the back of her mind and not even let it trouble her. He wondered if that manifested out of a cold dispassionate heart or if it was just her coping mechanism. He wasn't sure if it was to be admired or feared. The prospect could mean that given a set of circumstances she would throw him under the bus too without a sideways glance or a moment's thought. He considered his options. He could come clean which would ruin not only his career but his life and everyone else's lives too or he could keep his mouth shut and go about his life as normal. Sal was right the police had nothing, otherwise they would have been breaking down the down with arrest warrants not making an innocent phone call.

As he sat thinking about the conversation with the officer now, he was certain she hadn't been accusing him of anything she was just asking questions to form a picture of Cassandra. Afterall, enquiring about the amitriptyline and her drinking showed they knew she had issues. Also, on top of that he had remembered to mention about her low mood and the depression so Shona would have developed a picture of a woman on the edge. The supporting evidence is the distress the husband communicated pertaining to her bouts of erratic behaviour.

Thinking about it with more clarity Dr Carmichael was sure he had handled the situation indifferently without giving the police any leverage to shine the spotlight on to him or the surgery. Sal was right he had a responsibility to move forward without putting unnecessary pressure on himself. Besides wasn't it the husband who was always the first suspect so if the police did come knocking, they could always make something up to incriminate him.

He pressed the intercom through to the receptionist, thanked Janet for her patience and told her to send the first patient through. The Dr may have convinced himself he was in the clear but all he was really doing was buying himself some time. The problem with secrets is they are like a pressure cooker, sealed in a chamber but sooner or later, the steam builds increasing the pressure.

How he would regret his young foolish decisions like getting involved with Sal Carta, being dragged into this mess that would result in mentally torturing himself for years. Without a means to evaporate the pressure cooker steam to talk about the sins of the past it would continuously, steadily bubble under the surface until someone else let's that steam out for him. And woe betide him when that occurred, it would be too late for admissions or apologies, there would be no room for excuses, no sympathy, and certainly no mercy.

Chapter 12
Sally Carta: The Past is the Past

Sal Carta had been with a patient when the phone had rung, she apologised to the young woman who was redressing her child after having had a rash examined on his tummy. She didn't normally take calls whilst in surgery but the woman was taking that long, Sal's patience was fast running out and she hoped it might convey it was time for her to go. She pushed the prescription she had just printed out across the top of her desk towards the young woman to further emphasise her point before snapping up the phone. She instantly wished she hadn't bothered.

'They are on to us!' Carmichael bellowed down the phone at her.

'Good morning, to you too, Dr Carmichael,' Sally tried responding cheerfully without wanting to give too much away or to speak in front of the young woman and her child.

'Call me when your free,' he demanded and then remembering himself he said, 'Please.'

How rude, who did he think he was speaking to, she thought and why on earth would he contact her in the presence of anyone else let alone during surgery hours whilst she was with a patient. More to the point why didn't he have a stream of patients going in and out of his office like she did. Once the woman had sorted out her little darling and finally left the office, Sal Carta rang through to Janet on reception and asked her to give her a moment whilst she dealt with an issue. Afterall that is how she saw Richard Carmichael these days, an issue that simply required managing.

As a doctor he was charismatic, inventive, thought outside the box and was a hit with members of the practice. As a lover he was creative, attentive and caring but as a man he had turned out to be weak and uninspiring who could possibly bring about their downfall. She knew she would have to take charge of the situation and be direct with him as he was always so ready to catastrophise the smallest of situations.

In fact, she decided this was not a topic she was going to discuss with him over the telephone it needed to be face to face, he responded better that way. So, she walked the short way along the corridor to his office and without bothering to knock, she opened the door. She had all on not to go in guns a blazing but as soon as the door revealed he was on the telephone she had stopped herself. At least one of us has some self-control she decided, but the wide-open mouth dithering idiot in front of her looked decidedly pathetic over a bloody phone call.

After a brief conversation with him, she totally dismissed him then left as abruptly as she had arrived. She shook her head as she made her way back to her office scarce believing that he had got all uptight over something and nothing. No doubt if it ever came out and push came to shove, he would soon spill the beans and then where would they all be. She knew when they got home tonight, she would have to reassure him, give him a bit of attention and point him in the right direction so she decided she would cook dinner and they could have an early night. At least there was still one area that he was able to satisfy her in!

Sal Carta went through her day not giving the situation another second of her time, well why would she, the past was the past and it was high time he moved on like everyone else or moved out either worked for her. Sal was not the type of woman to be sentimental about anything whether that came under the category of places, possessions, memories, people, friends, relatives or lovers.

Some people admired her pragmatic, direct and often detached approach to life although her patients' opinions would differ, they thought she was cold, dismissive and rude. Sal viewed all their opinions with disinterest the only person in her life that mattered since her husband Malcolm had passed away 8 months ago was Jonathon.

He was and always would be her number 1 priority especially now whilst he was undergoing grief therapy. She thought about Jonathon for a moment and the impact the Millennium party had had upon him, then finding out his father was terminal with cancer, losing him and the aftermath of anguish. She wasn't stupid she knew that her son had been mentally scarred through the traumas he had endured and would therefore require many years of therapy. She just hoped there would soon be a breakthrough from his current catatonic state because not hearing his voice, not knowing what he was thinking or feeling was agonising for her. She just needed to know that he was ok, that he didn't blame her, didn't despise her but of course inside she already knew that the answer to all those questions was affirmative.

For now, all she could do was keep getting up every day, keep maintaining the façade of being the good doctor and hope that he would forgive her, one day. But for Sally Carta, she would wear that hope like it was a medal around her neck and she would fly the flag of peace in front of his face but for Jonathon Carta, there had not been any peace since 31 December 1999 the Millennium New Year's Eve.

Chapter 13
Jonathon Carta: A Little Mixed Up

Jonathon Carta had always been a fun-loving boy, he made friends very easily and absolutely loved life. He lived with his parents in a 3 storey Victorian house in Sandal, Wakefield. His mum Sally Carta was a doctor and his father Malcolm Carta was the director of a computer firm based in Leeds. Jonathon lived a life through the security of a stable homelife, continuity of school, gymnastics every Wednesday evening and playing football every Saturday morning. Each year the family would go away on at least 2 main holidays with trips to London to see his mothers' parents and Newcastle to see his fathers' parents. He loved both cities equally but for very different reasons.

With London, he loved the Monument to the Great Fire of London, he found it astounding that a fire of such magnitude destroying 86% of London only claimed 6 lives. It equally fascinated him that the year of the Great Fire was 1666 or as he viewed it I 666, seeing himself as the enemy. He could picture the sky being filled with huge glowing orange masses, the smoke filling the lungs of the thousands running for their lives, the crackle of the wood as it burnt, the sparks being carried along the night air igniting the next building. He had never told a living person but if truth beknown it filled him with great excitement and a deep burning desire to recreate something similar much closer to home.

His love of 221b Baker Street had created a fascination with the super sleuth Sherlock Holmes along with his archnemesis, the Victorian villain Moriarty. He loved how the museum recreated the feelings of yesteryear enveloping you in the early 1900s the moment you stepped over the threshold. Jonathon's other fascination was the Clink Prison Museum, here he loved the macabre exhibition of the heads mounted on to wooden posts, the executioners block and the theatrical moans, groans and screams a recreation of what it was like for bygone prisoners. It had a dank, dry smell a mixture of rotting flesh and damp with little natural light for added effects.

He had visited many landmarks throughout London on his stays with his grandparents zipping around through the many tunnels of the underground transport networks and he loved the maze and freedom it allowed not to mention the obscurity of being one of many faces within the crowd. He realised the talent of hiding in plain sight because when you blended in no one actually noticed you. He paid close attention to the skilful art of dual pickpockets as one skimmed past their target gaining the subject's attention whilst the other dipped in to their pocket to remove their prize. Jonathon's mind was always active he wondered if this was to do with having some kind of an undiagnosed condition because whenever he was forced to sit still for any length of time, he became fidgety so counteracted this by concentrating his mind thus sharpening his awareness.

He loved Newcastle because people were much more welcoming, they had a pleasing accent and everyone he had met seemed down to earth, real, genuine not fakes. No, not fakes like his mother. Here the pace of life seemed to be much more relaxed and he loved nothing more than sitting at the base of Grey's monument in Eldon Square to eat lunch and watch the day go by. Jonathon thought back to all the times he and his dad chilled out waiting for his mum whilst she went to "just one more shop". He smiled at the thought of his beloved father.

There were days he could scarce believe that his father had passed away and with it would come the overwhelming tide of grief as the realisation of not being able to embrace him ever again would engulf him. Both his mother and father had tried to shield him from the ravaging effects of the cancer and he knew they were only wanting to protect him but what he had needed was to be at his father's side. Jonathon had yearned to share what little time his father had left with him, not banished from the room and made to carry on life as normal. But life was not normal anymore and so he did not want to go to school, he did not want to go to gymnastics or soccer because none of these things were important to him anymore. However, his mother had forced him to go, she had stood in his way and literally blocked any form of passage to be with his dad.

Jonathon was still grief-stricken, hurt, emotional, in shock at his loss but most of all he was angry, angry at his mother for what she had done to his father, how she had readily accepted that he, Jonathon could have hurt those little girls and then of her lies. She wasn't concerned about him she never cared about how anything affected him all that concerned her was about how people may view her.

He hated her for it; he knew that maybe for the sake of his dad's memory he probably ought to try to be kinder to her but he couldn't. She was nothing less than a bare faced liar and a hypocrite preaching what was right and wrong yet committing adultery behind his dad's back whilst he was dying and then practically moving Carmichael in before his poor dad was cold in the ground.

Jonathon's life had been turned upside down on multiple levels during the past 12 months with each and every issue relating to his mothers' decisions, deceit and adultery. With the passing of each day, his hatred seemed to intensify further especially when she would sit there with her pleading eyes begging him to talk to her. Why on earth would he bother she didn't believe a word he had said, she hadn't supported him or helped him to navigate his way through the treacherous paths of false accusations being thrown at him.

No, she had simply believed the lies others had told when they pointed at him and convinced everyone that he Jonathon was to blame. Every time he closed his eyes, he could still see him over the top of her with his hand around her throat. He could still see the crowd of accusing eyes staring up at him as he tried in vain to stop her from falling, her crumpled body as it had landed at the bottom of the stairs. So, there was no possible way that Jonathon was going to forgive his mother anytime soon!

Jonathon thought lovingly of his dad's parents, the welcoming feeling they always bestowed upon him wrapped up in the warmth of their exuberant embrace. His grandma Frieda and grandad Arnie never seemed to have much by way of finances and the home that they shared was less grand than the one of his mothers' parents in London. However, it was the one place he had always felt accepted for who he was, loved enthusiastically, unconditionally and without measure. Since his father's passing, he had literally pined for the comfort and security of their presence knowing that in his loss it would help him to feel closer to his father.

But his mother had no empathy, no understanding all she had cared about was the surgery and not letting the partners nor the patients down. In reality, Jonathon didn't give a toss about his mother's work, it was nothing to him and at 13 years of age why should it be. For Jonathon as he observed his mother's decisions, he could clearly see that they openly demonstrated the surgery was all she cared about because his emotional needs were persistently ignored.

Jonathon thought of the times they had travelled by train from Jesmond station to North Tynemouth, the quirky little shops, the castle at the end of the main road overlooking the sea and beautiful coves. He had persuaded his father to take him down when he was about 7 years of age desperate to make sandcastles his mother remaining at the top unwilling to join them refusing the hike back up.

They had got the bus to North Shields walked down to the quayside taken the little ferry across to South Shields, then hopped on the coastal bus along Marsden beach, past the Grotto, on to Roker and Sunderland. He remembered the same new t-shirts he and his dad had bought at a little market because they had both spilt ice-cream down their fronts. He had been so proud to wear that damn t-shirt, a mini-me version of his dad. Tears began to well up in his eyes, as he recalled them singing, 'Oh I do like to be beside the seaside, oh I do like to be beside the sea,' as they trundled along on the bus much to his mother's embarrassment.

He wasn't sure at what point his mother had stopped joining in, had stopped being fun, had stopped loving him or showing him affection. He wondered if there had been a particular moment that had spoiled things for her, was it something he had done, his father or was it something at work. He had absolutely no idea whether it was someone else's fault or if she had just got up one morning and she didn't love them anymore. He knew she couldn't have possibly loved his dad because she had taken up with Dr Carmichael although he wasn't sure when all that had started either.

All he knew was that his dad was poorly yet his mother was out most of the time and didn't take any time off work until the last couple of weeks. His dad had become so weak, so pale that he had not resembled the strong, active, funny man that Jonathon had associated with his father.

The day of his passing had been a Friday, Jonathon had wanted to stay home, had invented a tummy ache but his mother had seen through his feeble attempts to get the day off school. The reality was that Jonathon had got a 6th sense that if he went to school that day, he would never see his dad alive again. His mum, a doctor had assured him he was fine and would still be there over the weekend but when Jonathon had arrived home there was an ambulance in the driveway.

He ran the last 100 yards but waiting for him at the door was his mother with the worst news possible as the coroners van pulled up to remove his father's body. He had screamed and charged at her attempting to fight his way through but one of the ambulance men had scooped him up and taken him to one side. Jonathon had sat trembling, screaming at the sight of the zipped body bag being transported out through the conservatory to the awaiting van. Bizarrely, he recalled thinking that his dad would suffocate and he kicked to get free to pull the zip down for him.

Jonathon could picture this scene with vivid accuracy and replay it through his mind at a slow-motion pace, the silver gurney reflecting flashes of the low spring sun. He could hear the wheels as they bumped along the paved driveway the tinny metal sound of the stretcher echoing as they moved along. The thud as the men hit it on the back of the van before they slid him in out of view, then the swinging down of the door, bang and his father gone, out of view. The stillness of the finality of death ringing out in his ears as the van pulled away out of the drive with his father inside, never to return. Who would he look out for now at the bay window, who would he wait for because his father was never coming back. He had felt a hand on his right shoulder, he had turned, looked up and seen his mother mouthing something to him but his ears heard no sound.

There was nothing but an unpleasant tingling running through him from her touch and a distorted water affect in his ear canal. He recoiled from her touch, he wanted to get up and run away but his legs wouldn't move. There was a bright light being shone into his eyes, he blinked his breath beginning to sound cavernous yet safe. He focused on his breath as it went in and out, he could feel it expanding his chest, filling his lungs. He imagined it circulating throughout his body, bringing the calmness he needed in the chaos and he knew this was where he wanted to stay here, he could protect himself from the outside forces of despair.

This was the place that Jonathon had remained for the past 8 months, unable to leave, unable to force himself out from beneath the cloak of protection he had afforded himself. His mother could hope, plead and beg but the grief-stricken anguish that kept him locked in also kept her locked out. He could not relieve her of the desperate bid to hear his voice telling her he didn't blame her, that he didn't despise her because the reality was, he did. Jonathon knew that his time would come to ensure she paid for what she had done to his dad, to him, to the little girls and their mum. Therefore, he was happy to wait it out for the long game and when he decided the time was right, she wouldn't know what had hit her.

Part Two
Fourteen Years Later

Time is so very precious
A time to think and a time to plan
A time to take action
And a time for retribution

(Juli Flintoff)

Chapter 14
Cortina Matthews (March 2014):
Life Goes On

Cortina Matthews was not looking forward to starting work she hated the brawling, touchy feely, drunken yobs that spilled into the bar and not for the first time did she think she needed to get another job. She thought back to last night's performance and the fool who had actually jumped up onto the stage as she was finishing with her signature tune of 'When We Were Young,' by Adele. Cortina pulled her legs up to her chest to comfort herself as she thought of the way he had mauled her. She cringed at the touch of his hand roughly cupping at her left breast and the stench of his cigarette-stained mouth as he had lunged forward towards hers. So much for having bouncers, what good were they, if any, Tom, Dick or Harry could actually get into her personal space and actually assault her.

Yeah, they had finally jumped up on the stage and grabbed the arsehole but by then it was too late. She could not believe her boss's lapse attitude just shrugging it off as "playful drunken behaviour" or that she should not "be so uptight". Apparently, she should expect drunks to behave inappropriately because they were under the influence of drink and unable to take responsibility for their actions. Cortina did not know how she hadn't got the sack on the spot when she had argued it was a "sexual assault" and warned him if his bouncers failed to protect her again, she wouldn't be responsible for her action. She had then enquired if he would also term *that* as "playful" behaviour "expected" in a bar?

Ordinarily she didn't mind Franko, her boss, he was a small rotund jolly man in his late 50s from the North East of England who'd had three wives all younger than himself and all of whom had fleeced him. Unlike most people, he did not tower over Cortina who was only a slight young girl and looked like she was barely out of school despite being almost twenty years of age. This was Cortina's first real job and as far as she could see, they'd had a good working relationship although she knew Franko had a soft spot for her. Cortina's young life had not been easy so if she could use Franko as a stepping stone to bigger things then she was going to exploit him for all she could.

Cortina did not want to get up. She uncurled herself and rolled over on to her back gazing up towards the ceiling. She breathed deeply, listening to the humdrum of life as the buzz of the city began to waft its way in through the thin pane of her bedroom window. Today was another day so she decided to put her negative feelings of the yob from last night to one side so she could enjoy her day. She glanced around her untidy bedsit with its greying, shabby lace hung at the dirty windows, the pile of clothes overflowing the wash basket in the corner, the pots she had been too tired to rinse from last night and the old, tiny portable tv that she was too broke to replace. She hated living in this shithole which she had told herself would only be temporary at the time however it had been two years ago now since she had left care.

Two years! Where had that time gone? Nowhere was the simple answer and neither had she. So much for the pep talk that Daniel her support worker had given her about how "the world was her oyster" and that "she would go far" and to see it as "an adventure without limits". Well, she hadn't gone far, she was still living in Wakefield, there were no opportunities for a kid fresh out of care and let's face it, her world was more of a clam than a pearl centred oyster.

'Life goes on,' she said out loud to the emptiness of the shitty little room wasn't that the phrase she had persistently been told.

'You may not want to go to school, but life goes on.'

'You might be upset that Daddy has another family now, but "life goes on".'

'You might not want little Jimmy to come and stay but we need the money and life goes on.' Her mother had told her on a daily basis until one day poor Cortina had been woken up in the middle of the night and went in search of her mum frightened by numerous fireworks. She was the one who found her mum hanging from the banister, when she was 6 years old. Ironically "life goes on" no longer applied to her mother who had decided to take her own life without leaving a note or explanation. All she could remember of the woman who gave birth to her now were the songs she played over and over again. She would grab Cortina by the hands and whirl her around whilst Gerald looked on from over the top of a book, he had his nose in. Maybe that was why Cortina had such a love for music so perhaps she had something to thank her mother for after all, her love of singing.

Cortina took a deep breath and told herself, 'You might not want to get up out of bed and you might not want to sing in a bar where Franko thinks it's acceptable for human riffraff to maul you but…LIFE GOES ON!'

Cortina threw back the quilt with its London emblazoned cover another reminder of her time in care. Daniel had wondered why she had chosen this particular design so she had told him if the "world was her oyster", she wanted to start it in London. Each day when she woke up, it would remind her to dream big and to not let today's mistakes cloud tomorrow's possibilities but all it did for her today was to remind her that she was stuck in this dismal, depressing rut of a life. Cortina opened the single glazed window to let some air into the room with the hope it would clear the stale fatty smell of the fish from the chip shop downstairs. It was always worse first thing in the morning.

She stood for a while watching the traffic imagining herself as one of the car's occupants having a purpose and a place she needed to go to too. Or of having friends to meet, a better job, money to go shopping with or more importantly having a welcoming home and a family to love her. A single tear ran down her cheek as it did every morning of every day that she tortured herself when she stood here at this window imagining a different life. Cortina gave her head a shake, put a smile on her face and told herself today will be different, also as she did every other day.

Cortina didn't know it yet but as she looked out of that window stood lurking in the doorway of a building opposite, there was someone watching her. Cortina would soon find out that today WAS the day that things would begin to change and in the most unexpected way which would end up taking her in a completely new direction. The chain of events that were beginning to slide into place would come through a bolt from the past where a chance meeting would literally change her life.

Chapter 15
Mick Denby: A Day Off

Mick Denby could be a slob of a human being; it wasn't that he lived in squalor he just hated the prospect of using his rest days on the tiresome job of cleaning the house. Mick had been brought up by his single dad his mother having run off with the postman, an old cliché but true nonetheless. He knew this because his father had drilled it in to him that his mother's boyfriend was a good for nothing son of a bitch who had dropped a letter through the door telling him she wasn't coming back. Denby was 13 at the time, he had grown up in a loveless household, had little in common with either parent but had lots of friends at school so used their houses as a form of escapism. The other place he'd use was the local library where he soon developed a love of reading imagining the main character as himself. He would lose himself in the books, their fictitious adventures becoming real within his own imagination, as the words spilled out of the pages chapter after chapter. On several occasions, the librarian whom he really liked the one with the tight-fitting pencil skirt, low buttoned blouse and kind smile invited him to become a member. The only problem with that was the fact that one of his parents would have had to come down to the library to fill out a form and he didn't want them there. This was his sanctuary and he certainly was not ready to invite them into this part of his life.

No, this was Mick Denby's space away from them so he didn't want either of them infiltrating it besides it gave him the excuse to stay there as long as he wanted to sit and read. His favourite book was Bridge to Terabithia by Katherine Peterson because he could totally identify with Jess the main character. Denby tried so hard to be the best that he could, he was helpful, he stood up for his friends and he had the heart of a lion. If life was becoming overbearing at home, he would grab his rucksack of fishing tackle jump on his bike then ride along the woodland paths out towards the lake where he would stay until nightfall. It was never about actually catching any fish just the need to get away from absorbing the negativity of his parents' arguments.

Denby wondered to himself if that was why he had a fear of commitment, why he could not be bothered with other people's drama and why he had a "love them and leave them" policy. Denby decided to make himself a brew whilst he considered what he was going to do with the rest of his day. When he entered the kitchen, he was pleasantly surprised it wasn't quite as bad as he feared, although the pizza box from last night was on the counter next to the kettle the lid at a 45-degree angle. He peered in to the box to find two uneaten slices along with a number of discarded crusts abandoned once the central delights had been sampled. He filled the kettle shifting the tap over the top of the smaller cutlery sink out of the way of the stack of washing up left in the bowl. He replaced the top of the kettle and put it down to rest on its cradle before flicking the switch.

He visually examined the contents of the sink before delving in to take out a mucky cup, then giving it a quick swill, he added a teabag. Whilst he waited for the kettle to boil, he selected a cold piece of pizza and scratching his boxer clad butt made his way back into the lounge. Upon the coffee table sat an overflowing ashtray, the tabs smoked almost down to the filters, a cheap refillable lighter discarded to its side. In a small mosaic purple dish sat his car keys and the change from his pocket that he must have emptied out the night before.

The curtains revealed a sliver of the morning sun glaring through trying its best to press itself in to the room. He deposited himself heavily upon the old settee, the seat cushions covered with a grey patterned throw to cover its worn surface, omitted a plume of dust particles into the air. Denby tried to waft them away as they danced in the more prominent path of light perhaps an admission that the place really did need a good clean. He heard the kettle switch itself off, he gave it a minute, before wrenching himself up and returned to the kitchen to make himself a much-needed beverage.

Denby stared out of the kitchen over the backyard and wondered how a grown arsed man in a professional position had ended up in a dive like this. He didn't own the place, paid a fortune in rent and if truth be known he had jack shit to his name. Basically, he got up, went to work, did his shift, came home, got changed and went for a few beers. He had to admit his existence was meaningless and as about as purposeful as the washing line outside that had laid across the grass for the past 6 months.

Maybe it was time to change up his routine and instead of going to the officer's club every night after work he might look for another venue and maybe pull a bit of skirt, if he was lucky. Mick decided he would have a quick tidy round then have a walk into town for a bite to eat. Afterwards he would use his afternoon off to sample some of the bars around Wakefield where he had been told on numerous occasions that there was plenty of live entertainment and karaoke on offer.

Denby had his brew, got a shower and with renewed hope washed up before picking up his keys from the little mosaic dish on the table, he pocketed the coins then found his wallet on the little hall table. He had decided to drive his car to work, get a spot in the overpopulated car park so that he could walk the short distance to town from there. If Denby was going to have the quantity of drinks he was expecting, then he would be in no fit state the next day to drive in for his shift and he certainly was not going to get a taxi both ways. Denby was in a very good mood when he easily found a spot to park, the morning shift having gone, with only the skeleton lunchtime shift in and the people on lates yet to arrive.

Denby knew what he was like after having one too many sherbets (pints) so there was no point in having keys this valuable on his person so he jumped out and hid them on top of the offside tyre. He had a quick look around but there wasn't a soul to witness his actions so he merrily went on his way out through the woodland walk towards the town. He was beginning to think it might have been a mistake to leave the car and walk this route when a colleague Darley Mays pulled alongside him.

'Need a lift?' Mays called across the passenger seat of her car.

'Where are you heading?' Denby enquired.

'Through Wakefield towards Featherstone,' Mays told him.

'If you could drop me in Wakefield that would be great,' he told her.

He heard a clicking sound as Mays opened the central locking system, 'Jump in.' She waited for him to get in, attach the seatbelt and settle himself in before she checked her mirrors, looked over her shoulder and then pull away from the side of the road. 'You not in your car?'

'It's off the road at the moment,' he told her not feeling too bad as it was stood in a car park so it was only a half lie. He smiled to himself in congratulations for being so smart. He may appreciate the fact that he did not have to walk the full distance to town but he didn't feel a need to share his business with this woman. Yes, he knew that she worked in the kitchens and served the dinners but that didn't give her licence to know his comings and goings. Besides as lovely as she might be, he was aware that she was a bit of a nosey parker who liked to gossip so the least she knew about him the better.

Along the route Mays chatted openly about how long she had worked in the kitchens, what she loved about her job, how the shift pattern worked well with being a mum and even what her favourite dishes were to prepare. Denby was mentally walking down the path of utter mind-bending despair when he realised, they were driving along Thornhill Street at the bottom end of town.

'Anywhere here is fine, thank you,' he said with a big grin on his face and as politely as he could muster.

'Are you sure? I can go round the ring road and take you to the town centre if that's any better for you?' Mays asked helpfully as she pulled up to the kerb.

'No really, you have done more than enough,' he began as he released the handle to the door, 'I am sure you will want to get back for little Lucy.'

Mays smiled at the usage of her daughter's name, 'Fair enough, see you the next time you're in for lunch.'

Denby was thankful to have gotten out of the car he could not have tolerated listening to more of her droning, whiney voice although he did automatically hold his hand up when she pipped her horn as she rejoined the traffic. 'What are you doing,' he scolded himself.

Mick Denby turned and instantly forgot all about Mays, the woman might have given him a lift and saved him walking the couple of miles into town but she had served her purpose and was of little interest to him now. He nipped into the street side entrance of the supermarket made his way through to the shopping mall, up the escalator through a department store and out on to the precinct.

Although he was familiar with the town, he had only been out to the bars once for a leaving do so, he wasn't quite sure where to actually go. He nipped into the Deserted Ship guessing exactly why it was so aptly named, not only was there no one in but it gave you the distinct feeling of wanting to run. He turned and walked straight back out. The Michael Angelo may have been a grandly named pub but it was one of the biggest dives he had come across and from the smell wafting towards him as the door opened, he knew it was no place for him. He was beginning to think he had made a terrible mistake when he nearly got side swiped from a car as he crossed the road.

'Watch out mate,' a voice called out.

In front of him was a young lad maybe about 20 years of age, 'Shish Kebab, that was close,' he said to Denby as he ran the remainder across the road.

Denby grinned and thanked the stranger then asked, 'You don't know which are the best pubs for an afternoon sess do you, I haven't been round here before and have only found the worst pubs in town so far.'

'I was just going to nip in here, you're welcome to join me,' the stranger told him, 'Carl is the name.'

'Cheers, Carl, I am Mick,' he said extending his hand out, the young lad shook it a bit too enthusiastically but seemed friendly enough.

He guided Mick into a back alley towards a bar that had more people on the inside than Mick had seen walking around the town. The stranger patted Mick on the back as he guided him through the bar and navigated him towards the bar, 'This alright for you?'

Mick suddenly felt elated not only had he got a drinking partner but the stranger also knew the area and which bars to go to, Mick relaxed, he was going to have a good day off after all. Little did Mick know but this new "friendship" had been no accidental meeting at all and Mick was being lulled in to a false sense of security.

Chapter 16
Mick Denby: The Stranger

The bar was long and narrow with an array of bottles stacked behind it, to the right was a pool table set back into a little alcove, opposite the bar were several high tables with people sat on barstools. The atmosphere was buzzing and a deep contrast to the Deserted Ship, past the high tables Mick could see people dancing and a young woman on Karaoke. Mick grinned to himself this was more like it, exactly what he had in mind.

'What you having?' Carl was asking a tenner already out of his pocket.

'No let me,' Mick offered scrambling in his pocket for his wallet.

'You get the next ones,' Carl dismissed and then asked again, 'So what are you having?'

'A pint of John Smiths,' Mick said delighted and noticing the bar maid was quite tasty too, oh yes this was going to be an altogether different experience to what he had first thought.

After having a couple of pints in what Mick later found out was called the Kick Inn, his new buddy Carl suggested they try another bar. Mick would have happily stayed where he was as the bar certainly lived up to its name, it really was kicking with the clientele out for a good time. Carl informed him that the courts were not that far away so people from the public gallery, the solicitors, families etc always came in to the Kick Inn as a means to celebrate a win.

The next bar that Carl took him to was back down the end of the passage and across a little side street this one didn't have quite the same buzz about it but the long list of beer pumps seemed endless. Not only that but it must have been happy hour or something because Mick could see a hand written price in the front of each pump. He couldn't believe how cheap it was for a pint with around a third having been sliced off the price of every lager and bitter on draught. He rubbed his hands in glee, it was now his turn to pat Carl on the back.

'Right Carl, my shout,' he called the bartender over and ordered the drinks then stood with his back to the bar surveying the other patrons, 'I think bumping into you today Carl was fate, my boy,' he said with such glee.

'Absolutely,' Carl responded with a huge grin on his face knowing full well there was no fate involved.

The two new buddies enjoyed the fullness of Wakefield's daytime drink culture from pub to pub unbeknown to Mick Denby, Carl was ordering himself non-alcoholic drinks. By the early evening, they stumbled upon a little club down some steps at the top of Westgate. By this point, everyone that Mick came into contact with, he was greeting them like they were a long-lost friend, stumbling around in a heavily intoxicated manner. On his way across the dance floor to use the toilets at the far end of the pub he was ambling past the stage, when suddenly the darkened area came to life. On his return, he was taken aback to see the most beautiful young girl who had the voice of an angel performing.

He stood transfixed for a while, taken in by her hypnotic tone reaching in and touching his very soul. There was something about her that he couldn't quite put his finger on, she appeared strangely familiar her magnetism oozing out of her that he seemed unable to take his eyes off her. For a moment, there was only him and her in the room and before he knew what he was doing he had clambered onto the stage and was trying to grab a hold of her. That was until two burly hands vice gripped his shoulders and literally manhandled him out on to the back street before the emergency exit snapped shut.

Mick sat a moment bewildered about his sudden extraction, trying to fathom out what had just happened. Without his mate around and inevitably not wanting to go through the front door of the club to be thrown straight back out of the back door again, Mick decided it was time to make tracks. He found a taxi rank across the street from the club though he did feel a little sad, he had been unable to let Carl know he was calling it a night.

He needn't have worried the stranger was more than aware that his drunken friend was leaving because he was in the cab behind monitoring his every move. Carl found it amusing the big dope had not even questioned him about who he was, where he was from or anything at all about him. All Mick Denby was interested in was himself and fulfilling his own desires sod everyone else around him, exactly how the stranger had remembered him.

Chapter 17
The Stranger: In the Shadows

The stranger had remained in the shadows keeping his eyes peeled on the alley waiting for the evicted Mick Denby to reappear. He didn't have long to wait. Mick a little worse for wear hobbled out of the arched entrance his shirt protruding from his vomit-stained trousers honouring the whole tramp look with victory. The stranger stepped back further into the doorway as Mick started to walk his way, then almost instantly turned and walked in the opposite direction towards the taxi rank. That was close. He watched Mick Denby staggering along the street a new level of despise for him having been achieved on seeing him scramble on to the stage grabbing and slobbering all over the young girl. He could see the dishevelled Denby making his way into the taxi rank office now so he quickly called the number emblazoned across the car's doors. As soon as he observed Denby fall into the back seat of the cab, he legged it to the car behind and got in grinning to himself as he told the driver to "follow that cab".

'Seriously mate? If you are going to the same place why not just get a car together,' he said turning round to face the stranger.

'Because that is my dad and he is a proud man I would hate for him to see me he would think I didn't trust him to get home alone,' he explained, 'You see, he has been unwell and this is the first time he has been out in a long time.'

'Alright mate,' the driver said and seemingly appeased he turned the key, indicated, checked over his shoulder and eased away from the layby to follow the car in front of him, keeping a very safe distance.

Throughout the whole journey the stranger was trying to decide just how Mick Denby would pay would it be fire, torture, disfigurement or trauma to the back of the head. He was beginning to salivate at the prospect of seeing this piece of shit suffer with his arrogant, selfish "*I am the only person in the world that matters*" attitude. Oh, how he wanted the bastard to scream, to be able to look him in the eye, for him to be cornered with no place to go in the knowledge he could neither escape nor talk his way out of it. Mick Denby was going to get his comeuppance for sure all the stranger needed to know was where he lived and the rest would fall nicely into place.

The drive took him around 5 miles out of town towards the village of Crigglestone where the cab suddenly swerved on to a side street then dipped down a hill before pulling up outside a row of terraced houses. The stranger asked the driver to pull up until his "dad" had gotten out of the car and once he was sure Denby would be out of sight he instructed the driver to continue. As they passed the house the stranger couldn't stop himself from taking a look at the house Denby now occupied.

He had come this far and felt that he at least owed himself that little morsel of pleasure and he was not disappointed to see the overall shabby, unloved frontage. The outer perimeter wall had several bricks missing at the corner of the gateway as though some vehicle had accidentally backed into it. The bricks were not visible but the damage was obvious.

The grass was overgrown, the borders a perfect mix of dead flowers and weeds. The window frames along with the door looked in desperate need of a lick of paint and there were old bits of furniture piled to the left of the gate. The stranger was disturbingly satisfied with the knowledge that the property Denby now occupied was as dilapidated as the dishevelled man himself. He continued along the road, until the car popped out on to the main road and seeing a petrol station, he told the driver '*Anywhere to the left would be just fine, mate.*'

He made a point of stating that he wanted to get an early night because he was flying to the States the next day. If the police found the cab driver, he wanted to make sure he threw them off the scent for a while. He paid the fare, walked into the nearest gateway then watched until the taximan was out of sight before leaving the driveway, then proceeding towards the petrol station. Just before the turning, he began to run so that by the time he got to the pump attendant his story would sound more kosher.

'Have you any green petrol cans, I ran out a mile up the road felt sure I would make it down here,' he said faking a look around the store.

'There must be something in the air I have had three people in today, they are over there in the far corner,' the young attendant said pointing hexagonally to the opposite corner of the room.

The stranger waved a hand up and made his way to the allotted corner. The store was like any other petrol station, bright strip lights donning the ceiling basking the goods below. There were two rows down the centre creating three aisles packed solid with groceries, drinks, sweets etc he found the petrol cans below the magazines, next to the maps. He walked coolly to the young man at the till to purchase the can.

'Do you want me to fill it first? Or pay for it and come back in when I have filled it?' he asked.

The attendant, Kevin, according to his name badge, gave him the once over and then asked, 'How much are you wanting?'

'I think £10 will be enough to get me home,' the stranger stated not wanting Kevin to expect him to return and give him reason to mention it to the police when they came sniffing. And he knew they would.

'Fair enough, you can pay for both now and I will put a cap on the petrol pump for a tenner,' Kevin said ringing the items through the till.

The stranger took out his wallet and selected his debit card then admonishing himself, *Nearly*, he thought. He paid Kevin cash for the goods then started to walk away before demonstrating an afterthought he patted his chest and jeans pockets. 'Oh, I would forget my head if it was loose, can I have 20 Regal please.' He casually selected a lighter from the pack at the side of the till and paid for the goods attempting to maintain a calm persona.

Kevin noticed the sweat begin to trickle down the stranger's forehead. The stranger batted it away with the back of his hand and feigned the issue as being unfit, 'Maybe it's time I started going to the gym.'

Kevin smiled, gave him his change. The stranger returned the smile, nearly there now he thought. He left the starkness of the store glad to be out in the cool evening breeze and made his way to pump 3. He selected a couple of the thin see through gloves available at the pump the last thing he wanted was to leave any prints or for his hands to wreak of petrol. He unscrewed the black plastic top of the can, set the can flatly on to the floor then lifted the petrol nozzle from its cradle and placed it inside the hole before depressing the trigger.

The colourless liquid began to dribble out at first and then flowed quickly filling the can the numbers zipping around on the pump until they finally hit £10.00 and then it stopped abruptly. The best £10.00 he was ever going to spend, he mused replacing the nozzle and tightening the top securely. He wanted to ensure he did not waste a single drop this was all for Mick Denby the dirty mauling drunken pig. Without even turning his head, he could see that Kevin was observing his every move so once he had stood upright, he raised his arm before turning and calmly walking back the way he had come.

On the return to Mick Denby's house he neither passed a soul walking nor in a car in fact the area was surprisingly quiet for an early Friday evening. The stranger glanced around as he approached Denby's house then sure of not being seen he snuck into the driveway and stepped back into the shadows. He waited a good 10 minutes before hiding the petrol can between the base of a huge bush and the neighbouring privet. When he was sure the can was completely out of sight and there was no possibility of it falling in to view, he slipped the lighter into one of the plastic gloves and secreted it underneath.

He waited a further 10 minutes before ducking out, back onto the pavement in the path of a lady with a golden retriever dog. She gasped at being confronted by a stranger suddenly emerging from behind the bush. The stranger unwittingly checked his trouser zip, 'Sorry,' he apologised. 'I couldn't make it all the way home.'

She shook her head disgusted, he on the other hand continued to walk on congratulating himself for his quick thinking.

Now, he had put everything in place it was just a matter of biding his time for the exact moment but first he had to give the taxi driver, Kevin and the dog walker an opportunity to forget their encounters with him. No point rushing things he needed to be prepared or be prepared to fail and that definitely wasn't an option. The stranger rang a different cab company several streets from the Denby house just to cover his tracks selecting a specific address but giving a bogus name. He had all the time in the world to put his plan into action but unfortunately for Mick Denby he would soon find out that time was not on his side.

The stranger took the taxi to Wakefield back to the club that Mick Denby had been extracted from. He walked past the bouncers, down the staired entrance, through the doors and into the bar at the bottom. There was still a hive of activity although the young woman who had been singing had finished so he made his way towards the bar and waited. It was not long before he saw her. She came out from a door at the side of the bar with a short fat man, really rocking the Danny De Vito look. He noticed she looked tired maybe too many nights singing at the club and not enough sleep or perhaps Danny here was a people pleaser and didn't look after his staff. He would make the time to analyse the man however the new focus of his attention would remain on the girl. She looked up maybe sensing that someone was staring at her so the stranger looked away, quickly.

He continued to watch her through the mirror from behind the bar, she seemed irritated, almost angry. Maybe she had hated how the man had grabbed and mauled her just as much as the stranger had hated it. He waited for the conversation to end and when she threw her coat over her shoulders and stomped off towards the exit it was time for him to go too. He finished his drink in one gulp, placed the glass back down on the bar and followed her out.

She made her way towards Wood Street, up past the police station then towards the college before taking a couple of side streets. He was intrigued to see where she lived, if she had anyone in her life, what she did and if life had been good to her. More importantly though the question was why would she so carelessly put her safety in danger walking along the streets of Wakefield so late at night. Was this something she did regularly, he wondered.

Intrigued, he continued to follow until she abruptly stopped along a strip of shops then took a key out of her pocket and slid it into a door half way along. He remained at the other side of the street where he ducked into a doorway and watched for a light coming on. He noted that the place she had chosen to call home was above a fish and chip shop, that did not make the stranger happy. Not only would it wreak in the flat but both her and her clothes would too and there would be too many people milling around, someone might see him. He elected to keep watch from a safe distance for now before deciding how or whether he would approach her, or not. Besides staying in the shadows gave him great comfort it was the place he liked to be, on the periphery keeping watch, maintaining a safe distance, remaining unseen.

Chapter 18
Cortina Mattews: Don't Let Go

Cortina decided to do what she always did when she felt a little low and that was to blast her music out whilst doing something constructive, so she decided to tidy the flat and clear the clutter. 'Tidy room, tidy mind,' wasn't that the mantra from when she was in care, perhaps there was something positive that they had taught her there after all, she mused. It did always help her mood and in no time at all she would be feeling happier especially when she had finished tackling the task, she was least keen on. Today, she decided, was not going to be such a bad day after all, the sun was shining, the sky was blue and soon she'd be feeling like brand new. She giggled to herself, 'I'm a poet and I didn't know it,' she said out loud to nobody and giggled to herself again.

Cortina believed she could manifest anything into whatever she wanted it to become as long as she captured the negative thoughts and concentrated on all that was good. So, she decided to make a start to get the flat cleaned firstly by bagging her laundry to take to the launderette, then changing her bed, next she attempted to tackle the washing up but found it needed to be left to soak and finally she tidied the small room she called home. Once she had refreshed herself with a warm soothing shower, had put on her favourite denim dress with the pretty little flowers running along the hem, she slipped on her favourite pair of Dr Martens, threw her bag over her head so the strap sat across her chest and decided to go for a walk.

By the time Cortina had stepped outside on to the pavement her mood was as light as the spring air, as sunny as the day ahead and her mind was as clear as the blue sky above her. With each step she smiled a little more, taking the time to greet anyone she saw to pass on to them the happiness that she now felt inside. Who knows, maybe other people's lives were as bleak as she had felt hers was this morning when she had stood looking out of the window, but that didn't mean to say she had to wallow in it. Maybe people would look at her as having a place to be, friends to see, a purpose to share and wish they were her. So, with that positivity she continued along her way hoping to make someone else's day that little bit brighter by being as friendly as she could.

As she waited at the pelican crossing near Lightwaves the public swimming pool, she noticed that her bus was already waiting for passengers at its terminal. She contemplated chancing it across the road but that would be foolhardy, it was far too busy. Luckily the beeping signal started to sound to alert her it was safe to cross and the cars began to slow. She shot off as quickly as she could, her little bag banging against her side hoping to catch the bus not wanting to have to wait another half hour. As she approached, the driver was just closing the doors when he caught sight of her, thankfully, he was kind enough to wait an extra couple of seconds.

Cortina didn't catch buses as a rule so wasn't au fait with their timetables besides, everything she needed was within walking distance of the city centre. This was the only bus she had taken in the past year; it was the same one she had taken 12 months ago on the same date and it would probably be the only one she would take throughout the next year too, also on the same date.

'Thank you so much for waiting,' Cortina panted.

'No problem love, where do you want to go?' the driver enquired.

'Sugar Lane cemetery please, Doncaster Road,' she told him.

'That's £1.50 love,' the driver told her which she had in her hand ready to give him.

He smiled warmly at her when she said, 'Thank you,' Cortina wondered if that was because other passengers weren't as polite or appreciative as herself or if it was because today, she was manifesting a good day. She wobbled down the bus grabbing hold of the intermittent bars fixed vertically from the ceiling to the seats and found a seat that she didn't have to share. She felt happy and content despite the fact of where she was heading enjoying the experience of trudging along on the single decker bus. She wondered to herself if she might have sat upstairs had it been a double decker but then quickly dismissed the idea because had that also been about to set off, she wouldn't have managed the stairs once it was moving.

Cortina watched the people as they meandered along the streets, noticed what she assumed were friends sat outside coffee shops and paid attention to the new shops that had opened up since she had ridden this route 12 months before. She had to admit she quite liked taking this journey it was soothing, it was a tradition that she was making all of her own and she liked to think of being independent. She thought back to her childhood, to Gerald, to her mum and the laughter they'd had dancing and singing.

She wondered what he was like now, where he was, what he might be doing, would he still look the same, would she know him if she saw him. And then a sadness fell upon her, why had she missed out on having him in her life surely social services could have done more to keep them together or at least allowed them to stay in touch. As she gazed out of the window, she absentmindedly glimpsed her reflection and as though talking to him she whispered, 'I love you Gerald, I wish you were here with me now.'

'Sugar Lane Cemetery,' the driver shouted looking through his rearview mirror at her.

She weaved her way through to the front of the bus and thanked the driver once more, then disembarked. As she stood at the side of the kerb waiting for the bus to pull away Cortina slid the scrunchie from her hair, regathered her hair up so there were no longer any straggly bits and replaced the scrunchie. She straightened her dress, repositioned her bag and looked up, she was ready now. It wasn't as though she had anyone to impress, she just wanted to present herself so she felt she looked her best. She crossed the road and walked towards the ornate railings that were embedded into a stone wall of around 3 feet high aiming for the gate around 10 feet from the roadside. As she entered the holy place of rest through its theatrical, squeaking, iron gate she took a moment to survey all that was ahead of her.

The tarmac path which wove its way upwards towards a derelict chapel-like building had seen better days. The tarmac had crumbled away in parts revealing a cobbled under-face she hoped that this had occurred through the wear and tear of mourner's footfall coming to pay respects to their loved ones. She did hope it was not due to neglect because the dead were long gone.

She couldn't help likening the cemetery to "The Secret Garden" a book she had once read with its wall enclosed perimeter cut off from life. This rundown, forgotten place with its village of forgotten headstones and towering skyscrapers of wealth memorials embedded amongst them, mapped out each little plot to commemorate the depth of love that once was. Cortina found it hard to imagine that all those inscriptions of names were real people who had lived a life, they'd had families, achieved goals, had jobs and meant something to the people around them.

Now they were no more than just a bag of bones laid in a box, way below where her feet would soon pass by. She decided to begin the uphill walk towards what she assumed would have once been a thriving chapel. The only part that remained today was the tower part of the chapel, the arched stone doorway bricked up to form a solid impenetrable structure. Above this was a stone, feature arch window, the glass long removed where ivy tentacles sprouted and upon it sat an exposed ceiling, the lead tiles stripped to reveal the carcass of wooden joists. Even the iconic cross that had sat on its pinnacle rooftop point the last time she had observed its beauty was now gone.

She looked from side to side as she walked noting the decay, the broken plinths, the illegible writing, the once grand expressions of love and sadness engulfed her. Life is like sitting on a bin bag at the top of a hill with its first fall of snow you feel great joy and excitement at the prospect of all that is a head of you then just as rapidly you shoot down that hill and before you know it, life has come to an end. Deep in thought at how unfair life can be she made her way past the chapel sweeping around to the right and on towards a crumbling smaller path to find the grave she had come to visit. It was only when she was almost upon it, did she see the figure kneeling down in solemn contemplation.

She stopped hardly able to fathom who this person was or what they could be doing. Her heart was beginning to race, her chest tightened as she tried in vain to process what her eyes were observing but her thoughts were not manifesting into anything her brain could absorb. She quietened her pace almost tiptoeing neither wanting to disturb the person nor wanting them to leave before she could get a glimpse of who they were. Despite the posture, she could tell that the figure would be taller than her if it were stood erect. It had an athletic build but from this angle she could not tell whether it was male or female due to the black hooded top and tracksuit bottoms it was wearing.

Tentatively, she stepped onto the grass careful not to walk across any other grave nearing the figure until she was almost within touching distance. As if now sensing her presence the spell of the figures meditative state disengaged from the headstone they had been focused on and they turned around. Cortina involuntarily gasped her hand instinctively shooting up to her mouth before tears instantaneously flooded her face.

'You weren't supposed to find me here,' the stranger began, 'I am sorry, I should go.'

An abundance of mixed emotions swept through Cortina simultaneously but the main one was the need to stop him from leaving so instead of allowing him to stride past her she grabbed him in her arms and held on for dear life. He was the only living soul she could call family and now that she had finally found him, she knew she was never going to let him go again.

Chapter 19
Gerald: Bath Time

Gerald had woken early eager to start the new day so was thrilled that the sun was out and the sky was blue. The hotel he had chosen was not a particularly grand affair but it was decent enough. The double bed had a freshly laundered grey quilt that had little round peaks sewn throughout its surface at 3 inch gaps to create tucks and giving it a patchwork effect from a distance. The two matching pillowcases at the top of the bed had extra ones beneath them covered in light grey, the fitted sheet was also light grey to match. Along the bottom of the bed was a light grey thin fleece with a herring bow pattern imprinted through it. At either side of the bed stood two solid pine bedside cupboards and not the cheap finish stuff either this was good quality. To the left of the bed was a double wardrobe to match and to the right of the bed a grey and black two-seater settee. In front of the bed was the door to a concealed ensuite shower room which he absolutely loved. The black and white diamond tiles along the floor were a complete contrast to the white London underground type tiles adorning the walls.

He made his way to the side of the roll top bath, pressed in the black plug that hung from a chain attached to a circular silver plate a few inches below the edge of the bath before opening up the taps full pelt. The water swirled from the old fashioned cross-topped taps gushing out its gravitational pull downwards to fill the awaiting tub. He selected one of the bath soaking gels from the complimentary tray on the laddered stand behind the door and squeezed lashings of it into the flowing water stream. Almost instantly, the bubbles began to foam. He unwrapped a small bar of soap and carefully placed this together with his sponge, shaving gel and razor onto the small bath caddy that sat neatly across the top of the bath.

At the large deeply squared sink which also housed the same taps as the bath, he proceeded to squeeze the toothpaste upon his brush and thoroughly cleaned his teeth. If there was anything that he hated, it was uncleanliness and poor oral hygiene. He removed a long sliver of dental thread and began to floss his teeth moving systematically along each cavity with care, discarding the thread and reselecting more continuously moving back and forth until he was absolutely satisfied. He then unscrewed the top of his mouthwash, poured a measure into the lid before emptying it into his mouth where he swished it around to achieve a fresh and thorough clean.

He loved the bite of the initial sharpness to his tongue and the dentist quality of his perfect routine. He checked the bath; it was filling nicely the bubbles up to 5 inches from the top of the water in peaks and troughs across the entire length of the water's surface. He noticed that the little shaving mirror above the sink had begun to steam so he popped open the little window to allow it to dispel outside rather than stay cooped up then overspilling in to his room. He dipped his hand beneath the water to assess the temperature, a little hot, he thought so he shut off the hot tap and added a little cold. He took a towel from a rack above the end of the bath and lent it over the top edge of the bath to rest his head upon and to also have to hand once bath time was over.

Despite the bathroom appearing pristinely clean, he was not able to place it on to the floor to then step upon, he would use the smaller bath mat. He arranged it neatly before wiping any dust particles from his right foot then stepping cautiously into the tub, repeating the same procedure with his left foot then easing himself slowly down into the water. He enjoyed the warm caress of the water engulfing his body, the heat an almost burning sensation creating a reddening to his pale skin. He lowered himself down from a seating position until he was lying down in anticipation of his complete submersion.

He opened his eyes knowing full well when he resurfaced, they would most likely sting, he didn't care it was all part of his daily routine. His ears no longer provided him with the clarity of sound the water now acting as a muffler like the silencer of a car's exhaust system. Only when the air in his lungs literally begged for freedom did he allow it to escape through the slow release of bubbles. He counted to 78 a new record, before raising himself up and giving himself the luxury permission of the intake of another breath. One day on the spur of the moment, without any notification, he would withhold the privilege of more air. He was determined that when he was ready, he would stay there beneath the water where it was warm, quiet and safe, whether Gerald was ready or not.

Chapter 20
Cortina: Happy Birthday Cort

Cortina did not know how long she had held on to him, all she did know is that he did not pull away so he must have needed her as much as she needed him. Perhaps he had been searching for her, yearning for her, wondering where she was, what she was doing too. Cortina was so afraid to let go in case he ran off and she would never find him again. Or worse still, would be if she looked closer into the figures face and found it was not really Gerald after all.

It was him who finally broke the spell of their embrace and gently pulled back from her as if he had been reading her mind and needed to see her face, but that was his only movement, he didn't leave.

'Where have you been Gerald?' Cortina asked.

'It's a long story Cort, maybe this is not the time nor the place,' he suggested.

"Cort" it was a long time since she had been called that yet it was still as familiar as the last time, she had heard it uttered from his lips. She had vivid memories of his distress at the sudden disturbance of being taken from his bed in the dead of night. All she could see was his face contorted from the pain of being manhandled ignited by the shock at being exposed to the lifeless body of her mother. He was shouting her name over and over again his distress like a volcano surging upwards and being expressed through that one word, her name.

As he was carried outside in those vice gripped arms kicking and screaming in an attempt to get free, his screaming voice could no longer be heard drowned out until she could only see him mouthing "CORT" to her. Yet Cortina was powerless to protect him, too small to prise the adults' fingers from her arm restraining her from stopping their forced separation. The sky ablaze with a multitude of shimmering lights, whirling sounds and explosions parallel to the flashing lights and sirens from the grounded emergency vehicles. Whilst the world celebrated the dawning of the New Year with renewed hopes and dreams for the future, both Cortina and Gerald's would turn out to be as black as the powder in the aftermath of those burnt-out spent fireworks. A fear ripped through them like the perceived "Millennium Bug" of the year before that the computer world had predicted would wreak havoc when the year changed from 1999 to 2000.

For Cortina and Gerald, the 31 December 2000 as the clocks struck 12 midnight was the moment their young lives were decimated. Cassandra Matthews was dead, cut down by the police, certified by the doctor and removed by the coroner like yesterday's garbage. The children, undeniably affected by the devastation of such a complex childhood trauma had their situation compounded by their forced separation. They had never experienced the "twin thing" where they felt one another's pain or of being able to sense that something was wrong, maybe that was due to them being different genders. However, what they had both experienced for the past 14 years was the yearning to have their individual hurts healed and the only strong emotional connection that could quench this need was each other.

They were the only ones who had experienced the same unquestionable terror of staring death in the face. A loss resulting in an incessant fear to connect, the separation an inability to trust and therefore rely on those who had become caregivers. They had grown into adults who found relationships hard to sustain which created a loneliness the depth and blackness of a cavern. Now here they were on the 3.5.2014 at the tender age of 20, clinging to one another just as they had been so desperate to do over 14 years ago.

'Happy Birthday,' she said with a smile.

'Happy Birthday Cort,' Gerald said relaxing a little and returning her smile.

'Shall we go grab a coffee from somewhere?' Cortina suggested, 'Perhaps we could walk back into Wakefield then we can talk and catch up.'

'I would like that,' he told her taking her hand as they used to do as children and then they made their way out back along the decrepit path towards the little gate to join the rest of civilisation.

It was a good mile and a half back to the city precinct with its cathedral and array of shops but they didn't mind a bit and Cortina would have gladly walked 500 miles as The Proclaimers had sung just to be with Gerald. They walked along Doncaster Road past the Hepworth Gallery, under the railway bridge and along Ings Road retail park until they came to the Royal Mail Delivery office. It was only as they reached this point having been so engrossed in their conversation that Cortina realised they had missed their turning. She quickly diverted him at the roundabout where Sainsburys stood off to the right so they could walk up the hill towards the top of Westgate. They found themselves a quirky little café where they could sit quietly in a corner and lose themselves in hushed conversation learning of each other's lives.

Cortina listened intently as Gerald revealed that he had been terrified seeing a strange man in his room, that he had never been able to get the image of Cassandra's face out of his head. More importantly he had not understood why Cort hadn't reached out to him and that he had always felt alone, forgotten and in the shadows since that day. The day he had no longer felt any measure of the peace, safety and security that he used to feel when they were together at 57 Park Grove.

No one had really taken the time to understand the despair that he had been in, his quietness seen as shyness, the endless bullying, of him never fitting in and always feeling alone. He had hated the loneliness, felt tortured by their enforced separation and the worrying of never knowing what had happened to her or if he would ever see her again. He had put his time and effort into studying and devised a computer programme that allowed you to intercept radio waves it changed the whole concept of communication. So, if the enemy was using a particular form of radio setting, he could intercept it and take control. He had also patented a listening device that the intelligence forces had commissioned rendering him a very rich young man.

Cortina stared in disbelief, astounded that the Gerald who relied on her like a comfort blanket and used to say nothing as he sat in the corner peering over the top of a book was destined to be so clever. She held his hands throughout his story, mesmerised, excited upon what the future might hold for both of them and so very thankful that they had finally found each other. When it was Cortina's turn to talk, she suddenly felt very foolish having not really accomplished anything, being really poor and of having to sing 3 nights a week, in a dive to make ends meet.

She didn't want to burst Gerald's bubble so she kept asking questions to encourage him to continue to spill out about how life had treated him so well. Inside Cortina was thrilled for him, she recalled the anxiety at not knowing where he was, how he was and more recently the fear of whether he was still alive. Cortina had not had it so easy and unlike Gerald she was not ready to divulge the extent of the suffering she had endured however by the end of their chat a plan was formulating in her head and she made him swear they would never to lose each other again.

Chapter 21
Cortina and Gerald: A Blast from the Past

At the club that night, Cortina sang with a renewed energy knowing full well there was a new member of the audience whom she was performing solely for, her brother Gerald. Each song took on a new meaning, each emotion felt with intensity and integrity to the point she completely lost herself in her music. Unlike every other evening she had performed, Cortina wanted to leave straight away so that Gerald and herself could celebrate her birthday without the glare of the other staff around them. This was their first celebration together in such a long time that they had no intention of sharing it with anyone else other than each other. As soon as Cortina had collected her wages from Franco and fended off his insistence, she should stay for a drink she nipped out through the back door of the club. Gerald was already in the alleyway only stepping from the shadows when he was certain it was Cortina. She led him along the back streets to her bedsit where they quickly ducked inside.

The bedsit wasn't anything like the comforts of the hotel room he was staying in, it was really small and he found it alarmingly claustrophobic but this was Cortina's home and he was glad to be here with her. She had told him she had lived there for almost 2 years whereas he could not imagine even being there for 2 nights so he decided he would invite her to stay with him. Cortina got 2 glasses and poured wine into them; it was far too sweet for Gerald but he drank it out of politeness. She put a compact disc into a small player, dimmed the lights and sat on the bed opposite him.

'It's so good to see you Gerald, I know I keep saying it but it is,' Cortina told him.

'It's good to see you too Cort and to be able to listen to you at the club your voice is amazing, I felt every word you sang,' Gerald said.

'Thank you, I think I felt it more tonight because I knew you were sat in the audience,' she confessed.

'There is something I need to tell you Cort and I am not quite sure how to start,' he said.

'You're not leaving already, are you? I couldn't bear to lose you so soon,' Cortina told him.

'It's not that I saw someone from the past last night Cort,' Gerald said tentatively.

She cocked her head waiting for him to finish silently observing the way he was running his finger around and around the top of his glass. He was nervous, that much was clear, but why?

'Just say it, Gerald!' she implored him.

'It was Mick Denby,' he let the cat out of the bag.

An ice-cold shiver ran down her spine as though someone had just walked over her grave. She could feel a multitude of emotions swimming through her fear, anger, hurt and a despised sense of loathing though she remained silent.

'He was in the club Cort, your club,' he told her.

'What? Last night? Do you think he saw me or even recognised me?' Cort stumbled.

'There was a flicker of recognition but I do not think he knew it was you Cort, did you not realise it was him?' Gerald asked.

'Who was him?' she asked puzzled.

'The man that got up on to the stage and grabbed you was none other than Mick Denby,' Gerald revealed.

The blood drained from Cortina's face, 'But he was this close from my face,' she said, holding her right thumb and index finger 2 inch apart, 'how can I not have noticed it was him.' She asked perplexed.

'Maybe your subconscious mind wouldn't allow it Cort, but I am going to make him pay for what he did to you,' Gerald said earnestly. 'What he did to all of us!' he corrected, 'but mainly what he did to you.'

'It is too late Gerald he has already got away with it,' she said deflated.

'It isn't too late Cort not for what I have got planned for him and I know how to cover my tracks,' then he went on to tell her about the petrol and how he had planted it in his garden and of the plan to go back much later when the taxi driver and the petrol attendant had forgotten all about him.

'But Gerald, I do not want you to have to go to prison because of something he did, it feels like a lifetime ago now.'

'That will not happen Cort and besides this is something I feel compelled to do Mick Denby needs to pay for his transgressions and we are going to make sure he does!' Gerald told her.

So, over the next two months, Gerald and Cortina rekindled the bond they had established as children each becoming engrained in to the others' lives getting to know one another intricately. Cortina continued to work at the club to maintain her normal routines whilst Gerald kept a watchful eye on Denby and his whereabouts. He knew it was only a matter of time before Denby would want to relive his experiences in Wakefield and when he did, they would be ready and waiting. This man had been living a pointless, futile existence with work, drinking, sleeping seemingly on repeat for years with total disregard for the lives he had shattered. Sometimes the past had a way of reaching into the present and dragging you back when you least expected it, well, Mick Denby had better get ready because he was soon going to be kicking and screaming back.

Chapter 22
Tony Lloyd: Not Funny

Tony Lloyd woke up feeling horny as he did most mornings but who wouldn't with this beauty next to him. He contemplated waking her but decided against it he just wanted to gaze at her for a few minutes. As she began to stir and stretch a lock of her untameable curly blond hair fell across her face, he smiled, reached forward and gently lifted it away. Her eyes opened.

'Morning,' Emma said groggily.

'Good morning you, beautiful creature,' he replied, grinning widely at her.

'Why are you looking like the cat that got the cream?' she asked.

He pulled back the quilt to reveal his erect penis, 'I was actually hoping that it would be your little pussy that would get the cream,' he told her.

'Bloody hell Tony I have just woken up,' she yawned then reached her hand down and took his manhood a bit too roughly into her hand.

'Careful, I am only delicate,' he recoiled, but when she smiled, he relaxed to allow her to caress him.

She softly rubbed him back and forth creating a hypnotic rhythmic movement then when his bum began to follow the same motion, she knew she had him in the palm of her hands, literally. Only then did she lean in and steadily trail the outline of his lip with her tongue. He wanted her but he was going to have to wait. She nuzzled his cheek, pushing his face away from hers kissing him in a path towards his ear. She traced her tongue around each of the grisly bits of his ear until she settled on to the lobe. Here she seductively stroked it with her open mouth whilst continuing to arouse him with her hand. She playfully sucked, released and licked at his lobe until she could feel his excitement building.

He tried to pull her to him hungry to enter her but she wasn't finished, he had woken her and now it would be at her speed not his. He slid his hand down between her legs but she simply knocked it away, no this was her show and it was going to be performed her way. She kissed along his neck and down into the crevice of his shoulder all the time maintaining the rhythmic pulsation of his penis. She brought her other hand up and wet it with her saliva, then on the upward motion of her right hand she brought the downward motion with her left. She circled the tip of his exposed helmet, he twinged in spasm at the sudden, heightened sensation it sent a bolt like current of electric through him. If he didn't get her soon, it would be over and he didn't want that, he needed to savour this, harness it despite the threatening eruption daring him to let go. She slid across him as she kissed his chest jibing at his nipples as she slid down to just below his belly button.

He breathed deeply at the anticipation that she would take him into her mouth so his hand instinctively cupped her head but she quickly shook it away. She moved across his stomach her mouth just out of reach then moved the direction of his erection to his right so that she could burrow into the crevice of his groin. She lifted herself up so she was in more of a foetal position her knees beneath her supporting her on the bed. She kissed across the flatness of his shaved pubic space, bringing him closer to her as she lifted her hand up and down his solid shaft. Her mouth hungry to take him she sucked and licked the entire length of his rigid organ up and down until his groans had almost reached a crescendo and only then did, she pleasure him with the moistness of her oral cavity. In a slow, controlled action, she applied a perfectly measured pressure to bring about a flawless pleasure.

Then without warning as he groaned and writhed, she suddenly raised her head and said, 'This might be the wrong time to say it but I bet that girl from last night wishes she was me right now.' Before he knew what was happening, she was up and off the bed, playtime over.

'What the flip, Emma why would you do that?' Tony asked.

'Do what?' she asked feigning innocence.

'Take me to such a height then leave me hanging? You're not funny you know!' he stated.

'Neither are you when you flirt with everything and anything that moves, not being funny Tony but I am not your dumb arse wife so if that is the game you want to play maybe you should go,' she retorted unapologetically.

'Leave, I am barely here as it is you are always sending me away and when I am here, I don't know if you really want me here or not?' he whined.

'Oh, not this old chestnut again....I feel like saying boohoo,' she turned to him displaying clenched fists with her index knuckles to the corners of her eyes, 'Boohoo,' she said again moving her hands back and forth.

'Don't patronise me Emma, that's not fair,' Tony told her.

'Watch out girls,' Emma said talking to the dogs huddled in their basket at the side of the window. 'Looks like it is going to be a pity party sort of a day, get out quick whilst you can,' she taunted and left him to wallow.

Emma walked down the landing towards the toilet and then into the bathroom where she turned on the shower. She took a fresh towel out of the airing cupboard not willing to go back into the bedroom just yet and climbed over the edge of the bath. She checked that the water was warm enough then ducked under its fast flow, allowing it to cascade over her hair, the miniscule water droplets massaging the top of her head. She grinned to herself, oh how she loved to wind Tony up it was just too easy sometimes but maybe she had gone a bit too far this morning. She pondered that if the roles were reversed, she wouldn't be particularly happy either but there again there were multiple times she hadn't reached a climax because he had spent himself far too early.

'Multiple times,' she said out loud and in the first six months of their relationship he had been downright useless in the bedroom, she remembered.

Emma took the soap and washed her intimate areas then applied the shower gel to her sponge and exfoliated her skin thoroughly before rinsing herself off and towelling her feet before stepping out of the bath. That was something else that annoyed her about Tony he always stepped on to the bath mat, leaving it drenched when he got out of the shower. In fact, when she came to think about it there were loads of things about Tony that frustrated her but one thing, she did love, was him making love to her now, oh and massaging her feet after a long day. She cleaned her teeth, then with the towel wrapped around her naked body she went back along the landing to her bedroom where she playfully allowed it to drop to the floor.

Tony was knelt on the floor rummaging through his drawer for a pair of boxers his nakedness exposed. The way in which he was knelt with his thighs pressed together had stretched and pushed his scrotum high so that it took on a shiny, almost plastic and translucent appearance. His penis no longer hard or standing to attention had regressed to a mere trace of its former glory.

Pointing to his now shrivelled up flaccidity she said, 'See, I told you it was tiny.'

'You're still not funny,' Tony told her.

'Yeah, you say that but we both know I am really,' she told him as their morning alarm "Wake up Boo" by The Boo Radleys began to play on the Alexa.

'See,' she continued even Alexa is in on the joke, and addressing his penis she said, 'Wake up it's a beautiful morning.'

'Why is it you can make me incessantly mad one minute and then reduce me to laughter the next,' he said giggling at her.

As she came closer towards him to get her own underwear out of the drawer he stood and took her in his arms and just held her. The warmth of her body as they connected skin to skin brought an instantaneous surge to his nether region. She felt the twitch and reluctantly pulled away.

'You know that woman from last night meant nothing don't you?' he said earnestly.

'In my heart of hearts I know, but I cannot help finding it disrespectful,' Emma told him truthfully.

'Why disrespectful?' he asked.

'You are more than aware that my husband cheated on me so when you do that right under my nose, of course I am going to find it disrespectful,' Emma explained.

'Don't you think that's like the pot calling the kettle black?' he asked.

'What on earth are you on about?' she asked quizzically as she slid on her underwear and began to get herself dressed.

'Well, how did we get together?' Tony reminded her.

'Don't you think that plays at the back of my mind as well? But equally, it was you who was married not me, Simon and I were divorced by then!' Emma stated.

'What worries me is that you could do the exact same to me as what you did to Cassie, but just know this, I will not stick around.'

'Don't be like that, we have been together 14 years now and I have never strayed not once,' he said hurt.

'You say that but once a man twice a child,' she retorted.

'What the hell is that supposed to mean?' Tony asked getting angry now.

'You're like a little kid that goes in to a sweetie shop every time a pretty little thing walks by, you have done the dirty before and your more than capable of doing it again,' she pointed out.

'For goodness' sake, Emma does it always have to come back to this sometimes being in your company is like sitting at a dinner party and wondering how long you have to wait until you can leave,' he said collating his things and walking off towards the shower.

She knew he was right to some degree but that was the problem when your relationship is bore out of the misery of doing the dirty behind another person's back, you always know you could be next. There again if he didn't play up to the attention when girls were flirting with him, dipping his head in close and whispering she wouldn't feel so paranoid. If she so much as got close to her male friends having to talk in their ear because the music was too loud, he would either leave without speaking or sulk for England for a couple of days. She did love him although she hated the way his behaviour created a substantial imbalance to the equilibrium of her life or the insecurity that it generated.

She knew he wanted her to marry him, he had made that plain almost instantaneously but she failed to see how her marrying him would change anything, he had been married when she met him. Also, their relationship had had too many ups and downs where he soon became complacent and failed to put the time in to keep it alive. She had continually felt as though it was her who was making all the compromises for the pleasure of allowing him to walk all over her. After all, it was her car that he drove, her place that he lived in, her sister's apartment that he used in Spain and yet it was eggshells that she trod on continuously in her own environment so he felt secure.

The worst experiences by far that she'd had with him was his failure to support her in times of need, of mentally draining her with his negativity, segregating her from her friends and ruining really important occasions through his thoughtlessness. Or worse still not even acknowledging his wrongdoing or delivering meaningless lip service and then persistently repeating the same behaviours. She found him self-centred, needy, selfish and blinkered most of the time but she was with him so she tried so hard to overlook these traits.

The only problem was that every few months she would get to a place of having "no more fucks to give" when she was outpouring everything and getting absolutely nothing in return.

No, there was no way she would ever sign her life away again to be the provider of somebody else's every need only to remain emotionally, mentally and spiritually barren in a relationship. If Tony Lloyd was not prepared to grow with her, then he could stagnate without her. It was time for her to cease being disrespected as a woman and disregarded as a human being.

Chapter 23
Emma Boulden: How Truthful are You?

Whilst Tony had his shower, Emma finished getting dressed then went down in to the kitchen to get a glass of milk and a banana before setting off for the hairdressers. Emma had waited for this particular appointment for over a month now unwilling to go to a different salon as Mel had been doing her hair since her mid-20s. Emma couldn't believe she was almost 51 years old now so with her grey hair pushing through she was glad she could finally get her roots done. Mel worked from home having firstly converted her garage into a salon and then upgrading to a property that had a purpose-built room. The salon was always a hive of activity with a number of clients of varying ages and backgrounds. The conversation was always light-hearted and with the reinstatement of Ruth, Mel's previous employee the banter was good humoured too. They made a great team working easily in sync together complimenting each other's skills for the greater outcome of their customers. Emma enjoyed the relaxed vibe of the place like you were almost part of the family it reminded her of the programme Cheers and the theme tune "where everybody knows your name".

As Tony entered the kitchen, his newly sprayed aftershave wafting in ahead of him Emma stopped scrolling through her Facebook page, grabbed her bag and keys.

'See yeah,' she said and was about to rush off when he stopped her in her tracks.

'You know it's not fair when you treat me as though I was the one who cheated on you,' he delivered stood in her exit path.

'What is that supposed to mean?' Emma asked.

'I am not Simon, so please stop hitting out at me for what he did to you.' Tony delivered.

'Wow,' Emma began, 'is that what you think I do? Really?'

'Yes, Emma you do, you hit out at me when you think I am following the same path that he did. But I am not Simon and not all men are the same.' Tony stated.

'You say that but you were married to Cassie when you hit on me,' she punched back.

'Yes, you're right and I utterly hate myself for hurting Cassie the way I did but that is a separate issue to how you treat me,' he tried.

'It isn't to me, you were married and you cheated on your wife with me therefore it is only reasonable to consider the prospect that you could also cheat on me in exactly the same way,' she argued.

'I know why you would think that but please try to consider how the circumstances are literally canyons apart. I did not love Cassie, I felt forced into marrying her because she was pregnant and whether you choose to believe it or not, I am not the kind of guy to shirk my responsibilities,' he tried calmly to explain.

'Really, Tony?' Emma retorted.

'Do you know what Emma sometimes there is no use talking to you, you are so closed minded and convinced I am the same so you just keep on kicking me down. We could be really happy if you would only let yourself but it's almost like you won't be satisfied unless it becomes a self-fulfilled prophesy,' he moaned.

'You're a man expecting me to treat you fairly that would be like 'expecting a bull not to charge at you because you are a vegetarian,' Emma blurted out feeling so clever with herself. Unbeknown to Tony she had just read more or less the exact phrase on her Facebook page by Dennis Wholey just has Tony was entering the kitchen.'

'Do you know what Emma, Simon may have lied his face off to you, he may have deceived you in the most hurtful way disrespecting your marriage but I would not do that. Please stop pushing me away as you may find that one day this search of yours to reveal I am lying may raise more than you want to see about yourself.' He turned and left her stood there trying to fathom out exactly what he had meant by his parting shot.

Emma knew that Tony was a good person and part of the problem was her inability to trust but when you had given your trust blindly and the last person had blown it out of the park and destroyed your whole world it wasn't that easy to let your guard down. When she had seen Tony's car pull out of its parking spot, she collated her things and locked up before driving to her hairdresser's appointment, determined to put it out of her mind and enjoy the pampering delights that Mel always bestowed upon her. She parked her mini behind a little blue smart car just before the bend where Mel's house stood. It was a beautiful stone 3 storey new build just outside the outskirts of Wakefield.

It had a little wooden gate set in a small stone wall and an inviting frontage that swept around to the left of the house. Emma followed the stone slabbed path surrounded by a multitude of flowering blooms, down the cascading steps at the side of the house to the back revealing a lawn with open woodland beyond. Mel had a variety of towels and paraphernalia pegged to the washing line blowing gently in the wind. Along the newly constructed raw wooden fence dividing the property from the one next door, Emma saw two squirrels scurrying along the length of it and then marvelled at their dexterity as one after the other they sprang up to explore the branches of an awaiting oak tree. Emma stood a moment or two scanning their progress across the branches expertly weaving, climbing and darting through the maze of interconnecting paths.

It was then that Emma couldn't help likening those branches to the paths in her life. The trunk where she was self-assured, strong upright and decisive in her thinking and actions, like when she had gotten married to Simon.

How they had interwoven their lives together until you could not tell them apart, they were as one. Yet as the tree got higher the branches got thinner and could barely take the same amount of weight thus the twigs began to break. She gave her head a shake and rebuked herself for being so melancholy, she was here to be transformed, to enjoy her appointment, to chat, to forget Simon, Tony and the past. She pushed down the handle on the door and entered the joyful little salon with its welcoming buzz, an array of nostril drenched hair solutions and her friends.

Emma's mood changed dramatically as she became an integral member of the little hair salon sharing stories, listening, laughing and fully participating in this select little group that passersby were completely unaware of. It was only when she was waiting for the colour to develop that Ruth passed her a cuppa, a piece of cake and the obligatory magazine that Emma's mind began to wonder again. It was really weird to Emma that whenever she was going through something in life it always seemed to be portrayed in some way through one of the soaps.

It was as though a great big spotlight was shining over her whether it was losing the only baby that she had miraculously conceived, the death of her brother-in-law or the life changing secret she had been sworn to keep. Now, Emma found herself reading stories of people's infidelity, of the lies they had told to cover their tracks, the devastation that had been caused but out of the misery, true love had prevailed. Some may call her a cynic but she doubted that very much more like desperation to be a twosome created a few rose-tinted glasses.

Emma Boulden had always seen herself as being a good person, she wasn't perfect but there again who was? However, if she was asked to describe herself, she would say she was honest, well up to a point I mean white lies aren't really lies, are they? She considered that for a moment and deduced that small white lies were ok especially if you were trying to spare someone's feelings. Say if a friend asked, does my bum look big in this and you reassure them, they look fine then that was ok. Or like when her and Tony first got together, he was useless in bed but she wouldn't have dreamt of telling him outright, she giggled not like today where she would tell him directly.

Emma had put it down to him being in a relationship that he didn't want to be in where Cassie had trapped him by becoming pregnant. Emma would never have contemplated that perhaps Tony was the one who hadn't used a Jonny and brought about the pregnancy or that the pill had failed. No, it was a downright acknowledgement that Cassie had been at fault, poor Tony had been trapped and ended up in a marriage he didn't want to be in so sex had become a "Wham Bam thank you Mam", kind of interaction. Besides he couldn't possibly have loved her otherwise he wouldn't have cheated on Cassie with Emma. Yes, she satisfied herself white lies were fine unless it was Tony telling them to her and then it wasn't ok.

As she pondered the thought about lies, she also had to admit that on the odd occasion there could also be times where you were exempt from wrongdoing for telling a great big fat lie. She considered the moment in her life where she had been forced into this very situation due to circumstances way beyond her control for the greater good of those around her. She still had nightmares about that time but who had they really hurt in the grand scheme of things she told herself? So, she reassured herself she was still a good person because she had done the best for the people she loved. Besides if she hadn't, maybe life would have been very different. Emma sat with the magazine in her hand still open at the same page with the heading "How truthful are you? Take our quiz and reveal the truth".

Emma glanced up at Mel unable to hear her voice due to the hairdryers seeing her mouth moving. Mel held up all the digits of her hands and mouthed "10 mins" Emma smiled in acknowledgement she had understood then went back to pondering the question about whether she thought lies were harmful. Thinking back to when her and her sister Sal were growing up, they would always tell white lies especially to the opposing parent to get their own way. Sal had been her greatest teacher of how to manipulate an adult.

'It's easy,' Sal had said, 'all you have to do is look sad, let your lip slightly protrude, make it quiver and think of the time your cat got run over.' At the thought of this, Emma had immediately burst into tears and the triumphant Sal had finished with, 'Bingo! You just learnt how to get your own way.'

Emma had been shocked at Sal's response because she had been genuinely upset about what she had said about her dead cat but afterwards she understood. Before long, whenever her parents said she couldn't have something or her mum was mean to her she would go tell her dad and vice versa perfecting her little act the more she rehearsed it. Emma brushed those lies off as just being a child and not really understanding it was wrong.

Emma thought through her early life at secondary school and at college where she had studied as a support worker for young children with additional needs and felt that she must be a good person to want to help others. She had so wanted to have children of her own so when she met and married Simon, she couldn't wait for them to start a family. Things hadn't quite been as smooth as she had expected because Emma had never lived away from home before so she'd had no idea of how much everything cost. She was shocked to think she would have to work for a few years before Simon and she could have even considered a child. It was a setback that was for sure, in her mind they would have a child, she would stay home and they would live happily ever after.

It had never crossed her mind that the house prices would suddenly hike up so that the mortgage each month would cost almost her entire wage. So, she covered the mortgage with barely any monies left over and Simon paid the bills and food saving the rest for their rainy day fund. Only what Simon omitted to tell her was that after the first two years of their seven years marriage he'd had affair after affair and the week before Christmas 1998, he was about to shack up with little Miss Twinkle Toes. Yes Simon, her Simon was shagging his secretary, so cliché and when Emma had gone to pick him up from the office Christmas party, he was tripping the light fantastic with Miss Twinkle Toes on the dance floor.

Emma saw herself during the whole of that Christmas period, so dejected, alone and miserable, unable to comprehend what she had not only seen but what his unfaithful lying arse now meant to her. Emma's whole world had been blown apart in that split second whilst Simon and Twinkle slipped off to enjoy the festive season together looking forward to a future playing happy families. The "*rainy day fund*" had become a rainy day for when Simon had bogged off with what *fund* was left after he had spent the rest on wining and dining a multitude of women.

The Christmas tree had stood in the corner of the room with its lights off, the array of presents covered in a range of brightly wrapped paper all left underneath until sometime during mid-March. They would have probably stayed there until the following year had it not been for Sal turning up and giving her a proverbial kick up the backside. She smiled at the thought of Sal, Miss Bossy Britches Extraordinaire, forcing her into the shower, laying out some clothes for her on the bed and taking down the Christmas tree.

'Enough is enough,' Sal had told her. Emma hadn't thought it was anywhere near enough at the time she could have wallowed in her self-pity a whole lot longer given the chance. But looking back Emma had to admit that she was glad Sal had intervened and forced her to pull herself together because there was no doubt in her mind now that Simon and Twinkle certainly were not worth it.

That brought her back to the magazine in her hands again and the question of whether lies were harmful and she had to concede that it depended upon which side of the fence you were sat. On Simon and Twinkles side life was rosy, they were enjoying life to the fullest and their deception wasn't hurting anyone until Emma found out and then the hurt was like having a red-hot poker in her eye.

Maybe, when her and Simon had got married, she had become complacent and had failed to assess how the relationship was going. Perhaps if she had taken the time, she might have noticed that she was meeting his needs but he had taken his eye off her needs and was also only meeting his own needs. Emma had become invisible not only to Simon but also to herself something she vowed never to become again.

If she was ever in a position where her security was being compromised, she felt her needs weren't being met like she did with Tony every now and again she made a determined effort to change it. As far as Emma was concerned being in a relationship did not mean putting the other person at the top of the tree and allowing them to stay there. For her, it was now about continually assessing that her own needs were being met too as she had forsaken them for far too long. Though maybe Tony had a point instead of waiting for the branches to break as she had with Simon, she was now not allowing him to stay at the top of the tree for long enough before she was giving it a damn good shake. She would then pat herself on the back for welcoming him to a new place back at the bottom with the other bad apples. Maybe it was possible to let Tony in a bit more, after all he was still here despite her reluctance to trust him and like he'd said it had been a good 14 years now.

Mel came over to remove the colour so she closed the magazine and was about to put it to one side when a young girl asked if she had finished with it. She smiled sweetly at her and handed it to her obligingly taking the magazine she was being offered in return. She was a sweet young thing with a beautiful smile Emma felt sure she would break a few hearts as she got older.

Then just as quickly Emma had forgotten her, smiling to herself at the thought of Tony getting all uppity that morning when she had left him wanting more, she had certainly shaken his apple tree and no mistaking it.

Chapter 24
Gerald and Cortina: Playing Games

'Did she recognise you?' Gerald asked.

'No, not at all, I was sat right there next to her Gerald and I actually swapped a magazine with her. She looked me right in the face Gerald. I was having serious palpitations; my hand was shaking as I held the magazine out to her but she didn't have a clue who I was,' Cortina told him.

'That's great, well done you for keeping your nerve,' he told her.

'It was awesome, scary as shit but equally as exhilarating!' Cortina told him.

'I think you are getting the bug for this cloak and dagger stuff next it is Mick Denby's turn,' he told her.

'No, Gerald I do not want to come into contact with him that is a step too far for me,' she stated feeling emotional.

'It's ok Cort, that's fine, besides I already have someone on the inside keeping an eye on him, just in case,' he told her.

'So, what is next on the agenda, I am beginning to like our role plays,' Cortina asked.

'I think it is time that we pay father dear a visit,' Gerald told her with a smile.

'You're not going to hurt him are you, Gerald?' She asked.

'Of course, not Cort I do not have a gripe with him he did his best for you when he could but social services blocked his application for residency so maybe he just thought it was better to let go. There is no way they would have informed him of where you were and I guess he did have a lot to deal with as well,' he reassured her.

'I don't think we should do anything to him Gerald maybe we could leave it until this is all over last thing, I want is for us to blow our cover so early in the game we have more important issues to address, like Sally Carta,' Cort urged him.

'Ok, if you think that is best Cort, we will play it your way,' he smiled.

Chapter 25
Sally Carta: Living It Large

It was the last day of Sally Carta's summer holiday so she had decided rather than having to clean her apartment she was going to chill by the pool before having to return to the rat race of life. It was 8 a.m. before she could finally throw back the sheet and tear herself away from the beautiful mountain view that her bedroom window displayed. She smiled as she poked her head through the open window to find early morning tourists already walking the beautiful Andalusian paths of Frigiliana. There was one main wide street that led visitors through the old town of the village called Calle Real and Sally's apartment bore off on a little side street to this.

If she turned and looked to the right, she could see the natural spring fountain called la Fuente Vieja people could often be seen filling their bottles with its spring water. To her left the cobble street met a steep set of steps taking you down to the main road Avienda Carlos Cano which took you to the mountain and beyond in front of her. Sally Carta loved this beautiful tranquil mountain village with its multifaith background, it's festivals, boutiques, tapas bars and white washed houses all sat above the town of Nerja. From the moment she had stumbled upon this hidden little gem, just after Malcolm had passed away 14 years ago, she had not been able to get it out of her mind. This was her little piece of paradise, her safe haven, her escapism from the ugliness of her real life. Here, she could be whoever she wanted to be lost in its soothing calm presence as she meandered around the many winding streets, sitting at a table enjoying a vino or simply lazing by the pool.

Sally grabbed herself a towel and made her way into the bathroom where she had a quick shower before slipping into her bikini. She checked her bag to ensure she had her towel, reading glasses, her latest book to read and sunglasses. Then she grabbed a bottle of water from the fridge, unplugged her phone, tied her hair back, slipped on her sunglasses and grabbed her keys. The good thing about Sally's apartment was that it had a really long terrace and it was only a short walk across a flat surface from her gate to get to the pool.

She slid the patio door back in place leaving a 4-inch gap to let the air circulate and then locked the secure metal gate. The lock always made a heavy sound regardless of how she tried to ease it into place so she instinctively looked up knowing Alberto the Weimaraner dog from the upstairs apartment would be inquisitively watching her. His little nose was already protruding through the bars of the Juliette balcony above her head, his large velvet dumbo ears hanging beside his cocked head.

'Morning Alberto,' Sally said to the 16-week-old pup as she had done every morning for the past 2 weeks, the apartment blocks newest resident. She could hear the whip of his undocked tail slapping against the sheets of her neighbours washing that hung over one side of the railings. He seemed such a happy little thing not that Sally cared that much for animals. Of course, he whimpered as she turned and ascended the stairs to the top patio level and then descended ducking under the overhanging purple jacaranda bushes but she was totally uninterested to his plights. Sally ambled along the lower terrace towards the tall green gate set into the high archway giving a cursory glance to the amazing countryside view to her right.

The tall palm trees shedding little shade on to the communal courtyard below, she breathed it in knowing that shortly it would be left behind her once more. Sally opened the gate and passed through choosing not to bother locking it as she had done throughout her stay. She made her way along the pristinely manicured gardens towards the pool breathing deeply and enjoying the warm early morning sun upon her body. On taking the steps down to the grassy area around the pool, she was pleasantly surprised to find that there were no other sun worshippers out yet so she could select her favourite place in the corner away from other people when they eventually did come and she knew they would. Today the weather report had given yet another scorching day and why wouldn't it be, here in sunny Spain. She threw her towel over her chosen sunbed, put her bag down onto it before kicking off her flip flops and taking the steps down into the pool.

Sally lowered herself under the cool soothing water firstly sitting upon the top step then fully submerging herself and stretching out her legs to feel the lightness of her body float and glide effortlessly. She tipped her head back thus allowing the water to gently massage her scalp in soft lapping movements with each paddle of her hands. The sound was intermittently distorted as her ears bobbed in and out of the water, lapping around her body as it held her upon its surface. Lying as still as she could, having surrendered completely to its embrace; her mind wandered as it often did to Jonathon, desperately trying to recall the last time she could remember hearing his voice. She tried to shut it out not wanting to hear his hurtful angry accusations but like the thin ice on a water's surface it easily broke through unwilling to be silenced.

'You killed my dad!' he had screamed at her, too young to understand the necessity of palliative care was about keeping him comfortable and pain free. She had tried to explain but Jonathon was in no mood to listen, unreceptive to hear words especially when Malcolm had passed away soon afterwards.

Jonathon might not believe her but she did miss Malcolm and had been absolutely devastated when he had told her about the diagnosis. It was true her first thought had been, *What about me?* and maybe that was selfish perhaps it should have been, *I am sorry that this is happening to you but we will fight it together.*

Unfortunately, that was not how Sally Carta's mind worked as far as she was concerned Malcolm would be gone, end of, she would be left to pick up the pieces so this was her focal point. Of course, she didn't want him to suffer so she had seen to it that he hadn't nor did she allow it to go on indefinitely at the end of the day death was imminent so what if she had helped it along.

Maybe one day when Jonathon was a little older, he would lose his innocent view of the world and perhaps then he would understand she had ensured he didn't suffer unnecessarily. After all, the code of conduct she had to live by was to make the care of the patient her first concern. It irked her though that he had still not broken his wall of silence despite the time she had devoted to him, the financial commitment to therapy she had invested in him and the patience she had endured all these years.

She could feel her mind wandering into the darkness a place she could scarce allow it to go without it sucking her into the black well of no hope and she did not want to go there. She did not want the goodness of this holiday to be dissipated so quickly, just like the affect Jonathon had had upon her life blood slowly being drained out of her these past years.

Sally placed her feet upon the floor of the pool then rested her arms on the top step her legs kicked out behind her. She listened to the song of the Spanish cicada among the gardens, dipping her face every now and again in to the water. She could hear the pool pump struggling as the strainer pot lid lifted and fell, the jets creating a stream of underwater bubbles as the water continually recirculated. She loved the peace and tranquillity of the small residential complex where she could simply soak up the atmosphere of this beautiful, mountain village.

Sally had been visiting Frigiliana for many years though she had never lost the magical connection it seemed to bestow upon you. She loved the variety of bars, restaurants and the people who lived here but its correlation with art especially painting was what inspired her the most. There was a vibrance in the colours of the work in the galleries that drew you in beneath the surface of the subject matter. She could look at an artist's painting and sit considering not what the artist was trying to convey but the personality of the people they depicted.

It was probably the only time she could really lose herself and maybe it had more to do with self-examination then it was about the portrait in front of her. She smiled to herself that it would undoubtedly astound her patients and staff to think that she would spend her precious time on such trivial things. However, as the artists canvases drew her in, so did the serenity of this beautiful whitewashed village in the heart of Andalusia.

Sally knew her time here was almost expired and she would have to drag herself away very soon for the journey back to Malaga airport to return to Leeds/Bradford. With a saddened heart, she climbed out of the pool and clothed herself with her towel, maybe if Sally Carta had known what was actually awaiting her, she would have quickened her step to save his life. Or maybe she would have taken the same easy way out she had chosen many times before, each time she had put herself before him.

Chapter 26
Sally Carta: Just Breathe

As Sally Carta's plane came in to land, she absentmindedly glanced out of the window to watch the runway tarmac edge ever nearer contemplating the next time she might be able to sneak away on another holiday. There was no doubt that she had made the most of her time away she had relaxed to the max, eaten a variety of cuisines, had a few too many on more than one occasion and generally just pleased herself fully. However, reality was now hitting home that it was back to the grindstone of everyday normality and this was not something Sally was particularly looking forward to. She bobbed her head down to reach her bag stowed under the seat in front of her, then removed her glasses and put them together with the book she had been reading into its centre compartment.

Once the plane had eased its way towards the terminal the captain did his usual announcement to request, they stay seated until the plane came to a standstill and that we would disembark shortly. He went on to state he trusted they had enjoyed their holidays, wished everyone a safe onward journey and thanked the passengers for flying with them hoping to see everyone again soon. Inevitably there was the immediate rush from the "I need a cigarette" brigade or the "I'm too impatient to sit and wait" ones who immediately jumped out of their seats the moment the plane came to a halt. What followed was the customary scrambling in the overhead lockers for luggage then the unavoidable delay whilst baggage in the hold was unloaded and the stairs connected to the plane before everyone was bid a fond "farewell".

Sally smiled to herself as she reached for her cabin case knowing full well unlike these other saps, she wouldn't have any need to stand 5 deep around the conveyor belts trying to spy overpacked baggage as she was travelling light. That was the beauty of owning your own apartment you could leave your clothes hung up ready for the next time no ironing, packing/unpacking or any messing about.

She glided through passport control and into departures looking for the ever-eager Richard Carmichael waiting to take her into his arms. She readily searched the sea of faces but for some reason was unable to locate him.

Feeling a little confused she visually scanned the café sure to find him finishing a coffee, but he wasn't there either. She was beginning to get somewhat irritated by the mild inconvenience when she saw a man holding a board up with her name emblazoned across it. Perplexed, she approached the young man.

'Hello,' she began and pointing to his sign she revealed, 'I am Sally Carta.'

'Good evening, Mrs Carta. I was booked by Dr Richard Carmichael to chauffeur you home, he said to send his apologies but an unexpected emergency had occurred at work. He said that you would 'understand',' the young man announced.

Sally was understandably surprised it was quite unlike Richard to be so organised although she was definitely pleased not to be inconvenienced because all she wanted right now was a glass of wine and a long hot soak. On a plus side, the young man carried her baggage to the car, opened the door for her and secured the case in to the boot.

'I trust you enjoyed your travels,' he said once they had secured their seatbelts and pulled out of the parking lot.

'Yes, thank you it was most relaxing,' Sally replied cheerfully then eased further into her seat and watched the world go by.

The driver was mindful of her need to release the stresses of travelling so allowed her the luxury of a none conversational drive home. However, his ears did pick up and his brow did furrow at her through the rearview mirror when she received a call just before they arrived at their destination.

Sally Carta raced from the taxi she had just taken from Leeds Bradford airport without even waiting for the driver to unload her bags. Her heart seemed to be pulsating up through her mouth as her shaking hands fought to get the key in, so desperate was her need to unlock the door to get to him. Sally who was always so composed, so calm, a clear thinker who paid close attention to every detail had missed the most important of all clues. He was there in the shadows at that very moment drinking in the depth of her terror enjoying the despair that had been in the palm of his hands to create.

He felt like a conductor waving his baton to the beat of her dread. In that precise moment, it was neon impossible for him to suppress the ecstatic joy bubbling up from the well of pleasure she gave him. And soon he would hear it that guttural howl of the loss of that person you held so sacred but who would no longer feel her love. The palpable excitement driven within those few moments of anticipation had risen beyond anything he had ever experienced before. He held his breath as he waited, like any good love making session, he was left begging for the climax. He was ready to be indulged he deserved it, and so did she.

Sally raced through the partial open door the strap of her handbag catching on the door handle in her rush to enter ripping at her shoulder. She felt no physical pain as her psychological torment was beyond despair and then she saw him suspended by his neck. Her immediate instinct was to grab him by the legs to try to support his dangling body but her training was at the fore. She grabbed the largest serrated edged blade from the knife block on the kitchen counter, ran up the stairs behind him and sliced straight through the noose just above the knot. Even in her distressed state she had instantly assessed what her eyes observed and was able to execute the swiftest, safest plan to best help her beautiful boy.

He fell with a thud into a crumpled state upon the newly laminated floor of the hallway, why on earth had she removed the carpet. She laid him flat loosening the knot around his throat, quickly checked that there was nothing obstructing his airways and covering his nose she took a deep breath and deposited it into his mouth so that he may have life. In each breath that she gave, she would have gladly relinquished it as her last if only he could be spared. She got herself into position at the side of him, then locating the centre of his chest she interlocked her hands and began the compressions. It was the first time that in her head she could actually hear the music of the Bee Gees tune playing "Staying Alive" despite having performed the task on so many other occasions.

'Come on Jonathon, please son, just breathe!' Sally implored him. 'Just breathe,' she said as she continued to incessantly pound his chest with all the energy her soul would expel.

At the door, the driver of the taxi was calling to her to tell her the paramedics were on their way but she heard nothing above the thud of the pulsating throb in her ears as she drove down hoping to restart his heart. Even the sirens of the approaching emergency crew didn't reach her, nor the crash team storming through and scooping her to one side. She sat at the bottom of the stairs clinging to the newel post in shock and thoroughly traumatised trying to fathom out what had just taken place.

There was a phone call when she was in the taxi, a male she was sure of that, but how did he know what Jonathon had done? Her mind felt absolutely shot, she couldn't process the facts not to mention having seen her only son hanging by his beautiful neck. The neck she had pretended to gobble as he squirmed as a child, the neck she had supported as she swaddled him as a baby and the neck, she had shaved for him when she cut his hair. Her mind took her to memories of Jonathon in the garden running round after their German shepherd Ruskin, of the dog jumping up trying to catch the water, Jonathan squirted at him from their hosepipe. It had been a bright sunny day filled with laughter but there was no laughter today just a paramedic shining a torch into his eyes trying to get his attention.

'Can you hear me?' another voice asked her whilst a blanket was being wrapped around her shoulders. She tried to look at their faces but could barely bring them into focus nor the surge of activity within the room. The distorted vision coupled with the adrenalin rush and imposed fear of the potential outcome she may have to face began to make her feel woozy.

Then there was nothing else but silence. Had Sally Carta paid attention to the details instead of reacting through the panic of her emotions she may have realised that things were not as they had first seemed. However, she would soon come to realise that her life was being launched towards a decidedly horrific downward spiral.

Chapter 27
Sally Carta: Confusion

The next time Sally Carta began to open her eyes she had an overwhelming sense of vertigo, her head was swimming like when she had been to the dentist as a child and had to have gas for her teeth extracting. She felt nauseous but her head wasn't pounding it just had a soft pulse but the silence was ringing out in her ears, like a small buzzing sense similar to tinnitus. Her mouth was parched and although her throat was lumpy when she swallowed, as she licked her lips, she was sure that she had tasted blood, though it was dry. She was trying hard to bring herself around but the woozy sensation was winning and her head continued to loll, its weight heavy and near impossible for her to lift. She felt her chest rise, could hear or feel her heart beating yet she wasn't quite sure which although she was certain she was alive.

She tried to formulate some kind of thoughts but she had no ability to assemble anything meaningful. She had observed this type of affect before, though she was unable to locate where? It was an administered drowsiness not normal sleep she was sure of it like when a patient had been under an anaesthetic and was coming round in the recovery room. Had she been in an accident? Did she need to be sedated for an operation? Why couldn't she think straight and then there it was again a deep breath out. It was all such an effort, too tiring to think to reach the right thoughts to make any sense of what was going on.

Sally attempted to focus on her body maybe she could try to evaluate things better if she did a kind of personal body mapping exercise. Maybe then she would be able to come round enough to focus her thoughts. She started with her breathing telling herself she would count to 10 breaths then start at her head and move downwards but this just made her want to sleep more. A sharpness somewhere around her mouth cut into her lip, making her wince; maybe that's why she had tasted the blood. She tried to move her jaw but it seemed rigid and her tongue felt as though it was protruding out of her mouth rather than sat comfortably within it.

She tried to swallow again but this time she was more aware that her throat wasn't just sore but there was some kind of an obstacle in the cavity. She became fearful that she really had been in an accident and perhaps she was waking up on the operating table with the breathing tube still down her throat. She tried to speak, to cry out to let someone know she was waking up but no sound emanated from her mouth in fact she could feel something not dissimilar to a ball in her mouth.

'Come on Sally,' she scolded herself, 'you have to wake up!'

Pushing through the fog she forced her head to move to a more upright position though she couldn't quite tell whether she was stood, laid down or on her side. To escape this discombobulated state, she knew she would have to reconnect with her whole being not just her inner self and that included her outer surroundings. Sally concentrated firstly on the digits of her hands trying to will her fingers to wiggle but although she was adamant there was some form of sensation no movement was possible.

However, she did find that she could wiggle her toes although her ankles seemed to be on top of one another and immoveable as though tightly bound. Her shoulders felt rigid almost pulled back at an awkward angle and her arms seemed to be somewhere behind her so she concentrated all her effort into regaining a more natural position. She heard the distant sound of a heavy chain engaging in some kind of mechanical pulley system then a searing pain shot through her entire body. An alarm activated instantly, her thoughts faded and her body went limp.

Chapter 28
Sally Carta: Pain

A new kind of rush for consciousness came over Sally Carta despite her desperate pull to want to stay in the comfort of slumberland. It came again the unmistakeable and overwhelming aroma of ammonia irritating her nasal cavity stimulating her oxygen intake and arousing her wakefulness. Sally's eyes flickered into life to reveal what was before her. She instinctively flinched, the jolt recreating the sound of the chain mechanism, then a scream of agonising pain and again, the alarm being signalled. She could see a person suspended about 4 ft from the ground trapped inside what looked like a sturdy dog crate. He was on his belly with thick metal collars clamped at his throat, wrists and ankles. A thick chain was fed through metal rings that were attached to the three collars and from what she could see Sally's startled reflex had caused the chain to tighten, harshly yanking his head back. His arms and legs were now stretched behind him at an unnaturally high angle, the hands bound tightly with the metal cuff. Whenever she tensed or slightly moved, pain was being administered directly to him. Sally could see that the base of the cage in front of her had razor-sharp blades standing vertically directly under the person's face so if he relaxed his face would be sliced to bits. She was trying hard to comprehend what was going on, where she was, who the caged person could be, how had she got here and why?

She tried to speak but her mouth was clamped open resembling the one her dentist had used on her last visit then she realised that her neck also had a metal collar clamped around it rendering her jaw rigid. She had some kind of gag on with a ball attached to it that was lodged inside her open mouth, preventing any movement of her head, neck or mouth. Her only available movement was to blink, breathe and at a push to painfully swallow. She knew she was seated with her arms bound up to the elbows behind her back her shoulders protruding slightly now generating acute pain.

Her knees were bent up high underneath the seat, her ankles strapped together no doubt the chain holding them tightly in place. Great thought had obviously been given to ensure the maximum discomfort knowing full well it would be difficult to keep this pose as to relax or straighten would induce pain for the other person. If she maintained her posture, he was safe if she didn't then pain was created. It was in her hands, maybe it was a test to see if she cared enough about the other person to ensure he wasn't physically harmed or whether she would just think about herself.

Utter panic was engulfing every fibre of her being despite her desperate bid to fathom out what was happening and why. She willed herself to wake up confident she must be enduring a nightmare that was seemingly far too real for comfort. It was impossible for this to be a wakeful moment so several times she tried in vain to snap herself out of it to regain her consciousness, but to no avail.

As Sally Carta became more compos mentis, she realised that not only did she recognise the other person's identity but that it was none other than Richard, her Richard, Dr Richard Carmichael. Her heart thudded violently in her chest as panic became the overwhelming factor in the knowledge that her past had finally caught up with her. She realised not only was she awake but this nightmare had only just begun and there was absolutely no way out of it for either of them. Her hearing seemed to intensify as she suddenly became aware that someone else was in the room with her and Carmichael.

She wasn't sure if she was in familiar territory or not but she could still smell the lingering effects of the ammonia tinged with something else maybe a cleaning product possibly bleach or some other chemical. She wondered if she was at the surgery but everything apart from the cage in front of her was blacked out so it was hard for her to establish this clearly enough. For all she knew, she could be in an abandoned building, a storage unit or an aeroplane hangar.

No that was untrue, she couldn't have been because she didn't have the sense of that kind of space or the cold air that it would generate. What she did know was that the room was not an office space because it was slightly larger perhaps the size of their double garage maybe bigger and it had to have something strong enough to suspend the cage from.

Her thoughts were interrupted by a sound coming from her left, instinctively she tried to move her neck again, but she couldn't it was too restricted. There was no way of telling how long she had been here or how long her neck had been held in this position but oh how she would love to bend it to make it crack just to ease the building tension. She heard the noise again only this time it came from her right. She looked as far over towards its direction that her eyes would allow but she was unable to identify anything.

Maybe, her mind was playing tricks on her possibly creating something out of nothing and sharpening her senses in a fight or flight protective response. Her legs from the knees down were becoming numb and a tingling sensation was radiating throughout her thighs as the blood was finding it difficult to circulate. She inadvertently attempted to straighten her legs, not registering the carelessness of her actions until she saw Carmichael's head, arms and legs being pulled taught and his scream of pain. She heard a blood churning crack just before the alarm sounded again signalling her to release the control of her legs. She did, just in time to see his head loll forward within millimetres of the razor-sharp blades, she gasped.

Sally Carta acknowledged the catch 22 situation that she found herself in, it was either him or her, as only one of them could possibly survive. She felt powerless to stop his discomfort and pain, unable to offer words of comfort by being rendered silent due to the gag and ball in her mouth. It was torture having to watch the suffering that she was unintentionally causing but what real choices existed. He was thrust up like a chicken awaiting slaughter whilst she felt like the butcherer with the proverbial knife.

Then the lights went out and there was silence.

Chapter 29
Sally Carta: Torment

'Sticks and Stones may break my bones but calling names won't hurt me.'
'Sticks and Stones may break my bones but calling names won't hurt me.'
'Sticks and Stones may break my bones but calling names won't hurt me.'

The same children's saying had been playing over and over again for hours as Sally Carta sat tethered to the chair in the darkness. Every now and again she had attempted to wiggle her toes and fingers in the hope that the circulation would reach her digits but almost all feeling had gone. She wanted to cry out to Richard to let him know she was there, that he wasn't alone but the gag was bound too tightly as the clamp bit into her dry open mouth. The faint smell of bleach was still in the air although she could now smell her own body odour and the urine that she had been forced to pass. Here she was Sally Carta the most in control, organised, strong, independent woman unable, incapacitated and helpless in a hopeless situation.

She still could not fathom her captor's motivation for her imprisonment and torture it simply made no sense to her. She tried to recall the last moments before she had woken up bound and gagged but everything was still so hazy, they must have drugged me in some way. She had been away on holiday that much she knew; she was sure she had taken the flight but had she landed? Ahh now she remembered Richard was supposed to meet her at the airport and she couldn't find him. Had she consumed a drink that someone had spiked? Could they have grabbed her in the car park using chloroform? No, maybe she was being a bit dramatic, she had watched too many films with that scenario maybe there was something else she was missing.

A bright light suddenly shone from behind her on to the wall to the left of Richard who was still strung up in the cage. Her eyes hurt instantly as a sharp pain shot through into the back of her head. It was of the same intensity and brightness used by the opticians when she had gone for her eyes testing. She instantly attempted to flinch but her movement was too restricted so she had to make do with shutting her eyes, at least she could protect herself in that small way. Ridiculously she felt "they", whoever "they" were had not been able to take that power away from her. In the now orange glow behind her eyelids, her mind suddenly revealed the last image she had seen before the blackness had fallen it was of Jonathon.

She recalled him hanging from his beautiful neck, cut down and a light being shone in his eyes but his life had been extinct. She tried to expunge the grief but no sound would come, no movement was possible, the anger, hurt, fear, loss, guilt flooded her every pore, organs, veins, senses like water swallowing buildings in a tsunami. She felt traumatised her mind shattered, splintering off in a thousand different directions, 'Noooo Jonathon, noooo not my baby,' she was screaming internally.

Somewhere in the darkness from the depths of her despair she became aware of a flashing light similar to that of lightning spasmodically bursting across the outer part of her eyelids followed by a clicking sound. She tentatively opened her eyes to find a series of photographs being displayed across the wall where the bright light had shone earlier. It was confusing, she saw pictures of fireworks but it didn't make any sense to her, she was going out of her mind she didn't understand the relevance.

There were party scenes people enjoying themselves, drinking having fun but she wasn't having fun. Then a recording came on of people laughing, it was loud, way too loud, she wanted to put her hands over her ears but she couldn't move them. She felt deep anguish being made to look on not wanting to participate but being forced to see the frivolities to hear the laughter. Her despair was rising to an intense altitude she needed to make it stop. She started to thrash around furiously, no longer aware of the catastrophic harm she was causing to Richard Carmichael, whose body was flipping around like a fish out of water reacting to each movement. His slender physique repeatedly contorting back and forth his face constantly thrust in amongst the sharp blades, piercing deeply up through every orifice until he was unable to feel anymore.

Then the projector stopped and the darkness fell again.

Sally Carta continued to thrash about her mind fragmented into a thousand tiny pieces no longer was she able to latch on to a single thought her brain was being decimated beyond recognition.

Chapter 30
Mick Denby: The Luckiest Man Alive

Mick Denby was giggling to himself as he made his way past the petrol station along Denby Dale Road on his way home from yet another night out at the officer's club. He glanced across the expanse of the forecourt to the window where the attendant generally stood at the till to find it was the young lad called Kevin. He was a friendly young chap, polite and was always quick to serve Mick and knowing what he did for a job, he never held him up unnecessarily. Mick noticed him look in his direction so he put his hand up and was about to continue when he suddenly remembered he needed milk. No doubt, come the morning, he would have the customary thick head which would undoubtedly require the assistance of a few strong coffees to see him on his way. He ambled across the deserted tarmac to the little latched window but Kevin beckoned him towards the door with a few quick gesticulations of the hand. Mick obediently staggered towards the full glass door and heard the automatic lock click so he pushed against it, entered the shop and heard the click lock behind him.

'You alright Kevin?' Mick asked.

'Yeah, just bored to death I hate doing the night shift especially on this stretch of road,' he admitted.

'I couldn't do it out in the middle of nowhere, you must worry that one day a customer is going to call for the till not the petrol,' Mick said jokingly.

'Chuffing heck Mick I didn't but I might now, thanks,' he said unappreciatively.

'How has it been tonight,' Mick asked trying to make small talk though desperate to get home to bed and out of the bright lights of the garage.

'I have had 4 customers in 3 hours,' Kevin admitted.

'Am I the 5th?' Mick asked.

'No, you're the 4th I was exaggerating,' Kevin chuckled.

Mick took a carton of full fat milk out of the fridge scrambled about in his pockets emptying the contents on to the desk to give Kevin the change. Kevin thanked him then the two men bid each other "goodnight".

As Mick opened the door a car pulled onto the forecourt, 'Looks like number 5 has arrived before you know it you will be into double figures,' he told Kevin before shutting the door.

Despite the summer evening the air was quite cold so Mick zipped his black prison issued, fleece jacket up to the very top to ensure he maximised his body heat. The walk up the hill from the main road seemed to take forever but he kept his stride until he finally arrived at the place, he called home. As he walked down the garden path, he noticed the bedroom light from the house adjacent to his go out old Mrs Baines was going to bed so he would try to be quiet. What he didn't notice was the dark form lurking in the shadows of the large bush at the side of the drive. Mick Denby fumbled in his pockets for his keys before realising he must have left them by the till when he was giving Kevin the change.

He made his way around the side of the house to the back door and on lifting the mat up he felt his fingers across the paving slab for the spare key. It wasn't there. Disgruntled, he dropped the mat back down and glanced around trying to determine what to do. There was no way he was going all the way back down to the garage tonight, he would just have to pick them up in the morning and it wasn't like he could knock at Mrs Baines.

There was nothing more for it, Mick Denby would just have to make do with the garden shed despite the inconvenience. He deftly crossed the garden no longer affected by his earlier inebriated state, entered the shed, grabbed an old picnic rug and bedded himself down on the floor hoping to get at least some rest.

It was approximately 1½ hours later that Mick Denby was abruptly awoken by a figure in the doorway looming over him. Startled awake he didn't immediately recognise his surroundings just seeing odd shapes and shadows illuminated by an orange glow reflecting through the Perspex window. The figure was dressed in a heavy dark jacket, with boots, a hat, mask and was very animated, his hand reaching down towards him. Denby's first thought was that he was under some form of attack so his natural instinct was to get to his feet to defend himself as he didn't stand a chance being on the floor.

As he jumped up the need to fight was instantly defused as he realised his house was not just on fire but it was blazing out of control. The firefighter grabbed the picnic blanket and threw it over him half rushing him and half dragging him out on to the street, where he was plonked safely next to Mrs Baines.

The whole area was packed with two large fire trucks parked diagonally in a V shape, cab to cab across the street their back ends one pointing at Mick's drive the other at Mrs Baines. Police cars were stood beyond the trucks their lights flashing blocking the road. As a precaution houses at either side of theirs were being evacuated and many of the neighbours were stood upon the walkway. Mick was bewildered unable to process what his eyes were observing, stunned into silence as the place he had called home was furiously being ravaged by flames. Amongst the spectators stood back at a safe distance in the crowd was a person who had been revelling in his handiwork that was until he realised that Mick Denby had somehow escaped.

'Are you alright, Mrs Baines?' Mick asked sadly, but the old lady did not respond she gazed vacantly at her home eyes glistening with moisture.

'Are there any other occupants known to be in the house?' The fire chief asked.

'No,' Mick said, 'we both live alone.' Mrs Baines nodded in agreement but never took her eyes off the blazing wreck praying her home and her precious photographs would be salvageable.

The next person to approach Mick and Mrs Baines was a policewoman, 'I'm Detective Chief Inspector Shona Williams. I am so sorry to meet you in such difficult circumstances but I wonder if I could ask you a few questions?' She asked and when they both nodded, she continued, 'perhaps we could go to the station it must be very distressing sitting here witnessing your homes go up in flames.'

Again, Mrs Baines just nodded allowing the young woman to guide her to an awaiting police car whilst Mick compliantly followed behind them both. As he sat in the back of the police car numb by what he had just experienced it was not lost on him that he had just cheated death. The young woman tried to make small talk but his ears had tuned out before the car had even set off and poor Mrs Baines looked like she needed to be seen by a doctor. When they arrived at the station, the young woman pulled through some automatic gates which brought them around to the back of the building.

There were a few unmarked cars whether they were privately owned or police Denby didn't know. The only other noticeable squad car was stood at the back door with its doors wide open where two officers were manhandling a man in handcuffs out of the car and they then propelled him in through the door of the building. Shona pulled into a space, jumped out, opened the back door for Mrs Baines ready to assist her leaving Mick to sort himself out. Again, Mick dutifully followed the duo into the custody suite where the man in handcuffs was being processed by the desk sergeant flanked by the two arresting officers. Shona Williams led the elderly lady down a corridor to her right, glancing back to Denby to ensure he was following.

'This way,' she told him. At the end of the corridor, she used her ID badge to gain access through some doors on the left, 'Are you alright with the stairs Mrs Baines, it's just one flight?'

The old woman didn't object and kept walking so Shona had to assume it was safe for her to proceed, Mick continued to follow. At the top of the stairs, she butted the door with her backside, stepped through still assisting the old woman and then led her to a comfy chair encouraging her to sit down.

'Would you like a hot cup of tea?' Shona asked trying to coax the old woman to talk but she just stared. She looked towards Denby, he nodded.

The room they were in appeared to be partially a chill out area which is where they were now sat and an open-plan work area, it had brown partitioning stands that sectioned off areas with desks and chairs on one end and offices at the other. Around 10 minutes later, the police woman returned with two steaming cups of tea accompanied by an older gentleman.

'I don't know if you take sugar or not but I have put two in as I always think in times like these, they recommend a hot sugary drink, I hope that is alright?' Shona Williams informed them.

'This is my colleague Detective Inspector Dion Jacobi I thought perhaps you and he could talk Mr Denby whilst the on-call doctor gives Mrs Baines the once over,' she said pleasantly as Mrs Baines started to get up. 'It's ok you can have your cup of tea here first; the doctor knows you are here and will be with us shortly.'

As they waited for the doctor to arrive, Mick gazed about the room yet not really seeing anything his mind was completely blank and as he looked down at his chest, he could see an exaggerated rise and fall of his t-shirt. Then he looked at the coffee and it struck him, if he hadn't remembered about the need for milk, he wouldn't have entered the garage which meant he wouldn't have left his keys.

Also, if the key had been under the mat near his back door he would not have ended up in the shed. A new sense of dread powered through him that if he had gone in and passed out on his bed like every other night he wouldn't be here, period. What a sobering thought to know he had just cheated death by the skin of his teeth.

'Are you ready, Mr Denby?' Jacobi broke through his train of thought apparently awaiting Mick's response, he stood obligingly and walked with Jacobi to a small interview room.

Jacobi sat at the furthest chair behind the desk leaving Mick to squeeze on to a seat that was fixed to the floor. Mick assumed this was for the safety of police personnel who might be interviewing unruly suspects though he was pleased to see there were no two-way mirrors. Maybe he had watched too many crime series.

'Mr Denby, I apologise for having to interview you so soon after what can only be described as a very traumatic experience but as you may appreciate these are extenuating circumstances,' Jacobi explained.

'I am sorry but I am still in shock, everything I own is in that house,' Mick told him.

'How long have you lived at the address?' Jacobi enquired.

'I moved here when I transferred to the prison which will be around 3 years ago and I began renting the property soon afterwards,' Mick said.

'So, you don't own the property then? In that case I will need the contact details of the owner so that we can inform them in the morning,' Jacobi said.

'It is owned by a Dr Carmichael, he lives at a place called Blenheim House which is on Elm Road in Sandal,' Denby stated.

'What is the nature of your work at the prison, Mr Denby?' Jacobi enquired.

'I am a prison officer,' he said flatly.

'Could there be anyone who has a grudge against you that may have started the fire?' Jacobi asked.

'Are you saying this is arson?' Denby faltered.

'At this stage of enquiries, we have to look at all possibilities, also the fact that the blaze became so intense that quickly suggests that an accelerant could have been used,' Jacobi declared.

Mick stared trying his best to gather some thought if only to reply but nothing was forthcoming.

'Mr Denby is there anyone that you can think of that would want to cause you serious harm?' Jacobi asked directly.

'No,' Denby stammered.

'Nobody at all, you're sure?' he asked.

'I am sure, there is no one at all that I have had a falling out with or with whom I am on bad terms with,' he assured Jacobi.

'What about the people you work with?' Jacobi pressed.

'I don't get on with everyone but I cannot believe a colleague would resort to such a crime,' Mick said.

'I wasn't talking about fellow officers Mr Denby. I was talking about the people you lock up on a daily basis. Could there have been an altercation with an inmate who maybe would want to get back at you?' Jacobi asked.

'I am sorry but I am finding it hard to think straight, I have had barely any sleep but there are no prisoners that I can bring to mind who might want to set my house on fire,' Denby said flabbergasted at the thought of being a target.

'Mr Denby this is not a matter of just setting your house on fire we are talking about attempted murder,' Jacobi said bluntly.

A cold shiver ran all the way through Denby like someone had just walked over his grave, the problem was had he not ended up in the shed then a grave would have been exactly where he would have been heading.

'Apparently the fireman who found you says you were asleep in the shed, a little odd for you to be in the shed whilst your house is ablaze,' Jacobi stated.

'Ordinarily I would agree with you especially if I owned the house, was in debt up to my eyes and had just taken out an insurance policy but it is very innocent,' Mick offered.

'Would you care to enlighten me?' Jacobi asked.

'I had been out drinking with friends at the officer's club as I am most evenings, I hate just sitting about the house especially after a long shift. Anyway, on my way back home I remembered I needed milk for the morning so I called in to the garage on my way past,' Mick was telling him.

'Which garage is this?' Jacobi interrupted.

'The one at the bottom of the hill where I live on the main road, a guy called Kevin was serving and he buzzed me in to get the milk,' Mick explained.

'He buzzed you in late at night on that long stretch of road and you say his name is Kevin?' Jacobi sounded doubtful.

'Yes, I go in most days to pick a paper up, milk or to get petrol,' Mick added.

'Is it customary to buzz someone in? I would have thought it would be a single post through the night I cannot imagine why he would put himself at risk that way,' Jacobi stated.

'Ordinarily, I guess he wouldn't but like I say I go in quite frequently and he knows what I do for a living so he didn't feel unsafe or threatened besides he was bored to death and glad of the company,' Mick reiterated.

'And this chap Kevin can collaborate what you are telling me, Mr Denby?' Jacobi enquired.

'Yes, yes of course in fact he told me I had been his 4th customer in a 3-hour period, so there isn't any way he will forget me,' Mick assured Jacobi.

'Ok, so what has this got to do with why you were found asleep in the shed and not in your bed like most folks?' Jacobi asked again.

'Sorry, so I was fumbling in my pockets looking for the change for the milk instead of having to break a note and in doing so I emptied some things on to the counter. It was only when I got back home that I realised I hadn't got my keys so I must have left them on the ledge near the till,' Mick explained.

'So why didn't you just go back for them, I mean that would be the most logical action don't you think?' Jacobi queried.

'I agree with you but I was absolutely shattered so I couldn't be bothered to go all the way back, besides I am supposed to be on a late shift today so it wasn't an inconvenience to simply pick them up this morning,' Mick stated.

'So not only can this chap Kevin collaborate your story but we will find your house door keys at the service station as well,' Mick suggested.

'That's correct,' Mick affirmed.

'A little convenient, don't you think, sounds to me like it was more of a plan to give you an alibi,' Jacobi inferred.

'No, no not at all, I had gone round the back of the house to get my spare key from under the mat but it wasn't there. As I said I was absolutely shattered so when I turned round and saw the shed, it seemed the easy option rather than having to walk all the way back down the hill and back. I just needed sleep, that's all,' Mick assured Jacobi.

'So, it comes back to why is your house suddenly on fire if you have no enemies and you haven't organised it then waited in the shed to escape harm,' Jacobi toyed with him.

'Honestly, I don't know but what I do know is I cheated death in a massive way tonight and I am here to tell the tale. So, if there is anything I can do to help I am more than willing to because I am keen to find out the same answers you do,' Mick stated.

'Right, that will be all for tonight I just need to speak with Ms Williams that brought you in and then we can release you. If you just want to wait here, Mr Denby I will be back in a moment,' Jacobi told him.

Whilst Jacobi went in pursuit of Shona Williams to relay the information, he had received Mick Denby pondered on the thought of his house being intentionally set on fire. He was thoroughly bewildered at the thought of someone seeking to deliberately harm him, why would they, he hadn't got any enemies that he was aware of, it just didn't make any sense. Also, what was he going to do now everything he owned was in that house and more to the point where was he going to live.

Oh my goodness, even his uniform would have gone up in smoke but he guessed he could at least see Grady in stores to get a couple of spares. But, where was he going to take a shower, have a shave, wash his clothes these everyday essentials were all now issues he would need to consider and perhaps what organisations that might be able to help him. Mick was beginning to feel overwhelmed by this imposed burden when Jacobi reappeared at the door.

'Sorry to keep you Mr Denby the boss has just said that as a precautionary measure we will need to take swabs of your hands including under your fingernails along with retaining the clothes that you are wearing,' Jacobi announced.

'Am I a suspect?' Denby asked stunned.

'It is just procedure to help us eliminate you from our enquiries Mr Denby so if you would like to follow me this way,' Jacobi said expectedly and without even waiting for an answer he walked back out of the room.

Denby followed Jacobi to a private area where he was expected to strip, his clothes handled with latex gloved personnel and bagged for testing whilst he was given a disposable, white, zip up the front suit to put on. His hands were photographed then swabbed and the contents from under his fingernails were removed with a file. Mick Denby felt like a common criminal yet all he had done was go for a drink with his colleagues, come home and then fallen asleep in his shed. He had to admit it did look a little suspicious on the surface but if someone had really set his house on fire expecting him to be inside it then he really was the luckiest man to be alive.

Chapter 31
Shona Williams and Dion Jacobi: Let the Investigation Begin

'So, what impression did you get of Mick Denby?' Shona asked.

'It's hard to say,' Jacobi said vaguely.

'How so?' Shona wondered.

'Inevitably he did seem genuinely in shock but I have seen people who have initiated a 3rd person attack not knowing when it is coming and therefore genuinely been surprised,' Jacobi said truthfully.

'Do you think he is capable?' Shona pressed.

'Let's face it given the right set of circumstances we are all capable of committing any act should the need arise. For instance, if Joe Bloggs saw a man sexually abusing his daughter, he is going to rip his head off,' Jacobi stated.

'So, are you saying we should dig deeper?'

'I am saying we shouldn't rule him out whether he is a prison officer or not,' Jacobi finished.

'Well, my thoughts on that matter are there are plenty of officers that succumb to manipulation, conditioning and coercion whether it is doing the odd favours, taking things into prison or inappropriate relationships. My gut says he hasn't got anything to do with it but we need to find the evidence that tells us he hasn't,' Shona evaluated.

'Precisely, did the old woman have anything to add?' Jacobi enquired.

'Not really besides the doctor concluded that she wasn't in a fit state to be interviewed so I got Betts to take her to the hospital. I contacted her daughter who lives in Doncaster, she was going to meet her at the hospital,' Shona said.

'How did she sound?' Jacobi asked.

'Scared to death like everyone else when they are woken by the police in the early hours of the night, I did explain the situation and urged her to drive carefully as we wanted her to arrive in one piece,' Shona explained.

'I guess we had better open an investigation then, do you want me to liaise with the fire chief or do you want to do that yourself?' Jacobi enquired.

'If you could visually inspect the building, assess the basic damage like whether it is going to be a right off need rebuilding or a good clean up then speak to the fire chief. I will speak to the sergeant, take the morning briefing and allocate positions then when you have got a good appraisal of the situation we will go and see Dr Carmichael together,' Shona concluded.

'Right boss, see you later,' Jacobi said and left.

Shona decided not to go home, there was no way she was going to sleep tonight so she began planning out the general necessary points of interest. Inevitably the first point was the establishment of whether or not it was arson and that would then tell her which direction this would take. She got a whiteboard, fixed an A1 size pad to it and an arrangement of markers then put pen to paper, it didn't work. She scribbled a few dead pens on the sheet until she found a purple one that did work, it would have to do. First, she would get a copy of the initial callers recorded call, find out who they were and arrange an interview taking note of what they saw before during and after.

She would get a team on the streets to knock door to door to gather vital information leading up to the fire, the fire itself and any knowledge about Mick Denby. Her and Jacobi would tackle the night attendant at the petrol station together. There would be the need for background checks, primarily upon Denby and Dr Carmichael then a look at the insurance details and whether there had been any high figure adjustments. Inevitably that would create a search of both Carmichael's and Denby's financial records to ascertain whether it was an inside job to pay off huge debts. She would also add in a chat with the governor at the prison along with any personnel or colleagues just to ensure she had a full account of who Mick Denby was.

The same would also be typical of Dr Carmichael's situation she would have to get some background on who he was from his partners and colleagues no stone could be left unturned. Hopefully this would establish a motive but if it created a dead end then she would have to rethink her direction but usually in the process it did raise unanswered questions. The telephone interrupted her thought process.

'Good morning this is Detective Chief Inspector Shona Williams Wakefield Police Incident room, how can I help you,' Shona said breezily for 06.35 hrs.

'Morning Shona, I hear there was a fire in Crigglestone last night, what's the news?' Superintendent of the Criminal Investigation Unit Gary Morgan asked.

'Good morning, Superintendent yes, it was a residential house fire; we are not sure of the extent of the damage yet but it was well alight when Jacobi and I arrived. The owner is a Dr Carmichael although he had the place rented out to a prison officer by the name of Mick Denby,' Shona briefed him.

'Any casualties?' Morgan asked.

'None known of at the moment nor are any expected the occupant was strangely asleep in the shed at the time and was awoken by the fire crew doing an area search. The adjacent neighbour was an elderly lady who was taken to hospital but more as a precaution than anything else. Jacobi interviewed Denby the prison officer earlier but that is all we have at the moment. I am expecting a call from Asher Blake once they have the fire under their control,' Shona told him.

'The occupant was asleep in the shed?' The super asked in disbelief.

'Yes, I know, if that doesn't arouse suspicion, I don't know what does,' Shona agreed.

'Ok, can you walk through the process, plan your route and deliver it this morning to the team?' He asked.

'Already on it, sir,' she responded.

'Good, good I didn't expect any less designate roles and execute them and we can have a catch up at the end of the day,' he said then rang off before she had a chance to respond.

The morning meeting was like every other update about ongoing investigations, new leads that needed to be followed up and information sharing. Shona informed the group of officers about the fire, that Jacobi would be on the scene this morning gathering vital information and that they were going to talk to the owner of the property. She delegated her list of responsibilities to available officers and then dismissed them to tend to their duties. Like cattle making their way to the milking shed, they filed out of the briefing room, down the hall and into the incident room, all but police constable Josie Petroni. Shona was collating her notes together when Josie coughed to get her attention so she turned around.

'Sorry to disturb you DCI but you said that the fire last night was at the address of a prison officer's?' Josie queried.

'Yes Josie, Mick Denby,' she repeated.

'The thing is my flat mate and I were at the officers club last night where we were sat with a group from the prison and I remember being introduced to a Mick Denby,' Josie informed her.

'That could be vital information Josie do you think you could provide me with a statement about what you remember from last night?' Shona asked.

'It's not much, I'm afraid but yes of course,' Josie agreed.

Shona made a call to detective Collins to get her in to her office to take the statement, she then collated her things ready to meet Jacobi at the scene of the fire when her phone began ringing.

'Morning Shona, it's Asher Blake, the fire chief,' Asher stated.

'Morning Asher, I was just on my way out to you,' Shona began suddenly on the edge of her seat, 'Do you have some news for me already?'

'I am afraid you will have to up your investigation.' Asher told her.

'So, it *was* arson then,' she stated.

'Oh, it was arson alright but we have also found a body,' Asher informed her, there was a pause, 'Are you there, Shona?'

'Has the medical examiner been informed?' she finally asked.

'Yes, she is going to organise the removal of the corpse but the autopsy and x-rays won't be taking place until tomorrow evening though as it is the first slot she has. I am going to organise for samples to be taken from around the body and once your photographer gets here, the positional pictures. Inevitably we will want copies of everything you get and obviously I will share our findings, photographs and evidence matter,' the chief advised.

'I know it is only early but have you any idea where the fire may have started at this point?' she enquired though didn't expect an answer.

'Officially no, but unofficially looking at the intensity burns of the debris, the directional flow, the concentration of the force and the visual aftermath I would say that petrol was poured through the letterbox. Samples will be taken from the door, the letterbox, flooring and surrounding areas, what's left of them, to confirm my suspicions but that would definitely be my guess.' Asher told her.

'Thanks Asher please keep me updated,' Shona said and rang off.

Shona made a note to enquire at the petrol station about the sale of petrol cans maybe it was possible someone had purchased a can from there, filled it up and used that to set the fire. When Shona turned from her desk ready to leave, she noticed the sudden change in pallor of Josie's face.

'Are you ok Josie?' Shona asked.

'I didn't mean to listen in to your conversation but I couldn't help overhearing what you said about the fact that a body had been found. I think I might know who that could be,' Josie said suddenly bursting in to tears.

Shona dropped her things onto her desk, ripped out some tissues from a box handed them to Josie and dragged a chair up beside her. She waited to allow the young woman to compose herself not wanting to apply any unnecessary pressure.

'I think it could be my flat mate Sandra, Sandra Clarke,' she said trembling, 'she wasn't in her room first thing this morning.'

'What makes you think that the body at our house fire could be Sandra's?' Shona queried.

'Last night we were at the officer's club, you see my friend Darley Mays works in the kitchens at the prison. Sandra and I have been trying to get her to come out with us for months but since she became a mum it is like the umbilical cord hasn't been cut. Anyway, last week she finally agreed but only if we went to the officer's club because there would be other people she knew there. I think she was feeling a bit insecure having not been out for so long and didn't want to feel left out if it was just the three of us. Sorry I am babbling.'

'We'd arranged to meet last night at the club and were sat at the bar waiting for her when Sandra received a message saying that she couldn't make it after all. I was livid and wanted to go somewhere else especially as we were only there because Darley had insisted upon it. Sandra couldn't be bothered with the walk into town besides she thought if we stayed it would be a great way to find out what Darley was really like at work,' Josie told her.

Shona glanced at her watch wishing Josie would get to the point of why she thought the body could be that of her friend Sandra but didn't want to appear too insensitive but she did also have a lot of work to attend to. Josie took the hint.

'Sorry. We stayed there all night just sat at the bar talking to various people as they came to order their drinks. Then this guy called Mick said that he knew Darley and she had given him a lift in to town a while back and that she seemed nice enough. Anyway, he was sat with a couple of fellas who called over from their table when they saw him talking to us and invited us to join them. Sandra was up and off her buffet before I even had chance to put my glass down,' Josie said.

'Do you know what the other men were called?' Shona asked.

'One was called Simon and the other was James but I am sorry I do not know their last names,' Josie apologised.

'No, that is great Josie. It collaborates Denby's story of his whereabouts but now we have a couple of extra pieces of the puzzle, who he was with,' Shona began, 'but that doesn't tell me why you think the body could be Sandra's.'

'We ended up having a right laugh with these guys and it was quite clear that Sandra had the hots for this Denby guy, sorry but it's a bit embarrassing, he joked with her about her trying his handcuffs for size and she said she'd rather try him on for size etc, etc. Anyhow when he found out that we only lived around the corner from him he said jokingly about having a spare key that he kept under the mat of his back door. He told her to feel free to use the key anytime she was passing. Just as cheekily she said she just might take him up on it, but I didn't think she meant it,' Josie said sniffling.

'Then what happened?' Shona asked trying to move the story on.

'Well, I had to be up early the following morning so she begrudgingly got a taxi home with me but promising Mick and his pals that we would call in again. Mick followed us outside and when I had gotten into the taxi, I turned around to see them snogging. He gave her his mobile number then reminded her about the key under his back door mat before playfully slapping her on the bum as she got into the cab,' Josie stated.

'So, do you really think she would have gone to a stranger's house, let herself in and waited for him? It is quite a bold move,' Shona asked puzzled.

'Ordinarily I would say that it is so unlike her but last night they just sort of clicked, so I would say that anything is possible,' Josie stated.

'What was different about last night?' Shona enquired.

'Normally when we get back after a night out, we will hit the shower and go straight to bed. However last night she had another couple of drinks whilst I was sorting myself out, maybe a bit of bravado juice I don't know but when I came out, she was on about Mick and the spare key under the mat,' Josie told her.

'So, what exactly did she say?' Shona asked.

'Just that he was a really good kisser and that she had a good mind to call his bluff, go round and use the key to surprise him when he got back. Like I say I didn't think she meant it I thought she was just messing about but when I got up this morning, her bed hadn't been slept in. That's why when you revealed the occupants name of the fire, I felt I had to let you know we were in the club with him last night. I would hate to be accused of withholding any evidence, but when your caller said a body had been found…' she trailed off becoming upset again.

Detective Collins had stood intently at the door of the office not wanting to break the flow of the conversation but now stepped forward. 'Maybe a cup of tea would help, Josie?' she said kindly.

Shona nodded and requested that Collins bring in one of the liaison officers just to sit with Josie and perhaps support her whilst they took a formal statement. Once they were in place and Josie had composed herself Shona made her exit her head swimming with this new evidence. This was not going to be a clean-cut case after all; in fact, it was becoming more like spaghetti junction with many leads going off in all directions.

Chapter 32
Shona Williams and Dion Jacobi: Two for the Price of One

When Shona arrived at the scene, she was shocked to see that the house had all but been incinerated completely, the windows downstairs had blown, the upstairs had melted and there were only threadlike splinters of the roof visible. As soon as she got out of her patrol car, she felt the thick, black remnants of smoke at the back of her throat. She reached into her car for a face mask despite what little protection it would give her she decided that anything had to be better than nothing. As she approached from the front of the house, she could see Jacobi stood with Fire Chief Asher Blake and they looked deep in conversation.

'Hey guys how is it going?' Shona greeted them.

'Just look at the state of the place,' Jacobi said. 'Whoever did this definitely did not want Mick Denby to survive.'

'Well, someone didn't survive, someone lost their life,' Asher Blake said solemnly.

'We have a lead who that someone might be,' Shona told them.

'Already?' Asher asked.

'Yes, one of our young constables, Josie Petroni was apparently at the officers club last night and says she thinks it could be her flatmate, Sandra Clarke, apparently her and Mick Denby hit it off,' Shona informed them.

'That's strange, he never mentioned it to me when I questioned him earlier and why on earth would he have been in the shed whilst the house was burning down with her in it,' Jacobi said sceptically.

'That is a very good question Dion one that we will put to Mr Denby once we have interviewed Kevin the petrol attendant and Dr Carmichael,' Shona informed him.

'Can you have Mr Denby do a sketch of the rooms to assist with our investigation we will need to put whatever is salvageable back in their places to help us analyse the flow, damage patterns etc. My guys are recording the after affects with photographs/videos then we will be using the table over there,' he pointed to a newly erected table which had a variety of equipment, evidence bags, tags, pens, clip boards, paper and labels, 'as an evidence collection area.'

'Can you feed everything through to me, please Asher?' Shona requested.

'All the necessary samples and results will be filtered through as and when the information is available, Shona,' Asher Blake told her then said, 'Looks like the medical examiner is here now.'

Jacobi and Shona turned around to see Sallyanne Peters making her way towards them. Sallyanne was a lovely lady in her late 50s, she had thick ginger shoulder length hair that she always wore down with a hairband across her head. She was an astute woman, who was dedicated to the complexities of her work and loved nothing more than problem solving how someone had died. Unlike a few other people in her profession, Sallyanne was very pleasant, she was always willing to prioritise where necessary, was responsive, reliable and very thorough. Jacobi, Shona and Blake had all had the pleasure of working with her in the past so all three were so glad she had been assigned to this particular case.

'Morning,' Sallyanne said, 'looks like a welcoming committee have you been waiting long for me?'

'Not at all,' Asher was the first to respond, 'and we think we have a name for the corpse.'

'Good that will make my job a little bit easier,' she responded.

Jacobi and Shona made their exit whilst leaving Sallyanne and her team in Asher Blakes care still contemplating the impact the fire had caused to the damaged building. Jacobi followed Shona in his car down to the petrol station pulling into the space next to hers on the forecourt. They made their way towards the shop noting the cameras scanning the entire length of the frontage, then went inside and over to the desk.

'Is Kevin the attendant who was on duty last night available or do you have a contact detail that we might be able to reach him on?' Shona enquired.

'I am sorry his shift finished at 6am but he will be back on duty tonight at 10pm,' the young man wearing the name badge "Paul" informed them.

'Do you have an address or phone number it is essential that we get in touch with him as soon as possible,' Jacobi tried.

'The manager will have it on file, just give me a moment,' Paul told them and pressed a buzzer from somewhere under the counter. Within a few seconds, a small chap with a thick Irish accent appeared from a door at the back of the store and made his way towards them. 'The police were asking for details about Kevin.'

'Is there something the matter officer?' The manager enquired.

'Nothing to worry about as you may have heard there was a fire up the hill last night and we believe that Kevin who was on duty last night may be able to help us with our enquiries. Paul here has just told us his next shift starts at 10pm tonight but we could do with speaking to him before then. Have you got his contact details available?' Shona asked smiling at the manager hoping to put him at ease.

'Yes, would you like to come into the office? I will get you them now,' he told them.

The office was very small and looked over crowded with its one desk, chair and small filing cabinet. On the desk were two monitors one that was assigned to a computer and the other where the screen was divided into four parts displaying 2 each of the interior of the shop and 2 projecting the outside camera footage. 'Do the camera's record 24/7?' asked Jacobi.

'Yes, unless there are any incidents that we need to extract for evidential purposes it automatically rerecords every 14 days,' the manager explained.

'Would it be ok to send one of our technicians down later today to take a copy from last night, it may be possible you have footage that will help with our investigations?' Shona queried.

'That's absolutely fine although I will only be here until 6pm,' the manager stated.

Whilst Jacobi waited for the contact details of Kevin, Shona excused herself contacted the station and spoke to Mike Dennings to arrange for him to extract the information that she required. Once Jacobi had joined her outside, they made their way towards their awaiting cars.

'The manager said it would be alright to leave one of our cars here so that we could nip up to see the doctor together rather than going in two separate cars,' Jacobi told Shona.

'Good call, Dion the planet will be thankful of the greener option,' she said playfully.

'To be honest I thought it better for us to arrive together as a team, give the impression of unity,' Jacobi explained.

'You mean it was not to experience my scintillating repertoire of conversation and wit?' Shona joke.

'Oh yes, that too boss,' he said getting into the patrol car. 'And the fact I feel much more important sat in an actual patrol car, it's like re-living my childhood dream,' Jacobi laughed.

As they took the dual carriageway towards Pugneys with the intention of moving on towards Asda Durkar and on to Sandal an emergency response came in over the radio. Shona and Jacobi looked at each other in disbelief.

'Did I just hear that right?' Shona asked.

'You did, and the address was Blenheim House on Elm Road exactly where we were heading,' Jacobi stated.

Shona hit the blues and twos sped round the car who had been avidly maintaining the speed limit due to the patrol car behind him and shot off towards their given destination. When they pulled up at Blenheim House there was mayhem with patrol cars, an ambulance, neighbours and the general public gathered at its walled building. Shona pulled as near as she could to the house and haphazardly parked the car before both her and Jacobi jumped out.

'Good job we only had one car, Dion,' Shona said looking at all the people and lack of parking space.

There was an officer posted at the door, 'Apparently it's not pretty,' he told them.

'Who else has entered the building?' Shona asked the constable who had a clip board in his hand.

'Myself and Officer Clarkson were first on the scene, we entered the property went down the hall and into the lounge to find two paramedics dealing with the casualty. Marianne Chambers the occupants cleaner and Jonathon the occupant's son were also in the lounge. Stefan Garforth the ambulance driver made the discovery of the body and called it in, to my knowledge he was the only person to have ascended the stairs. He opened the door but did not enter the bedroom as he could tell from the injuries sustained, the amount of blood lost and the colour of the deceased that life was extinct. He retraced his steps to preserve the scene.'

'Officer Clarkson is sat with Marianne Chambers in the kitchen whilst I remained at the door to ensure no other personnel entered the property. It looks like our scenes of crime guys have just arrived too,' Constable Collins informed them.

Shona and Jacobi quickly made their way through the inner door and along the hallway where they could hear a woman who sounded hysterical in a room to their right. Shona peered around the doorway to find the person being given a shot of something by one of the ambulance crew, a startled eyed young man was sat to her right. Hearing their arrival Constable Clarkson made his way out of the kitchen towards them.

'What's going on here then?' she asked.

'It is hard to say, by the state of her I would have guessed she'd woken up to find him dead beside her. She was absolutely hysterical when we arrived.' He announced.

'Or she is a cold-blooded killer who has cleaned herself up after committing the crime herself hoping to make it look that way,' Shona said.

'I take it the young man is the son, Jonathon?' Jacobi asked.

'Yes, that is, Jonathon,' he told them.

'So, do we know who the deceased is?' Shona asked knowing full well what the answer was going to be.

'We think it is her partner, a Dr Richard Carmichael but the ambulance driver said he is in a right mess so it will be hard to identify him. We have not let anyone else into the house and no one else has been up the stairs or anywhere near the room,' Clarkson reaffirmed.

Jacobi looked at Shona perplexed and together they made their way up the stairs to the offending room but were not at all prepared for the carnage they saw. The grey plush headboard of the bed was pressed up against the wall directly opposite the door. There was a large bay window to the right which seemed to drench the corpse in the sunlit rays that were pouring through it. The body was to the left side of the bed and laid upon red-drenched white sheets.

To the right of the door was a dressing table, most of what appeared to be the surface contents were strewn across the floor. Shona tried to steal a look at the body without going too far into the room as she did not want to contaminate the area of what was one of the worst bloody crime scenes she had come across. Jacobi took his turn to peer around the door to take in the scene.

'What do you make of it, Dion?' Shona asked.

'With such a colossal blood loss I would have expected there to have been splatters all over the wall, headboard and floor yet it is predominantly in the one area, on the bed,' Jacobi surmised.

'My thoughts exactly, also with the curtains open and the contents of the dressing table on the floor it does appear that the lady downstairs could have woken up, opened the curtains, seen the body and ran out of the room,' Shona said.

'But how does anyone stay asleep whilst the person next to them is being slaughtered?' Jacobi asked.

'Or, how do they not wake up if the body was placed there after the fact?' Shona mused.

'Perhaps the only person who can answer those questions is the hysterical woman downstairs,' Shona said.

'She looked around the door jamb again hoping to find something she hadn't noticed the first time but nothing was forthcoming, she gazed at the position of the body and noticed marks on one of the visible wrists. Hmmm, possible wrist binding or bondage for that matter, she was letting her imagination run away with her. She tried to glance at the face but it was an undetectable gouged out bloody mess.'

'Guess the first place to start would be to talk to the occupants,' Shona told Jacobi. She followed him down the stairs to the front room where the woman who had been sedated was strapped into an ambulance chair staring glassy eyed and ready to be transported to the awaiting ambulance.

'Has she said anything?' Jacobi asked the ambulance team.

'She was muttering incoherently when we arrived but nothing came out that made any sense, she pointed upwards so my colleague made his way upstairs to see if there was anyone else who needed help. I have given her a sedative but as you can see, we need to take her with us to get her checked out,' the guy behind the chair responded by tipping the chair back to start making his way out, clearly not wanting to be delayed.

Jacobi followed the other paramedic out into the hallway to ask if anyone else had gone upstairs and to obtain their contact details.

'No,' he confirmed, 'there was only me, then I came straight downstairs and went outside to call you guys, the name is Stefan Garforth.'

'What is the lady's name?' Shona asked the young man who was stood in the lounge with her.

'It is Sally, Dr Sally Carta and I am Jonathon her son,' he told them.

'Is there anything you can tell us about what has happened here Jonathon,' Jacobi asked as he re-entered the room.

'Not really, I was working the night shift at the secure part of the hospital so I didn't know anything was wrong until the cleaner called me this morning, she comes in twice a week on Tuesdays and Fridays,' Jonathon said.

'What did she tell you?' asked Shona.

'She just said that she had arrived as normal and was surprised to see that the lounge curtains were still on so she had come into the room to pull them back. She had apparently found mum sat on the mat there in front of the fireplace,' he said pointing to the mat.

'Did she say whether your mum had spoken or if she had been anywhere else in the house other than the lounge?' Jacobi asked.

'No, she just informed me that Mum appeared to have had some kind of mental breakdown and that she was sat on the floor in the lounge rocking back and forth with her hands clasped around her legs, muttering,' Jonathon recalled.

'What happened then?' Jacobi asked.

'I told her I would get straight over and advised her to make Mum a cup of tea. I told my manager something bad had happened to my mum and that I had to leave immediately, so she said she would fill in for me and I left,' Jonathon told them.

'What is your manager called Jonathon?' Jacobi asked getting his notebook out ready to take down the information.

'Her name is Cheryl Connors,' Jonathon said.

'So, take us through what you saw and did, step by step when you arrived,' Shona guided him.

'Do you mind if I get a glass of water first, I am parched, I think it is the shock,' he requested.

'Of course, sorry we should have considered that,' Shona stated and then once he had left the room she turned to Jacobi, 'What do you make of him, first impressions?'

'He seems genuinely bewildered probably hasn't got a clue what is going on and if he has been up all night, we may have to talk to him again later,' Jacobi suggested.

'You're probably right but we need to get as much detail as we can now otherwise his brain may shut down too,' Shona said as Jonathon re-entered the room.

'Thank you I needed that, won't you sit down,' he said to the officers. Shona and Jacobi sat on the settee leaving a spare seat between them whilst Jonathon sat in the chair to their left.

'When I got here, I drove in at speed so I didn't pull into my usual spot, I just jumped out of the car and raced in. Marianne, the cleaner must have been watching for me out of the window because she had the door open as I raced up the steps. She just told me she still hadn't managed to get any sense out of her and that she seemed locked away somewhere. I came into the room and knelt down on the floor in front of her but as soon as she looked up and saw me, she became hysterical. I tried to comfort her but she started thrashing out at me, screaming,' he said visually looking upset.

'What do you mean she wouldn't let you comfort her surely you would be the one person she would need to give her some support right now,' Shona asked.

'As Marianne told me she was just staring intently pretty much as you have just seen, she didn't seem to notice anything going on around her at all but when she saw my face she suddenly started screaming. I reached out to comfort her but she started lashing out at me hitting my hand away and screeching uncontrollably. I have never seen her like that, ever, it reminded me of the patients we have at the hospital who suffer with serious disorders. It was exceptionally distressing to see and not be able to help her so I told Marianne that she had better call for an ambulance,' Jonathon said looking quite worried.

'Did she calm down at all whilst you waited for the ambulance to arrive?' Jacobi enquired.

'No, in fact she became a lot worse as soon as she heard me telling Marianne to get the ambulance. You see my mum is a doctor so she would know being in this state that there would be a high possibility she could get sectioned under the mental health act,' Jonathon explained.

'Did you go upstairs at all?' Shona asked him.

'No, I had no reason to but I did use the toilet down the hallway near the kitchen,' Jonathon revealed.

'Did Marianne venture upstairs?' Jacobi asked.

'Not to my knowledge I think she came in to open the curtains, found Mum then stayed with her whilst I arrived and she didn't leave Mum until the ambulance came,' Jonathon told them.

'Where is she now Jonathon?' Shona asked.

'She is sat with one of your officers in the kitchen drinking a cup of coffee, is everything ok?' Jonathon asked, 'she hasn't done anything wrong has she?'

Jacobi and Shona looked at each other then back to Jonathon.

'What?' he asked.

'Does anyone else live at the property Jonathon?' Jacobi enquired.

'Yes Richard, why?' Jonathon asked.

'Is Richard your father?' Shona asked innocently.

'No, my dad passed away many years ago Richard is my mum's partner, Dr Richard Carmichael they work at the surgery together,' Jonathon began then stood to take his mobile from his jeans pocket, 'Oh, my goodness I never thought, I must ring him and let him know what's happening.'

'Would you mind just holding off on that Jonathon whilst we have concluded our interview, is that ok?' Jacobi said.

'Is this a formal interview? Am I being accused of something, I don't understand,' Jonathon declared.

'Why don't you take your seat,' Shona guided him. 'Do you know if your mum was seeing anyone else apart from Richard?'

'No, definitely not!' he stated.

'And what about Richard, could he have been seeing someone else and your mum has potentially found out?' Jacobi queried.

'I doubt it very much they work together and live together but I guess anything is possible, why?' He asked.

'We are just trying to ascertain what could have happened to traumatise your mum so dramatically that it has seemingly rendered her incoherent, confused and hysterical,' Jacobi told him.

'We must inform you that we believe Dr Richard Carmichael is deceased,' Shona delivered bluntly monitoring his every response to see if there were any telltale signs of previous knowledge, there were not.

'What, no that's not true he will be at work, please you must let me ring him he will want to be by her side,' he said standing again. This time they let him make the call whilst they sat in silence. After a couple of seconds, the tune "Bohemian Rhapsody" by Queen could be heard faintly playing. Jonathon removed the mobile from his ear, tilted his head with a puzzled expression then seemed to realise the phone was somewhere in the house.

'Jonathon please sit down,' Jacobi said, Jonathon slowly obeying slid back down into his chair.

'I don't understand, what is happening?' Jonathon asked.

'We have reason to believe that Dr Richard Carmichael is not only deceased but that his body is in the bed upstairs that he and your mum shared, his face is so badly mutilated he will have to be identified by some other means,' Shona explained.

Jonathon sat open mouthed trying to process what he was hearing, 'and you think my mum has done that to him?' he stammered.

'We are not ruling anything out at the moment, we will know more once we have gathered evidence, conducted interviews and investigated numerous components. Inevitably Dr Carmichael and your mum are the only people who truly know what has happened here, one is dead and the other appears to have had a mental breakdown. Hopefully she will be fit to talk to us at some point very soon and then we will be able to get to the bottom of what actually happened here. In the meantime, Jonathon you will need to make alternative accommodation plans as the house is now an official crime scene,' Shona informed him.

Shona supervised Jonathon whilst he collected some belongings to last him for a few days whilst Jacobi guarded the door to the offending room the last thing, they wanted was for any evidence to be compromised. Once he was ready, they took his mobile number and requested that he keep in contact with them and for him to provide them with an address when he was sorted. Shona walked him out then welcomed the scene of crime guys. Before long, the ominous white tent was erected outside the property, equipment unloaded, an evidence collection area designated and a team of whited suited people were on the case. There were now two serious crime scenes to investigate but unbeknown to Jacobi and Shona there would soon be a third.

Chapter 33
Shona Williams and Dion Jacobi: Establishing the Facts

'What do you make of that?' Jacobi asked Shona as he slid into the patrol car beside her.

'Very strange, it would be impossible to remain asleep whilst someone next you were savagely mutilated,' Shona began, 'although I have to say the shock and distress did appear real, there was no way that could have been an act.'

'So, the cleaner arrives, the curtains are on, she lets herself in and finds her in a distressed state,' Jacobi repeated.

'Yes, although we do know the cleaner regularly works Tuesdays and Fridays so it could be planned for her to be an innocent bystander set up accidentally on purpose as a witness,' Shona stated.

'Or it could just be a coincidence,' Jacobi tried.

'I don't believe in coincidences, maybe the son planned it knowing full well the cleaner would be going in this morning and being on night shift he would have an alibi,' Shona mused.

'How could he commit the crime when he was working at the secure hospital?' Jacobi asked.

'We will give his manager a ring when we get back to the station, see what she has to say about Jonathon,' Shona told him, 'But first I think we need to pay Kevin a visit and then get Mick Denby in again.'

'Do you think the cases are connected?' Jacobi asked. 'I mean the house that belongs to Dr Carmichael is torched and then he is murdered, now that is definitely not a coincidence!'

'Connected yes, how, I am not quite sure yet. We will need to look into the Dr's affaires, when Clarkson and Collins get back, they can cover his bank records, debts and that sort of thing. We will pay the surgery an initial visit just to get a feel for the people there before delving further I wouldn't want to alert anyone nor upset the running of the place just yet,' Shona said.

On their way back towards the city, they passed Sallyanne Peters the medical examiner, 'we are keeping Sallyanne busy today,' Shona commented raising her hand to her as she went by.

'I wonder how long it will be before she can fit our new dead body with the mangled face in, I don't know how she has the stomach to dissect them and then sit and eat her lunch,' he joked.

'This is the street Forest Dyke what number was Kevin's house again?' Shona enquired.

'133 the even ones are on my side so 133 must be on yours, hold on a minute that one is 45 so it must be quite far down,' Jacobi instructed. As they continued to move along the road, he kept his eyes peeled until he located the correct number, 'It should be the house just after the white van,' he said pointing over to his right.

Shona pulled over towards the kerb where Jacobi had indicated glancing at the house in question, 'Looks like he could be in bed, the upstairs curtains are drawn,' she told Jacobi.

'Then we will just have to wake him up,' Jacobi said with a smile undoing his seatbelt.

'What did the manager say his last name was?' Shona enquired.

'Maltby, Kevin Maltby,' Jacobi said then followed her out of the car and down the path.

The house was a stone fronted mid-terrace property with three steep steps that lead up to the front door. The edges of the steps had an inch thick white line painted around them. It reminded Shona of the steps going to the back door of her grandma's old house as they had the same white border, a sign that elderly people had once lived there. Shona smiled as she pictured her young tomboy self, kicking a ball on the track that lay between the yard and the garden beyond.

Funny how something so insignificant could arouse such a detailed memory and ignite a wealth of emotions. Jacobi knocked on the door perhaps befuddled at her sudden hesitation, then stood back down next to her to wait. When no answer was forthcoming, he knocked again, a little harder this time then stood further back glancing up at the window to see if there was any movement, there wasn't.

'I will go check around the back,' Jacobi said taking a little archway that was neatly excavated between Kevin's house and the one to the left.

Shona knocked on the door again and then shouted through the letterbox to see if that would stir a reaction. The curtain moved slightly but did not open, perhaps Kevin had finally heard them, got up and the draught had caused the movement. As Jacobi reappeared Shona was looking through the letterbox and was about to call out again when sure enough two feet appeared at the top of the stairs, so she stepped back into place beside Jacobi. When the door opened, they were stunned to see that it was none other than Mick Denby standing in front of them.

'That was quick, I have only just informed you lot where I was staying,' Denby revealed.

'Sorry?' Shona said.

'You told me I had to keep you informed where I would be, well I rang and left a message for you about an hour ago,' Denby began. 'Isn't that why you are here?'

'No,' Jacobi answered. 'We were given this address by Kevin's manager from the petrol station, I take it this is the right address?'

'Yes, it is but he is in bed at the moment,' Denby replied.

'You will need to get him up Mr Denby we need to speak with him, may we come inside please?' Jacobi said.

Mick Denby stepped aside, closed the door and showed them into the front room before going back upstairs to fetch Kevin. The room was typical of a young bachelor's pad on minimum wage, with mismatched furniture, empty takeout boxes, an overflowing ashtray, posters haphazardly stuck to the wall and little warmth. Shona and Jacobi could hear the objectional groans from upstairs of Kevin's displeasure at being woken from his deep sleep then the heavy footsteps that someone barely awake makes.

Jacobi suddenly elbowed Shona and nodded to a small shelving unit that stood to the left of the cream tiled fireplace, Shona followed his glare. A small quantity of drug paraphernalia had been cast aside, blackened foil, a spoon, lighter and a small homemade plastic tube most likely used as a makeshift pipe. There were also some cigarette papers and a strong whiff of cannabis emanating in the room. When the door opened, they were greeted by a young lad in his mid-20s stood in his boxer shorts looking confused.

'Hello are you Kevin Maltby who works at the garage on Denby Dale Road,' Shona asked him.

'Yeah,' he replied groggily scratching his head.

'I am Detective Chief Inspector Shona Williams and this is my colleague, Detective Inspector Dion Jacobi,' Shona said as the horrified Kevin glanced straight towards the items, he had left strewn on the unit.

'We did come to ask you a few questions but I can see from the remnants over there this may not be a good time,' Jacobi said nodding over to the drug paraphernalia. Kevin looked from one to the other not quite knowing what to do or what to say so he remained silent and motionless.

'You will need to come down to the station before you start work tonight, Mr Maltby as we need to ask you some questions with regards to Mr Denby,' Shona told him.

'I am more than capable of telling you what you want to know now although I am not sure how helpful it will be,' Kevin assured them as he suddenly decided to walk fully into the room where he sat down and offered them a seat. Jacobi sat whilst Shona remained standing near the window overlooking the frontage of the house.

'Fair enough,' Jacobi began, 'what can you tell us about Mick Denby?'

'I know him from being a regular to the garage he swings by at least once maybe twice a week for petrol and walks past most evenings,' Kevin said.

'He walks past most evenings you say, why does he have a dog or something?' Jacobi enquired.

'No, he generally drives to the officer's club in the evening, has a few pints and then walks back. Sometimes if he is on an early shift, I might see him on a morning walking back for his car as I am leaving work at 6am,' Kevin explained.

'Yet you have offered him a place to stay?' Shona interrupted.

'The guy is down on his luck some prat has just burnt his house down what else could I do?' Kevin shrugged off.

'So would you consider yourself friends?' Jacobi continued.

'Not essentially, he will bob in like he did last night and we will chew the fat (chat) but he hasn't got any family up here. No doubt we will become friends now though as it is situations like this that create deep friendships, helping people out I mean,' Kevin said.

'Speaking of his house burning down did anyone come to the station last night to purchase any petrol using a can rather than depositing it into their car?' Jacobi asked.

'No, not last night,' Kevin assured them.

'But you do get people purchasing the green and red cans for petrol then filling them,' Jacobi enquired.

'Sure, that is what they are there for, sometimes for lawnmowers, chainsaws or when people have broken down,' Kevin answered.

'When was the last time you sold one?' Shona intervened.

'I don't know maybe a couple of months or so ago, I remember one day I must have sold 3 or 4 on one shift?' Kevin told her.

'Would there be any records of those sales and do you remember anything about the people or circumstances you sold them,' Jacobi asked.

'Not really, I think it was just a matter of people running out of petrol not far from the garage you know that sort of thing but nothing relevant about anyone comes to mind,' Kevin said honestly.

'So, going back to last night,' Shona broke in to change tact again. 'About what time did you see Mr Denby?'

'It would have to be about 1.30 a.m. I remember telling him I had served 4 people in 3 hours and I started my shift at 10pm,' Kevin said.

'So, you didn't just see him, you spoke to him too,' Jacobi confirmed.

'Yes, I am not supposed to open the door but I did last night because it was only Mick not like he was going to nick the register or anything being a prison officer,' Kevin grinned.

'One would hope not,' said Jacobi, 'so what happened then?'

'He bought some milk; we exchanged a few pleasantries and then he left. There was nothing of any importance he just popped in and left,' Kevin said then suddenly worried, finished, 'please don't let my boss know I opened the door I would get the sack. Company policy and all that.'

'How did Mr Denby pay for his milk; did he use a card or cash?' Shona asked.

'He used the small amount of cash that he found, in fact the idiot took his keys and bits of rubbish out of his pockets but then forgot them and left them on the counter. That is why he came back to the garage early this morning so he could collect the keys. I was astounded when he told me what had happened, maybe if it wasn't for me opening the door he would have gone home and been in the house when it was burnt down,' Kevin stated.

'That is possibly true Mr Maltby, anyway I think that is everything for now if we need anything else from you, we will be in touch. In the meantime, if something springs to mind that you haven't already told us please don't hesitate to give us a call,' Jacobi said handing him a small business card.

'Yes, we will let you get your rest now Mr Maltby but before we go it might be an idea if we have a quick word with Mr Denby?' Shona said opening the door with a wry grin on her face knowing full well that Denby was at the other side listening in. 'Won't you come in?'

Mick entered the room looking a little sheepish whilst Shona and Dion threw each other a knowing look however Kevin was thankful to be able to get back into bed so left without giving it another thought.

'I am sorry for any inconvenience Mr Denby but we need you to accompany us to the station we have a new line of questioning we need to investigate,' Shona told him.

'What, now? I have been up most of the night and really do need to sleep,' Mick began.

'I know you have been through the mill on this but the quicker we can get some answers the sooner we can find out who is responsible for the fire that has destroyed your home,' Jacobi coaxed.

'Fine, let me throw some clothes on unless you are expecting me to go like this,' he said then took off to get changed.

On the way to the station, Jacobi sat in the back whilst Shona drove the conversation keeping it light and generalised. Once they had arrived Shona parked up and they led Denby to a spare interview room. They made it clear that he was not under arrest and that he could leave at any time although it hadn't felt like he'd had any choice about going in with them. They explained the procedure for recording the interview to which Denby had no objections, as far as he was concerned, he wanted it over with as soon as possible so he could get out of there.

'Right Mr Denby firstly thank you for agreeing to accompany us today and just to reiterate we have a new line of questioning with regards to the investigation upon what appears to have been an arson attack upon your home,' Shona said.

'You told me earlier, that last night you had passed the garage whilst on your way home after a night out, is that correct?' Jacobi asked.

'Yes, I had been to the officer's club like I do most evenings,' Denby replied.

'Did you arrange to meet anyone at the club, Mr Denby?' Jacobi wondered.

'No, it's the kind of place where you don't need to make arrangements you just turn up and there is always someone there that you know?' Denby revealed.

'So, who were you with last night?' Shona asked.

'I was with the two colleagues that I see most nights, Simon Donelli and James Swan,' Denby said matter-of-factly.

'Are they the only people you were sat with,' Jacobi asked emphasising the word sat. Mick glanced from Jacobi to Shona and then back again with much confusion across his face he desperately tried to fathom out what they were getting at but had absolutely no idea.

'Think very carefully before you answer Mr Denby,' Shona warned him, but he was blank.

'I seriously have no idea what you are getting at, I went to the club on my own, I sat with Simon and James, had a few pints, left the car and walked back,' Denby said.

'Then let me be specific,' Jacobi began, 'did you entertain any female company last night?'

'Oh, my goodness why didn't you just ask outright then I would know what you are on about instead of all the cloak and daggers. Last night, two women were sat at the bar waiting for Darley, Darley Mays who works in the kitchen but she stood them up. One of them wanted to leave but the other one didn't so they came over to join us, but left soon afterwards. I had a laugh with one of the girls and a bit of a flirt before we shared a snog when she was going home in the taxi,' he finished.

'When was the last time you had guests stay over with you,' Shona changed tact.

'What?' he said thrown by the sudden change of direction.

'At your home, do you entertain regularly, have friends, family or a partner stay over at all?' Jacobi asked.

'No, hardly ever in fact the only person I ever remember staying over was James when him and his Mrs had a spat about 5 months ago, why? How is that relevant?' he asked perplexed.

'According to one of the young ladies from last night you told her she could stay anytime and that you kept a key under the mat of your back door, is that correct?' Shona jumped in.

'Hold on a minute exactly what am I being accused of here? I want to make it absolutely clear that I haven't done anything wrong and when the girls left in the taxi, I did not see them again,' Denby stammered suddenly very hot under the collar.

'We are just trying to establish the facts, Mr Denby,' Jacobi stated.

'But they are the facts,' Denby stated.

'Didn't you tell me in your earlier interview that the reason you were asleep in the strange place of your garden shed was because the key that you usually keep under the mat was missing?' Jacobi asked.

'I'd had several pints was a bit worse for wear, I was feeling around for it but I couldn't find it simple as,' Denby said getting a bit annoyed with the questions back and forth.

'I can see how this may seem tiresome to you Mr Denby but the fire brigade found a body in the wreckage of your home so any information in finding the identity of that person would be very much appreciated,' Shona delivered.

The colour in Denby's face drained rapidly and he looked as shocked as a newborn calf hitting an electric fence. Both he and Shona knew without a shadow of a doubt that Denby was not aware of anyone having been in the house during the time of the fire. Shona excused herself to get a cup of cold water from the bottled water fountain then passed it across the table to Denby. They waited for him to regain his composure, noting how his hand shook uncontrollably as he drank, it took him several minutes for him to speak again.

'You mean that she came to my house, took the key and let herself in and that is why the key wasn't under the mat?' he asked.

'Yes, that is exactly what we think may have happened because her flatmate reported her missing this morning also the last thing that Sandra had told her was that she had a good mind to take you up on your offer,' Jacobi informed him.

At that moment, Mick Denby did something that neither of them expected, he began to cry, 'I cannot believe that she liked me enough to come round to my home, I was only joking.'

'I can see this has been an enormous shock to you Mr Denby but as you can imagine this is now a murder investigation so there is no more room for joking around. Right, we now also need to ask you about Dr Carmichael,' Shona began, 'what kind of a relationship do you have with him?'

'Sorry, I am confused what has Dr Carmichael got to do with Sandra?' he wondered.

'I don't think she has anything to do with Dr Carmichael but we need to establish if the potential arsonist was targeting you or the owner of the property,' Shona concluded.

'He was my landlord, that is it,' Mick said flatly.

'So, you do not have a personal relationship with him it was merely formed from a landlord/tenant perspective,' Jacobi asked.

'Absolutely, he was the landlord and I was simply renting a property off him,' Denby replied.

'Ok Mr Denby I think that is all for today,' Jacobi concluded.

'For today?' Denby said, 'does that mean you might want to talk to me again tomorrow or the day after?'

'It is an ongoing investigation Mr Denby so yes we may need to ask you more questions depending on any new information that arises,' Shona said, standing to indicate the end of the interview.

'If you would like to just wait in reception, I will organise transport back to Mr Maltby's for you,' Jacobi told him opening the door for him to walk through.

'Oh, there is just one other thing Mr Denby,' Shona thought, 'has anything strange happened to you lately?'

'Strange? Like what?' he queried.

'Have you met anyone new lately, like accidentally bumped into someone or has someone recently ingratiated themselves into your circle, asked inappropriate questions or consulted you about your landlord, Dr Carmichael,' Shona wondered.

'No, nothing like that has happened to me well not that I can recall,' Mick said.

'If you do recall anything please inform us as soon as possible you never know it could be that crucial bit of information that we need,' Shona urged him.

'Also,' Jacobi reminded Shona. 'Asher Blake wants the sketch of the rooms in the house to investigate the fire.'

'Sorry Mr Denby we may need you a little longer I will get Sonja Bell down to sketch it out for you then we can send it straight over to Asher it will prevent any delays,' Shona told him as Denby rolled his eyes.

Once Denby had left the room to be escorted to reception by Jacobi, Shona put a call in to arrange for Sonja to attend reception to take the sketch and then for her to drop him back at 133 Forest Dyke. She was just on the phone with Mike Dennings when Jacobi returned.

'What was all that about asking Denby if anything strange had happened to him?' Jacobi asked as soon as he came back.

'I know it is grasping at straws but there could be something that has been made to look so insignificant yet it is the very detail we need to crack the case,' Shona delivered.

'Really?' Jacobi asked very doubtful.

'You never know Dion we sometimes find the answer in the detail but failing that if Denby has kept a nugget of information back afraid it might incriminate him this will give him the opportunity to unburden himself,' Shona said wryly.

'Anyway, Mike Dennings is going down to the petrol station to extract the information from the camera's now,' Shona reminded Jacobi. 'You might as well go along with him to pick your car up.' She looked at her watch, 'Meanwhile I will speak to the super to update him on what we have so far, looks like this investigation is hotting up and I am not just talking about just the heat from the house fire.'

'Two bodies in one day, a house fire, a hysterical woman and an intricate web of information to plough through, oh how I love this job,' Jacobi joked.

'And tomorrow will be just another day in the mad house,' Shona said, but she could not have known just how true her words would become!

Chapter 34
Mick Denby: An Unfortunate Encounter

Mick Denby was already scanning the car park for spaces as he pulled up to the barrier. So, once it had begun to automatically rise and had just cleared his windscreen, he was off the mark like a sprinter at the Olympics. He accelerated quickly, changed gear and darted passed the little silver Toyota that he had been tailgating from the main road and throughout the entire woodland approach. That was more than long enough. Mick could not understand the need to dilly dally about behind the wheel as far as he was concerned people driving that slow shouldn't be in a car and might as well get a mobility scooter. Funny, whenever you were in a rush you either happened to get stuck behind a tractor, an elderly couple plodding along like 2 mile an hour Tess or some kid on a moped driving down the middle of the road. He had neither patience nor time and today was no different, he should have been on the landings 10 minutes ago where no doubt the day staff would be getting seriously pissed off by now.

It wasn't his fault he had simply forgotten to reconnect Kevin's Alexa after being out on the lash with Simon and James. He hadn't been intending on staying late but when he had told them about the fire and the body, they had inevitably encouraged him to have a few stiff ones. Once he had got back, it had consisted of a staggered stumble to the bottom of the stairs, where he then nosily ambled up them to what was now his temporary bedroom. On flicking on the light switch and collapsing in a heap on to the unmade bed, the room began to spin in unrelenting swirls like a ballerina on acid.

Almost immediately, the light headedness won the battle over sleep and was quickly superseded by the threat to puke. In his eagerness that the contents of his stomach should hit the bottom of the toilet bowl and not the jamb of the bathroom door, he suddenly sprung up from the bed. His single-minded determination that it should reach its final destination in tact left him blinded to the artefacts in his peripheral vision. Inadvertently in his inebriated and somewhat animated desire he knocked the damn Alexa clear off the chest of small drawers at the side of the door. Subsequently in doing so he failed to realise the Alexa had totally freed itself from its electrical connection. Way before he had any chance to kneel down, the contents of the past four hours of drink began to spew from his mouth mixed together with the beef stew he had eaten earlier.

The brown goo splattering the white of the toilet seat like a Jackson Pollock painting. His stomach convulsed in a rhythmic motion to pump the liquid upwards and outwards until only thick saliva mixed with the acidic taste of bile was left. Mick Denby sat half bent over the toilet bowl half hugging it wondering why he did this to himself. As he clung on, more to stop the dizziness from stealing his balance than anything else he knew that the morning would begin with the obligatory throbbing head.

There was no point in telling himself that he would take it easy the next night or that he would drink less or have more water because he knew this would never happen. He had lied to himself for far too long now, that even he didn't believe them anymore. No, Mick Denby knew he was a functioning alcoholic although at this very moment he was spent and ready to surrender into the depths of a snore worthy sleep.

Originally, Mick Denby had started going to the officers club to socialise with his new colleagues but that was almost 3 years ago. He had continued his nightly sessions supposedly for the company, well that's what he had told himself but it had soon become part of an essential routine. The reality was that he couldn't get through the day without the need for a drink which is why he had taken a quick nip of vodka before setting off for work. At least it had taken the edge off and the bounding in his head was beginning to lose the solid beat of the Jamaican Ska band it had been banging away to.

He checked his watch he was only 10 minutes late but there again he still had the issue of having to get through the gates, where, if Officer Flynn was stationed there was sure going to be some pointless further delay. 'Today of all days, please just let me get through quickly,' he thought as his attention was refocused on the present.

He deftly sped around the Toyota taking no notice of its occupant, then cut sharply across the front of it pulling in to the only available space with the ease and swiftness of a hawk seeking its prey. He smirked at the stupidity of the driver to think they could beat him and pleased with himself he shut off the engine. He wouldn't care to admit it but his car was definitely an extension of how he saw himself fast, flashy, and fun, a true babe magnet if ever there was one. Opening the door careful not to knock the car next to him he slid out then grabbed his gym bag from the back seat and only as he stood up straight on closing the door did, he realise that the Toyota had stopped close to his rear bumper. He was about to react in his usual loud, arrogant, brusque manner when he quickly pulled up tight like a jockey about to release the horse over a jump. The driver was none other than the number 1 governor, Diana Burrows!

'Ermm, good morning, Ma'am,' Mick stammered as he began to flush with embarrassment of his judgemental stupidity.

'Good morning, Officer,' the governor replied sternly. She paused for a few seconds to ensure her displeasure was felt to the maximum before continuing. 'I hope you take more care in the execution of your duties within my prison than the lack of safety you display on the road.'

'I am so sorry, Governor, I am late for the unlocking so was rushing. I did not mean to be so reckless, my apologies, Ma'am,' Mick hesitated, not wanting to appear rude but clearly, he needed to leave. He checked his watched again.

'Well, unfortunately for you, your colleagues and the prisoners who will be waiting for your untimely arrival will be forced to wait a little while longer,' the governor declared, nodding towards his car.

'Sorry?' Mick responded, completely oblivious to the governor's reference.

'In your keenness to cut me off to secure this space, I think you have failed to notice the sign displayed over there,' she said pointing to the front of his car. 'Perhaps you would care to take the time now to read it and then kindly move your car.'

Mick Denby walked to the front of his car unsure what he was expected to find and then he saw it. Defeat engulfed him as he realised the foolishness of his mistake. On a small wooden stand was mounted a metal plaque of approximately 30 cm x 20 cm that stated, 'Reserved for the number 1 Governor.'

Mick Denby got back into his flashy, red car and slapped it into reverse whilst Diana Burrows had already pulled forward, positioned herself and was ready to reclaim the space that was rightfully hers. Once she had squared her car evenly between the parked vehicles she disembarked and trotted off as fast as her heels would carry her towards the huge prison gates. Mick Denby was left humiliated and as deflated as a punctured inner tube in the wake of her absence.

He knew he had no time to waste so he simply parked his pride and joy down the centre of the car park hoping to find it in tact at the end of his shift.

As he approached the pedestrian gate, it was immediately and uncharacteristically buzzed open before he even had a chance to reach for the bell. He ducked through, secured it behind him and walked through into the initial foyer area. It was completely empty further highlighting his lateness. He located himself a locker placed his mobile phone, wallet and keys inside then applied his belt and key chain. As he absentmindedly turned to face the window of the gatekeeper's office, he noticed Officer Flynn with two of his OSG's (Officer Support Grades) staring intently at him. One of the young trainees held his keys ready to dispense them down the key shaft to him. He removed his tally and threw it into the slot, the OSG slid the bolt back removed the tally, dropped the keys in and slid the bolt back in place so Mick could receive the keys.

Mick then made the mistake of looking up to see all three of them with a knowing smirk plastered upon their faces. How he hated Flynn the smug bastard with his condescending, power tripping attitude that he always displayed as though this was his own private domain. No doubt on the outside he was one of those sapless bastards whose wife wore the trousers which is why he was so power hungry at work. Mick snatched his keys up and clipped them to his chain before slipping them in to his right trouser pocket.

Once through the final gate he made his way into the bowels of the prison with its customary high green fencing topped with razor wire, towards B wing fondly known as the Bronx. It was a two-storey building with 36 cells, 20 downstairs and 16 upstairs which predominantly held prisoners who had completed their induction and who had either been allocated an area of work placement or given an educational course. He hated it.

To him these little scrotes were nothing more than drug fodder awaiting their next fix. As far as he was concerned, all prisoners should do hard labour in a bid to stop the revolving door of their constant return to prison. They were a drain on resources, were as uncouth as alley cats and not fit to breathe the same air as him. But it was a job and it paid the rent so he would continue to take great pleasure in locking their sorry little arses up each and every day. He strode past the reception area, the visitors centre, works department and along the edge of the exercise yard until he finally arrived onto B wing. This was undoubtedly going to be another long shift.

'Where the fuck have you been?' Jerry Sanders, the senior officer bellowed.

'Sorry sir there was an incident in the car park I had to deal with?' Mick muttered.

'When you work on my wing, you arrive on time do you hear me? This is the second time this week you have kept my officers waiting, there had better not be a third!' Sanders delivered into Mick's face. 'Right let's get unlocked before we have a bloody riot on our hands.' He turned on his heel and shot off towards the first cell.

Mick followed close behind not deaf to the sniggers and mutterings of "fucking prick" and "what a waste of space" from his colleagues.

The day took on the same format as every other in this stinking place so he might as well just grin and bear it. Besides, it was only 36 pay days to retirement, if only that was days and not months he thought. His mind awash with the blurry effects of last night's escapades, he unwittingly opened the third cell door without noticing the details on the name card, trust him to open Nina bloody Spalding's door.

'Hey up, it's Mick the Prick, the girls will be tingling today sir,' came Nina's unorthodox greeting.

Nina had a tiny frame, was unkempt and sported shoulder length brown matted hair. Her skin was a grey pallor and Mick couldn't help thinking that she always looked like she could do with a good scrub. From the back, she could easily have been mistaken for a teenager but the full-frontal version demonstrated the effects of heavy drug use. Her skin bore signs of scabbing probably where she had scratched at it fearing she had things crawling under the surface. She had obviously experienced a runny nose as there were snail like trails downwards towards her mouth which her yellow stained tongue absentmindedly and hungrily slid across it.

'Hey Mick, I got my clit pierced when I was on the out, you want to have a look?' she enquired unashamedly.

Repulsed, Mick turned away but not quick enough to miss the cracking of the thick crusted mouth ulcer that was embedded into the corner of her mouth. Mick chose to ignore her in the hope she would find something or someone else to occupy her tiny little self.

'Fucking hell ignorant twat, I was only being friendly not like I was asking you to lick it or owt,' she spat at him hurt.

Mick continued along the landing unlocking each door quickly moving to the next to ensure there was no room for any further unwanted interaction. He had almost made it when the dulcet tones of the office OSG (Officer Support Grade) came through the tannoy system summoning him to the office for a phone call. With a deep sigh, he retraced his steps back along the landing and down the stairs thankful that Nina bloody Spalding was nowhere in sight.

He locked and unlocked the gate that took him through into the small office area and picked up the phone receiver that had been left sat on the desk.

'Hello, this is Officer Denby, B wing how can I help,' he said in the most professional tone he could muster.

'Good morning, Officer Denby, this is Janice Waring, the governor's secretary,' she paused for effect. 'The governor has requested your presence in her office at 10 am sharp. Do not be late.' The line was abruptly disconnected.

Mick Denby stood in silence for a few seconds sometimes his life felt like he kept banging his head diving into the shallow end somehow expecting that one day it would surprise him and actually be the deep end. He checked his watch knowing full well he had time to supervise the cleaning of the cells and breakfast before he would have to make his way towards the big red door of the governor's office.

Mick gave a thin tight-lipped smile to the questioning look of the OSG as there was no way he was explaining anything to her. The problem about working in this place was that Chinese whispers were rife but they acted more like tumbling rocks of gossip that were dropped from a great height by relentless lying carrier pigeons. No matter what the situation, the dinosaurs as the old staff were known were so out of tune with reality, they feared new blood so attempted to annihilate any competition. The weak were so scared of being the next round of fodder that they would hide behind the dinosaurs rather than challenge their inappropriateness.

Mick couldn't abide either party so he kept himself to himself, did his job but then left a little more soul destroyed each day. As he walked back out onto the landing, he noticed Officer Marks had already started the daily job of checking the cells downstairs, he was about to make a start on the upstairs cells when the first alarm bell of the day suddenly pierced through him. Officer Davies quickly responded to his radio's information call to attend a fight on the hospital wing. It was now Mick's time to smile his lateness rendered him radio free for the day. He locked the inner gate at the front entrance of the wing behind his colleague to maintain the security and took the stairs to check the bars, lights and integrity of the cells.

What neither Davies nor Denby was aware of was that Marks had also responded to that same alarm bell at the hospital and had exited through the bottom gate of B wing.

Mick Denby made several mistakes that morning, getting up late for work, taking the governors parking space, delaying unlock and failing to notice both his colleagues had attended the alarm bell thus resulting in mismanaging his own safety on the wing. However, the major mistake Mick Denby had been making for the past 6 months was underestimating the prisoner he knew only as Nina "bloody" Spalding. He failed to recognise how she had initially started systematically grooming him with her words, coercing him to do things for her or how she had made him feel good about himself as she separated him from his colleagues.

Mick Denby's life was so pitiful she had formed such a relationship with him that she could say practically anything to him and he would just walk away like the good little puppet he had become. More importantly was the persistent conditioning of her 1 daily act that had been as regular as a bodily motion yet appeared as innocent as child's play. Mick Denby had been so carefully and expertly conditioned throughout her entire sentence that he hadn't noticed a thing. Nor had he any idea that her textbook manipulation of him would soon reach its pinnacle point and that as a result his ultimate downfall.

Chapter 35
Mick Denby:
In the Execution of One's Duties

Mick Denby made his way back up the stairs of B wing to the first cell; he turned the main light on and off repeated quickly by the night light, he shot the bolt on the door to ensure he could not be locked inside and made his way towards the bars to check their solidity. He gave the cell a cursory glance around before removing the build-up of fruit that was sat along the window sill and exited the cell.

'Where you going with all my fruit boss?' came a voice from a female walking up the stairs.

'You have too many pieces stored up, it is against regulations so I am removing it,' Mick said sternly.

'What, they are mine what gives you the right to take my property?' the unknown prisoner screeched.

'Rules, that's what, you lot have too much time on your hands without getting any ideas of making hooch into your heads,' Mick Denby stated as he ignored any further protests and continued to the next cell.

It was a boring laborious task that had to be performed each morning so to some degree he continued on autopilot unaware that his safety was about to be compromised more than he could ever have imagined.

Meanwhile across the prison a dozen officers were responding to the emergency pertaining to a fight in progress. As the prisoners sat eating breakfast chatting amicably in the hospital dining room a whole host of officers suddenly burst in through the main door. The medical practitioner left his office to find out what the commotion was all about and stood with a perplexed look upon his face at the mention of a fight. He grabbed his role check board, called each prisoner's name in turn and then acknowledged that everyone was accounted for.

Davies used his radio to connect with Comms to enquire who had raised the alarm but no one seemed to know anything about an emergency. Officer Marks and Officer Peters from the gymnasium did a walk through the various areas of the hospital to satisfy themselves the area could be sanctioned as clear.

'It came over the radio 5 minutes ago!' Davies was heard saying into his radio.

'There was no communication sent from here regarding a fight,' the communication officer stated.

Unwilling to get into an argument about it in front of other members of staff Davies motioned to Marks with a quick sideways tilt of the head and they headed towards the door they had just arrived through. The other officers followed suit a little disappointed that their sudden adrenalin surge had nowhere to dispel itself. As Davies and Marks made their way back along the maze of corridors, locked doors and across the exercise yard back to B wing they discussed the alarm.

'If the emergency wasn't generated from Comms (central communication) then where did it come from?' asked Marks.

'I don't know because it is impossible for it to have come from anywhere else because we all got the call at the same time it doesn't make any sense at all,' Davies stated.

'Yeah, I hear you although you can request to connect between each other's, can't you?' Marks enquired.

'You can, but you have to get Comms' permission. I didn't really take any notice of the person's voice; did you recognise it?' Davies asked.

'No, I just focused on the mention of a fight and the hospital wing, that was it,' Marks told him.

'Yes, me too? There is more to this than meets the eye let's just hope we haven't been duped into leaving our posts for some other ulterior motive,' Davies acknowledged.

'Oh shit,' Marks declared. 'We left Denby on the wing on his own, the S.O will kick our arses for this!'

'Sod him, why should we give a damn it's not like he gives a shit about his job turning up for work stinking of last night's alcohol. I am fed up to the back teeth of covering for him do you know the last time he did a set of nights the OSG reported him for sleeping the entire time. When Peters worked with him, he also reported him for having a hip flask during work time, Jerry Sanders gave him a right bollocking.'

'Is that why Jerry went off at him this morning?' Marks asked.

'Yes, I think he is as sick of having to carrying him as we are, it's about time he either started pulling his weight or got the boot, the lazy sod,' Davies stated unrelenting and without any sympathy at all.

On returning to B wing, Marks and Davies were greeted with a queue of prisoners lined up behind the inner entrance gate. Marks made his way on to the unit whilst Davies went into the office for the role board.

'Come on back up a bit,' he instructed to the women closest to him. 'Back up,' he instructed again. There was a slight surge forward from some idiot at the back so Marks closed the gate again, 'When you are ready let me know.'

'Sorry sir,' Nina said before turning round and bellowing, 'Get the fuck back I want to get out of here even if you lot don't.'

After a few shuffles here and there, the herd of women stepped aside so that Marks could open the gate. 'Thank you,' he acknowledged.

Davies stepped out on to the wing from the inner office gate with the roll board and handed it to Marks who systematically checked off each prisoner going to their respective places of work and education. Once each person had departed Marks returned the board to the office and Davies called the cleaners to him and gave them the tasks they were to perform for the day.

'Where the heck is Denby?' Marks enquired returning to the wing.

'No idea,' Davies stated looking puzzled.

'I have just asked the OSG and she hasn't seen him since she called him to the office for a phone call, that was about 20 minutes ago,' Marks informed him.

'Who was the phone call from?' Davies enquired.

'Apparently, the number one governor's secretary and she did not seem pleased,' Marks said.

'He must have been summoned to her office it's the only plausible reason he could have left the wing,' Davies tried to reason but even he knew that there was no way the wing would have been left unattended.

At that moment, a blood churning scream was heard coming from the upstairs landing. Both Davies and Marks shot up the stairs 2 at a time in pursuit of the bearer. Seven cells along the corridor Sally Ryder the head of the cleaners stood hysterically screaming the look of shock emanating from her rounded face. Davies reached the door first and stopped so abruptly, Marks collided into him.

From the doorway, they could both see that Mick Denby was deceased his throat cut in one full sweep from ear to ear. There was no movement, no blood choking gurgles or evidence that his life could be saved, he was gone and had been for the duration of their absence. Davies and Marks took in the scene before them with both terror and concern for themselves as both of them had left the wing leaving Denby alone. They would both get disciplined for sure.

Marks tended to Sally Ryder whose screams had now subsided as he stood outside the locked door where Denby's body lay. This was the first time he had seen a dead body and the first thing he thought of was how unkind he had been just because Denby had been late for work. Not that it mattered, in fact nothing really mattered now especially for Denby.

'Comms this is Bravo, one over,' Davies spoke into his radio.

'Go ahead Bravo One,' came the response.

'We have a code black emergency on B wing please phone the hospital wing for the doctor's assistance, do not use the airwaves. I repeat DO NOT use the airwaves. Over and out,' Davies said.

'Copy that Davies, medical attention is on its way,' Comms confirmed.

Davies locked the door and walked quickly back down the stairs, through the locked gate and into the office where he picked up the phone and dialled the appropriate extension number. Whilst he waited for it to be connected, he asked Caroline the OSG to tannoy the cleaners to tell them to return to their cells. Caroline Simms did as he was asked then retook her seat.

'Sorry to disturb you Ma'am but we have a serious incident on B wing that requires your immediate, full attention and we will need the medical examiner,' Davies stated.

The OSG lifted her head and looked quizzically at Davies but he was in no mood for a question-and-answer session, so he ignored her.

'I understand Ma'am but this IS exceptionally serious it will require a police presence, the preservation of the area, the prisoners to return to their cells, a full lockdown and the potential of a full prison search,' Davies informed her.

'Right,' he said. 'I will notify Marks now he is the one stood outside cell 31 guarding the door.'

Davies went back out of the office on to the wing and back up the stairs to the upper landing towards cell 31. He couldn't help but notice the shock beginning to radiate through Marks whose hands were shaking uncontrollably, his colour had paled, his breathing was shallow and he seemed to be looking straight through him.

'Marks,' Davies said. 'Marks,' he tried again a little more forceful but he was neither hearing him nor seeing him. It was no use he would have to wait with him until help arrived.

The first people to arrive on the scene were the doctor Simon Proctor along with one of the hospital wing nurses Marrion Stevens. Davies requested they tend to Marks first before he opened the flap in the heavy metal door to reveal the body of Denby laid on the cell floor. Proctor nodded agreeing there was nothing he could do for Denby and assisted Marrion along the corridor towards the upper offices where he disappeared momentarily before reappearing. Davies then pointed Proctor in the direction of the empty cell that Nina Spalding had vacated where he would find Sally Ryders, whilst he continued to maintain a vigil outside the offending cell. As Davies stood looking along the full length of the upper landing, he realised he had failed to inform Jerry Sanders, the wing's senior officer. Another mistake he would be reprimanded for and have drilled into him.

Chapter 36
Nina "Bloody" Spalding: Playtime

Nina woke at 06.30hrs as the officer opened the flap at her door and peered through the tiny slit of a window known as the viewing hatch. This was one thing she definitely would not miss about being in prison being woken up every morning when the day shift took over. Apparently, the dicks did a role check every morning which not only down right pissed her off but when you considered that they'd completed one before locking her in the night before where else did they expect to find her. The other things she wouldn't miss were the slamming of the doors, the jangling of the keys, the "jail bent" women, the constant shouting, swearing and the stench of the place. There was nothing she had ever come across before that could be described as a mixture of body odour, puke, diarrhoea and grime. Unlike a lot of the women who used the main gate as a revolving door like a career path, once she had walked through them later today, she could safely say she would never look back. Her eyes would be firmly fixed on looking forward as there was no room for a rearview mirror in her future. Nor would she miss the heavy counterpane covers, the rough sheets, net type blankets, solid pillows or the limp mattresses that dipped in the middle which you would be hard pressed to even find at a tip. No, her part in this particular scene had well and truly been played to the fullest and she was more than ready to hot hoof it out of here.

She got up and threw on the dirty tracksuit bottoms and scraggy t-shirt that she had purposefully kept for this morning. She gave her face a quick cat-lick before throwing all her belongings into the black bags the officers had given her to pack them in before being discharged to reception. Here, she knew full well everything would be carefully checked and cross referenced against her possession chart before she was allowed to pass through the front gates. If truth be told, there was not one solitary item within these bags that would make it beyond the visitor's car park. Now all that was left to do was to wait for her door to be unlocked.

At 08.00 hrs when the door failed to open, she wondered what was going on but by 08.30 she was beginning to get worried that the past 6 months might have been all for nothing. Then she heard the familiar jangle of keys as heavy boots made their way up the metal steps, doors were unlocked and heavy steel banged open, before footsteps moving to the next cell. She couldn't believe her luck when none other than Mick the Prick threw open her door and then she was on it giving him grief like she always did, feigning hurt when he was repulsed by her.

Poor sap, he had absolutely no idea this would be the last time he would ever get the opportunity to look down his nose at her. Nina didn't know how she had managed to keep in character all these months so could scarce hold in her excitement knowing the finale was about to commence. She decided to take herself off downstairs to get some toast along with the thick, white slop that went for porridge in this place, it was more like a paper paste of glue. Nevertheless, she had to keep up appearances.

Out of the corner of her eye, she watched "Mick the Prick" up and down the landing with his usual cocky swagger. She couldn't stand his arrogance or the demeaning way he spoke to the women like they were the shit he had just scraped from the bottom of his heavy prison issued boots. She could see he was a bit more sluggish than usual, probably got pissed again last night, she smirked. Maybe that was why they had been late getting unlocked for the second time this week. It didn't matter to her, tomorrow morning she would be getting out of a warm clean bed at her leisure and tonight she would be relaxing in a hot soapy bath. Nina couldn't wait she was so excited but knew she just had to suppress it a little while longer in order to maintain her focus so she could execute the plan with precision.

When Denby was at the far end of the wing, an announcement came over the tannoy system calling him back to the office for a phone call. Nina was rooted to the spot, teeth clenched almost holding her breath the entire time her eyes darting back and forth, until he finally appeared again. Thank goodness she sighed, what if he had been called to another wing so late in the day then all the planning and attention to detail would have been for nothing. As Mick the Prick took the staircase up, that was nearest to the office to begin the daily cell checks she waited with bated breath.

The timing had to be perfect and then the alarm sounded. She calmly stood, scraped her plate into the food bucket, dropped her cutlery into the metal serving tray and then slowly walked to the staircase at the opposite end of the wing. Nina did a cursory look around and darted into cell 31. Here she would wait for Mick the Prick to discover her as he had done in different cells along the landing, every day for the past month. As usual, he would get all authoritarian, kick her out for being in someone else's cell then threaten to write a bad comment in her personal file.

Only this time, it wouldn't quite follow the same format as it had done every other day throughout the month, today would bring a different chain of events. As she heard him draw closer, she thought she might be physically sick with the size of the lump that had taken residence in her throat and that felt like it was partially blocking her airways. Nina took her place at the window, the shaft concealed in her right hand held deep in the pocket of her tracky bottoms, and then it came the bellow that was Mick the Prick.

'How many times have I told you to stay out of other people's fucking cells? Go on, get out!' he bellowed turning the lights on and off. When she didn't move, he continued, 'Selective hearing is it today, Spalding? Go on, out!' he demanded striding towards her.

She turned in the almost slow-motion movement that she was known for and then without warning and at a speed he didn't even realise Nina bloody Spalding was capable of, her hand came up and sliced across his face. Nina took a moment to drink in the confusion, the shock, the realisation that his mouth had been sliced from ear to ear. He swallowed the excess blood that suddenly filled his gaping mouth, his fear filled questioning eyes as her hand came up again piercing the carotid artery at his throat. She smiled as he teetered backwards grasping his neck as the blood gushed through his fingertips then as deftly as her attack, she sprung behind him to block his escape from the cell.

He knew there was no way he was recovering, this was the place she had chosen for him to die, left on the squalid floor in the shithole of B Wing she had been forced to live for the past 6 months. Mick the Prick had finally got his comeuppance and she Nina "bloody" Spalding had been the one to dish it out to him, she was elated. Only when she was sure he was dead did she sneak out of the cell and back in character she shuffled down the landing to her own cell.

Here she removed her clothing, stashed it into a spare black bin liner and quickly swilled any trace of blood from her person. She snapped the blade from the end of the toothbrush that she had spent a week melting it into, then she wrapped it into some tissue paper until the only trace was ironically a heart shaped blot. Amazing, she thought love was a lot like that blade sharp yet fragile, at times it could be painful but when supported from the right angle it could serve you well.

She decided to keep the blade close on her person so embedded it deep into her pocket ready to disperse of when she got off the wing. That should bide her a bit more time. Once she was ready, she gathered up all her bin liners, secreting the bloody bag inside another and made her way to the gate ready for dispatch. A queue was beginning to form so she took the steps nearest to the office and the exit as Davies and Marks were arriving from their little jaunt across to the hospital wing.

Now all she needed to do was get to reception and out of the godforsaken shithole. Once she had been checked off the wing, she took a little detour past the kitchens where she threw the bag containing the bloodied clothes into their skip. On arrival at the reception, she waited for the officer to resume her duties and then ducked into the toilet where she deposited the blade into the sanitary bin flushing the tissue it had been in down the toilet.

Nina "bloody" Spalding was quick to be processed probably because her unnaturally putrid stench was too much for the staff to tolerate not to mention their unwillingness to let it linger for the rest of the day. Soon she was queuing at the big green gates of the prison set for freedom waiting for Officer Flynn's lacky to open it when she saw him, stood back beneath a tree. As the gate opened, he signalled for her to continue to walk forward as though she was like any other prisoner being released until she got out of the camera's view. He then joined her before they raced to his awaiting van.

'Wait,' she said, running back to the bin where she deposited the black bin liners taking the time to secrete other rubbish on top of it. She then ran back to the van jumped in, slammed the door and secured her seatbelt.

'Oh my goodness, you smell like shit,' he stated starting the engine so he could fully open the windows.

As the vehicle pulled away heading up through the woodland towards the main road, they suddenly heard a siren blaring out.

'He's been found!' They said in unison.

Chapter 37
The Investigations Continue

Jenson Parker attended the early morning meeting as per usual with no real expectations that it was going to be any different to all the others, he had attended in his 20 years+ career. He couldn't remember the last time his creative juices had flowed so there was little motivation nor interest just another day in tinpot house. He knew he should have more respect for his profession but over the years he had been passed over that many times and handed only the crap to sift through. Today, well he had less motivation than yesterday but mused the fact it was probably going to be more than he would rally for tomorrow. Having changed careers late in life he was on the countdown to retirement. He knew it wasn't a productive way to live but he had absolutely nothing else in his miserable life to look forward to. His beloved Gloria had passed away eaten from the inside by cancer, his old army buddies had either not survived or suffered horrendous PTSD and having never had children he was alone. So, after Gloria's untimely death he decided that once he reached retirement he was going on cruise after cruise after cruise. He had no ties, no one waiting for him, no one loving him and so nothing to keep him in this "dirty ol' town" any longer. He grinned at his reference to his favourite Pogue's song. Hence the somewhat despondent view of his life and approach to his job, it was all just a matter of banking that wage and sailing off into the proverbial sunset.

As Parker took his seat, he conducted his usual cursory inspection of the room. The three new recruits Taylor, Betts and Davidson were larking about near the door like schoolkids, 'What a lot they have to learn,' he smirked to himself shaking his head. Shona Williams, was back on the local circuit and known as Wakefield's newest blue-eyed girl. She was dressed in a crisp blue two-piece suit with a white blouse peeking out beneath it. She had her hair neatly scraped back into a ponytail and wore just sufficient make-up to enhance her clear, youthful pretty face. He liked Shona she was the only one who hadn't changed despite promotion after promotion.

She was always polite and made a concerted effort to acknowledge each colleague she came in to contact with. Parker remembered the cases he had worked with her, he had found her to be conscientious, resolute, reliable and tenacious in resolving crimes. The one case that had never sat right with him had been the Cassandra Matthews investigation and he knew Shona Williams was equally as disturbed by it. Many times, over the years he had wondered what had happened to the two kids who had woken up to find her body hanging in the hallway.

Shona aware someone was staring at her glanced around the room before her eyes fell on Parker, she smiled at him and he nodded in acknowledgement.

'Right chaps and lasses let's get this show on the road,' Damien Clarke chief inspector of basic command said addressing the crowd. 'Yesterday we had a body at a house on Blenheim Road, our guys are still processing the scene as we speak and we are still unaware of the circumstances. We have one suspect who had to be sedated at the scene and whom we are waiting to interview pending a mental capacity clearance. This is a very delicate situation that we have on our hands and the utmost care needs to be applied although I still expect a robust investigation. As the suspect was in a dire mental state, we will need to proceed cautiously ensuring we do everything by the book, so cross the t's, dot the I's and so forth ensuring all the mental health boxes are ticked. Apparently, it is impossible to identify the body at this point because the face has been sliced to shreds.'

'Who is the suspect?' asked Collins.

'It is a Dr Sally Carta,' he replied.

'Is it her postal address?' Parker asked.

'Yes, it is, she lives there with her son Jonathon who is 26 years of age, he was at work at the time, called home by the occupant's cleaner. Inevitably he had to find alternative accommodation and as yet, we are unaware of his whereabouts, is that correct, Shona?' the sergeant told the room.

'That is correct, I contacted Jonathon's manager Cheryl Connors this morning and she has confirmed he was at work when Dr Carmichael was brutally murdered. Jonathon has provided his mobile number and was asked to let the department know where he will be staying,' Shona confirmed.

'Couldn't he be a suspect too, Sergeant?' Betts the new recruit piped up much to the amusement of Taylor and Davidson.

'Everyone is a suspect until we eliminate them lad, didn't they teach you anything at the police academy?' Damien Clarke asked shaking his head.

Parker grinned to himself he had seen the same performance every time new kids came on to the block all they wanted to do was make their mark and show off well that was until the chief embarrassed them. He wasn't being malicious; he just wanted to teach the young recruit a lesson in manners, respect and to nip any bravado or exhibitionism in the bud.

'Right Constables Parsons, Murgatroyd and Samuels, I want you to partner up with our new recruits over there and make some door-to-door enquiries see if anyone saw or heard anything and find out as much as you can about the occupants at Blenheim House. Peterson and Parker, I want you to get me some background checks on Sally Carta, Dr Richard Carmichael and the son Jonathon Carta just to be on the safe side. You can also delve into their financial records too.'

'What about the rest of us, Chief?' Clarkson asked.

'I thought that would be obvious Clarkson, we need everyone else back on the Denby case,' Damien Clarke began then he threw open to the floor, 'over to you, Shona.'

'We know that Mick Denby lived alone, he rented his home from none other than Dr Richard Carmichael,' Shona began.

'So, is it safe to assume it was Carmichael that the arsonist was after or warning,' an officer enquired.

'At this stage, it is not safe to assume anything until we find a strong positive connection, we have to treat them as separate cases, for now. Right so where was I, yes Mick Denby was a prison officer…' Shona tried to continue.

'Did the uniform give it away?' someone heckled.

'For all of you who do not know her, this is DCI Shona Williams from the Senior Criminal Investigation Unit so simmer down and show some respect we have two deaths to investigate and I want everyone focusing their attention please!' Damien commanded.

'As I was saying Denby lived alone, he doesn't appear to have any known enemies. On the night of the fire, he was at a club having a drink with two colleagues named Simon Donelli and James Swan. He left the club at approximately 01.00 hrs passing the petrol station on Denby Dale Road at around

1.30, the night attendant Kevin Maltby let him in for milk. He subsequently left his keys on the counter and ended up sleeping in his shed unable to gain access to his house. The fire brigade was called by a neighbour named Connie Webster who had been woken up by her dog persistently barking. At the time of the fire, Mick Denby was found asleep on the floor of his shed.'

'That's a bit suspect, couldn't he have set it on fire and hidden in the shed?' Clarkson asked.

'That was our initial thought but he was found fast asleep, there were no traces of petrol on either his hands or clothing and besides it is far too obvious a solution,' Shona explained.

'So why be in the shed?' Clarkson continued.

'Whilst at the club Denby liaised with 2 young females one of which we believe went to the Denby house before he arrived home, she used a hidden key to gain entry hence Denby couldn't get in and ended up asleep in the shed,' Shona stated.

'He is one lucky man. I wonder if he is giving out numbers for the lottery,' someone said.

'Asher Blake, the fire chief, then informed me that a body had been found, Sallyanne Peters the Medical examiner will be performing an autopsy on it later today. We have yet to formally identify the corpse but it is highly likely it's the young woman Denby liaised with earlier on in the night,' Shona stated.

'Do we know the name of the young woman?' Damien queried.

'Yes, Sandra Clarke and can I make it clear that if we are correct, she is the flatmate of one of our own, Constable Josie Petroni so please no wise cracks let us find out what happened and who is responsible,' Shona stated.

'Right, I have the list of jobs you wanted delegating Shona so if I read them out the rest of you can put your heads together and get on with them,' Damien began. 'We need the particulars of the Insurance company for both the Denby House and the Blenheim House, a deed search on both properties and find out if Dr Carmichael owns any other properties. Also look into whether there have been any high figure adjustments to the insurance policies. We need door-to-door enquiries to find out if any of the neighbours saw anything on the lead up to the fire, ask any dog owners in the vicinity too. Clarkson, I want you to go down to the petrol station and get the till records for the last 6 months,' Damien was saying.

'Six months?' Clarkson echoed in an exaggerated tone emphasising his shock.

'Yes, if this was arson the perpetrator is not going to have toddled down to the garage, filled up a can, come back and merrily set the house on fire. He is going to have been a lot shrewder than that so we need to go back, find out about the dates that the petrol cans were bought and used, especially at night,' Damien explained.

'Also, whilst you're in that area I want you to call upon Connie Webster she is the woman who called the fire brigade, find out every detail of what she saw. Peterson and Parker can you also retrieve the caller tapes for both the fire incident and the request for an ambulance response to Blenheim House,' Shona requested to Clarkson. Lastly track down Jonathon Carta we need to know where he is staying.'

'Right any questions?' there were none, 'Good, let's get to it,' Damien said as usual.

Shona turned to Jacobi, 'Right our first port of call is to check up on Sally Carta and see if she is medically fit enough to talk to us, then we will pay the staff a visit at the surgery.'

'Oh goody, goody I get to go on another field trip, are we travelling together too?' Jacobi asked sarcastically.

'Before we set out, I just want to organise a meeting with the Number 1 Governor at the prison we need to know what kind of a chap our Mr Denby is and what his colleagues think of him. If she knows we are going I am hoping she will organise interviews for us with Simon Donelli and James Swan too about the night Sandra Clarke and Josie Petroni joined them,' Shona told him.

Jacobi went through to the drinks machine whilst Shona returned to her office to make the call on her return Jacobi was fiddling with those plastic lids trying to press it upon the cups without succeeding. 'I swear, these things are not the right size for these cups they never fit properly,' Jacobi said before looking up and on seeing Shona's face, he waited knowing whatever she said was not going to be good news.

'You're not going to believe this?' Shona said.

'Judging by the look upon your face I am not sure I want to hear it because I know I am not going to like it,' Jacobi waited.

'I rang the prison and was put straight through to the number 1 Governor without any delay which I thought was strange but apparently the officer thought the governor was awaiting my call,' Shona told him.

'Awaiting your call, but how does she know about the fire and our investigation into Denby, no information has been released yet,' Jacobi puzzled.

'She doesn't know about our investigation she wanted to inform us that there has been a death at the prison, Mick Denby's!' Shona revealed.

Chapter 38
Meeting the Governor

When Shona, Jacobi and her team of specialists arrived at the prison their patrol entourage was immediately waved straight through the usually double locked 20ft high solid green gates. There was no waiting in the central gate lock for the car to be checked as both were wide open, a sign of a very serious incident. Normally there would have been a physical escort in the form of someone walking alongside the car to ensure it wasn't tampered with or used as a means of escape. Today there were several personnel at pinnacle sites to point them in the right direction. Each person appeared downcast and in mourning but then that was what the whole prison seemed to scream out through its unnatural and overpowering silence. As they pulled up to the highlighted space by the outer gates of B wing, the governor stepped outside obviously having tracked their journey through the prison on the cameras. She was dressed in a grey skirt suit with a cream blouse underneath around her neck she wore a lanyard. Shona couldn't help thinking of the potential safety risk that could pose should a prisoner decide to use it as a means to strangle her. She shook the thought away; stepped out of the car and took the hand she was offered before exchanging introductions.

The wing wasn't overly big there was an office section to the left of the entrance gate surrounded by a bubble of windows obviously designed to see anyone and everyone on the wing, along with who was coming onto and going off it. From this open central foyer area were two gates leading on to separate wings one had a massive B emblazoned upon it the other A. From where Jacobi and Shona were stood, they could see that B wing was the smaller of the two, having arrived at the scene safely the governor lead the way.

As they walked, the governor handed Shona a clipboard. 'You will find everything documented on there that will help you in the execution of your duties DCI Williams,' the governor told her.

Shona gave the board a cursory glance it stated who was the first officer on the scene, what actions they'd taken, like securing the area, appropriate assistance and emergency medical attendants, the name of the person who found the body and people in the vicinity at the time. All were meticulously documented with times, names and contact details stated, one that particularly stood out to Shona was Sally Ryder.

'As soon as we were aware there had been a serious incident the women were returned to their prospective wings and a full lock down initiated. Until the scene has been processed and the body removed, we will remain in lockdown. Looking at the injuries from the observation panel it appears his face has been sliced with a knifelike object. At this point, we are unaware whether the weapon is still in the cell or if it has been discarded somewhere within the prison. Inevitably a full search will commence as it is imperative, we locate the implement as soon as possible,' the governor informed them.

Shona was unsure if she was always this stoic or whether it was her way of telling them to get on with their tasks so she could regain some measure of control. Either way neither her nor Jacobi would be rushed.

'Do we definitely know that the identity of the person who has been murdered is Mick Denby, what else have we got so far?' Jacobi enquired.

'At the moment, we have nothing to go on,' she said as she approached the cell, 'This is officer Davies, he was the first person on the scene with Officer Marks and has maintained a vigilance at the door throughout.'

'How are you doing, Mr Davies?' Shona asked gently.

'Not so good, Ma'am,' he responded truthfully.

'Why don't you stand down, Mr Davies, get yourself a hot drink and we will have a chat later, by the way, please call me Shona or DCI Williams,' she said pleasantly.

'Thanks, Ma'am, I mean DCI,' he looked towards the number 1 for confirmation and only when she nodded, did he continue. 'Thank you, I really could do with a drink,' Davies admitted.

'Has anyone else entered the cell apart from the person who found the body?' Jacobi queried.

'From what my staff tell me as soon as the body was discovered, Ryder ran screaming out of the cell. Davies and Marks attended but did not enter. The door was immediately sealed, the medical examiner contacted but more for the benefit of Officer Marks and Ryder. Davies has maintained his position keeping meticulous notes as requested, specifically noting times everything occurred, who was on the landing when the body was found, what they saw and how they proceeded. I am sure he will have made very precise notes,' the governor informed them.

'After we make our initial observations, we will want to interview any witnesses, prison staff and prisoners who were present. I am sure you will want me to move quickly, so any available staff who can assist me to speed things up would be very much appreciated,' Shona stated.

'All personnel you will want to speak to are in the association room at the end of the landing with the senior member of staff's office and tea room delegated for you to conduct interviews in,' the governor said.

Shona was beginning to like the governor; she was very methodical, organised and wanted the least disruption to the running of her prison as possible. It seemed to Shona that she had never attended a crime scene that had been text bookly secured and ready for her to operate. When Shona looked through the glass pane, she could see a colossal pool of blood had seeped out and collected under his neck. Whatever the weapon used, it had been executed with precision slicing through his cheek to his mouth and across through to the other side.

Mick Denby had a gaping hole for a face and Shona couldn't help wondering if this was a none too subtle sign to say he was a blabbermouth. Maybe Mick Denby had known something about Dr Carmichael after all and having been interviewed rigorously by the police it had concerned the perpetrator that he might have talked. Shona took a pen out of her brief case, a new sheet of paper, gloves, a mask and tied her hair back. She then requested that the governor open the door and stand back at the railings. From this viewpoint, she was still able to observe everything that Shona was doing.

When the door was opened, Shona knelt on her haunches looking at the scene from a different perspective. She glanced around the floor area to see if there were any foreign bodies unwittingly dropped or that had been torn from the perpetrator in Denby's bid to get out. She couldn't see anything obvious and probably like every other cell on the landing it had a fine covering of dust, dirt and loose hair. The bed was unkempt just pulled over not made but let's face it, it wasn't like the occupier was going to be entertaining. She took her paper, noting the angle of the body with a quick diagram and its relation to the fabrication of the cell to accurately identify the positioning in relation to the toilet, the sink, window and bed. She noted that the front of Denby's shirt had a huge pool of blood down the front to indicate he had remained standing, but why hadn't he run out to get help.

Perhaps the attack was so quick, unprovoked or by someone he least expected, so it had shocked him, rooting him to the spot. There was also a puncture wound at his throat where his carotid artery sat the poor beggar had bled out knowing full well, he was going to die. His hands were infused with his own blood, inevitably a sign that he had grabbed at his throat attempting to stifle the flow of blood. Shona noted the splatters of blood on the wall to the right side of the window and the adjacent wall where the bed was situated. The splatter direction from top to bottom along with the most dominant collection told her the perpetrator had been stood with their back to the window.

Denby had obviously approached, the person would have had to use a right to left motion for the blood to land at that side. There was another patch of blood on the floor that had a messed-up footprints in it and from a visual check, she could see that the sole of Denby's shoe was covered. He must have received the second attack in quick succession before he'd even had time to react then slowly pivoted round as he bled. No doubt the culprit had darted past him to secure the exit determining that death was the intended outcome.

Shona also noticed that the desk to the left of the window had some clothes draped over the chair where some more faint splashes had landed. When Denby had gone down, he had tried to grab out to stop his ultimate fall but weakened by the blood loss his attempts were futile and the prisoner's blanket lay beside him a smeared bloodied handprint evident. Shona noted all that she could see then handed over to her team directing them in minute detail of the photographs she wanted and the evidence that needed collecting.

Shona had almost forgotten that the governor was behind her so she quickly included her in order to maintain a good cordial relationship. 'Are there any of your specialist search teams available, Governor,' Shona asked.

'Yes, the security office is on standby to conduct a full prison search once the body has been removed,' the governor said.

'Would you mind if they started now by doing a perimeter search of this building, any bins within the vicinity and then the communal areas of the wing.

That would be of tremendous help and allow Jacobi and I to interview the witnesses,' Shona divulged.

The governor agreed to Shona's request and went down to the office on the wing to ring for a team to commence the search, inevitably it was the weapon and any discarded clothing that were the vital components. Shona appointed one of her team as a recording officer to document the footfall in and around the cell along with keeping accurate records of times in and out.

Jacobi elected to use the staff tearoom as his interview room not giving Shona the office out of superiority but more that he wanted access to have a cuppa whenever he wanted one. Shona decided to speak with Sally Ryder first as she was her most valuable witness. When she entered the office, Shona couldn't help but feel for the girl no doubt in a different situation, she portrayed herself as an harden con whereas right now she was anything but. She stood at approximately 5'5" had greasy dyed hair pulled back with a thin bobble, was dressed in white kitchen gear, had a light grey hoody tied around her waist and poor random tattoos down one arm. She had a grey pallor to her like she could do with a bit of sun and looked worried to death.

'Come in Sally, there is nothing to worry about,' Shona said gently, 'I am DCI Shona Williams and I just want to ask you a couple of questions, is that ok?'

'I haven't done anything, I didn't see anything, I wasn't even there. I just walked into my cell and found him,' she blurted out.

'No one thinks you have done anything,' Shona tried to reassure her, 'we are simply here to find out what has happened, why it has happened, who has committed the crime and when it occurred.'

'Ok miss, but honest I didn't do it. I am due out next week and I don't want it to stop me from seeing my bairns,' she wittered.

'Let's start by me asking you a question and you giving me a precise answer then we will get through this quickly, is that ok?' Shona asked.

'Yes, miss,' Sally said.

'Right, good. What job do you do here at the prison,' Shona asked.

'I work in the kitchens, miss,' Sally told her.

'And were you working in the kitchens this morning, Sally?' Shona continued.

'Yes, I serve the breakfast on the wing, we clean up afterwards and then I usually come upstairs to give my room a clean before changing and then cleaning the wing,' Sally said.

'So, what you are telling me is that throughout the morning you were in the kitchen and only when you came upstairs were you on the wing?' Shona asked.

'Yes miss,' Sally spoke.

'So, when you came upstairs did you see anyone leaving your cell or hanging around by the door, anyone at all?' Shona enquired.

'No miss, I remember Mick the Prick,' her hand suddenly shot up to her mouth, 'sorry miss I mean Mr Denby.'

'Why did you call him Mick the Prick?' Shona jumped in.

'Everyone did miss but that is what he was known as round here, he spoke to us girls like we were a piece of shit. He was really arrogant, looked down his nose at us and waltzed around like he owned the joint. But it wasn't just us none of the officers liked him either, ask anyone,' Sally blurted out.

'Was there anyone in particular who would have wanted to seriously harm Mr Denby, not just didn't like him?' Shona enquired.

'I can't really say miss, I mean I didn't particularly like his attitude but at least you knew where you stood with him. There was no point asking him to do anything for you because you knew it wouldn't get done, it was like he had lost any interest in himself, never mind the job,' Sally explained.

'When you had finished work and took the stairs what happened?' Shona asked, cutting through to get to the point.

'I walked over to my room and I remembered thinking why is the door unlocked because I had specifically asked Mr Davies to lock it before I started work,' Sally said.

'Are you sure Mr Davies locked your door, Sally?' Shona asked.

'Yes, I am positive. On here, we get new girls in all the time so when they realise who works in the kitchen, they know they can nip in and out of your room without being detected. Last week I had a packet of chocolate digestives and half a pouch of baccy taken from under my pillow. I know we are in prison, Miss, but it doesn't mean our stuff is fair game,' Sally explained.

'So, you are sure he locked it?' Shona reiterated.

'Absolutely, I stood here and watched him to make sure as I have also had a problem with one of the wings scrotes going in and out of my room. She doesn't take anything but she stinks to high hell so today I wasn't taking any chances,' Sally told her.

'Is it possible that this prisoner had anything to do with Mr Denby's death?' Shona enquired.

'Spalding? No way, she is a pathetic little junkie who shuffles up and down the landings no one takes any notice of her she is harmless and just wandering here and there. I think she has something wrong with her upstairs,' she said pointing to her head, 'She isn't capable of swatting a fly never mind taking down Mick the P…er Mr Denby,' she corrected herself.

'So, talk me through when you opened your door,' Shona guided her.

'As I was going up the stairs, I noticed Mr Marks and Davies coming back on to the wing together. I thought it was odd because normally when the alarm bell sounds only one officer goes but I saw both of them coming on together.' She began.

'Hold on a minute you say there was an alarm bell?' Shona broke in.

'Yeah, to some fight somewhere?' Sally offered.

'Are you telling me Mr Denby would have been left on the wing on his own?' Shona asked.

'He must have been,' she said innocently.

Shona furiously made a note to question Marks and Davies about leaving Denby alone on the wing as this could just be the decoy our perpetrator orchestrated to commit his or her crime. Could either one of them be in on the act was more of a question she wanted answering. 'When you got upstairs was anyone else around?'

'No, no one. I went straight to my door pushed it open and was about to walk in when I saw him dead on the floor?'

'I know this may seem like a stupid question, Sally but how do you know that he was definitely dead,' Shona asked.

'He was staring, there was no movement not even from his chest rising and there was so much blood, I just screamed and staggered back out,' Sally said, beginning to sniffle.

'Did anyone else go into the cell after you?' Shona asked.

'No miss. Mr Davies and Marks came bounding up the stairs, they were about to go in but stopped dead, they didn't set a foot inside. In fact, they locked the door and Mr Marks stayed with me whilst Mr Davies went down to the office and the next thing, I remember was that the doctor and a nurse were here,' Sally said concisely.

'Is there anything else, Sally, anything at all that you can think of that you might have forgotten to tell me?' Shona pressed.

'No miss that is everything,' Sally assured her.

Shona rang down to the main office to ask if there were any empty cells on the unit and then requested that an officer escort Sally to it, so that she might get some rest. Shona was more than aware of the impact that this type of incident had on a person and if Sally Ryder had been up early working too then she would need the space to decompress. Shona thanked Sally for her assistance, encouraged her to get some support and to chat about how she was feeling to the medical staff. It was then time to talk to someone else.

Dr Simon Proctors interview was run of the mill he had nothing more to add as his attendance had been after the fact and only to confirm the death and manage Marks and Ryders shock. Marrion Stevens the nurse took exactly the same format so Shona dismissed both and decided to meander along the corridor to see how Jacobi was doing and if she could interrupt to get herself a cuppa. As she approached the door Marks was just leaving.

'Perfect timing, I was hoping to get in for a cuppa,' Shona began, 'how is it going have you got anything yet?'

'No not essentially but those two will be in for it, you will never guess what happened,' Jacobi said, his grin almost as wide as the unfortunate Mick Denby's.

'What, that they both left the wing to attend an alarm bell giving our perpetrator the opportunity they needed to slice their colleague's carotid artery?' Shona said without breaking stride much to the annoyance of Jacobi.

'What? I thought I had found a juicy bit of information to investigate, you ought to have seen their faces when I said their actions could potentially be seen as being accessories to murder!' Jacobi delivered.

'How many times do I have to tell you to play nicely,' Shona jokingly chastised him.

'But you left me to my own devices, so technically you're at fault too,' Jacobi joined in.

'So that's the way you're playing it is it, counsellor?' Shona said using her best impression of a judge's voice. 'Have you got anything else?'

'No, diddly squat? Although one thing did raise an eyebrow the fact that both Marks and Davies said that the bell, they responded to was a false alarm despite it coming over the radio. And, they both affirmed that the guy on the Comms desk denied that a transmission had been sent by him regarding an altercation on the hospital wing,' Jacobi informed her.

'That doesn't sound like diddly squat to me in fact that has just piqued my interest by 100%, I think we need to have a chat with our communication fellow straight after we have our cuppa,' Shona said.

The security team's hub was on the way to the heart of the communication centre so the governor walked with them on her way back to her office. On interviewing the staff, both Jacobi and Shona were dismayed to find that nothing had been found to support their investigation. The security team were pleased though at finding numerous contraband that had surreptitiously been discarded out of the prisoners' windows probably knowing a search was on the cards. The communications officer was adamant that he had not broadcast any incidents on the hospital wing nor had anyone else had access to his radio equipment. He actually came across to Jacobi and Shona as being quite possessive over his position that he alone was the controller. In fact, humorously they felt as reprimanded as a child at the headmistress's office he was that authoritarian in his delivery.

As they made their way back over to B wing, Sallyanne Peters was just arriving right on cue, 'We are going to have to stop meeting like this DCI Williams that is 3 bodies in a matter of two days, I am beginning to wonder if you think I have too much time on my hands,' Sallyanne joked.

Shona collected the completed documents of the scene and secured them into her briefcase to go through in detail at the station. She knew it would be a laborious task of sifting through what was vital to ascertain what happened from what was required for legal reasons. The accuracy of measurements within the cell, the placement of the body, each article documented, photographed, items collected, evidenced, sketches and the records kept. She finished up assisting her team to pack their vehicles and then she waited for the extraction of Mick Denby's body.

Only yesterday, she had been interviewing him about the circumstances in which he had almost died and today he was being scooped up his life blood unceremoniously drained. Shona thought it was safe to say that this was no coincidence whoever had it in for Denby may have failed once but they were making sure they did not fail a second time. But how on earth did Dr Richard Carmichael fit into the picture they were from opposite realms of society both socially and economically. Was it just a coincidence that Mick Denby was renting a house that happened to be owned by Carmichael? Or did Mick Denby have something on Carmichael and was using this to blackmail the Dr into giving him a roof over his head.

No doubt their financial records will identify any misdemeanours and reveal if Denby was paying rent or getting a freebie. Now that would open the door to delving deeper into what was being covered up. Then Shona had another thought, there had to be a third-party involvement because both of them were dead and both were brutally murdered.

Perhaps Sally Carta isn't as innocent as she appeared and there is more to this than meets the eye. It had been a long day and all Shona wanted to do was get home, kick her shoes off and take a long hot bath but first she needed to take everything she had into the station and log it all. As she looked up the body was being wheeled out onto the yard to be deposited into the back of the coroner's van.

On their way back to the station, Shona and Jacobi independently mulled over their day evaluating their actions and scrutinising their performance. One thing they both couldn't help but ponder was the fact that when Denby had opened his eyes this morning he could never have imagined that it would be the last day he would ever see. This sobering thought stayed with them throughout their journey to propel them to think not only about their own mortality but the importance of finding out what happened.

Right now, the questions were: who made the transmission, how did they get access to control the system, was it purposefully used as a decoy, why did both officers leave Denby alone, who killed him, what weapon was used, where is it now and why did he need silencing? Today had seen enough drama goodness knows what tomorrow would bring.

Chapter 39
Damien Clarke: The Investigation Hots Up

The next morning as the team assembled in the briefing room there was an unusual buzz of excited chatter. The first officers to arrive were the ones who found seats others were sat on the edges of tables or leaning against walls. As soon has Chief Inspector Damien Clarke entered the room it went quiet. There was a pause as people turned to the door expecting to see Shona Williams and Dion Jacobi following behind him. They were not.

'Right chaps and lasses let's get down to business, Parker what do you have for me?'

'Sally Carta was as clean as a whistle, no convictions spent or otherwise, she had a parking ticket issued 4 years ago but it was overturned due to an emergency house call saving a patient's life. She is financially secure, not only having a tidy doctor's salary but the house is mortgage free and she owns an apartment in the town of Frigiliana in Spain. She was widowed in early 2000, inevitably inheriting a few more thousand and has a son, Jonathon, 26. There is little to say about Jonathon, no convictions, works at the secure unit, still lives at home, he is single and has a healthy bank account for a lad so young.'

'His bosses had nothing but good to say about him, hardworking, dedicated, has a keen interest in mental health and very reliable. Apparently, he has an almost intuitive ability to connect with patients and has had ground breaking improvements with individual cases they cannot sing his praises enough. Carmichael's parents bought the Denby house in 1982 which he inherited in 1998 after his mother passed away. This was just before he finished his doctorate at Sheffield University.'

'Electoral records show he lived there until 2001, he rented it to a couple, both prison officers until 2011 then Mr Denby became his tenant. It would be logical to assume that the couple gave Denby Dr Carmichael's details as this was the only connection we could find. Denby had a few hundred in the bank but seemed to earn his wage, pay his rent and each month he spent what was left.'

'So, there isn't a lot to go on there, have you got anything else to add Parker?' Damien asked.

'Not much sir, Shona asked us to do some digging at the surgery but again there was nothing forthcoming. From what we can gather Carmichael and Carta have been together for around 12 to 14 years, they appear happy according to their work colleagues. It was clear from what they were saying that Carta definitely wears the trousers in the relationship, she is strong and independent bordering on domineering whereas he is easier going. There were no negatives, no back biting in fact the surgery was thriving and appeared well run,' Parker finished.

'Come on guys there has got to be something, Collins what about you?' Damien asked.

'I teamed up with Davidson sir and again the only information was Denby pretty much kept himself to himself. He was pleasant enough but seems he went to work, came home, went out then staggered back home late at night. One of the dog walkers we spoke to said she saw a young fellow lurking around maybe about 2 months ago but was only taking a leak. Nothing else,' Collins said.

'Clarkson please tell me you have something,' Damien pleaded.

'Again, not much sir, I got the till receipts but it is going to take an age to go through all 6 months of them on my own, I could do with a couple of new recruits to help if that's ok sir?' Clarkson said.

'Fine, Davidson and Taylor can give you a hand but I want something by tomorrow morning, is that clear?' Damien insisted.

'Yes sir, the caller tapes have been retrieved and are ready for you to listen to. I have an appointment with Connie Webster at 10 a.m. the lady who called the Denby house fire in. I am seeing Stefan Garforth the ambulance driver who called the Blenheim House murder in straight afterwards,' Collins revealed.

'I paired up with Betts we door knocked around the Denby house chatted to residents and the odd dog walker but again nothing sir, sorry,' Parsons said.

'There was something,' Betts said, 'when we were outside the Denby house a car pulled up, it was Mrs Baines daughter,' he spoke.

'How do you know that lad?' Damien asked.

'Well, when I took Mrs Baines to the hospital, I stayed with her for a while until her daughter arrived, so when I saw her car, I thought I would ask how her mum was doing. She told me that Mrs Baines was devastated about her home but that she had decided to have a drive over to see it for herself but then she wished she hadn't done. I enquired whether Mrs Baines had recalled anything about the fire and she told me that she had noticed Denby coming home, because she was just drawing her curtains and that she thought she had seen a shadow to the right of the bushes. However, with it being dark she had dismissed it putting it down to the dark and her eyes playing tricks on her. I don't know if it is anything,' Betts finished.

'Well done lad, that is exactly what we want, building connections and acting on your intuition do you know what, we might make a copper out of you yet,' Damien said.

'Right, Parsons lets follow up on that, get the daughters address then take young Betts with you to have a chat with Mrs Baines. You know how it goes, care in the community, checking in with her, it was a terrible shock and we are here to help. Get as much information as you can,' Damien said. 'Any reports back from Asher Blake or Sallyanne Peters at the coroner's office?'

'The body found in the fire was confirmed to be that of Sandra Clarke, police liaison officers are going out to inform the family this morning, Asher Blake states his findings will be sent through by the end of the day, tomorrow at the latest,' an officer informed them.

'I was able to retrieve the footage of the night Denby allegedly stopped at the garage for milk and I can confirm he did and also that he fumbled about for change and unwittingly left his keys,' Mike Dennings added.

'Right, what about the murder at Blenheim House, where are we with this one?' Is the body that of Dr Carmichael? Damien enquired.

'We won't know until Sallyanne has done the autopsy and formally identified him sir but it is looking that way. Shona and Jacobi were on their way to the hospital but were diverted to the prison murder,' Dennings revealed.

'Speaking of the prison incident for those of you that haven't heard yet the murder victim at the prison was none other than Mick Denby,' Damien said as gasps and hushed chatter began to ripple through the room.

'Shona and Jacobi were called back first thing this morning, during a full prison lockdown a thorough search was conducted resulting in items found. It is possible that the murder weapon along with the perpetrators clothing has been found. These items will be brought back shortly for forensic examination with our guys poised to process them as soon as they arrive. Right, let's get those till receipts analysed, the tape callers interviewed and Mrs Baines visited. Parker, I want you to pay a visit to the hospital and find out what condition Sally Carta is in,' Damien told him.

Jenson Parker did a look around as though he hadn't quite heard correctly, 'Me sir?' he asked.

'Yes Parker, why have you got something more pressing to be getting on with?' Damien asked sarcastically.

'No sir, err thank you yes I will get on to it,' Parker said not used to being given any real responsibility.

'Anything else?' When no one spoke he dismissed them, 'Good, let's get to it.'

Chapter 40
The Prison Revisited

Shona and Jacobi had arrived at the prison early and got stuck behind a long queue of officers going through their security procedures to enter the prison, no longer were the gates wide open nor were they a priority. So, they waited. Shona was deep in thought eager to get inside to see the exhibits that the security department had found when Jacobi suddenly nudged her.

'What?' she asked in a hushed whisper.

'The guy over there with the handle bar moustache is James Swan and I wouldn't be surprised if the guy with him isn't Simon Donelli,' Jacobi said.

'What makes you think that?' Shona asked.

'He has just thrown his tally down the shaft and said to the gatekeeper Donelli Keys 129,' Jacobi said smirking and raising his eyebrows at her.

'Just a minute,' before the men could go anywhere Shona stepped forward, 'Is it Simon Donelli and James Swan?' she asked directly.

The two men looked at each other in confusion and then back to the woman, 'Who is asking?' Donelli said.

'Sorry, I am DCI Shona Williams and that is my colleague DI Dion Jacobi we were investigating the fire that occurred at Mick Denby's and subsequently we are now probing a murder enquiry. Do you mind if we have a word with you before we leave, it would really help with our enquiries and if needs be I can clear it with the governor first,' Shona said.

'If there is anything at all we can do to help we are more than happy to answer any questions you may have but to be honest I am not sure how much it will aid your enquiries,' Donelli said.

'We will both be on G-wing,' Swan said and then they moved forward with the crowd as it propelled them along.

'That was a stroke of luck,' Shona said.

'Stroke of luck,' Jacobi mused. 'That was good old fashion police work of keeping your ear to the ground and paying observational attention to the details.'

Once inside the prison, a member of the security team was at the other side of the gate, having been contacted by Officer Flynn, the gatekeeper, and was waiting to escort them up to the security office. Principle officer Mark Jennings was waiting in his office with Senior Officer Judy Pickering ready to discuss the finds.

'Good morning,' Jennings said heartily, extending a shovel of a hand to Shona that she was surprised felt very soft and gentle until she saw the tight grip, he held Jacobi's hand. They made their introductions and got straight down to business.

'So, what do you have?' Shona enquired.

'The teams worked in groups of fours taking it in turn to do all the cells, two to remove the prisoner, strip search them, then remove them to sterile area whilst two others conducted the search. Any evidence was bagged, labelled and brought here. Once the cells, landings and congregation rooms were cleared we systematically moved on to all the other areas. We have kept the prison in lockdown, with skeleton staff operating so that we could blitz the place and I have to say we have had a great response from everyone coming in on their day off,' Pickering was saying.

'Anyway, those were our operational duties and we have had some tremendous finds but more importantly for you and why I wanted you to come in today are these exhibits,' Jennings said unlocking a secure evidence cabinet.

Shona glanced over at Jacobi and without realising it held her breath in anticipation. When Jennings turned back round, he was holding a small evidence bag which contained fragments of a blade that had been snapped. Has Shona looked closely she could see that there was some red plastic coating on parts of the blade. The bag was clearly marked as being found by officer Evelyn Crowther in a sanitary bin, of a toilet in the reception area of the prison. Immediately, Shona's eyes sprung up.

'Reception receives inmates from court but I am also guessing that prisoners pass back through reception on their way to release?' Shona queried.

'That's right, all prisoners due for release are searched along with their possessions and have their items checked to make sure they are not stealing anyone else's property or taking prison property through the gates,' Pickering explained.

'If the blade was found in there, I am guessing it wasn't from one of the cleaners but a prisoner who was being released,' Jacobi said.

'But surely no one could have left because as soon as the body was found the prison was put into lockdown,' Shona said in disbelief.

'That is correct however one person was processed and released minutes before the alarm was raised and this person resided on F-wing,' Jennings explained.

Shona's mouth was suddenly dry could a prisoner really have just committed the perfect murder, in a prison, then been able to just walk out? She was waiting with bated breath, swallowing the hard lump down and trying to block out the deafening boom of her heartbeat. She looked at Jacobi, he appeared as nervous as she did, 'So who was it then?' she finally asked not able to take the silence.

'The prisoner that was released was known as Nina Spalding, I am told she was a junkie of slight build, was always picking everyone's dips up, shuffled along slowly, was a loner and stunk like pig excrement,' Jennings delivered.

'That doesn't sound like our killer at all,' Jacobi exclaimed. 'The person who took Denby down would have had to be quick, strong, athletic and have a motive.'

'Did this Nina woman and Denby have issues, had she threatened him or anything?' asked Shona.

'No, not essentially but it seems a bit of a coincidence, that she had been on F-wing giving her the opportunity, that the blade was found at reception and that she was the only prisoner who passed through reception that morning to be released,' Pickering argued.

'I hear what you are saying and inevitably we will investigate your theory but when was the last time that sanitary bin was emptied or searched?' Shona enquired.

'According to our records reception was searched 10 days ago and the waste was emptied 4 days ago,' Pickering said reading from their logs.

'Then anyone who has been in and out of reception could have either planted the blade as a decoy to assume it was someone who left but they are actually still here or it may not even be the murder weapon,' Shona concluded.

'I hear what you're saying but the entire prison has been searched and this is the only discarded implement that could have been used. Also, the red plastic that you were observing is identical to the toothbrushes we provide. It seems to me that Spalding used this blade as a shiver, chive, shank or whatever you want to call it and then expertly made her getaway,' Jennings summarised.

'Sorry I am not buying it,' Jacobi said. 'She is a slight young woman who shuffles along, is a loner picking everybody's dirty dog ends up but she has masterminded killing one of your officers?'

'I understand that it may seem implausible but don't the best criminals hide in plain sight?' Jennings probed.

'Obviously we will take the information and I promise you we will look into it, thank you. Have you anything else for us?' Jacobi asked not sounding very hopeful.

'Actually, yes we have,' Jennings began before pulling out 2 bags each containing an item of clothing. Shona's eyes nearly popped out of her head, 'What do we have here then?' she asked glancing at Jacobi to catch his response.

'Officer Martha Randall who was searching with,' Pickering paused to check the name on the bag, 'Daniella Forsythe found these items of clothing discarded in the kitchen waste skip. It was in a black bin bag so it stuck out like a sore thumb as the kitchen only use blue waste bags.'

'Has you can see there are what look like blood stains across the t-shirt and here on the tracksuit bottoms,' Jennings said.

'Is there any way of tracing who they belong to?' Jacobi asked.

'No, whilst female prisoners are allowed to wear their own clothes in prison all our cleaners, farm hands and women without possessions are issued with the same grey sweatshirts, bottoms and t-shirts,' Pickering stated.

'So, it will be a job for our forensics team to pick at then,' Shona said jovially.

'Please tell them to have a peg ready,' Pickering commented as Shona and Jacobi looked at each other puzzled, 'the clothes smell like pig shit.'

Shona and Jacobi signed out the evidence bags, took a photocopy of the prisons chain of evidence form stapled it to the police evidence forms then obtained Jennings and Pickering's signatures before taking charge of the items. Shona enquired about interviewing Swan and Donelli which Jennings facilitated by lending them his office. They collaborated everything that Denby had told them and were unable to extract any new information so they plumped for interviewing the officers Crowther, Forsythe and Randall about the evidence they had found. Once they had completed their investigations, they were escorted back down to the gate, to pick up their belongings and finally out through the main gate to freedom.

'I am not sure how helpful our visit has been today but let's just hope forensics get a match with Denby on that blood and DNA to find out whose clothes they belong to,' Jacobi stated.

'It would be nice but I am not holding my breath nothing about this case has been straight forward yet,' Shona replied without hope.

They had just deposited their things into the boot and were closing the lid when they noticed a woman across the car park at a low-level building frantically waving to them.

'Excuse me, can I have a word?' she asked then dipped back inside the building through the open fire door. Shona and Jacobi looked at each other puzzled.

'Curiouser and curiouser!' Jacobi declared then they started walking towards the building to find out what the woman wanted. As they arrived at the door, she suddenly appeared again holding some bin liners in her hands.

'I pulled these out of the bin over there,' she said, holding the bag up in her left hand to indicate the bin by their car. When she could see they were confused she continued, 'I was working in the officer's mess early yesterday morning when I saw a woman with a young man getting into a white van. I didn't think anything of it at first, as lots of people getting out are picked up by their visitors here but then she suddenly ran back and stuffed her bags into that bin. Normally what they are carrying is all they own so I thought it was a bit odd and then the alarm went off and the van sped off up the lane. I went over and retrieved the bags, just in case there was anything in it that was important,' she told them.

'Was the young woman shuffling as she walked?' Jacobi asked.

'She was when she first walked to the van but then she turned and ran to the bin to secrete these and ran back,' the woman explained.

'Did you recognise the woman?' Shona asked.

'No, but she was obviously a prisoner because she had the telltale tracksuit on,' the woman said.

'Would you recognise her if you saw her again?' asked Shona.

'Sorry she was too far away and like I said she shuffled towards the van with her head down and then ran back and forth to the van as though she was in a hurry, and then the alarm sounded,' she repeated herself.

Suddenly Shona and Jacobi felt as though their trip to the prison had not been a waste of time after all and, they had just got their first real breakthrough.

'Have you looked in the bags?' Jacobi asked.

'Not really I just opened the top saw that it was a number of dirty, clothing and it absolutely stunk so I didn't want to touch it,' she told them.

'Sorry, what's your name?' Shona enquired.

'It's Darley. Darley Mays,' she told the astonished officers then turned around and went back inside leaving the bags in front of them.

Shona knelt down and tentatively opened one of the bags then rapidly closed it.

'What is it?' Jacobi asked.

'It smells like pig shit,' she responded.

Chapter 41
Out in the Field

Damien Clarke was in the car park as Shona and Jacobi reached the station their heads practically hanging out of the windows of the car gasping for clean air. Bemused he walked over to them as Shona swung into her allotted space and immediately jumped out.

'Everything alright?' Damien asked concerned.

'I don't know is Dion still with us?' she asked as Jacobi scrambled out of the car.

'Just,' Jacobi managed to gasp.

'Would one of you mind telling me what's going on,' Damien asked.

Shona put her hand through the backseat window grabbed a bin liner and threw it to Damien. Instinctively he put his arms out to catch it but immediately wished he hadn't. 'What the heck died in there?' He asked.

'Possibly Mick Denby's murderer,' Shona spluttered.

'Our guys are going to love you,' Damien said as he retraced his steps chuckling.

'Can you take it and get it booked in Dion whilst I take the evidence that Jennings and Pickering gave us?' Shona enquired.

'If you are taking that in you might as well take them all together,' Jacobi said light heartedly.

'I cannot manage to carry it all,' Shona said trying to pass it off.

'Well, as the senior investigator I think you should be awarded the pleasure and subsequent notoriety,' Jacobi added.

'I think you are right,' Shona began, Jacobi smiled thinking he had won but then she continued, 'As the senior investigator I am delegating you with the job.' Then she selected the pieces that the security officers had given her and strode off leaving him with no other option but to take charge of the smelly bags.

When Shona opened the door to her office, she immediately noticed that both the autopsy and fire reports were sitting centrally on her desk. She took a deep breath then began flicking through them in turn. Shona lent back in her chair so, Asher Blake was right it was arson and the body was that of Sandra Clarke.

Interestingly a key shaped object had been found embedded into Sandra's hand indicating that Josie Petroni was right she did return and use the key that Denby had told them about. If only Darley Mays had turned up, if only they hadn't got chatting to Denby and they hadn't clicked then Sandra Clarke would still be alive. So many ifs and buts, now Shona would have to organise police liaison to visit Sandra's next of kin and she would need to break the news to Josie Petroni. Shona shook her head, talk about the wrong place at the wrong time. Shona's thoughts were suddenly interrupted by the telephone.

'DCI Shona Williams,' she said snapping the phone up to her ear.

'Hi Shona, its Anita Collins I was tasked with interviewing the person who called the fire in this morning and I have got to say it has been quite an interesting conversation,' she began.

'I'm listening,' Shona waited suddenly sitting upright on the edge of her chair.

'So, the caller is a woman called Connie Webster, she has a golden retriever dog called Charlie who wouldn't stop barking on the night of the fire. Connie gets up to let him out in case he needs to do his business in the garden, but once out Charlie bolts out of the gate, round the corner and up the road. Connie runs out to see that the house fire has started but cannot see where Charlie has gone. She grabs her house phone set, rings it in and with slippers on and dressing gown flapping in the wind makes after Charlie. Connie said she thinks that the arsonist was still in the vicinity, possibly lurking around to watch the fire but that Charlie must have picked up his scent and chased him off.'

'Anyway, when she caught up with Charlie, he was sniffing around the bushes along the side of Mick Denby's drive. This reminded Connie of an encounter she'd had around 2 months ago again when she was out with Charlie when a fellow had appeared from the same area of bushes. She remembered seeing some old bits of furniture to the left side of the drive which she had thought were an eyesore that Denby has since removed. Anyway, she said she thought it was strange at the time due to the hour and the person being dressed in black like they didn't want to be seen,' Anita said.

'Did Connie confront the person or ring it in?' Shona asked.

'She did confront the person who passed it off as not being able to make it home as though he was having a pee, however she did not call it in as she thought it could be innocent and she didn't want to waste police time,' Anita concluded.

'I don't suppose she could pin point the date more accurately?' Shona queried.

'She was very specific, it was Friday 27 June,' Anita said.

'How could she be so accurate?' Shona asked, a little doubtful.

'It was her wedding anniversary, she had been out for a meal with family and it was the only night she took Charlie out so late,' Anita delivered.

'Well done, Anita I will get someone out to see Connie again so she can identify the exact area and I will have it searched. Is Connie willing to come into the station to give us her statement?' Shona enquired.

'Oh yes, more than willing, in fact she said she could come in this afternoon at 3.30. I am just on my way to see Stefan Garforth now the ambulance driver who rang the Blenheim House murder in I should be back by the time Connie arrives, if you want me to take her statement?' Anita asked.

'That's perfect, well done I think we are slowly beginning to move forward,' Shona said ringing off.

When Shona walked into the incident room to locate herself and Jacobi a coffee one of the new recruits, Taylor beckoned her over.

'Sorry to disturb you but I think we might have found something interesting in these receipts,' Taylor began. 'We have been sifting through looking at the purchases of the petrol cans then cross referencing them with ones where the can was actually filled. We decided to see if anything stood out about those purchases, the only differing factor was that 4 were sold in one day, of these, 3 were filled but only 1 of the 3 was paid for in cash. We rechecked all the receipts again and found that this particular one was the only cash transaction during the past 6 months,' Taylor concluded.

'What was the date of the transaction?' Shona asked hoping to hear the right words.

'It was at 22.25 on Friday, 27 June,' Taylor stated.

'Well done, Graham, excellent work this date ties into our dog walkers account of seeing someone in the area 2 months ago, excellent!' Shona told him.

Shona grabbed herself some coffees and had only been back in her office 10 minutes when the telephone started to ring again, it was Jenson Parker who was up at the Fieldings Secure Unit.

'Shona it's Jenson, Damien sent me up to the hospital to check on Sally Carta's condition, I am afraid her prognosis isn't good in fact she had been sectioned on an emergency 24-hour observational watch under the mental health act. This has now been extended to 28 days with a view to extend it further should the need arise. The doctor I spoke to, a Mirriam Davies said it was highly unlikely that Sally Carta would leave the unit any time soon and that she was a very unwell lady, mentally speaking. Unfortunately, there is nothing I could do as Mrs Carta is not allowed any contact with the outside world, not even her son can visit her,' Jenson said sadly.

'Oh dear, that doesn't sound hopeful at all. Are you free now?' Shona asked.

'Yes,' Jenson replied.

'Can you make your way over to 79 Peterson Road, it's on the corner of Jacobs Well just below the Denby house the home of Connie Webster our dog walker who called the fire in. I will organise a search team now for the garden area at Denby's and will meet you over there, she will be expecting you,' Shona said.

She was just finishing the necessary calls when Jacobi walked in, 'I feel contaminated by the stench of those pig shitting clothes,' he said exaggeratingly holding his arms up, curling his nose and walking stiff legged.

'No time for that now, here,' she said handing him the coffee, 'it's a bit lukewarm but get a good swill we have to go,' she said grabbing her things and rushing towards the door.

'Oh, haha "swill", yes good pun,' he said managing to get a gulp of coffee before leaving it on the desk and following her out.

Chapter 42
Searching

Shona took the opportunity to fill Jacobi in on the new developments whilst travelling to Connie Websters house, the excitement in her voice erasing his earlier experience with the contents of the bin liners. When they arrived on the scene, Parker was walking towards the house from the direction of Jacobs Well with a woman in her mid-40s. She was around 5'5" had an athletic build, her hair neatly scraped back in a blond ponytail and sported figure-hugging fitness gear. She looked as bright as a button like she had just finished her run and the endorphins were kicking in. This woman obviously used the gym not like any of those lardy arsed, lumpy chicks with more cellulite than a surgeon's waste bin. Connie Webster was hot and Shona could see that Jacobi thought so too.

'Your type is she, Dion?' Shona jibed.

'Give over,' he began, 'but you have got to admit she is stunningly beautiful.'

They got out of the car and were busy making their introductions when the search teams pulled up in their vans.

'Oh, I love it when a plan comes together,' Shona said.

'Wasn't that the famous line said by the character John Hannibal Smith in the A-Team?' Connie asked.

'Beautiful and brains,' Jacobi muttered as the team busied themselves collating equipment and organising themselves.

'Right Mrs Webster, can you show us the direction you were coming from and point to exactly where you saw the man coming from on the night of 27 June?' Shona asked.

Connie explained that she had been coming down the hill having just finished her walk and that as she came to the opening of the Denby driveway she had been startled by the man coming from the left out of the bushes. If Mrs Baines was looking out of the window and had seen something to her right then the man could have stored his petrol on the 27 June and sat in wait for Denby to come home on the night of the attack. What had Denby done to warrant such a brutal attack? To want him to burn to death was to want him to suffer, so there was no way this was not personal. Whoever had done this had meticulously planned it, attempting to cover their tracks by playing a waiting game.

Shona decided she needed to speak to Swan and Donelli again there had to be someone who had made threats, or befriended him to find out where he lived or a disgruntled prisoner but there was no way this was because Dr Carmichael owned the house. Shona liaised with the search team to direct the specific areas of interest and then they took Mrs Webster up on her offer for coffee whilst the team worked. It was a good excuse to have a less formal chat with Mrs Webster on her own territory and with her defences down.

The house was a dormer style bungalow with two huge protruding extended windows on the roof, the side of the house had a double extension with a wraparound garden. There were a range of manicured Hebe mature plants, shrubs and other flowers bordering a finely cut circled lawn that had a small Salix tree at its centre. The white PVC door sported red, flowered tulips with a smaller window at the top reading Jacob's Well. Mrs Webster saw Shona's gaze resting on the name.

'It is symbolic of the biblical reference to Jacob's Well, being a holy place where Jesus asked for a drink from a Samaritan woman. It reminds us to be kind, giving, to love our neighbours and those in need, not to mention being thankful of all that we have,' Mrs Webster explained.

'That's lovely, I like that,' said Parker.

They were welcomed into a hallway that had a staircase up to the right, a doorway to the left and a small corridor towards what they assumed was a small kitchen area. The hallway had a highly polished solid wood flooring, half panelled walls and a beautiful balustrade. Mrs Webster walked along the hallway so Shona, Jacobi and Parker followed. What they were not ready for was the humungous kitchen space that sat behind the door. The kitchen itself was a good 20' by 20' the units were of a gleaming white with a black speckled marble top, running left to right along the centre was a stunning island with 6 tall bar stools immaculately polished.

Mrs Webster led them to the top right corner of the kitchen through an archway into a garden room with huge bi-folding doors and an inlaid glass roof.

Two settees one golden and the other light grey sat at right angles a perfect viewing position of the huge flat screen TV that was secured to the wall.

'What an amazing house you have, Mrs Webster,' Shona gushed.

'Please call me Connie, Mrs Webster sounds too much like Chris's mother!' Connie said.

'Sorry Connie, how long have you lived here?' Shona enquired.

'Coming up 9 years, I love the place. It was a bit of a wreck when we bought it but Chris is a builder so we did most of the work ourselves,' Connie beamed.

Shona immediately thought she needed to get herself a builder for a husband, it was a truly spectacular space. Connie busied herself making the drinks whilst Jacobi stepped out on to the decked rear garden, Parker hovered and Shona walked back into the kitchen area to accompany Connie.

'Would you be able to identify the man you saw or at least provide our forensic artist with a description?' Shona asked Connie.

'To be honest I really don't think I would, it was very dark with only the briefest of encounters besides he seemed to keep his chin down so I didn't get a clear look, I'm sorry,' Connie said honestly.

'I knew it was a long shot but still thought I would ask,' Shona said kindly but really feeling quite gutted.

'Do you think it was arson then and that he was the one who set the house on fire? How dreadful!' Connie said aggrieved. 'What could possibly drive a human being to want to burn someone alive? I can't imagine it, well not unless they had hurt my kids. Mick was a prison officer, he kept himself to himself, I really do not understand it and so close to home. It has unnerved our community but at least it has instigated more to join the neighbourhood watch programme,' Connie babbled.

Although Shona was physically present throughout what turned out to be Latte's and M&S double chocolate biscuits with Connie Webster, she could not shake the comment that it would have to be 'someone hurting her kids.' It was true mothers would do anything to protect their kids it was as though an inbuilt primal instinct switch got flicked once motherhood came into force. Shona wondered whether there were any reports or allegations against Denby from young prisoners that maybe she needed to investigate. Perhaps a young prisoner had found it hard to adjust when they had got out and committed suicide that would definitely drive a mother, brother, father to want to seek revenge.

Hadn't Sally Ryder, the woman who had discovered Denby's body stated that they called him Mick the Prick and that he treated them badly. The only trouble with this theory was he had been working there for 3 years and there would be hundreds of prisoners he would have come into contact with. Shona was beginning to feel overwhelmed by the enormity of possibilities when the search team rang through to say they had something. It had been Shona's intention to thank Connie Webster for her hospitality and then leave quickly but it seemed Connie Webster saw herself as part of the team and there was no way she was apparently going to be left behind.

Some members of the team were sat on the front perimeter wall of the Denby house whilst others were either stood about or glued to hand held devices perched on the edge of the flooring of their open, back doored vans. Samual Morrison saw them approaching so moseyed over towards them.

'What have you got for us Sam?' Shona asked.

'The petrol can was obviously embedded under this bush here, not only can you still see the indentation but parts of the bush have been broken by whoever squeezed down into the space to secrete it. We have taken in depth photos but interestingly the soil has particles of petrol absorbed into it so my guess is that the perpetrator lit the fire and hid the can back here afterwards. Let's face it, no one would be looking for the evidence under here but being in the possession of a can of petrol when there was a house on fire would be a bit damaging.' Samual said.

'So, the culprit must have been on foot otherwise they would have stashed it in the boot of their car,' Shona surmised.

'Which means our man could quite easily have been in and amongst the crowd watching it burn pretending to be one of the neighbours,' Jacobi offered.

'Oh my,' Connie Webster shuddered.

'There are no samples of fabric from the perp's coat or anything but we did find one of those thin, see through plastic gloves provided at petrol pumps, it's possible it fell out of our man's pocket as opposed to being discarded. We had a quick look through the rest of the garden but didn't come up with anything although under the back mat there was a key,' Samual stated.

'A key? How is that possible? Mick Denby stated that the key was missing when he fumbled around for it, unless whoever started that fire knew about the key and had been noseying around Denby's house when he was at work,' Jacobi wondered.

'Or Sandra Clarke had heard Denby fumbling around, remembered she had the key, went down to surprise him, unlocked the back door but found he wasn't there so replaced the key leaving the door unlocked for him,' Parker stated.

'But Sandra Clarke had a key on her person when she died,' Shona stated that the autopsy referred to it.

'Couldn't that just have been the key to her own home?' Connie Webster joined in.

'If the key Sandra had was hers, then the back door would have been open all along but Denby didn't think to try it. Who knows maybe being in unfamiliar surroundings Sandra had put a light on that our perpetrator believed demonstrated that Denby was in the house, hence he proceeded to ignite the place,' Shona said sadly.

'There was one other major find Shona, in the shed was a green petrol can containing remnants of liquid. The outer parts of the nozzle side are drenched with petrol symptomatic of being haphazardly poured, splashed or ejected from the can.' Samual told them.

'So, if your theory is correct that the culprit was on foot so stashed the can back by the bushes because he didn't want to get caught, he must have been watching things unfold to know that his plan had failed. If he realised Denby had been asleep in the shed then what better place was there to come back and stash the can to frame Denby for the fire,' Shona concluded.

'I don't know how you manage to stay sane with these kinds of puzzles to solve give me my sudoku book any day of the week,' Connie said bidding them a farewell.

'Right send me all the photo's through and let me know if you get any prints from the glove, the can or the key, I have a feeling this is going to be another long week,' Shona said before making her way with Jacobi to the car.

'Where do we go from here boss?' Jacobi enquired once they were inside the car.

'I think we need to get back to the station, Josie Petroni will be starting her shift in half an hour and I want to be the one to tell her about Sandra Clarke. Can you get on to the prison to talk to either Swan and Donelli there has to be something that we are missing either somebody has a grudge against him or our culprit has befriended him recently. I will arrange for us to pay a visit to Sandra Clarke's parents this afternoon, then I want to find out about the body at

Blenheim House and make my own enquiries at the hospital about Sally Carta,' Shona told Dion.

Shona started the engine, took a deep breath and tried to remind herself that finding the answers to puzzling crimes so that she could put bad people away was why she did the job, she just needed a breakthrough. So far, she had three bodies, a prison officer, a doctor and an innocent bystander that posed numerous questions with too few answers. Her gut instincts were telling her that Dr Carmichael's death and Denby's were somehow connected she just had to keep following the trail, unearthing the stones and joining the dots. She knew she would find the answers she just needed it to be sooner rather than later.

Chapter 43
Breaking the Bad News

Back at the station Shona got a coffee then hung around reception waiting for Josie to arrive whilst Jacobi made calls to the prison, the hospital, the forensic team and Sallyanne Peters. When Josie saw Shona step forward as she arrived, she knew, her face instantly crumbled and she turned and ran back outside. Shona found her at the side of the building literally sobbing her heart out.

'I should have stopped her, why didn't I talk some sense into her,' Josie broke her heart.

'It is not your fault Josie there is no way you could possibly have known that this would happen,' Shona tried to console her.

'It wouldn't be half as bad if she had died through an illness, a car accident or doing something she loved. But to have her life meaninglessly taken for being in the wrong place at the right time is such a senseless waste and I cannot help but feel responsible,' Josie punished herself.

'Josie, the blame is on the person who set fire to the house, not on you,' Shona said kindly.

'So, it definitely was arson?' Josie asked.

'I am afraid it was; Asher Blake has confirmed that petrol was poured through the letterbox,' Shona advised. As Josie crumbled again, Shona stepped in to take the young woman's weight to give her what little comfort she could.

'There is something else Josie, we need to locate Sandra's parents to inform them of her death and I wondered if you would like to come along with me when we break the news,' Shona asked.

'I think they would get more comfort if it came from me than from someone they didn't know. Although I don't know how I will find the right words, Sandra was a very dear friend that I grew up with, we went to school and college together she wasn't just a flat mate,' she said and broke down again at the enormous reality of her loss.

Shona got Josie a drink then led her through into her office so that she had the privacy to make a call to Sandra Clarke's parents before she caught up with Jacobi in the hall, 'What have you found out, anything,' Shona asked.

'My call to the hospital didn't raise anything of value they basically echoed exactly what Parker had said that Sally Carta is unable to give an interview, however undeterred I have booked an appointment for you to liaise with her doctor at 2.30 pm tomorrow. Forensics surprisingly don't have anything for us but Sallyanne Peters has confirmed that the body at Blenheim House is that of Dr Richard Carmichael. She said his face looked like it had been savagely gouged out in a frenzied attack whilst he was still alive with some puncture wounds delving deep into his brain,' Jacobi told her.

'Do you think he could have had an affair and this was Sally Carta's revenge?' Shona surmised.

'It's quite a psychotic reaction to take his face off!' Jacobi shuddered.

'I just think that like the Denby case it was a brutal and personal attack. I don't know maybe it tipped her over the edge and she was making a statement that he wouldn't be able to look at anyone else ever again. Remember the case of the married woman who was a hooker but her husband didn't know, he killed her, cut her head off and sat it in the microwave. Then he would take women back, screw them in the kitchen in his macabre subconscious he was taking back control by making her watch him,' Shona said.

'Yes, I remember, but he was completely looney tunes,' Jacobi said inappropriately.

'My point is, that the woman's deceit, infidelity and pleasure at his expense sent him completely over the edge. No doubt beforehand he was a regular Joe earning a crust going about his normal life,' Shona pushed.

'It seems a bit farfetched though, really?' Jacobi was not convinced.

'Think about it, there was no one else in the Carta's house, no signs of forced entry, the other key holders were the son who was at work and the cleaner. It is amazing what the mind is capable of look at the gay man who killed his boyfriend because he had a roving eye, he boiled his eyes and ate them to make sure he couldn't ever look at another man again. It is another case of being mentally pushed over the edge, this could have been the same for Sally Carta,' Shona threw in.

'You don't think that they were having an affair with each other, do you?' Jacobi asked.

'Who?' Shona wondered.

'Carmichael and Denby!' Jacobi exclaimed. They quietly pondered the possibility and had to admit anything was possible so they couldn't rule it out.

'Did you manage to get through to Swan or Donelli at the prison?' Shona enquired.

'I am glad you asked because this is where it gets exciting, apparently…' he stopped as his mobile phone rang, so Shona pointed to him that she would be in her office.

'Thanks for getting back to me, Mr Donelli were you able to pinpoint the date in question? Ok, brilliant, that's great. Thank you so much, yes that is of enormous help, bye,' Jacobi rang off and entered Shona's office with a self-satisfied grin on his face.

'Ok, you look like the cat that got the cream, spill,' Shona insisted.

'That was Simon Donelli and as I was about to tell you he mentioned that Denby had forfeited one of their fortnightly Friday afternoons at the club. Apparently Denby had chosen to broaden his horizons and go out round Wakefield instead. Here, he met a young lad who took him to a host of different bars in the city but the night ended abruptly when Denby was kicked out of the back door of the Paradise. My thoughts are that he would have called it a night and walked across to the taxi rank opposite the club. I was just waiting for Donelli to confirm the date and guess what? It was the 27 June,' Jacobi said delighted.

'We are getting closer, Dion; I can feel it! Give the taxi rank a call and find out if any of their drivers took a fare to 79 Peterson Road, Crigglestone any time day or night on the 27 June,' Shona said getting excited.

'Right Josie, how did you get on with Sandra's parents?' she enquired.

'I asked them what time they were going to be in because I needed to pop round to pick something up. I feel awful for lying to them but I didn't want to cause them to panic before we could get there,' Josie said empathetically.

'I am sure it will be the least of their worries Josie, so when are we going?' Shona asked.

'They said I could go now if I wanted, is that ok I just want to get it over with,' Josie admitted.

Shona looked at the clock and there was nothing more pressing so she agreed ringing the police liaisons to let them know she was making the trip instead providing them with the details so they could follow it up the next day. The Clarkes lived in a three-bedroom detached house at Darton just on the outskirts of Barnsley. Although it was a 20 minutes' drive the journey throughout was in complete silence Shona knew that Josie was stealing herself to give her friends parents the devastating news. It felt to Shona that remaining silent was somehow paying respect to the young woman who had innocently lost her life. Shona could feel the nerves vibrating through Josie's body, her hands were visibly shaking and her eyes stared vacantly through the window.

When they pulled up outside the Clarke's home Shona made sure the car was not visible, she wanted to give Josie the space to deliver the news without the fanfare. As they approached the house the door swung open to reveal a very tall, slender lady in her early 60s, she had a brown, bobbed hair style, wore a long-sleeved thin cherry jumper and a brown long A-line skirt. She had been smiling when she first thrust the door open but now, she was looking questioningly between Shona and Josie. There was a moment when Shona thought Mrs Clarke had guessed and was going to slam the door shut in a 'if I don't hear it then it hasn't happened kind of way.'

This was going to be a pinnacle moment of both hers and Mr Clarke's lives; one that Shona was now not happy to share. Shona suddenly felt uncomfortable, it was wrong that she was here like a spectator of the matador securing its first kill. As soon as those words were spoken this poor woman's life would never be the same again nor would she be able to greet Josie without being reminded of her precious daughter. Life could be so cruel; people could be so heartless and the devastation caused was slapped away to become some other person's cross to bear. This was the part of the job that Shona hated and if it had been up to her, she would have had someone else deliver the news but she could not have let Josie do this alone.

'Is everything alright, Josie?' Mrs Clarke asked looking quizzically at Shona.

'Do you mind if we come inside Maureen? I have something to tell you,' Josie said swallowing hard to stave off the tears.

'You're worrying me now Josie who is this?' Maureen asked.

'Please Maureen let's discuss it inside and I will be able to answer any questions you have,' Josie said comfortingly.

Maureen stepped aside to allow them over the threshold, Josie walked straight through into the lounge like it was her own home whilst Shona waited for Maureen to close the door then followed behind her.

'Hello Josie, how lovely to see you is our Sandra not with you?' Mr Clarke could be heard greeting her but there was no reply.

Josie stood, waiting for Maureen to enter the room then when Shona followed confusion hit Mr Clarke's face. The newspaper across his lap slid to the floor, his glasses at the end of his nose balanced precariously as he stared in anticipation of the news he was about to hear.

'Maureen, won't you take a seat,' Josie said professionally as the older lady silently obeyed without taking her eyes off of her. 'I am very sorry to have to tell you…' Maureen's hand shot up to her face, her eyes instantly teared, her breathing became rapid and she screamed knowing exactly where this was going. '…but a body found at a house fire has been confirmed to be that of Sandra's. I am so very sorry.'

The grief-stricken howl of her best friend's parents was far too much for Josie to bear so she crumbled onto the floor next to the woman who had been more like a second mum to her. Shona found the outpouring quite overwhelming the poor mother was beside herself with the torment of a deep anguish and loss that Shona had never experienced before. Mr Clarke was dumbfounded, rendered speechless and unable to process neither what his ears had heard nor his eyes were witnessing. Shona knew that once the news had sunk in there would be so many questions, they would need answers to and only Josie could provide them so she made her exit giving them the dignity and privacy they deserved.

She had been sat in the car for almost 40 minutes when Josie reappeared, her eyes were red, her cheeks blotched and she looked like she had been put through the wringer. She opened the door, slid into the passenger seat and applied her belt then said softly, 'Is it alright if I have the afternoon off Shona, I don't think I will be of any use today,' she said quietly.

'Shall I take you to your parents?' Shona asked, 'I really don't think you should be on your own and if I were your mum, I would want to give you the support that you need right now,' Josie just nodded and provided the address.

Once there she simply said, 'Thank you' then closed the door, mentally drained and with her emotions spent she walked down the drive of her parents' home. As Shona sat in quiet contemplation her mobile rang, she glanced at the caller ID to see it was Jacobi, 'Talk to me!' she said.

'I have been in contact with the taxi company and spoken to a driver called Fred Boocock he took a man, a bit worse for wear matching Denby's description, to Peterson Road on the night of the 27 June at around 10pm,' Jacobi informed her but Shona's thoughts were elsewhere until he carried on and then they were crystal clear.

'Another taxi driver, a Patrick Roberts followed Fred's vehicle carrying a younger man who said he was the drunk man's son and wanted to make sure he got home alright. Patrick said that once they had seen the man walk into his house, he was asked to drop the son at a house on Denby Dale Road by the petrol station. I think this is our man, Shona,' Jacobi insisted.

'The only problem is, who is he and what is his connection to Denby? Did Patrick get a good look at him?' Shona enquired.

'It was pretty dark and again he kept his chin down so not enough to give me a description though he did say he was roughly 20 to 25 years, maybe 5'10".'

'Not enough to go on, but we are making headway, we now know a young male did befriend Denby, that he followed him home at around 10pm, was dropped off by the garage at a time when petrol, a can and a lighter were purchased together. We also have a sighting of a man at the scene of Denby's house later that night purportedly taking a leak right where the petrol can was evidently stashed. What we do not know is what has Denby done to attract an attempt on his life, moreover who actually succeeded on the second attempt. Also, what on earth is the connection with Denby and Carmichael it just doesn't make any sense at all,' Shona said chatting it through as much to hear herself say it out loud than anything else.

'So, what now?' Jacobi asked.

'Put some pressure on the forensics for the samples from the prison and what they have collected from both the Blenheim House and the Denby scene. In the meantime, I am going up to the hospital to have a chat with the Carta's doctor this cannot wait until tomorrow,' she said cutting the call.

Shona sped through the city to the Fieldings, drove through the barrier and did a couple of circuits of the car park before a couple walked towards a car. Shona sat drumming her fingers on the steering wheel whilst she sat waiting endlessly for the couple to get in, fasten their seatbelts, adjust mirrors and move. She was about to get out and ask them if they were actually leaving when she saw the reversing lights finally appear and the car slowly rolled out of the space. Shona pulled the car in, quickly jumped out and made her way towards the reception area. It was pretty much like any clinical waiting area with a mishmash of posters on the wall, a stand full of leaflets, magnolia walls with white paint work and a receptionist behind a glass partition.

It wasn't at all welcoming and from first impressions she hoped she wouldn't be here for very long. There were two ladies behind the glass each sat at their own individual desks with monitors in front of them. Charlotte was the first to spot her at the window and immediately rose sliding back the partition. She fixed her eyes on Shona's and beamed so intensely at her it was hard to tell if Charlotte was a patient that they were indulging or whether this really was her workplace.

'Good afternoon may I help you?' Charlotte asked pleasantly putting Shona at ease.

'Yes, I am DCI Shona Williams I am here to see Mirriam Davies about a new patient that has been admitted,' Shona explained.

'Was Dr Davies expecting you?' Charlotte enquired.

'Yes, my colleague DC Dion Jacobi rang to arrange the appointment,' Shona said.

'I am afraid Dr Davies is not available today but Dr Sykes may be able to help you. If you would like to take a seat, I will ring through and check for you now,' Charlotte said helpfully. Within a few minutes, the glass partition slid back again, 'You will need to wear a visitors badge, if you could just look at the camera here it will take your photo and then I can print it for the badge.'

Charlotte directed and then on handing her the ID said, 'Please make sure you do not talk to any of the patients and ensure your badge is securely clipped to your clothing.'

'My colleague Pauline will escort you to Dr Sykes' office,' she said.

Pauline was not as talkative as Charlotte the most she said was 'If you would like to come this way?' and then she wandered off along a maze of corridors, through doors that required an authorised swipe card to get through or heavier more secure doors that they had to be buzzed through. Shona noted that at various points cameras were monitoring their passage until they ultimately reached their destination. Here there were people physically milling around but who did not seem to be mentally present, others appeared to be statue like in a suspended animation. It was quite a distressing notion to think that they were someone's mother, father, sister, brother and Shona thought, *For the Grace of God go I.*

Her contemplations were interrupted when a man stepped out from a door on the left about 25' down the corridor. Shona could see him intently observing her as she walked towards him and suddenly, she became incredibly self-conscious something she was neither comfortable with nor used to. As she neared him, he suddenly thrust out his hand and said, 'Good afternoon, I am Dr Martin Sykes, I believe you had an appointment with Dr Mirriam Davies but wasn't that for tomorrow?' he questioned her knowingly.

'I am afraid it really couldn't wait until tomorrow Dr Sykes I have 3 murders on my hands and no suspect in custody. I believe your patient Sally Carta may be involved or at least she may know the culprit in question, it is imperative I speak to her as soon as possible,' she said honestly.

'Please won't you come into my office,' he said turning for her to follow him and then shut the door behind her. 'The thing is detective Mrs Carta is in no fit state to be able to help with your enquiries as I am sure your colleague will have been informed; ordinarily I wouldn't have taken the time to talk to you but I have to say I was intrigued.'

'Intrigued?' Shona asked not following his thread.

'Yes, intrigued, it is quite a bold move on your behalf to come and spin the story that you just have.' He suggested then smiled surreptitiously before continuing, 'I am not permitted to discuss Mrs Carta's case due to patient confidentiality; I am sure you understand that.'

'I just want to know when she can be medically fitted for an interview?' Shona pushed on regardless.

'A prediction in time of when the mind will heal is an impossible task, the trauma that she has sustained has been cataclysmic reducing her to a shadow of her former self. She may never regain the memories that you wish to question her about because her brain has simply shut down to protect her, the experience being far too damaging for her to deal with,' the Doctor explained.

'Is it possible that she is faking the symptoms, after all she was a doctor herself, so wouldn't she know how to mimic the effects of a breakdown to avoid having to stand trial for murder?' Shona asked bluntly.

'There are two things I am prepared to do for you detective chief inspector the first is to categorically affirm that there is no way Sally Carta is acting and the second is to give you the opportunity to observe her yourself,' he told her.

'Thank you, I very much appreciate your assistance,' Shona acknowledged and then stood as he moved towards the door.

Shona followed him further down the corridor to a small room that had a two-way mirror to the far-right hand side wall where she stood beside him looking out into a dining room. There were people sat with their fingers in their bowl, others attempting to lift food to their mouths using cutlery but it was falling off before it arrived at its final destination. One woman in a long open backed hospital gown was pasting her food on to the glass of the two-way mirror and then she spotted a pitiful sight.

There was a male nurse attempting to feed a woman slumped in a wheelchair but nothing was staying in her open mouth each spoonful dribbled back out. Her eyes were shut, her head cocked at an irregular angle and there was a collection of sputum down the side of her mouth with a wet patch on the top side of her right breast.

'I see you have located Mrs Carta,' Dr Davies said calmly.

Shona looked at him in horror, 'You mean that is Mrs Carta?'

'Yes, detective chief inspector that is Mrs Carta, now do you see why a timeframe cannot be placed upon her wellness and why it is impossible for her to be interviewed?' he finished triumphantly but Shona was too dumbfounded to muster an answer.

Having made his point Dr Sykes was about to turn away when a young woman suddenly ran across the room and grabbed hold of the impassive Sally Carta shouting and screaming in her face, the food, the caregiver was holding went up in the air. The doctor instantaneously slammed a big red button fixed to the wall at the side of the mirror and an alarm immediately penetrated Shona's ears, four members of staff raced to the scene grabbing the young woman and hurled her out of the dining room. Shona scrutinised the occurrence in minute detail as it was happening, the astonishing lack of a reaction from Sally Carta compared to the excessive anger in the young woman's face.

She was sure that this was not a spontaneous action there was something beneath the surface that had provoked this young woman's reaction. As Shona sat for a moment pondering the thought, she was sure it had been stimulated through recognition. Shona pictured her face, contorted through anger, the rage, but it was mostly born out of pain expressed through her anger that had peeked Shona's interest. Carta had obviously caused this young woman serious harm but who was she?

It was a good 20 minutes before Dr Sykes rejoined her, 'Sorry you had to witness that I could never have predicted such an outburst that patient is usually so placid.'

Shona decided to keep her theory to herself but enquired. 'Who was she, the young woman?'

'She is a very perplexing case that we are still trying to fathom out. At the moment I am unsure whether it is simply an underlying personality disorder but she keeps displaying psychotic episodes of hallucinational disassociation with reality. Very intriguing yet also mystifying we just need to study her for a little while longer,' Sykes explained.

'Has she been here for a long time?' Shona enquired.

'No, no not at all maybe 6 to 8 weeks in total she was picked up wandering around the town in just a nightgown apparently suffering from amnesia so she was transferred to us,' Sykes said. 'There are not many cases that hold your attention quite like a puzzling one but then you know all about that detective.'

'Does she at least have a name?' Shona asked as nonchalantly as possible but with the intention of doing some investigations of her own.

'Yes, she was able to tell us that her name was Cortina or at least that is what she is answering to?' Has Sykes spoke the name a shiver ran through Shona it was a name she had never forgotten nor ever heard of again since the New Year's Eve suicide of Cassandra Matthews. 'If you would like to follow me detective, I will walk you out.'

Shona's mind was running on overtime so as they made their way back through to reception, she refocused her questioning on to Sally Carta 'Has anyone else enquired about her well-being? I know she has a son, Jonathon who works here but does she have any other family?' Shona enquired.

'She also has a sister, Emma Boulden who I believe is down as her next of kin but I am unaware of anyone else?' The doctor informed her.

'Mrs Carta appears subdued now but when I saw her at the scene, she was hysterical, has she had any more of those episodes?' Shona asked.

'Yes, astonishingly she only becomes distressed if she sees her son or hears his voice, the poor lad is beyond distraught,' Sykes told Shona.

'Do you have the sister's address and contact details on record?' Shona asked.

'Yes, Charlotte or Pauline on reception will be able to retrieve them for you. Here we are, it has been a pleasure to meet you detective, good-bye?' Sykes said turning around and leaving.

Shona's stomach was doing somersaults and her gut instinct was telling her that there was a link here somewhere, she could feel it. This may not turn out to be the massive breakthrough that she had been looking for but there was something. The problem she couldn't quite fathom out was how the heck did Denby fit into it or was he a red herring?

Chapter 44
Revelations

She called Jacobi as soon as she was back in her car and gave him the address of Emma Boulden instructing him to do some digging into the Cassandra Matthews case.

'Cassandra Matthews? You mean the New Year's Eve suicide? What has that got to do with Denby, Carmichael and Sally Carta?' he asked totally perplexed.

'I don't know yet but I am sure that we will find some missing links just get digging I am on my way back now!' she urged him.

When she arrived at her office, Jacobi was stood at the door with a look that told her he had something, 'Spill it,' she said as she dragged her jacket off and raced to the desk with its numerous leaves of paper strewn across it.

'You are not going to believe this,' he began.

'Hit me with it,' she was in no mood to play cat and mouse.

'So, it turns out that Carmichael was the doctor who was treating Cassandra Matthews for depression before she committed suicide. He had been working at the same surgery as Dr Sally Carta for approximately 15 months prior to this. As you will recall Cortina Matthews was found wandering the streets late that night after finding her mother's body suspended from the banister. Surprisingly she ended up in care, though it is unknown why because she did have a father, Tony Lloyd. I was unable to access the file beyond this due to data protection and confidentiality as the child was a minor. We will have to get a judge to warrant further investigation. However, we may be able to find out via a much simpler route,' Jacobi toyed.

'Dion, just tell me,' Shona said impatiently.

'Tony Lloyd is the partner of one Emma Boulden!' Jacobi threw in victoriously.

'I knew it! I knew there was a significance,' Shona stipulated.

'There is also something else forensics have been able to retrieve DNA from the blade and it does have blood on it but having been secreted in the sanitary bin this will be inadmissible due to the contamination of other bloods. The clothing found by security has numerous stains and whilst it could be linked to the Denby murder there are no camera's covering the kitchen bin areas.' Denby revealed.

'What about the Spalding woman? The prison takes photographs of every new prisoner along with their number there has to be a facial source to work from. Plus, map the route she took from when she left the wing to when she arrived at reception, count the bags she is carrying to ascertain if she had one less on arrival. What about the clothes in the bins at the car park that Darley Mays gave us?' Shona asked.

'Now that is interesting and I thought it was possibly our killers one vital mistake, however the DNA on these clothes does not match the clothes that the security office handed us. It matches Sally Ryders the woman whose cell Denby was found in,' Jacobi stated.

After a brief pause, he continued, 'How is it possible for Sally Ryder to be held in the prison, to have been working at the time Denby was killed and yet be the person stuffing the clothes into the bin witnessed by Darley Mays?'

'What was the number of the cell room that Sally Ryder occupied where Denby was found?' Shona suddenly asked.

'I don't know but I will check, why?' Jacobi asked.

'I think we have a very clever person on our hands who has almost masterminded the perfect crime and like the Denby's case has sported someone else for the murder. Perhaps it is not only to revert our attention from themselves but to also identify that we have missed something in the Cassandra Matthews case,' Shona stipulated.

'So where do we go from here?' Jacobi asked.

'Ask Parker to check whether Carmichael had any life insurance and I bet your bottom dollar Sally Carta made a high-level alteration just weeks before he was killed. Although, whether it was her personally or just made to look like it was her, now that is the real question. If I am correct, we are being pointed to the wrong people committing the murders of the right people who escaped justice,' Shona advised him.

Energised by this new lead Shona Williams set up an interview with Emma Boulden not at her home or work but at the station in order to apply some pressure on whom she perceived would be the weakest link. Jacobi instructed Parker to delve into the life insurance theory, then it was a waiting game until Emma Boulden arrived.

Chapter 45
Full Disclosure

'Thank you for coming in to see us today Mrs Boulden may I...' Jacobi began.

'It's Ms Boulden if you don't mind, I was divorced many years ago or if I am honest, I would prefer it if you just called me Emma,' she interrupted.

'Sorry Emma,' Jacobi continued. 'As I was saying thank you for coming in today, we just wanted to ask you some questions with regards to your sister Sally Carta and the death of Dr Richard Carmichael.'

'I am not sure I can be of any help sorry,' Emma immediately dismissed.

'The thing is, we believe that Dr Carmichael's murder could be linked to a suspected suicide that happened on New Year's Eve 2000,' Jacobi revealed whilst Shona scrutinised Emma for the minutest sign of recognition and there it was, her brow furrowed slightly as her eyes widened.

'Can you tell us what you know about Cassandra Matthews?' Shona dropped in.

'I didn't know her that well she was my partners ex-wife who made our life a misery when we first got together,' Emma delivered flatly.

'But you do remember the incident?' Jacobi continued.

'Yes,' Emma said giving little more.

'Then you will remember the name Cortina Matthews and this is primarily who we want to talk to you about,' Shona revealed, expecting a small glimmer of recognition but what she was not expecting was a full disclosure of a very grave secret that she had been forced to keep. A secret that explained absolutely everything.

At the end of the interview, Shona contacted Dr Sykes to arrange for her and Jacobi to meet him at the hospital. It was imperative that he knew who his patient was, if he was going to successfully treat her and that they were able to observe her when Cortina was questioned.

The three doctors who had been assessing Cortina gathered together to process the information then arranged for an interview to take place whilst Jacobi and Shona Williams stood at the other side of the two-way mirror. An ear piece was secreted inside Dr Sykes right ear so that Shona could give him direction divulging information to push her buttons.

Part Three

There is a time to deceive
And a time for the truth
A time to keep quiet
And a time to speak out
A time to let go
And a time to move on

(Juli Flintoff)

Chapter 46
Cortina Matthews: Something is Missing

Cortina Matthews examined the room around her, there was nothing particularly interesting nor inspiring about it. In front of her behind a nondescript wooden desk were three people sat upon three old wooden chairs. She noted that the small window out on to the yard with its heavy bars was particularly dirty and the parquet flooring needed a good polish to revive its tired and well-trodden surface. Cortina was so disinterested in their formalities, the same questions over and over again, she just wanted to scream out yes it was my fault, move on, get over it but here she would sit again. The room was silent but for the rattling of papers and their hushed whispers.

Her head was kind of fuzzy a bit like cotton wool there were no thoughts just clouds passing through. She felt no emotions and if truth beknown she just wanted to be left alone. She gazed up at the ceiling her eyes resting upon the decorative moulding that surrounded the thick electrical cord upon which hung a naked bulb. She thought of the bulb suspended in midair but for the cord attached to its neck, it made her think of her mother, so she blinked and looked away. The bright light gave a clinical stark glow leaving blind spots in her eyes as soon as she had glanced away. She looked towards the huge mirror in front of her but the light was reflecting off it so she averted her gaze. She traced the cornice along the edges of the ceiling with her eyes then back to the central rose.

There were two outer ridges, then a thicker band followed by a row of inner beading. From the centre moving outwardly were circular rows, gradually getting wider. It reminded Cortina of the time her and Gerald were at a lake and it had started to rain, heavily. They had thrown stones to see who could skim them along the water's edge, then got heavy rocks and dumped them in from above. The heavy splash had caused a rippling affect with full circles being cast outwards, just like she would expect an echo to do if she could actually see it.

There was another memory somewhere deep inside, attached to that day but she couldn't recall it, so she brushed it away.

The main feature on the decorative moulding was an interlocking wreath of flowers just like the ones Cortina's dad had hung on the door that Christmas, again there was something else trying to push through but she couldn't see it. She closed her eyes and saw her parents excitedly opening the presents that her and Gerald had made in Mrs Piper's class, in year 1. Her and Gerald had been able to sit next to each other, a lump of damp grey clay in front of them had a white gauze cloth over the top. Gerald had been impatient and with his curiosity getting the better of him, he'd started to peel back the gauze to take a peek when Mrs Piper began to scold him. She then made him wait whilst everyone else was able to unwrap the gauze and examined their pieces, a punishment for him being too eager, too impulsive.

'Fools rush in where angels fear to tread,' Mrs Piper had told Gerald, 'Now, let it be a lesson to you that when we do a project, we do it together,' she had admonished him.

Cortina smiled to herself now, just as she had done at the time when she'd ignored Mrs Piper, unwrapped her clay and handed it to Gerald to hold, 'She is right Gerald, we will do it together,' she had told him. They had then moulded their clay lumps as instructed, pressed their tiny hands in to it and left it to dry for a week. Mrs Piper had later allowed them to paint their masterpieces. They had felt so proud taking them home, wrapping them up and hiding them under the Christmas tree. They had laid them side by side, together, always together.

No one had ever been able to separate them, not really although many had tried by making her go to a different class, or sleep in a different room but they were still together, in their hearts. Cortina knew that they were in this together and nothing would ever keep them apart, not even death.

As Cortina sat on the hard seat she breathed in his scent, she clasped her hand as though she was holding his, she visualised his body squirming around in her mother's womb with hers, her brother, her partner in crime. And she smiled again lost in the warmth of his love.

'Right, we are ready to begin again now Cortina,' the man in the middle said addressing her directly.

Cortina opened her eyes and smiled still thinking of him.

'The last time we spoke it was about why you had attacked the defenceless woman in the wheelchair do you remember Cortina?' He asked.

'Yes, I remember, but I told you she just reminded me of someone, I did say that I was sorry,' Cortina said.

'I know you did but I think that you have left something out about the woman in the wheelchair Cortina,' the man in the middle suggested.

'No, I haven't,' she said sullenly.

'We know that you have and you know that you have Cortina,' he told her whilst the two women at either side of him stared intently at her.

'What do you think I have left out,' Cortina asked addressing the woman to the man's left.

'The reason, why you attacked her? That is the big question, that is what we are missing,' the woman glared at her now.

'I told you she reminded me of someone,' Cortina repeated herself.

'Did she remind you of someone or is she really the person that you know?' He asked her.

'You are confusing me; I don't know what you are wanting from me,' Cortina said agitatedly.

'Isn't it obvious?' He asked her.

'No, I don't think it is obvious,' she replied.

'In previous sessions you have been resolute that your mum's death was not a suicide and were specific about it being her doctors who had killed her. You were adamant that they had got away with murder. Can you tell me the names of the doctors?' the woman to the right asked.

'I don't remember,' Cortina dismissed.

'Does the woman in the wheelchair remind you of one of the doctors whom you say killed your mum?' The woman to the left asked.

'I don't know,' Cortina said trying hard to remember not to give them too much information.

'The last time we chatted you had attacked the woman in the wheelchair when you saw her in the dining room, since then you seem to have been creating an obsessive fixation with her and are now accusing her of being some kind of a psychopath?' The man stated redirecting Cortina's attention from the woman on his left back to himself.

'Are you saying that you think I am the psychopath, is that why you are holding me here?' she enquired bemused.

'You are here because you were found wandering the streets in a highly disassociated state, we are here to determine how best we can help you,' the lady on the man's right interjected.

'Interesting,' Cortina smiled, the drugs he had given her were beginning to wear off.

'Why is it interesting,' the same lady asked.

'That you should even consider the possibility I could be a psychopath, please tell me how you could even think that?' Cortina enquired.

The woman looked to the man for guidance knowing that conflict of any form could become detrimental to the case and perhaps even result in a dangerous outcome. Shona spoke through the earpiece asking him to continue. Surprisingly, his colleague nodded, maybe wanting to see how the subject would respond when challenged with her own behavioural traits and whether she would take any responsibility. So, she continued, 'there are many things Cortina, firstly your inability to express any guilt or remorse for your actions.'

'How can I show remorse when there is nothing that I need to be sorry for, there is a difference between being able to express remorse and being sorry.' She argued.

'Does the lady in the wheelchair remind you of Dr Sally Carta?' The man in the middle asked the question he was prompted to ask and Cortina was immediately emotionally triggered as soon as she heard the name.

'The doctors were not sorry for what they did, they intentionally caused physical and emotional harm, they had no concern for the distress they caused to my mother, my brother or myself. She lied to get what she wanted; she manipulated the doctor to make him do what she wanted to cover up what they did. She lied over and over again unwilling to give us peace, our rights to live as a family unit was obliterated by her just so the truth didn't get out, are they not the traits of a psychopath?' Cortina reacted raising her voice.

'We are here to study your patterns of behaviour Cortina so that we can determine how best to help you,' the man said very carefully and in a quiet voice hoping to bring her back down to a manageable level.

'Dr Carta was a callous, cunning, manipulative narcissist only interested in herself and saving her career. The doctor saw it, he knew, why don't you ask him?' Cortina queried.

'We can't, can we Cortina?' the woman to the left asked.

'Why can't you? He was just as much a victim as we were, ask him?' Cortina demanded.

'We can't Cortina because he is dead, but you know that don't you?' the man stated.

'What? No, that is not right,' Cortina stated confused.

'What is not right?' the man asked.

'That he is dead it wasn't me or Gerald, is that why you think I am a psychopath?' Cortina asked confused.

'Gerald? Who is Gerald?' The woman to the right asked.

'My brother Gerald,' Cortina was becoming irate.

'But you don't have a brother, Cortina,' the woman to the left told her.

'I do have a brother, I am a twin, his name is Gerald!' she asserted beginning to get upset.

'Cortina there is no record of you ever having a brother the truth is you had a sister, didn't you?'

'No, I had a brother his name was Gerald,' she affirmed putting her hands over her ears and not wanting to listen.

'Cortina, you were born as a set of triplets the boy died at birth, the girl, your sister lived until she was almost 6 years of age,' the man said softly.

'That's NOT true, why are you saying this? Gerald and I were there when the doctors came into the house and killed my mum,' Cortina screamed.

'No Cortina, that is not true. Your mum committed suicide on New Year's Eve 2000,' the lady to the left stated reading from the records in front of her. 'The only person found in the house that night was a little boy that your mum was looking after from next door called, Jimmy.'

'It was Gerald not Jimmy!' Cortina screeched.

'No, Cortina his name was James Gerald but everyone called him Jimmy, you treated him as your brother to fill the gap when you lost your sister,' the lady to the left identified.

'No!' Cortina yelled.

'It is true Cortina,' the same lady said softly.

'Your mum was unable to cope with the loss of her child and the breakdown of her marriage so she took her own life, didn't she?' the man pressed.

'Dr Carta was having an affair with Dr Carmichael when my mum found out, she threatened to tell on them so they killed her to make it look like a suicide,' Cortina revealed.

'Cortina, it was ruled that your mum did commit suicide,' she continued, 'we know it is very hard on the people who have been left behind especially when the deceased does not leave a suicide note.'

'That is not true she was depressed like you said about my dad leaving us but they did kill her, I was there I saw them,' Cortina yelled recollecting the truth that she had actually seen them there that night. Behind the glass, Shona Williams punched the air in triumph but poor Cortina was broken sobbing her heart out suddenly wanting to get away from them and the distress they had initiated.

She tried to stand but found that she couldn't. A hand pressed down on to her right shoulder from someone that was stood behind Cortina, she tried to lift her hand up to push it away but she couldn't her hands were shackled. She looked down in disbelief, distress filling her terrified heart what was going on where was she who were these people? Then it abruptly stopped.

The lady to the man's right whispered, 'I fear she could be experiencing a delayed but chronic mental breakdown due to the effects of the trauma's she sustained as a child.'

'I think you could be right and it was triggered when she saw Dr Carta,' Davies told her.

'What is the meaning of this, why are you upsetting my poor sister,' a cold calm voice emanated from Cortina's mouth.

The three people sat at the desk looked from one to another, then towards the mirror and began to talk in a hushed whisper.

'I asked a simple question I would like an answer please?' the voice came again.

'Go with it,' Shona urged Dr Sykes.

'I do not think we have been introduced,' the man tried. 'I'm Dr Martin Sykes I am one of the Psychotherapists here and you are?'

'Gerald, Gerald Matthews,' the voice informed him.

'Nice to meet you Gerald, Cortina was just telling us about you. May I introduce Dr Mirriam Davies,' he said placing a flat left hand out in front of the lady to his right, 'and this is Dr Sarah Ashley,' he said putting his flat right hand out to the lady on his left.

'Nice to meet you I am sure, if there are any questions you need answering it is probably better to ask me as Cortina gets quite emotional in times of stress especially where our mother's death is concerned. You see, she never quite got over it,' he told them.

'What do you remember of the time your mother passed away, Gerald?' Davies asked indulging in this new element of the subject.

'She didn't just pass away she committed suicide,' Gerald said matter-of-factly.

'Do you know the reasons surrounding her suicide?' Dr Sykes asked.

'Yes, it was New Year's Eve but to fully understand you have to go back to the year before, it started on 31 December 1999, the New Year's Eve of the Millennium,' he began.

'Can you tell us please what happened?' Gerald shifted himself around in his seat to make himself comfortable and then began his story.

Chapter 47
Gerald: Mirror, Mirror on the Wall

I will set the scene first before I tell you about what happened, you see Mum and Dad should never have gotten married they argued all the time and life was not very happy for any of us. Cortina and I used to hide in the bedroom our hands over our ears. It probably affected her more than me because I would block it out and play with my Brio train set. I loved that train set but Cortina smashed it to pieces when she thought I spent more time playing with it than I did playing with her dolls. She could get in to a rage for no apparent reason Mummy was terrified of her and didn't know how to deal with her escalating behaviours. Mummy was desperate she begged Daddy to help her but he was too caught up with his new girlfriend. So, having escaped he had no intention of being dragged back to deal with Cortina, I think he just thought Mummy was being dramatic and that she should be able to deal with a 6-year-old. The trouble was Cortina was not like any other 6-year-old something really bad happened that spiralled everything out of control and which pushed Mummy over the edge.

At the end of her tether, mummy needed to talk to daddy because she couldn't keep the secret any more so she rang him but he wouldn't take her calls. She kept ringing until he turned his phone off, she rang Emma's number but they unplugged that, she turned up at their home and they had her removed. She tried in vain to get him to help her but to no avail. So, one night at her wit's end when she couldn't take anymore, she took her own life, but she wasn't on her own.' He smiled menacingly.

'What do you mean she wasn't on her own?' Davies asked enthralled by this new piece of information.

'Cortina has been right all along it was an assisted suicide,' Gerald delivered.

The three adults looked at each other astounded at what they were hearing, then urged Gerald to continue.

'To understand fully what I am about to tell you I need to convey what happened the previous year at a Millennium New Year's party and about the people who attended it,' Gerald informed them.

'We are all listening,' Dr Ashley told him. 'Please, feel free to begin at whatever point you are comfortable with Gerald.' She looked at the mirror and then at her two colleagues seated at the desk for confirmation. They smiled and agreed.

'As I said my parents didn't get on, they argued about absolutely everything.'

Chapter 48
Tony Lloyd: Pointless Protests

New Year's Eve 1999

'For goodness' sake, Cassie, it's New Year's Eve; why the heck would the kids want us dragging them out to go to someone else's house when they should be at home in their own beds?' He challenged his wife.

'We don't have to go for long, just to show our faces,' Cassie tried to coax him.

'It's alright you saying that now, Cass, but I know what your like once we get there you will forget about me and the kids. We always end up being like bookends, stood there like spare parts and at the end of the night I will be left having to hold you up,' Tony Lloyd retorted.

'Tony, it's New Year's Eve, what does it matter if the kids stay up besides, we should bring it in together,' Cassie tried.

'We can, we can bring it in together here at home then everyone gets what they want,' he said playing devil's advocate.

'I told Sally that we would go, she was really looking forward to meeting you,' Cassie said protesting.

'Well, you and I could go for an hour and get young Jenny from next door to nip in and watch the kids,' Tony offered.

'Tony, it means everything to me to go tonight, I couldn't believe it when she invited me especially as I have only just started at the clinic. This could help me get to know the others there not to mention help me get settled in,' she moaned.

'Fine me and you can go for a couple of hours and get home to bring the New Year in with the kids,' Tony compromised.

'That's the beauty of it the kids can come too, Sally has a young son called Jonathon so the kids will have a great time,' Cassie pushed further.

Tony Lloyd knew his wife; he knew that if she had made her mind up about something there was no point protesting as she wasn't listening. Her goal was only fixed upon what she wanted, so knowing full well he wasn't going to get anywhere he succumbed to the inevitable. He went upstairs to run a bath for his children taking great delight in their enjoyment of the warm soapy water as he filled the sponge and squeezed it over their backs. He mused how relaxed, content and at ease they were oblivious to the tensions and unrest between their parents.

Tony Lloyd had been married to Cassie for 6 years, after knowing her for only 4 months when he found out she was pregnant. Many times, during those 6 years he had questioned himself would he have married her if she hadn't been pregnant and the simple answer every single time was a resounding NO. He loved his children but Cassie had been a drain on his finances since the day he had met her and the debts she kept running up were getting greater and greater. To date they were £63,000 in debt due to credit cards she had ordered and maxed out on and also bank loans. She had used every excuse that she could come up with for her untamed behaviour but the number one always came back to it being Tony's fault because he was never home.

Cassie did not seem to grasp the concept that the credit on these cards was real money that it was not free and somehow it had to be repaid to the credit card companies. The very first time he had found out about her spending issues was through a Bailiffs letter because she had hidden several demand letters from him. Now, it had been escalated so unless he worked every hour that God sent to meet the demands, they were soon going to face court action. Tony still remembered the shock, there had been no indication of lavish goods suddenly appearing or grand gestures of presents just a bill for £7235 including costs.

At the time he had thought £7235 was a vast sum to be in debt, oh, how he wished that was all that they owed now, instead of the colossal amount of £63k. A blackness started in the pit of his stomach and had radiated throughout his whole being at just the sight of the letter, a threat to his family, his home and his security through her selfishness. He wasn't sure if it had started with the feeling of contempt towards her on receiving that letter and whether that had just steadily grown towards disgust.

He just knew that as the letters continued to arrive a deep loathing began to bubble under the surface until he had gotten to the point that he couldn't abide anything about her. What do they say act in haste and repent at leisure? As he looked back over the time that he'd had the unfortunate displeasure of knowing Cassie, he certainly felt that he wished he had known then what he knew now. If he had, there was no way he would have made Cassandra Matthews his wife.

Chapter 49
Cassandra Lloyd: In Control

Cassandra Lloyd was thrilled to get an invite to Sally Carta's NYE Millennium party, what a privilege. She didn't tell Tony until the last minute because she knew if she gave him any indication beforehand, he would have put his foot down. No, she knew if she stood any chance at all she had to wait until the last minute and then put him on the spot. She also didn't tell him that she hadn't got an invite as such well she did but it was a bit of a back handed invitation. Gosh if he had known that there was no way he would have entertained it at all. She hadn't lied she just hadn't told the whole truth, yes, she got it there was a lie in not fully disclosing all the information but she didn't care she wanted to go to the party and that was that.

She had only just started working at the surgery and maybe to everyone else she was just the cleaner but she was thrilled to be able to get out of the house and "do her bit" as Tony kept saying. She knew she wouldn't hear the last of the debt situation until it was paid off so she had to show willing and get a job but this was the only thing she could get being unqualified for anything else. It didn't matter to her she loved having her own little locker, a cupboard for her work materials and the regularity of getting out of the house. So, when she was cleaning the offices and happened to overhear the excited buzz about Dr Sally Carta having one of her famous parties, she knew she had to get an invite. She tried dropping hints but no one was forthcoming with any information and then an opportunity arose that she couldn't have orchestrated if she'd tried.

Thinking that the surgery was empty she had walked into Sally's office to complete her evening clean when she stumbled on the young Dr Carmicheal giving Sally more than a bit of pleasure over the examination bed. Cassie had not thought to shut the door and walk away, nor did she know what to say so she had just stood frozen to the spot. Talk about passion killer, the doctors dived up, covered themselves and rearranged their clothes all whilst Cassandra just stood there. The young male doctor brushed past her and rushed off down the corridor whilst Sally Carta composed herself.

'What?' she said unapologetically.

'But you're married,' Cassie stuttered.

'Oh, come on Cassandra haven't you ever needed to spice things up a bit, let yourself go and take life by the balls once in a while?' Carta shrugged off her infidelity.

'No, I haven't,' she said truthfully.

'Look I can see you are a bit shocked but hey-ho, how do you think we felt having someone barge into my office? I thought everyone had gone home,' Carta complained as though it was Cassie's fault for being there rather than anything she was doing wrong.

'I am sorry Dr Carta,' Cassie said as she shut the door and walked away from the office.

Sally Carta may have been a brussen woman with an over inflated sense of superiority but she was not stupid and the last thing she needed was this young woman blabbing her mouth to anyone who would listen. Therefore, once she had thought about the harm her exposed secret would generate, she decided some damage limitation procedures where necessary. She followed the woman back to the main reception area, where she found her stacking some cleaning products in the cupboard.

'I am sorry that you had to witness that,' Sally Carta lied, she was far from sorry she couldn't have given a hoot this woman was nothing more than an inconvenience, 'I am sure we can come to some arrangement.'

'Arrangement?' Cassie asked unsure what the doctor's nisus was.

'Maybe I am being a little vague, so I will be more direct if that is what you prefer,' she began and when Cassie said nothing she continued, 'I trust that we can keep our little (pause looking for the right word) indiscretion between ourselves.'

'I have no interest in getting involved in your business. Dr Carta what you choose to do has nothing to do with me. I just want to come to work and do my job, nothing more, nothing less,' Cassie told her.

Chapter 50
Gerald: Present Day

'Sally Carta may have walked away that day feeling triumphant but the next day she wasn't quite as smug,' Gerald told Davies, Sykes and Ashley.

'Why, what happened next?' Davies enquired.

My mum had always felt like a nobody, she had been invisible to everyone around her all her life, putting other people's needs first but never quite making it to their lists of being important. One night she met a guy, had her first sexual experience and as luck would have it, she found herself pregnant, she told him and he couldn't get away fast enough. So, when Tony Lloyd came on to the scene there was no way she was going to make the same mistake twice, she passed the pregnancy off as his, they got married and the rest is history.

'So, what you are saying is Tony Lloyd isn't even your father?' Davies asked.

'Bingo,' Gerald smiled, 'why do you think he wouldn't take her calls and he insisted she changed our names from Lloyd to Matthews, her maiden name?'

'But what happened with Sally Carta?' Ashley asked.

'The next day Mum hears the excited chatter about Sally's Millennium NYE party, of course she wants to go, but there is no way the cleaner is going to get an invite, or is there?' Gerald toyed with them.

'Come on Gerald the suspense is killing us,' Sykes urged him.

'Basically, Mum had seen the way the good doctor had manipulated the people around her to get what she wanted so Cassandra decided to emulate her and beat her at her own game. When she insinuated in front of everyone that she too was invited actually joining in on their chatter of course doctor Carta did not correct her. So, Cassandra now knew she had Carta over a barrel. There soon became an unwritten agreement that Cassie would not say anything of the doctors' indiscretions as long as she kept her happy. The problem with having someone over a barrel is that the more you roll over, the dizzier you become and sooner or later the contents of the barrel end up depleted.'

'Are you saying that Cassandra pushed things too far and that the doctor retaliated by assisting her to commit suicide, because if you are that is quite a claim?' Ashley said looking at her colleagues in disbelief.

'Oh, there is far more of this story we still need to explore first,' Gerald told them.

'Then please continue Gerald, I think it's safe to say we are all spellbound!' Davies told him.

'Yes, you certainly have my full attention please continue,' Ashley affirmed.

'Ok, so I think at this point it is probably a good time to introduce you to the other party goers who have a part in what happened that night. Emma Boulden, who is Sally Carta's sister,' he began.

'Isn't she the woman who was with your father, I mean Tony Lloyd?' Ashley asked.

'She is,' said Gerald, 'and she was also part of the cover up.'

'What cover up, your mother's suicide?' asked Davies.

'Patience, patience Dr Davies to understand Cortina, my assisted mother's suicide and the carnage that followed you need to get to the finger that pulled the trigger that sent the bullet out to hit the target,' Gerald was really beginning to enjoy himself.

'Ok, so tell us about Emma Boulden,' Ashley guided.

'Emma Boulden was not a party animal and was not interested in going to one of her sisters' raucous parties. She had recently split with her husband so was devoid of the seasonal spirit and had no perceived hope for a better year ahead therefore the last thing she wanted to do was to celebrate. However, like everyone else in Sally Carta's life she manipulated her sister no end to fulfil her own desires and NYE of the Millennium was no different than any other day in Emma's life. Sally Carta had decided Emma was going to be a part of her New Year's celebration and she was not going to take no for an answer,' Gerald told Ashley, Davies and Sykes. He was loving the fact he had got their undivided attention and he was going to milk it for all it was worth.

Chapter 51
Emma Boulden: The Millennium NYE

Sally Carta was hosting yet another one of her raucous parties no doubt lots of her friends from work, their partners and other family members would be there so Emma had declined the invitation. She thought back to the previous New Year celebrations where she had been spectacularly dumped the week before on Christmas day. She had settled down on the settee in seasonal PJ's, a plush blanket wrapped around her, book in her hand, all Christmas presents from Sal when there was a knock at the door. She tiptoed to the door, looked through the little spyhole to decide whether she was going to open the door or ignore it when she saw Malcolm, Sal's husband. She threw the door open wide without a greeting and walked back towards the settee to retake her position knowing full well Malcolm would follow. He did.

'You can save your breath Malcolm I am not going!' Emma told him and picked up her book dismissing anything he might have to say.

'Emma, I don't want to be here as much as you don't want me to be but Sal has sent me to come get you,' he stated.

'I can see that but I am more than happy here thank you very much,' Emma reiterated.

'Look, you know what Sal is like…' he trailed off as Emma's mobile began to ring.

'Hello Sal,' Emma sighed. 'Yes, I know, he has just got here now.'

'No, I do not *need* to come over and no you're wrong I *can* stay here if I choose to,' Emma responded.

Malcolm stayed where he was there was no point going anywhere because he knew Sal would get her own way she always did and by the way Emma was responding he also knew full well what Sal was saying.

'For goodness' sake Sal, we don't all need to be reminded that yet another year has come to an end and that here I am in the same sodding rut. For all I know, the next bloody year could be just as bleak what is there to celebrate in that?' Emma's voice raised to the point of being upset.

Malcolm looked away; he was a quiet man who didn't do female hysteria very well it wasn't something he could handle so chose to ignore it. Then it was there, the words he knew he would hear.

'Fine, I will come to your bloody party, just know it is under duress I don't want to be there, I will not enjoy it and you are actually spoiling my New Year's Eve!' Emma finished throwing the phone on the settee next to her.

'Your wife is a bloody nightmare, Malcolm; how do you stand for it!' Emma said stomping off towards her bedroom door to presumably get dressed he thought. When she returned, she had simply thrown on a pair of jeans and a white blouse which gaped slightly at the breast bone with her hair now tied back. He couldn't help but notice how pretty her face was without make-up and wondered why he hadn't noticed before. She was much slender than his wife, generally had a good disposition the present situation accepted and a dry sense of humour. It beggared Malcolm's belief and not for the first time why her husband had cheated on her, she was everything in a lovely little package.

'Are we going to this bloody party then or what?' Emma asked him directly, snapping him out of his trance-like thoughts.

'Err yes, ready when you are,' he said walking through the open door.

Chapter 52
Malcolm Carta: The Sad Truth

Emma closed the door, locked it and then tried the handle to make sure it was secure, a habit she had formed since living alone. She followed Malcolm's lead down the stairs instead of taking the lift as she often did. He had parked in the small area adjacent to the flats, she mused at the fact he had managed to get a space especially tonight when everyone would be celebrating. She felt sure this would have been the one night of the year to leave your car at home if ever there was one. He clicked the remote on his keypad the car coming to life responding by igniting the interior lights and the flashing of the orange indicator lights. An indication it was now unlocked so she depressed the handle and slid inside, Malcolm walked around to the driver's side and got in. Emma couldn't help but notice Malcolm's loss of weight from the last time she had taken a ride with him and recalled the conversation she'd had with Sal about his rapid weight loss.

'How's it going with you then Malcolm?' Emma queried as much to break the silence than actually caring.

'Ok, plodding along as always,' he told her. Malcolm didn't know why he did that brushed off his thoughts and feelings, maybe to avoid what was really going on because if he voiced them perhaps, he would have to face matters.

'Sal said you had an appointment at the hospital before Christmas how did it go?' Emma attempted to be more direct in the hope that she could get some conversation going.

'Oh, did she, I didn't realise she had said anything,' Malcolm stuttered.

'Sorry Malcolm I didn't mean to make you feel uncomfortable if you'd rather not talk that's fine, I understand,' Emma said kindly.

'It is not that Emma, it's just, I don't know how I feel about it yet,' Malcolm admitted.

'I get it Malcolm you are married to my sister and we have never really been that close so don't sweat it I am not offended if you don't want to talk to me about it,' Emma offered to let him off the hook.

'It's not that either, Emma,' he said.

'So, what is it, you're not going to die or anything are you?' she said jovially trying to lighten the air.

'Actually Emma, I think I am, yes,' he said solemnly and then clammed up and continued to drive like he hadn't uttered a thing.

Emma sat in silence unable to speak not knowing how to respond or what to say so she said nothing. They sat in silence throughout the whole journey across town. Malcolm deftly managed each red light with exaggerated care, his approach slow, his gear change smooth ensuring the maximum comfort of his passenger. Malcolm wanted his mind on something more constructive than his failing health and certainly did not want to voice what was in his heart. When the lights changed to green, he accelerated skilfully gliding through each gear to attain the maximum legal speed limit for each section of their drive. He was in a quandary of wanting this journey to be over yet not actually wanting to arrive at his final destination.

Why was life so brutal? The last thing Malcolm wanted or indeed felt that he could cope with was a house full of people. People celebrating their hopes and dreams for the coming year. People who were happy. Excited. People who actually had something to celebrate, a future something he knew he did not have. Before he knew it, he was pulling in along Elm Road, and in to the drive of Blenheim House as he had thousands of times before yet right now, he wanted to turn his car around and get out of there. But he couldn't, it was New Year's Eve and his place was next to Sal as it had always been and where he would always be until he could be there no more.

He pulled into his space, the one he had used for 26 years since they had moved there during the May of 1973, the space he had vacated only an hour ago. As he cut the engine, he inadvertently glanced up towards the red entrance door with its frosted glass insert which now sported the Christmas wreath as it had every single Christmas they had celebrated together. He saw himself carrying Sal over that threshold collapsing in fits of giggles as they started their married life together. A life that had been blessed with love, with foreign holidays, with laughter, hope, good careers and opportunities, he smiled but his heart was sad. If he had a penny for every time, he had stepped over that threshold he would have been a multimillionaire but money had never mattered to either of them it was the memories and the moments that took his breath.

Like the day Sal revealed she was pregnant, he may have crossed the threshold that day but his feet never touched it because he was floating on air. Then there was the day her waters had broken, right there underneath the storm porch and he had run down the staircase from the upper level to assist having heard her yelling for him. He could then see himself carrying Jonathon his newborn son through that door with Sal waddling close behind when they'd arrived home from the hospital.

'Jonathon,' he whispered tears beginning to fall freely down his face completely forgetting that Emma was sat beside him. She stayed absolutely still not wanting to sever the connection from whatever deep thought he was locked away in.

Jonathon only 12 years of age his whole life ahead of him and yet what would be in store for him without the protection of his father. Malcolm shook his head at the prospect of not being able to watch his son grow up, not know the grades he would achieve, the career path he may take or the wife he would choose. Malcolm's involuntary sobs shocked him as much as it did Emma having never seen him cry before she was transfixed and knew she had to allow him to expel those tears not knowing each one held such deep sadness. Malcolm came to the realisation that he would also never hear that precious future child or children call him "granddad" and his heart grew heavier still.

Sal would have all these new memories but they wouldn't be with him. Her life would continue, yes, she may be heartbroken for a while but even so she would continue forward without him by her side. He wasn't sure how he felt about that no doubt it would take a little time to process but that wasn't for right now.

# Chapter 53
Sally Carta: Let the Party Commence

Sally Carta loved nothing more than to throw a party. She was so proud of the privileged position she had found herself in that she wanted to share it with those around her. Well, maybe "share" was not really the right word the truth was she wanted to show off, rub it into other people's faces. She wanted to take the scorn of the past: her mother who had always belittled her, her teachers who had told she "Would never amount to anything" and the school ground bullies. She wanted to take her two fingers and stick them up in their faces and tell them to well and truly F off. However, being unable to do this practically or personally, she had to settle for the next best thing and that was to revel in her position imagining the saps at work were her little minions. Inside she felt the hollow ground of the past but outwardly she expressed the present and today would be no different.

The day she had met Malcolm Carta she knew he would be her golden ride to a better future so she had held on with both hands and never looked back since. She remembered her wedding day, Emma had been her chief bridesmaid dressed in a ¾ dusky pink satin dress that was low at the neck, tapered into her tiny waist with tiny puffy sleeves. Sally had the most flamboyant, white silk gown with tiny pearl buttons which ran down the back.

The train was only short as she didn't want it to get creased nor did she want to have to hold it up for the entire day she just wanted to be the elegant princess she had always imagined. As the wedding planner had adjusted her tiara and placed the veil over her face, Emma entered the honeymoon suite. Sally's eyes had almost popped out of her head when she had seen that Emma was wearing her mum's old silver locket.

'How are you feeling Sal, nervous?' Emma had asked.

'No, quite the contrary,' Sal responded through gritted teeth unable to take her eyes off that damn locket that Emma was inadvertently sliding back and forth up and down its chain.

'Not too late to back out,' Emma threw in jokingly without taking any notice of what Sal had just said.

'I am fine thanks, in fact I haven't been as sure about anything as I am of marrying Malcolm Carta right now,' she responded clearly.

'Gosh it will be really weird, you will have to get used to signing your name as Sally Carta and not Sally Edwards,' Emma told her still sliding that infernal locket up and down its chain.

'Emma I cannot wait to change my name it's the only thing I have thought about since I met Malcolm. If the truth be known I have been practising a swirly signature, softer one that flows like my life with Malcolm definitely will,' Sal admitted. 'I cannot wait to become Sally Carta because people will be looking *up* to me then not down *at* me like they have my entire life.'

'I have always looked up to you Sal,' Emma smiled at her older sister. 'I couldn't be prouder of you as I am right now,' Emma gushed.

'Thank you, babes,' Sal responded with a smile her features relaxing and less harsh.

'Oh, I forgot to tell you look,' Emma said, holding the locket between her thumb and index finger then extending it forwards towards Sal, 'I found Mum's old locket. I have put her photograph inside so that she can be with us on your wedding day. No doubt she will be watching and be as proud of you as I am,' Emma beamed.

All Sal wanted to do was grab that bloody locket, rip it straight from her sister's neck then flush it down the toilet and into the sewer where their dear mother belonged. But this was her wedding day so she was not having that woman spoil it like every other stinking, drunken day she had ruined throughout her miserable life. No, today was the day that Sally Edwards life ended she would be gone, forgotten and buried forever.

Soon she would rise out of those ashes a new woman, with a new life and new possibilities. She would dispel the forlorn image of the ugly duckling and become the swan she was always destined to become. Today was the day she would shed her old life and take that step up to be at the side of Malcolm Carta where she would have all her needs met and where she would stay no matter what. As she looked to Emma all she could do was smile.

'Where is Daddy?' Jonathon asked for the umpteenth time breaking the intensity of his mother's thoughts.

'I have told you darling he has gone to fetch Auntie Emma and he will be back soon,' Sally told him.

'You don't think anything has happened on the way back, do you, Mummy; it has been snowing quite heavily all day and the roads may be slippery?' he pondered.

'No darling I don't, Auntie Emma will be dragging her heels because she doesn't want to come out tonight,' Sally told her young son.

'Why, Mummy, doesn't she like us anymore, has she fallen out with us like I fell out with Paul Mackie at school,' Jonathon innocently enquired.

'No Jonathon it is not like when you and Paul fell out love she is just being a misery guts, but don't worry they will be here soon,' she said soothingly.

'I hope so because I am starving and want to eat some of the trifle you have made,' he said.

'Why don't you go into the lounge and watch for them out of the window,' Sal said trying to get Jonathon from under her feet, 'I won't have it all set out if you keep getting under my feet.' She smiled.

Jonathon had always been such an inquisitive child with 1001 questions about everything that surrounded him. Sometimes it amazed her how he would connect with the world around him but at other times, like when she had just got back in from a long day at the clinic it was mentally draining. All she wanted to do right now was to finish the food and a couple of other tasks then she could kick back and enjoy the party like everyone else. Finally, she was able to step back, survey her efforts and know everything was complete then she strolled across in to the lounge where some of the guests were intermingling, enjoying a drink and chatting.

'Here she is,' Barry a technician from the clinic said, 'we were all wondering where you were.'

Everyone cheered as Jonathon returned to his spot at the window and heaved the heavy curtain aside. Sal made her way over to the mantelpiece to retrieve her wine glass. He cupped his hand to the window so he could see out and that's when he saw the familiar car in the driveway. He turned to the people in the room and said excitedly 'Daddy's here and so is Auntie Emma, Mummy!'

Sal weaved her way to the window, saw that it was Malcolm's car, she turned around, smiled at the people in the room and said to them, 'Let the party commence.'

Chapter 54
Malcolm: Putting on a Brave Face

At the edge of the bay window, the heavy grey ribbed curtains were effortlessly pulled back and a little boy's head peeped out, his hand cupped to the glass to give him clarity. He looked back into the room an animated expression of excitement because his dad had returned before Sal came up behind him and also peered out. Malcolm bit the corner of his lip at the thought of the day they would be standing there looking out for him yet knowing that he would never be coming home again. Malcolm gasped; the sobs heavy, his shoulders rising with each one unable to fend off the inevitable. Emma overwhelmed by this surge of emotion reached out and touched his hand but instantly recoiled due to Malcolm's startled reaction. So deep in his thoughts was he that he had completely forgotten Emma was there, then panic shot through him as she had witnessed his outward expression of sorrow.

'What is it Malcolm, you are worrying me?' Emma asked not sure if she was actually ready for the answer.

'The doctor told me I have cancer, Emma,' he said matter-of-factly.

'There are lots of treatments now Malcolm, the doctors can do so much more than they ever used to,' Emma told him trying to sound hopeful.

'The problem is Emma, the doctor has told me that it is terminal and has given me less than four months,' he delivered in a monotone voice.

Emma sat rigid in her seat unable to say or do anything as Malcolm unbuckled his seatbelt and reached for the door handle. 'There is one other thing Emma, Sal doesn't know anything about it I haven't told her yet,' he informed her.

Emma stumbled to unfasten her seatbelt and to get out of the car before he had the chance to walk off. He couldn't just drop this on her and then walk off expecting her to go inside, say absolutely nothing and bring in the New Year knowing he was not going to be here for another one. By the time she had got herself out of the car, he had shut his door and was now striding towards the door evidently no longer open to any further conversation. Emma had to reach him before he got to the door, had to stop him she could not just let what he had said go.

'Malcolm wait, what do you mean Sal doesn't know?' she asked in desperation.

'Just that Emma, I haven't told her that this is our last Christmas and our last New Year because I didn't want anything to change, I wanted to celebrate it the way we always have, as a family. I did not want to spoil it with unnecessary doom and gloom. When something happens to me, she needs to be able to look back on this time and remember our last one with fondness as being one of the best not the worst. I owe her at least that much, Emma and one day she will thank me for it. I need to give her something to hold on to it,' he explained turning away and then changed his mind. 'Just promise me one thing, Emma.'

'What's that?' she asked tentatively as silhouettes of people began looming into view as they walked down the hallway towards the door.

'Make sure you look after them for me!' he said, turning away as the door was flung open and the excited chatter of a party in full swing bellowed out into the night air.

'Always,' Emma muttered though she was unsure whether he had actually heard her as he was engulfed in the loving arms of Jonathon.

Chapter 55
Emma Boulden: Being Useful

Emma hung back allowing both Jonathon and Sal the pleasure of enveloping Malcolm, a luxury that they could ill afford to waste. She only edged her way up the two steps onto the storm porch when Jonathon began propelling his dad forward in towards the long hallway. Then it was her turn.

'Come on misery guts,' Sal said grabbing her by the hand and almost dragging her inside.

The house was awash with light and life a stark contrast to the car from which she had just left. She could see the back of Malcolm as he disappeared into the front lounge still being guided by his son. The entrance hallway had always been a firm favourite of Emma's probably because in her small flat you basically stepped in from the outside corridor straight into her lounge. She loved the fact that at Sal's house you had an extra inner door it gave the sense of privacy when you answered the front door and stopped anyone from looking straight into the core of the house. She couldn't help wondering if like her it might make Sal feel more secure especially in the coming months and years when she too would be living alone.

Obviously, Jonathon would be there but perhaps Sal would become more protective feeling a need to somehow shelter him more in a dual responsibility when his father was no longer around. She berated herself Malcolm had only just told her of his diagnosis how dare she talk to herself this way as though he had already passed away. The poor guy was only at the other side of the wall, no doubt living it large and being the life and soul of the party as he always was.

When Emma had seen him on her doorstep, she was so angry not at him but at her sister who never knew when to let people just be. Sal might be the incessant party animal who loved to fill her house with guests and feed them until they were absolutely stuffed, but she Emma was totally the opposite. All Emma really wanted to do tonight had been to chill on the settee and lose herself in her book. The last thing she would ever have contemplated was having to be in a room full of people, probably all coupled up or worse still as a family.

She could think of nothing worse. When she and Simon were together, she had thought he was the reason for her infertility only to have a sledgehammer smacked in her face to prove she was wrong. It had been only 12 months since he had walked in, told her he was having an affair that not only was he leaving her but this other woman was pregnant. He might as well have said, 'Put that in your pipe and smoke it! The child, a boy was born four months later so he would be eight months old by now, they were still together. Emma had been in town Christmas shopping when she saw them out with one another Simon actually navigating the pushchair. It had cut her so deep.'

'So, shoot me Sal if I don't want to come to your bloody party,' she absentmindedly said out loud.

'What? Shoot you, why would I shoot you,' Sal asked.

'You might want to shoot me now, I was just saying. I cannot believe you sent Malcolm over to mine to drag me here,' Emma said trying to recover from her unintentional expression.

'Well, I knew you would come if I sent him besides, you're here now so you can at least get in the mood and look like you intend to have a good time,' Sal said heading towards the kitchen whilst Emma removed her shoes.

If only Sal knew, Emma was coming with the intention of not looking like she was enjoying herself because sulkily she had been annoyed at being forced to come out into the cold. However, after hearing Malcolm's news she would be trying to put a brave face on and look like she was enjoying herself though not for the reasons that her sister might think. At least she wouldn't pester her as to why she wasn't as excited about the New Year as everyone else, as she would just assume it was not only because she was billy no mates but a single pringle to boot.

Emma walked along the geometric black and white tiled hallway glancing at the black and white photographs displayed in their black frames set in white mounts. If she were a stranger entering the house the impression, she would form about its inhabitants would be that they were a very happy family with strong bonds drenched in love. Their happy smiling faces told a multitude of stories as they shone out of each picture propelling you to look at the next and then the next.

They were like a good story that unfolded with each page, not allowing you to put the book down so engrossed were you in their story. She felt a deep yearning for that same story in a chapter of her own life but she knew it would never be possible as she couldn't have children. Emma had an overpowering surge of mixed emotions, heart-warming as she looked into the faces of these beautiful people yet heart-wrenching as she considered the prospect of the devastation, they would all soon suffer.

'Come on Auntie Emma everyone is waiting for you,' Jonathan called as he came into the hall to find her.

'I'm coming bossy britches,' Emma responded playfully and chased him back into the front lounge.

There were quite a few people some sat on the odd dining room chairs that Sal had obviously brought in from the other room, others on the settee or balancing on the edge of its arms. Mostly there were people milling about in the centre of the room but most looked like they were deep in conversation so she decided to go through to the kitchen to see if there was anything she could help Sal with. She needn't have bothered as usual Sal had everything under control with a whole host of foods spread out to feed a battalion.

That's when the doorbell rang so Emma decided to make herself useful by answering it. She made her way back down the hall, opened the inner door to reveal a cluster of obscured shadows of people on the doorstep. She opened the door to reveal a family unit. There was Dad who held a child in his arms and Mum with a young girl of approximately 6 years old who stood between her parents.

'Hi,' Emma said.

'Hi, have we got the right address for Sally, Sally Carta? I am Cassie Lloyd; I work with her at the surgery,' the mum said introducing herself.

'Hi, yes sorry,' Emma offered stepping aside, 'please won't you come in.'

The family stepped inside as Sal appeared into the hallway and enthusiastically greeted the woman Emma now knew as Cassie Lloyd. Emma watched as Sal whisked Cassie away noticing how she glanced to her husband for confirmation it was OK and the slight nod he gave her before removing the child's coat that he had been holding. The other girl tried taking her own coat off but then the dad had to help her with the buttons. Emma closed both the exterior and inner doors then asked if they would like to have a drink. It was only when the man stood up with the light upon his face, that she actually got a really good look at him. She could not help noticing just how handsome he was.

'Where should we put our coats?' he asked.

'Oh, I will take them and throw them on the bed,' Emma said innocently.

'Maybe I will keep mine on then,' he said playfully, but Emma looked puzzled so he added, 'when you throw it on the bed.'

Emma wasn't sure how deep her face had flushed before she managed to steal herself away but she was certain there was no way he could have missed it. She quickly grabbed the pile of coats his hand accidentally on purpose sweeping across hers in the process. She ignored his penetrating eyes along with the attention she knew he was giving her backside as she ran up the stairs. Emma felt completely out of her depth; she had not had a man come on to her since before her relationship with Simon and that was years ago so she was unsure how to respond.

Also, this man had just walked in with his family so why would he be coming on to her it didn't make any sense. Perhaps she was seeing in to things that weren't there, let's face it, her mind was all over the place since Malcolm had disclosed his news. So, she decided to go back down the stairs to rejoin the party and enjoy the night as much as she could before being able to get home to snuggle down into her bed.

However, what Emma did not realise was that tonight she was not going to make it anywhere near her home never mind her bed. Tonight, something horrendous would occur sending them all into a quandary that would result in a sworn secret that would haunt her for the rest of her life.

Chapter 56
The Party

Sally Carta mingled in amongst her guests throughout the night ensuring that their glasses were full, people were introduced to each other and everyone was enjoying themselves. For Sally remaining the centre of the attention being the "hostess with the mostess" as the saying goes was her favourite role to play. She loved her home, her job and her family so she couldn't think of a better place to be than entertaining in and amongst this crowd to bring in the New Year. Well, it wasn't just a New Year it was the Millennium New Year so she was especially excited. Each person had been handpicked to share this momentous occasion with her, well almost apart from that Cassandra woman who had practically invited herself. The cheek of her, and she had turned up with the husband and her brats in tow. Sally's eyes fell upon the woman at the other side of the room whilst she took a sip of her drink. She glared at her over the top of her glass still unable to believe the audacity of her to actually turn up at her home. She made a mental note to make sure she did not open herself up to further manipulation of this woman who was after all a bloody cleaner. Sally could scarcely comprehend how she had let this happen but she was surely going to keep a lid on the woman's ability to exploit any future situations. Tonight, she would let it slide because nothing was going to spoil the celebrations.

Sally casually glanced around the room her eyes falling upon Carmicheal inadvertently licking her lips what she wouldn't give to be able to feel the warmth of his skin next to hers, his tongue exploring the depth of her mouth. She delighted in being able to cast her eyes over him visually examining his lean athletic body. She focused in on his dark, neatly cut hair that was perfectly shaped across the back of his neck, the neck she'd smothered in kisses numerous times. His white perfectly ironed shirt, skimming his slender back packed tightly into the top of his black chino's that hugged his tight, firm buttocks. Lost in her lust for this younger man, she failed to see Cassandra observing her hidden desires. And then Malcolm disconnected the reverie with the tapping of his glass to bring about a hushed silence amongst the room.

'Sorry guys if I can just have your attention, please,' Malcolm said.

'Is it food time already?' a guest piped up.

'Not quite,' Malcolm said, 'although it won't be long, I can assure you,' Malcolm looked to his wife for confirmation.

'Everything is prepared and ready maybe another drink or two and then we will open the buffet,' Sally conceded.

'Buffet, it's fit for a king,' Dr Jameson said.

'You can always be sure of a good spread if Sally Carta is doing it,' another chimed in.

'Here, here,' two or three said as Sally Carta gushed, not out of being humble but from pride as she always put in 110% to ensure it wasn't just good but the best. She knew that her staff, close colleagues, family and friends would be talking about the spectacular feast for months and remembering it next New Year hoping for another invitation.

'Right, thank you everyone if I can just have your attention for a moment,' Malcolm began. 'Sally Carta and I have lived at this house for almost 27 years, we have loved it, we have shared it with our good friends and we have brought our family up here. I just want to thank old and new friends for coming tonight to celebrate with us the momentous occasion of bringing in the Millennium New Year. If you would all like to raise your glasses, 'To friendship, to love, to laughter and to the future, may all your hopes and dreams be fulfilled in the coming year. Cheers!' he finished.

Glasses around the room were readily thrust into the air to a resounding chorus of "Cheers" only one person stood, tears in her eyes overcome by Malcolm's sincerity and blessing.

'Come on, misery guts,' Sally elbowed her sister playfully. 'This could be your year you never know you might find your Mr Right!'

But Emma couldn't swallow down the lump in her throat never mind take a drink from her glass so she plumped for just squeezing her sister's hand and smiling letting her think her sadness was due to her being on her own. She looked across to where Malcolm was stood surrounded by a group of well wishes laughing, drinking smiling and a new admiration swelled within her heart for this amazing husband, father and friend. Lost in her thoughts she hadn't noticed that the handsome stranger she had met earlier was edging his way towards her.

'Happy New Year,' a voice said to her left she turned about to say something like it isn't midnight yet to find him stood next to her with 2 glasses in his hand.

'Oh,' she began a little startled, then noticing the two drinks he was proffering she said, 'isn't one of those for your wife?' Emma did a cursory glance around the room but couldn't see her.

'No, this one is for you,' he told her extending his hand further towards her until she felt obliged to take it from him.

'Thank you,' she said feeling a little hemmed in all of a sudden.

'So, tell me about yourself,' the stranger said.

'Maybe you should introduce yourself first and then I wouldn't feel like I am talking to a complete stranger,' Emma toyed playing for a bit of time to think about what was actually going on here.

'I am Tony Lloyd,' he told her.

'Cassie's husband?' she asked directly.

'I am her husband on paper but we haven't had a relationship in the marital sense for years,' Tony Lloyd informed her.

'Isn't that what all the married men say,' Emma blurted out.

'I married her because she got pregnant but we have never shared a loving man and wife connection. To be honest I only married her because of the children and now I only stay for the children but we tend to live separate lives,' he stated.

'That sounds like quite a sad existence,' Emma said sympathetically.

'It is not the best but like Malcolm has just said I am hoping that next year all my hopes and dreams will be fulfilled,' he said.

'And what are they?' Emma couldn't stop herself she was the ultimate 'Happy Ever After,' love story queen.

'I want to dare to hope I will find my true love then we can start to build on a future together where we can realise the dreams of our hearts,' Tony said.

'That's a big ask, I think at our age love has passed us by,' Emma said cynically.

'That is where you are wrong Emma all it takes is for two like-minded people to meet by chance at a Millennium party, to fall in love and then choose to take the path that they both want,' he said smoothly.

'You're quite the charmer, I will give you that, smooth, confident but a little bit too much up yourself for me, thanks anyway,' she said swiftly sidestepping him and mingling in to the centre of the crowded room.

Tony watched her go. He knew he had come on really strong but didn't want her to think he was some kind of creep although he wouldn't have blamed her if she had. He was not usually so upfront but from the moment he had set eyes on her he had felt a draw to her. There was something about her that touched his spirit maybe she had been trapped in a loveless relationship too or perhaps she had been let down by someone she trusted. He decided he needed to know more about her and would definitely make sure he was somewhere close to her when the countdown began, he wanted her and he was going to make sure he got her.

The trouble was a very different kind of countdown had been initiated the very moment Tony Lloyd allowed his wife to railroad him into agreeing to attend Sally Carta's party.

Chapter 57
Gerald: Present Day

'So, what are you saying Gerald, that something happened at the party?' Davies asked.

'Have all these people that you are telling us about somehow played a part in something? It is awfully confusing,' Ashley said shaking her head looking to her colleagues to see if they could shed any light on the situation.

'And what has it got to do with Cassandra Matthews' suicide?' Davies enquired.

Gerald was loving playing to his audience of baffled doctors who still hadn't seen it yet, but they would when he was good and ready to reveal it, when he had taken all the time he required.

'All will be revealed in good time but first you need to know about the people and the turn of events that caused the cogs to shift. The lies, the secrets, the despair and suffering that those people caused and how it created the whole situation and the reason I sit before you today,' Gerald informed them.

'But I don't think I do understand Gerald, even I am not sure about what is true and what isn't right now?' Ashley stated.

'To understand you need to be fully aware of the whole truth as this may give you a completely new perspective to deliver your verdict of what is right and what is wrong,' Gerald said.

'But how can we be sure what is right or wrong if we do not know what has happened?' Davies asked perplexed.

'What right do we have to be any kind of judge? What is right for one person may not right for another?' asked Sykes.

'Exactly, Dr Sykes because we all make mistakes, no one is perfect the question is with whom does the culpability lie, who is to blame and why. To find the answers we must return to the beginning and it all started on that fateful night,' Gerald continued.

'So, what happened next?' Davies asked.

Chapter 58
The Guests

The party was in full swing, the guests merrily enjoying the gastronomical delights, drinks were flowing, the children running in and out of the rooms excited and having fun. Tony was keeping one eye on his wife to make sure she didn't embarrass him and the other eye on Emma. Ordinarily he hated these kinds of affairs especially being in and amongst people he didn't know but tonight he was enjoying just being. He would engage in the odd chat that was offered but took more pleasure in just observing, able to watch Emma interacting, mingling amongst the many different people. She had a certain sadness about her, where he could tell she was trying to keep others at arms-length all the time wearing the same false smile that he had worn for years. He wanted to tell her he had noticed, tell her she needn't feel invisible, unloved, unwanted but he couldn't just blurt it out he didn't know her well enough. Although he was sure that if he waited, his time would come as long as he was patient.

Emma was becoming more and more self-conscious knowing full well that Tony Lloyd was watching her every move. To some degree, she felt a sense of unease at his sustained and prolonged attention but on the other hand she was enthralled by it. He was quite a captivating individual, mysterious and yet somehow familiar who knew, maybe what he had said about his unhappy marriage was true, but then again it did seem like a cheesy chat up line. The one thing she couldn't deny was that she was flattered by the attention he was giving her.

Maybe she would find a moment to ask her sister what Cassie was like at work and try to get some information about their relationship that way. At least then she wouldn't feel so bad, although was this any different to what Simon and Miss Twinkle Toes had done to her. She had been devasted at the break up of her marriage so she could not imagine ever doing that to someone else. Was it selfish to think she also did not want to be on her own either? She knew that didn't make it right to take someone else's husband, oh my goodness what was wrong with her, was she really this desperate?

The person that was desperate was Sally Carta, desperate to get her hands on the fine young doctor it was torture having him so close to her but of her being unable to reach out her hand and to even touch him. She walked into the kitchen and found his aftershave filling her nostril cavity, she reached over to take a canapé from the table to feel his lithe body press against hers.

The sensation of his mere presence and her not being able to have him was beginning to send her wild. She tried her best to stay away from him, to maintain her usual stalwart composure telling herself it was for the sake of her husband but really it was to maintain her image. The risk of exposure being too great to take not to mention this being her home with her friends, family, son and more importantly, her husband so close. So, she decided she would just have to settle for watching him from afar, for now.

Unbeknown to Sally Carta not only was Cassandra Lloyd monitoring her behaviour but so was Malcolm. She must have thought he was stupid not to have noticed her sudden need to have to stay at the surgery longer, the impulsive, carefree, wild abandonment associated with a new love. He had suspected something was amiss the day she had arrived home from the conference in London. Unlike every other one she had attended, her mood was energised, overly chatting and giving details about the people she had met, the topics of the lectures, quite unlike her. During the past few months, he had noted the number of times she had missed dinner, had secretive conversations or sat poured over her phone and then he did something that he never thought he would, he followed her.

The deceit had hit him like a wrecking ball hits the side of a building totally destroying his heart, knocking him crumbling to the ground his world demolished. Malcolm Carta had never so much as looked at another woman because Sally Carta was all he wanted yet he was being confronted with the fact that he was not enough for her. He had spent his life loving her, he had supported her through medical school, had a child with her, built a life around her and this was what he was left with. He may not have shared this knowledge with Emma but the reality was that if he had lost her to another man then he didn't want to go on living. This had contributed to his decision to not bother to fight the cancer because as far as he was concerned, he had nothing worth fighting for.

Yes, there was Jonathon but he loved his son far too much to put him through the heartache of a broken home where his parents got divorced and he spent the rest of his days wondering if it was somehow his fault. No, if Sally was moving on then he had no choice but to let go gracefully and to do it with the same dignity in which he had lived his life. It was too late for him to have regrets, too late for her to be sorry, he had neither the energy nor the time to fight, but more importantly he did not want to die alone a broken man. So, he would continue with the façade a little more disappointed with each lie that she would tell him in the knowledge that when he did pass, the guilt would hopefully consume her in grief.

Dr Carmichael was deep in conversation when he noticed Malcolm Carta staring at him so to dissipate any knowledgeable thoughts about him, he called him over, 'Hey Malcolm come and tell this fella to stop giving me grief,' he said aptly.

'Why is that, Richard?' Malcolm enquired.

'Dr Jameson here is just telling me that it's time I started to think about specialising in a specific field of medicine but it's far too early,' Carmichael laughed trying hard to make light of the situation.

'Maybe fertility services,' Malcolm suggested. 'I hear you are quite a hit with the ladies at the surgery.'

'The girls in the office definitely swooned the first day you walked in,' Dr Jameson noted.

'Oh, I wouldn't say that,' Carmichael said modestly.

'They did and the patients think you're marvellous, in fact my numbers have drastically reduced since you came on to the scene,' Dr Jameson reiterated.

'Perhaps a specialist in women's services would hamper your career, maybe stay as a general practitioner Dr Carmichael then you cannot get yourself in hot water with the ladies,' Malcolm said walking away before retorting, 'or their husbands.'

Dr Jameson's belly laugh could be heard throughout the ground floor but there was someone upstairs who was not laughing, a child. Tony Lloyd's children had been playing hide and seek with the Carta's son Jonathon, one little girl was hiding in the bottom of the closet waiting to be found. She was beginning to think that no one was coming to find her until the bedroom door slowly began to open. She could see from the outline that there were two people so she crept back down in to the shadows straining her eyes to peer through the venetian style wooden louvre slats.

Then the light went off. A tiny squeal escaped from her mouth; her breath became heavy she was sure they would hear her but their breaths seemed heavy too. Perhaps they were as scared of the dark as she was. She closed her eyes, imagining that she was bathed in light with only her eyelids blocking it out. She could hear them moving about on the bed, could see their silhouettes cast from the street light but had no idea who they were. She wanted her daddy but he was too busy keeping his eyes on his prey. She wanted her mother but she was too busy mingling amongst the party goers enjoying her own experience, she wanted her sister but she was hiding too. The people were moaning, gasping but then it stopped abruptly and the woman left giggling telling the man he'd have to wait until later and to give it 5 minutes before coming out.

The little girl moved her foot knocking some coat hangers on the floor of the closet alerting him that someone was in there, that someone had seen him and the woman. He stood up, the doors were flung open and a hand flailing blindly down hit her in the face. She yelped. He grabbed her harshly by her clothing and dragged her out depositing her on the bed. She could smell his drunken breath, could feel his rough hands on her tiny body grabbing, mauling but she could not get him off her he was too strong. He held her by the throat no sound able to squeeze past the vice clamped to her neck, unable to suck in any oxygen. She tried to grapple with his hand to get it off her furiously kicking, wriggling but the pressure in her head felt like a pop bottle when it had been shaken vigorously.

Then a million knives shot up through her tuppence ripping her internally and discharging the contents of her stomach but there was no cavity for the vomit to escape. It gurgled in the back of her throat then as her eyes began to shut, the door was suddenly flung wide open.

'We know you are in here because we have looked everywhere else,' Jonathon was saying, as the room was suddenly illuminated followed by a high-pitched scream.

The man his rage at being teased by the woman to be left high and dry let go of the child's neck suddenly lucid, aware and fearful of his drunken actions. In a split second, he'd hauled himself away whilst the other Lloyd child had fled to the top of the steps. Jonathon tried to stop her, tried to grab her not sure what action to take, but knowing she was as shocked and terrified about what she had just witnessed as he was. In her attempt to curve around the top of the stairs, she went over on her ankle misplaced her footing and tumbled cracking her skull on the sharp edge of the small radiator.

The house was suddenly filled with screaming, the guests rushing to the bottom of the stairs to find out what had happened only to witness the young girl banging her head like a pinball machine as she was propelled down the stairs. By the time she had landed at the bottom in a crumpled heap, there was nothing anyone not even the doctors or clinicians could have done to save her. The guests looked up to see Jonathon Carta stood, his hands still outstretched staring wildly at the child's lifeless body.

Behind him the door to the bathroom opened, Mick Denby strolled out, glared at the commotion at the bottom of the stairs and then looked back to Jonathon saying loud enough for all to hear, 'What have you done?'

Downstairs the countdown to the Millennium New Year could be heard ringing out on the TV, '10, 9, 8, 7, 6, 5, 4, 3, 2, 1 Happy New Year!' Followed by "Auld Lang Syne" ironically depicting the futility of planning for a hopeful future in the face of unforeseen circumstances.

Jonathon turned around to see the other little girl dazed and staggering from the bedroom her clothing ripped, with marks around her neck and blood dripping from between her legs. Thousands of fireworks simultaneously began to fill the night sky as the Millennium New Year was being celebrated locally by neighbours. The reds, greens and golds casting their array of colours across the landing and hallways, rockets zipping up, bangs all around then in that split second as quick as the flashing display Mick Denby saw an opportunity to save himself, 'oh my goodness it looks like he has raped this little child.'

Aghast the crowd froze, Jonathon so innocent and scared froze, the child screamed but no sound came out and Mick Denby stood, his accusing face focused upon the scapegoat.

Chapter 59
Gerald: Present Day

Davies, Sykes and Ashley sat in silence horrified at what Gerald had just told them neither of them wanting to break the silence first. It took a good fifteen minutes before Sykes took up the gauntlet.

'That is quite a story, Gerald,' Sykes confessed, 'I am not quite sure how to respond to what you have just told us.' He looked to his two colleagues for some kind of support but neither one was forthcoming, they were equally as stunned.

'As I said earlier, we needed to go back to the beginning to be able to judge what is right or what is wrong. You have now heard what kind of man Mick Denby really was, a child rapist. He chose to save his own neck, he lied, he blamed someone else for his actions and that person was none other than another child.'

'But surely the truth came out? I mean, Jonathon would have denied it,' said Ashley. 'His mum would have known he couldn't do such a thing.'

'Oh, it is true she should have known better but he was stood there at the top of the stairs with his arms outstretched the little girl seemingly pushed. She could not deny what her eyes had seen, no one could,' Gerald declared.

'But surely though tests would have been conducted upon the child to confirm that Jonathon couldn't possibly have been the culprit,' Ashley stated.

'In an ideal world, but here we have a woman who was quick to judge the situation based upon how other people would view her, of how it might affect her career. She wasn't interested in the truth or of meeting the needs of her son nor how he might feel. So, she chose to believe he was guilty and took evasive action to eradicate the problem,' Gerald explained.

'But what about the other doctors surely they would have spoken up?' Sykes asked.

'You may think so but they were worried about their own reputations and that of the practise, so everyone was bound by silence as there was nothing, they could do for the dead child but together they could ensure the live child had the help she required,' Gerald said.

'So, what you are saying is they covered up the death of one child as being accidental and also the rape of another child by taking care of her inhouse at their own surgery? There are far too many unethical practises breeched to even mention here, this is wrong on so many levels,' Davies stipulated. 'It is just too farfetched and simply not possible.'

'What is impossible to comprehend my dear Dr Davies is how Mick Denby got away with ruining the lives of these two children not to mention inadvertently causing the death of the third child,' Gerald told him then continued, 'Do you know how he spent his miserable life, by drinking to block out his depravities rather than choosing to confess his transgressions. Mick Denby knew what he was doing, yet he chose to take the cowards way out and chose to remain silent.'

'Surely your mum and your dad, sorry Tony Lloyd,' Ashley corrected herself, 'fought for their children's right to gain justice?'

'You see it was this course of action that created the huge divide between my mother and Tony, she wanted her daughter to be treated independently, she wanted the police involved,' Gerald said.

'So, what stopped them?' asked Sykes.

'Malcolm Carta,' Gerald said simply.

'How could Malcolm Carta possibly stop them from calling the police?' asked Ashley.

'Firstly, he emotionally blackmailed my mother using the shame of a scandal it would bring to her child for her school friends to learn she had been raped and then he bought Tony's silence,' Gerald told them.

'Bought him how?' Davies asked.

'Remember Malcolm Carta knew he was dying, he also knew his wife was having an affair so it was a matter of two birds, one stone,' Gerald toyed with them.

'What is that supposed to mean, Gerald "two birds, one stone"?' Sykes enquired.

'He had worked hard all his life; he had saved and had amassed a healthy sum but if he was dying, he had no use for any money, it was meaningless to him. He knew his wife was having an affair however he wasn't prepared to fund her relationship after he passed so he bought Tony Lloyd's silence.'

'There is no way as a mother Cassandra Lloyd would have gone along with such a hair brain plan, no way,' dismissed Ashley.

'You are right in part Dr Ashley; don't forget Cassandra Lloyd had run up £63000 worth of debt and the family were drowning so Tony talked her into accepting the offer because there was no other alternative. At the time, they were on the brink of losing everything of being thrown out of their home and on the verge of splitting up so where would her daughter be then?' Gerald explained.

'So how did this result in her suicide?' asked Davies.

'Cassandra went along with the plan but it consumed her every waking minute of every day and so she turned to drink to blot it out. She became locked in a cycle of despair and spiralling bouts of depression. She became consumed with hatred for Tony Lloyd and eventually blurted out that he wasn't even the father of her children. Not realising what she was saying and focusing on her only having the right to make parental decisions, she inadvertently absolved him from any responsibility to her or the remaining live child,' Gerald finished.

'So that was the reason they split up then?' asked Sykes.

'Yes, that was the final nail in the coffin, so to speak, sorry poor choice of words,' Gerald said apologetically not for their benefit but more for his sister.

'That was the reason he finally abandoned her and would not take any of her calls or entertain her in any way,' Ashley assumed.

'Tony Lloyd had been manipulated into a loveless marriage believing he was going to be a father; he was battling high levels of debt and none of it had anything to do with him. So, as soon as he had the chance to get out of there, he fled straight into the arms of Emma Boulden who was also bound by the same secrecy of that night. The other common ground that they shared was the fact they had both been lied to and deceived by their spouses,' Gerald detailed.

'What happened to Cassandra and Cortina after Tony left?' Asked Ashley concerned.

'Good question, Dr Ashley,' Gerald complimented, Ashley brimming with pride at finally feeling that one of them was at least getting something right.

'My mother had to take local children in to make ends meet but this didn't sit well with Cortina, she was jealous and would act up having temper tantrums her behaviour becoming impossible at times,' Gerald told them.

'Is that why your mum sought help from Dr Carmichael and got the antidepressants?' asked Davies.

'She sought the help of Dr Carmichael alright but it wasn't to ask for antidepressants she wanted him to help her get justice for her daughter. When Tony wouldn't answer her calls, she started on Dr Carmichael believing he was the weakest link to the chain. She started pressuring him threatening she would go to the police and ruin all their careers if he didn't help her, didn't tell the truth,' Gerald said.

'So, what did he do?' asked Sykes.

'He told Sally Carta. She had neither patience nor sympathy for Cassandra Matthews who as far as she was concerned shouldn't have even been at the Millennium party in the first place. Sally's opinion was that if the woman hadn't invited herself then Jonathon wouldn't have been accused of the dreadful crimes and that it wouldn't have rendered him catatonic. She blamed my mother for her son's condition so she wasn't going to be threatened or backed into a corner for a second time,' Gerald announced.

'But prescribing antidepressants wouldn't have shut her up!' stated Ashley.

'No, but by prescribing antidepressants and biding their time for a few months and using the exact date of my sister's death as a smoke screen they were able to make her death appear to be a suicide,' Gerald declared.

'But how?' asked Davies.

Dr Carmichael arranged to meet with my mum late on New Year's Eve when he knew that everyone would be out celebrating and entered the house by the back door to ensure he wasn't seen. She was in quite a state but he calmed her down and made her believe he was on her side and that they would go to the police together. He stayed for a drink and then another before mixing a quantity of amitriptyline into her glass then encouraged her to keep drinking. When she became drowsy, Dr Carta assisted him to move her to the staircase where they placed a noose around her neck. They then heaved her lifeless body upwards pulling the rope from the top of the stairs and securing it over the banister,' he told them.

'But surely the police would have found evidence to suggest a crime had been committed,' Sykes said disbelievingly.

'You would think so and they nearly did but for Emma Boulden going back to the house to wash the glasses that her sister and Dr Carmichael had forgotten about and she almost got caught,' Gerald revealed.

'By whom?' asked Davies.

'By the police woman Shona Williams, you have the file in front of you when you view it again with all the answers you will piece it together and begin to see the truth,' Gerald spoke, 'but as I said at the beginning you needed to go back to the very beginning to have all the correct information and then you could judge!'

'One of my sisters died, the other was brutally raped and then my mother was assisted to commit suicide when she wouldn't just accept it. Is there any wonder Cortina sought the truth, that she needed to avenge the sins against her mother, her sister and herself. She needed redemption, she needed peace, she needed to be released from the perpetual torment,' Gerald pleaded his sister's case for her as she was unable.

'How are Cassandra, Cortina, Daisy or myself guilty of any crime we are merely products of the circumstances that these people inflicted upon us? On the contrary, Mick Denby knew exactly what he was doing but chose the cowards way out. He chose to stay silent condemning the children to a life of torment due to the childhood trauma he inflicted upon them. He was to blame but got away with it because everyone else agreed to remain quiet through some misplaced loyalty,' he said setting out his case.

'That is fair and well, Gerald but Dr Carmichael was murdered, Mick Denby had his throat cut, Dr Carta is in a mentally destructive state and by what you are saying, no doubt Malcolm Carta would have been murdered had he not passed away due to cancer. Surely you are not suggesting that Cortina is blameless and that we should absolve her from any wrongdoing?' asked Davies.

'Yes, that is quite an outrageous assumption Gerald if that is where you are going with your story,' stated Ashley.

'When a child is so severely damaged and they do not receive the help support or love that they need to learn how to heal from such horrendous childhood traumas, how can they be blamed for their adult reactions later in life?' Gerald queried.

'There has to be culpability otherwise society would be like the Purge films with every Tom, Dick and Harry taking the law into their own hands,' Sykes determined.

'There was no accountability for anyone who attended that Millennium party every person lied by not telling the truth, worse still they covered up what had happened and brushed her death away as accidental. Not one person spoke up about the rape because Dr Carta swore everyone to secrecy to protect her beloved son. How it must have irked him to know she didn't believe him. Then he had the further impact of losing his father to cancer giving Dr Carta and Dr Carmichael the green light to conduct their affair openly. Again, here she was putting her wanton desires before the needs of her only son,' Gerald argued.

'I agree she does come across as being a selfish, manipulative woman but the question remains did she really deserve to end up the way that she is now?' Ashley enquired.

'No one was prepared to listen to mother, or give Cortina and Daisy a voice, no one stood in the gap for them, no one told the truth so yes they all got what they deserved,' Gerald responded adamantly.

'I am not so sure we can agree with you Gerald,' Davies said.

'Surely a child should not have to pay for the rest of their lives for not understanding the gravity of what is right or wrong. Should the lesson not be in how we learn from those mistakes and how we try to grow by challenging the psychological damage of the concealment of the truth?' He asked.

'So, are you trying to tell us that Cortina is not responsible for her actions due to the effects of childhood trauma, not having access to appropriate therapeutic services causing a diminished responsibility mentally?' Ashley asked.

'I believe the driving force behind her actions was born out of her early experiences yes. She was severely affected mentally freezing her emotional development and fragmenting her mind to create personalities assisting her to cope. I would therefore not consider Cortina to be compos mentis and believe me I should know,' Gerald stated with a wry grin at his predicament.

'Yet we are still bound by law so there will always remain the issue of justice,' Sykes stated with a shrug.

'Perhaps justice is in the confrontation of the adults who scheme to save their own skins, who lie and choose to forget their actions. There has to be retribution, there has to be a consequence for their actions and an atonement for what they did whether the subject was willing or otherwise. Should Cortina be punished further, hasn't she been through enough? Should she spend the rest of her life paying for impulsively reacting when she came face to face with the people who took everything from her?' Gerald asked.

'But murder is murder whatever way you look at, Gerald though I hear you in terms of the case you build for diminished responsibility,' Sykes conceded.

'It would be easy for a jury to look at Cortina and vilify her for the murders you feel that she has committed but first you would have to be able to place her at the scenes of the crime and I am afraid that would be impossible!' Gerald declared.

'I have confidence that our justice system would find the evidence Gerald,' Davies affirmed.

'I know 100% that it will be impossible for any police officer to find the least bit of evidence to put Cortina Matthews at the scene of any crime,' Gerald said emphatically.

'I am sorry, I don't follow,' Davies said looking at the other two doctors.

'Then let me enlighten you, what about Daisy how would you view her?' Gerald wondered.

'Daisy? I am not quite sure what you mean Gerald what has Daisy got to do with this she died at the bottom of the stairs so without being disrespectful, Daisy has nothing to do with the case of Cortina,' Ashley said.

'Is that what you think too Dr Davies?' Gerald asked.

'Yes of course she was the innocent party in this,' Davies answered.

'And what about you Dr Sykes what do you think?' Gerald queried.

'Of course, I agree she has no culpability at all!' Sykes clarified.

'Daisy, Jonathon and Cortina were all innocent children in this,' Gerald affirmed.

'I hear what you are saying Gerald but I think what we are all in agreement with is that Daisy cannot be blamed for the actions of what Cortina committed as an adult,' Sykes said as both Davies and Ashley nodded vigorously.

'Then I would like to introduce you to the person sat in front of you this is Daisy Matthews, the young girl who was raped by Mick Denby, the girl who never grew up because her innocence was stolen from her,' Gerald finished.

'Gerald what do you mean? Daisy died at the bottom of the stairs this is Cortina Matthews,' Davies protested.

'Gerald, Gerald,' Ashley raised her voice but there was silence for several minutes.

'I think he has gone,' Sykes stated.

'Cortina?' queried Davies but there was no answer.

The patient was taken back to her room whilst the doctors reconvened with Shona Williams and Dion Jacobi to discuss the case, the information they had just heard and decided they needed to arrange a field trip before a decision could be taken. Sugar Lane was bleak that day, there was not a living soul to be seen on its premises apart from five adults three women and two men. They made their way through the wrought iron gate, along the crumbling tarmac path, past the part demolished church and around to the right. The headstone they stood before stated it was the resting place of one Cassandra Matthews, who had died on 31.12.2000. It also contained the body of her child, Cortina Matthews born 5.3.1994 who had died 31.12.1999 aged 5 years 9 months.

The five figures could be seen huddled together in quiet contemplation around one gravestone, their every move having been observed from a safe distance by the stranger who preferred to remain in the shadows. Always in the shadows.

Epilogue
Twelve Months Later

Daisy Matthews sat on a blanket which had been laid on the grass for her in the centre of the lawn. Arranged in a semi-circle in front of her were Mr Rabbit, Geraldina her favourite dolly and an old brown teddy bear with several tiny cups and saucers, a beaker of juice in the centre. Daisy was busy chatting happily whilst serving each one in turn under the watchful gaze of her favourite male nurse Jonathon Carta.

'How are things today, Jonathon?' asked Dr Ashley.

'Much the same Dr Ashley, she is having another tea party and enjoying the sunshine,' Jonathon replied.

'Have there been any signs of any visitors at all?' Ashley asked.

'No doctor, the treatment has superseded all expectation, the only person present has been Daisy for the past 5 months and there have been no signs of either Gerald or Cortina,' Jonathon confirmed.

'It has to be the strangest case I have come across,' the doctor mused.

'Why is that?' Jonathon asked.

'Well, as a multi-disciplinary team we have unsuccessfully been able to ascertain a specific diagnosis because the personalities she has created existed through an actual multi-birth,' Ashley stated.

'So, these were not just figments of her imagination or parts of her personality but actual people?' Jonathon enquired.

'Yes, Gerald and Cortina did exist but they have somehow become amalgamated within Daisy and become established personalities within their own right. It's fascinating that they have their own personalities, character traits and history. Gerald knew Daisy and Cortina intimately though he actually died at birth, yet neither Cortina nor Daisy was aware of him or each other. Now she has somehow managed to disassociate herself with them both yet has intricately become them as a whole,' the doctor tried to explain.

'That sounds a bit too technical for my brain a mere mental health nurse, doctor,' Jonathon feigned a lack of all knowledge.

'We have studied her physically, looked for legions or tumours in the brain, significantly analysed her symptoms, her historical loss of memory, the different personalities she has created through her birth, even whether there is any genetical insight. Normally a patient with split personality would be unaware of each of the others and someone with a dissociative disorder it can be a coping mechanism for dealing with childhood trauma,' Dr Ashley said.

'So does she not come under either category then?' Jonathon asked.

'To be honest she comes under both and other disorders but not one definitively. You see she seems to have needed Gerald for comfort, strength, wisdom and calmness, yet she needed Cortina's inner assurance, her social skills, independence and confidence.'

'So how does Daisy fit into it all?' Jonathon queried.

'This is the most interesting part, Jonathon when Daisy was raped, it stunted her emotional development thus the trauma encapsulated her therefore, she has remained as a child. As doctors we need to concentrate on developing Daisy's maturity and our success is linked to how her needs were met through Cortina and Gerald. This will allow her to move forward into adulthood thus supporting her to lead a normal and fulfilling life,' Dr Ashley explained.

'So, her progress is going well, will she be able to leave here?' Jonathon asked.

'Oh yes Jonathon Daisy just needs our support there is plenty that we can do here but the majority of her progression needs to take place in the community,' Dr Ashley readily stated. 'Sorry Jonathon I forgot to ask, how is your mother doing these days?'

'There's no change unfortunately, she just stares out of the window,' Jonathon replied.

'Very, very sad case do they know what drove her to attack her colleague yet?' asked Ashley.

'I think the trauma of suddenly losing my dad to cancer had been bubbling under the surface, work had been getting on top of her and she had been very erratic at home,' Jonathon replied vaguely.

'But to snap in such a vicious, frenzied attack is quite extreme,' Ashley stated, 'why repeatedly stab him in the face and neck area?'

'I think one of the psychologists referred to it as wanting to obliterate his face from her memory. You see she had been having an affair with Dr Carmichael for a few months when she found out about my dad's diagnosis. It did go on afterwards for a good number of years but apparently, he had been seeing a much younger woman. The hypothesis was that she couldn't live with the guilt of cheating on my father, especially when he went off with someone else and seeing him every day was eating away at her,' Jonathon gave his spin on it.

'Love can be very passionate but out of its intensity can also come many other emotions especially where infidelity is concerned,' Dr Ashley said politely.

'Yes, the theory is that she found out he had been seeing someone in secret and this is what set off the devastating chain of events,' Jonathon told him.

'And her ultimate breakdown,' Ashley said.

'Yes, apparently, she may never be fit to stand trial for his murder, obviously it was committed through diminished responsibility, but as you say she has had a complete breakdown,' Jonathon feigned sympathy.

'Of that there is no doubt my boy, your mother will be held at this facility for a very long time I am sad to say,' Ashley said.

'I feel like I have lost both my parents now, Mum may be here physically but mentally it is excruciating,' Jonathon stated.

'Does she still scream and lose her mind every time she sees you?' Ashley asked.

'Yes, she is quite delusional she believes I am a ghost who has apparently come back to haunt her. The doctor stated her condition worsens if I speak to her so I have been asked to leave her in their care now and just focus on my own life, which is what I am trying to do,' Jonathon replied.

'It must be hard but if that is what the doctor has ordered we must give her every chance of recovery,' Ashley said supportively.

'It has been tough whilst I have been working at the same facility so I have had to make the difficult decision to hand my notice in,' Jonathon informed her.

'I think under the circumstances perhaps that would be the best decision all round,' She agreed, then pointing to Daisy 'I think it is perhaps time Daisy was going in for tea now,' she smiled. 'She has responded exceptionally well to her treatment perhaps if we can get her a place in the community, we can start to make the transition soon,' Dr Ashley said as she walked away.

Jonathon smiled to himself as he casually approached Daisy, sat down next to her, their backs to the hospital building as they always did and they began picking the flowers off the grass.

'So, what did she say?' asked Daisy.

'We are all good, no one suspects anything. Mother darling will be staying here indefinitely,' Jonathon informed her.

'What about that police woman?' Daisy enquired.

'The police are not looking for anyone else in connection with Carmichael's murder as their only suspect is too mentally ill to be questioned. With Denby there were no witnesses, no uncontaminated DNA, no trace that anybody called Nina Spalding ever existed and so the file will be left unsolved. As for yours truly, poor Jonathon was forced to leave his job because he couldn't bear to see his mum's demise,' Jonathon sneered.

'It was a perfect smoke screen bringing me into the dining room so we could make them believe I was just having a delayed breakdown,' Daisy said.

'Yes, and I am sure that she recognised you too, hopefully it will screw with her mind even more,' he said uncaringly.

'Thank you for protecting me and encouraging me to stay in here whilst everything played out. If you hadn't mentored me on how to behave, I don't think I could have pulled it off,' she confessed.

'It is all thanks to having a doctor for a mother along with having access to the books I needed to perfect the plan,' he told her.

'It was a sterling idea to make her think you'd hung yourself,' Daisy gushed.

'Both her and Carmichael drove your mum to a breakdown covering up what happened to both Cortina and you at that bloody Millennium party. When they thought, your mother was going to expose them, they drugged her and strung her up leaving you and little Jimmy to find her. So yes, we had to mirror that to create the right level of despair and give her some of her own medicine,' Jonathon declared piercing holes in the stalk of one flower then pushing the head of another one through it connecting the flowers together.

'How is Jimmy, I really did miss him when we were torn apart,' she said sadly.

'I know you did, Daisy and he missed you too, it was very clever of you to call him Gerald,' Jonathon praised.

'When Cortina died, I was devastated, left alone to cope with not only what had happened to me but to also grieving her loss. I really did see him as my brother, Jonathon we drew close together and helped each other,' she said sadly.

'Don't be sad Daisy, it is over now, we got them and it is finally time to move on,' he soothed her.

'I am glad I can finally be me though and use my own name,' Daisy said.

'Yes, if Barry Jarman hadn't mixed you up all those years ago you probably wouldn't have gone through life as Cortina, but it has worked in our favour,' Jonathon noted.

'And if you hadn't been stood at the window when they drugged her and strung her up no one would have ever found out. But do you think we went too far?' Daisy asked selecting another flower from the grass.

'No, they killed your mum besides I was her son her own flesh and blood yet she was still quick to believe that I was capable of pushing poor Cortina down the stairs. She wouldn't listen that I was trying to stop her from falling or how that pig of a man Denby had raped you. She was more interested in saving her own reputation than of knowing the truth or standing up for justice. She wasn't protecting me she believed I was the child rapist, she refused to discuss it, so that's why I stopped talking altogether because there was no point, she wouldn't listen,' Jonathon explained.

'So, what now?' Daisy enquired.

'She will be the one condemned to silence tormented by what she has done and accused of a crime that she hasn't intentionally committed.' he smiled.

'Perfect retribution all round,' Daisy agreed. 'And how long do you think I will have to stay in here?'

'Shouldn't be too long Daisy, they are arranging cognitive behavioural therapy, no doubt it will be supplemented with medication but you don't have to take it and I am pushing for a referral to a supportive community treatment programme. You have played the parts of Cortina and Gerald perfectly we just need Daisy to start to grow up and then we can blend them together. This is not something they have come across before so we can continue to blame your mum's suicide, the rape and death of your sister as the historical traumas for the reasons you have blocked out important memories,' Jonathon coached.

'I cannot thank you enough Jonathon for helping me to get that bastard Denby, I finally feel free to be able to get on with my own life now,' she said earnestly.

'And I cannot thank you enough for helping me to get my mother and Carmichael, all I need to do now is work my notice here and then I am free to get on with my life too,' he stated.

'Yes, then we can start preparing for the next part of the plan,' she said excitedly.

'I am meeting with Jimmy and his girlfriend Anita tonight, to discuss the people they want destroying then I will fill you in tomorrow,' Jonathon informed her.

'You mean Carl/Gerald and Nina "bloody" Spalding,' she corrected him and they began to laugh together.

'Until you get out of here, we need to continue playing our parts, keep an eye on mother dear and any sign of her improving I want to know so that I can pay her a little visit.' He urged her with a tight-lipped smile.

He stood, offered his hand to the woman he loved, assisted her up, placed the daisy chain around her neck and watched as she skipped off towards the hospital entrance maintaining the illusion of being a 6-year-old child in an adult's body. He left the toys to their tea party ready for the next time he and Daisy needed a private chat. He smiled to himself, thinking about Daisy, his lover and his secret partner in crime.